Royal drama and intrigue…
Who will take over the throne?

Capturing
the Crown

Three exciting, intense royal romances from
favourite Mills & Boon authors

Capturing the Crown

MARIE FERRARELLA

KAREN WHIDDON

LINDA WINSTEAD JONES

First published in Great Britain 2012
by Mills & Boon, an imprint of Harlequin (UK) Limited,
Eton House, 18-24 Paradise Road, Richmond, Surrey TW9 1SR

CAPTURING THE CROWN © by Harlequin Enterprises II B.V./S.à.r.l 2012

The Heart of a Ruler, The Princess's Secret Scandal and *The Sheikh and I* were first published in Great Britain by Harlequin (UK) Limited in separate, single volumes.

The Heart of a Ruler © Harlequin Books S.A. 2006
The Princess's Secret Scandal © Harlequin Books S.A. 2006
The Sheikh and I © Harlequin Books S.A. 2006

Special thanks and acknowledgement are given to Marie Ferrarella, Karen Whiddon & Linda Winstead Jones for their contributions to CAPTURING THE CROWN.

ISBN: 978 0 263 89683 1

05-0312

Printed and bound in Spain
by Blackprint CPI, Barcelona

THE HEART OF A RULER

BY
MARIE FERRARELLA

USA TODAY bestselling and RITA® Award-winning author **Marie Ferrarella** has written over one hundred and fifty books, some under the name Marie Nicole. Her romances are beloved by fans worldwide.

To
Nickolas J. Gardner
One of the best Test Leads ever.
And to one of the most Incredible teams ever,
Brooks Rowlett, Craig Scheile,
Jarded Hickman & Paul Adriano.
You guys are the greatest!

Chapter 1

"What's the big deal?" Reginald, the crown prince of Silvershire, asked with a laugh that only partially echoed with humor.

The other viable emotion that was present, and more than a little evident in his retort, was irritation. It was common knowledge that Reginald had never liked being challenged or questioned by anyone. His was the right to do or say whatever pleased him. Explanations did not please him. The only other person in the kingdom who dared question him—on rare occasions—was his father. For the most part, King Weston doted on him as Reginald was the single living testimony of his late wife's love.

Obviously struggling with a temper that rarely resided in check, Reginald paced about his bedroom. He shot the companion of his childhood an impatient look.

Reginald frowned, his handsome features taking on a malevolent appearance. "It's not as if I'm asking you to marry her in my place. Just go and fetch the damn woman and bring her back."

"Fetch her." Lord Russell Southgate, the present duke of Carrington, repeated the phrase the prince had thrown out so cavalierly. Because he knew her, or had known her when they were children, he took offense for the woman who wasn't there to do it for herself. "Amelia is not a dog, Reginald, she's a princess."

Russell watched Reginald square his far-from-broad shoulders. Only in the privacy of Reginald's chambers was he allowed to address him by anything other than his title. By the look on the prince's face, Russell knew he was rethinking that. Rethinking everything. And changing. Because someday, very soon, he was going to be king. And Russell knew that once Reginald was king instead of his father, a great many things were going to change, including their relationship. Because too many people liked him, Russell thought, and the prince viewed that as a threat.

It was just a few days before the wedding, a wedding that would forever bind Silvershire with Gastonia, and it was obvious that Reginald did not want to spend the last days of his publicly recognized freedom playing the dutiful fiancé. Not when there were women to be enjoyed.

Abruptly turning on his heel, the prince looked at him. "You're right, she's not a dog. Dogs are fun. Dogs are obedient. Princess Amelia," he emphasized her title with a sneer since he'd made it known that only *his* title mattered in this union, "is neither. And, there're rumors that since we last met, she's developed a nasty independent streak. Having you bring her back to Silvershire in my place will take the little tart down a peg or two." A smile that was known to make the blood of those on the receiving end run cold spread across his full lips. "Besides," Reginald continued loftily, "I'm going to be busy."

Russell leaned against the overly ornate desk that Reginald felt befit him. The one the prince had yet to use for anything other than bedding a very starstruck young woman who had managed to sneak into the palace as one of the cleaning staff. Observing his future monarch, Russell wondered, not for the first time, if perhaps, in light of the century they were living in, the monarchy had outlived its usefulness and purpose. By any standard except that of birthright, Reginald hardly seemed suited to ruling over the small, independent kingdom.

Russell supposed it was up to him to somehow pull off a miracle and make the man suited. He owed it to his fellow countrymen. The question, as always, remained how.

"Busy?" Russ's deep voice rumbled as he pressed, "Doing what?"

For a moment, Reginald looked incensed at being questioned, but then he let it pass. Instead, he smirked and replied, "Having my last fling of bachelorhood."

Without another word, Reginald began to walk out of the room.

Russell straightened. Though his tone was deceptively easygoing, he wasn't through trying to convince the prince not to ignore his obligations. For him not to go to the princess in person was an insult. What really galled him was that Reginald knew that.

"Forgive me, 'Your Highness,' but you've been 'flinging' ever since you discovered you had something to fling." Moving swiftly, he got in front of the prince, aborting the latter's getaway. He'd endured enough of Reginald's evenings to know exactly what was on the prince's mind. "Don't you think going to Gastonia to bring back your future bride is a little more important than having some nameless, vacant-headed woman pour herself all over you?"

Reginald pretended to pause and actually reflect on the question. "Well, since you put it that way—" His eyes narrowed as his expression became cold. "No." He sighed, irritated. "Look, Carrington, this marriage is for my father, for Amelia's father who wants to keep that poor excuse of a little country of his safe." His tone increased in its sarcasm. "It's for the people of Silvershire so they can litter the streets, rubbing bodies against one another as they jockey for position, pathetically waving the flag and getting a small thrill into their dull, dull lives when the royal carriage passes them by. It's for the news media, who just love 'storybook weddings.'" His eyes narrowed into dark, almost malevolent slits. "It's for every damn person in the universe except me."

Russell struggled not to allow the contempt he felt show on his face. If this was a play for sympathy, it fell well short of its mark. All of his life, the crown prince of Silvershire had had everything he'd ever remotely asked for or wanted. King Weston had never learned how to say no to his only heir. Sadly, abundance and indulgence did not give birth to a wise, magnanimous leader. Reginald had been the Playboy Prince ever since he'd reached his sixteenth birthday.

But despite the fact that the prince was accustomed to women of dazzling beauty, the woman who was to officially share his martial bed was not someone who would fade into the woodwork. He'd seen recent photographs of Princess Amelia and thought that Reginald was getting far better than he deserved.

"Princess Amelia isn't exactly Medusa," he reminded Reginald.

The prince shook his head. He'd made it known more than once that he hated having no say in the matter, hated having any part of his life dictated to him. And this marriage pairing him with the twenty-six-year-old princess had been arranged years before he'd even known what the term meant.

"No," Reginald agreed, "she isn't. But she is undoubtedly a cold fish, because she is a princess, which means she's pampered. And," he recalled, "she had a willful streak as a young girl. I always had to remind her that when we grew up, she was going to have to mind me if she knew what was good for her." He placed his hand on Russell's shoulder. Rather than a show of affection between friends, it was a way for him to remind the duke of his powers over him. "This will be a good start. Come on, be a sport, Carrington." The edges of his smile became slightly brittle as a sharp edge entered his voice. "Don't make me command you."

Russell's face never changed, but inwardly, he felt his resentment flare. He could not remember a day that he hadn't known Reginald. He also couldn't remember a day in which he'd felt that the milk of human kindness even marginally flowed in the prince's veins. They were companions because of proximity, because their ages were similar and because Reginald, although never verbalizing the thought, cleaved to him as a protector.

That was his role more than any other, more than the royal title that he bore or the fact that King Weston had appointed him as Reginald's political advisor. He was Reginald's protector. He knew the political climate, knew the ways of the people. But his first loyalty had always been and would continue to be to the crown, and so, to the prince.

He was Prince Reginald's confidante, his protector and, at times, he was the man's scapegoat. The latter occasion came about when either Reginald's temper got the better of him or when he got into trouble and couldn't bear the close scrutiny of his father or the kingdom for his misdeeds.

A scapegoat was one thing. Serving as a lackey was another. Russell balked at the latter and this certainly felt as if it came under that heading. Bringing the princess back was something Reginald should be doing himself. To send someone else in his place was clearly a veiled insult to the kingdom that was the place of her birth.

He considered what it was that Reginald was telling him. So Amelia had gained some spirit, had she? Good for her. Russell remembered the princess, a fair, shy girl with vivid, violet eyes, who, for the most part, attempted to hide whenever the prince and he accompanied King Weston on royal visits to Gastonia.

On those visits, the adults would converse, leaving

Reginald and him to their own devices and wiles. Reginald would entertain himself by ordering around everyone—especially the princess—like a spoiled child while he, well, he had to admit he wasn't exactly an angel in those days either, Russell remembered with a smile. He loved to play practical jokes. Still did, actually, although it was no longer dignified for him to indulge himself that way.

The poor princess had been his chosen target for water balloons. Hers was always his bed of choice when it came to depositing the vast variety of bugs that the almost fairy-tale-like kingdom of Gastonia had to offer. If he closed his eyes, he could still hear her high-pitched, blood-curdling scream the night he'd slipped a huge black spider in between her sheets.

He remembered that Amelia always looked so relieved whenever their royal vehicle would be pulling away from the palace, signaling an end to their visit. Hers was always the last face he saw as he left the country. He'd focus on her, standing there, beside her father, a small vision in pinks and whites, her blond hair moving in the breeze, her smile widening as they disappeared into the distance.

And now she was going to marry Reginald. He wondered if he would ever see her smile widening again.

That was none of his concern, Russell reminded himself. Reginald was his prince, his soon-to-be king.

The man was going to be unbearable then, Russell thought, feeling sorry for Amelia.

Reginald was shifting from foot to foot, anxious to gain the door.

"There's no reason to bandy this about any longer,"

Reginald said in a dismissive tone. "You will go in my place and you will bring Princess Amelia back. End of discussion."

Russell found his own impatience difficult to bank down. Maybe because, as an adolescent, whenever he'd heard Reginald ordering Amelia around, something inside of him had rebelled, softening to the look in Amelia's eyes. It was a necessary political alliance, but that didn't mean that Reginald should be able to treat the princess like chattel. "Do you intend to be so careless of her feelings once you're married?"

"Feelings?" Reginald jeered incredulously. He looked at Russell as if he thought that he'd lost his mind. "She doesn't have any feelings. She's a princess," he pointed out. "She has duties. I'm sure she makes love that way, too. Like it's her duty." Reginald smirked. "It will be our royal duty to make the Princess Amelia attempt to make love like a flesh-and-blood woman." Smug superiority highlighted his features as the prince delivered another patronizing pat to his shoulder. "That's a royal 'our' in case you think that's an invitation to sample the royal goods before delivery."

Russell shrugged the prince's hand off. "Have I ever told you that you disgust me?"

Reginald took a step back, hatred flashing in his eyes. Hatred, Russell knew, because the prince knew that in a contest of wills or strength, he was more than Reginald's match.

"Frequently. With your eyes." And just so that there was no mistake in intent, he added, "You're the only man I've ever let live who did that." The smirk on Reginald's lips grew larger. "Because at the end of the day, I will be King and you will not."

Russell knew Reginald thought he was taunting him. Russell was next in line for the throne. The rules of the kingdom were such that if the King had no male heirs, then the Duke of Carrington would be the next King of Silvershire. He doubted that Reginald believed that there was nothing that he would have wanted less than to be King. But his ambitions had never taken him in that direction.

As far back as he could remember, he had always hated being in the limelight. Hated being singled out for any reason, for any amount of time. He would have shrugged off the order of succession in a heartbeat, but it wasn't his decision to make. And he was too loyal to his king, and his family's honor meant too much to him, to ever do more than simply contemplate walking away. His path was clear. He had his duties.

As did Princess Amelia. Hers were harder, Russell thought, looking at the prince. At least he didn't have to marry Reginald.

He supposed there was no point in arguing. Reginald wasn't going to be dissuaded from his planned revelry. Maybe the prince did need to get it out of his system one last time. At least, Russell thought, he could hope.

Inclining his head, Russell surrendered. "All right, I'll do it. I'll go and bring the princess back for the wedding."

Reginald smiled coldly, triumphant. "Of course you will. Was there ever any doubt?"

Before Russell could trust himself to safely respond, the prince had left the room, slamming the door in his wake.

* * *

Princess Amelia of Gastonia stood on the palace terrace, overlooking the lush green gardens she loved so much. The gardens where she had played with almost reckless abandonment as a child. While other little girls might have fantasized about being princesses, she, as a princess, had fantasized about being just like any other little girl.

But even then, she'd known that she wasn't like every other little girl in Gastonia, the once-quaint country that her father had brought into the twenty-first century. She was different. On her shoulders was the weight of the kingdom. The welfare of her people. That had been taught to her from a very young age.

And if, by some wild fantasy of fate, she ever forgot for a little while, there had been Prince Reginald's visits to remind her.

She sighed inwardly.

Prince Reginald. The toad. Her fiancé.

Not that the Prince of Silvershire was actually ugly. As a boy, he'd been decent enough to look at. Not like his companion, Russell Southgate, the current Duke of Carrington, of course, whom she'd secretly had a fleeting crush on, but decent. It wasn't the prince's face, but his soul that was ugly.

Amelia strove now not to shiver even as she wrapped her arms around herself for comfort. In another lifetime, she was fairly confident that Reginald could have been, and probably had been, Ivan the Terrible, the blood-thirsty Russian czar.

At least, that was the feeling she always had whenever Reginald was around. He treated everyone around him as if they were less than the bugs that were so plentiful in her garden. She was accustomed to being treated with respect, yet Reginald would order her around as if she were, in his mind, a lowly peasant.

It was Russell who would intercede, distracting Reginald and getting the prince to leave her alone. Russell who reminded her, in those instances, of a medieval knight in shining armor. With his sandy-brown hair, charismatic smile and beautiful dark brown eyes, he had been her hero.

He had also, she remembered, been her tormentor. Russell had never missed a chance to drop a water balloon on her head, or infest her bed with a myriad of bugs. Weeks after the royal party had left, she would have trouble rounding a corner beneath a balcony or getting into bed at night without first stripping off all the sheets, shaking them out and then remaking the bed.

Still, she thought, of the two, Russell was far preferable to Reginald. So when her father had just now come to tell her that Lord Carrington, not the prince, would be the one coming to take her to Silvershire, she'd received the news with a wave of relief, though she was acutely aware that her reprise was only temporary.

She'd always known this day would come, that she would be required to fulfill her obligation as Gastonia's princess. Amelia tried not to shudder; the full impact was only now setting in. She was going to be marrying Reginald. Sharing a crown with Reginald.

Sharing a bed.

Oh, God.

Perhaps if she'd had siblings, someone could have taken this burden from her. But there weren't any siblings. She was her parents' only child. And her marriage was Gastonia's only hope of security.

Still, knowing it would come intellectually was one thing. Absorbing the full impact with her heart was really quite another. Now that it was happening, she felt trapped by honor, duty and circumstance. If she hadn't been born a princess, this wouldn't be happening to her.

"It's not fair, you know," she murmured, more to herself than to the regal man who stood behind her.

Did he feel as helpless as she did? she wondered. Did some part of her father regret having to sacrifice his daughter's happiness in order to insure his country's continued safety?

Amelia turned around to look at her father. "In this day and age, it's not fair, you know. Not fair to have to marry a man who, if not for his lineage, would have trouble securing a date even on the Internet."

King Roman frowned deeply. His eyes looked sad, she thought. There was never any doubt on Amelia's part that her father did love her. And, she hoped, if there were some other way, he would want to see her happy. But King Roman was steeped in tradition and so, she knew, should she be.

With an air of frustration, the king waved an aristocratic-looking hand at her comments. "Be that as it may—"

She wasn't going to make this difficult for him. She was her father's daughter, and well-taught. Amelia nodded. "Be that as it may, I will honor the treaty and my obligation, even though it's obvious that Prince Reginald doesn't think very much of me." She saw her father raise his eyebrows in silent query. "Otherwise, he'd have come here himself."

"I'm sure that Prince Reginald has other pressing business, my dear."

Amelia laughed softly. She, like everyone else in both her kingdom and his, knew of Reginald's reputation. "I'm sure 'pressing' is involved."

Gray-and-white eyebrows rose high on her father's forehead in shocked disapproval. King Roman was an enlightened man, but not where his daughter was concerned. Even though he had given her the best tutors and trainers he could find, in some areas he tried to keep her unworldly. "Amelia."

Amelia forced a smile to her lips. "I will not disappoint you, Father," she promised.

Even though I'm horribly disappointed myself, she added silently.

King Roman took her hand in both of his and then raised it to his lips. "You have always been my treasure," he told her before he left.

Amelia turned toward the garden again. She heard her father's footsteps recede on the stone terrace until they faded away altogether. With a sigh, she made her way down the terrace steps to the garden. Maybe the flowers and the vast green scenery would help soothe her agitated state.

They didn't.

She was a princess; was it so wrong to hope for a prince who lived up to her expectations, not some personification of self-indulgence and sloth such as Reginald? The prince's escapades were well-known. His face had graced covers of *People* magazine, not to mention that the tabloids loved him. She frowned to herself. Not exactly the prince she'd hoped for.

And this, Amelia thought darkly as she picked her way through a passageway where the shrubs were as tall as trees, giving her a measure of solitude, was what she'd been saving herself for all these years. This was why she'd remained a virgin in a day and age when abstinence and virtue were not so highly prized as they once had been. In some circles, virginity was even viewed with skepticism and no small amount of pity.

She'd done it by choice, and she felt cheated. Royally. Pun intended, she thought, her lips twisting in a self-deprecating smile.

Involved in numerous charities and educational programs throughout Gastonia as well as in matters of state, she was acutely aware of the fact that she hadn't really lived life to the fullest. Not where it counted, she thought ruefully. She'd traveled the world over and was still sheltered.

How could she love her people, be compassionate, if she'd never experienced real love herself? If she'd never wanted to give of herself until there was nothing left to give?

She wished now that she had been a little freer, a little more resourceful where her own pleasures were concerned. She knew of a great many high-born girls who'd been ingenious when it came to satisfying their curiosity and their appetites.

But that was just it. She'd wanted it to mean something. She hadn't wanted the experience just to have it. She'd wanted it to be something to remember to the end of her days. And now, what she was going to remember was that horrible rutting animal mounting her. Probably issuing orders to her while he did it.

It made her want to run away. It made her want to have an affair, however brief.

She sighed, shaking her head. She knew better than that. She was the Princess Amelia and no more able to have an affair than pigs could fly. Especially not only days away from her wedding.

Oh, well, maybe she was being too hard on Reginald. Maybe he'd changed. Maybe he had gotten all the wildness out of his system and would be the good, decent husband and ruler she was praying for.

And maybe, just maybe, she thought as she turned around and began to walk back toward the palace, hell would freeze over before her wedding day. The odds, she knew, were more in favor of the latter than the former.

Chapter 2

The soft ticking of the antique clock that had once belonged to her grandmother seemed to fill the spacious bedroom, nestling into the corners and gently stroking the shadows. The sound became more audible with every passing moment.

Amelia couldn't sleep. Try as she might to will herself into an unconscious state, she couldn't achieve it. Usually, all she needed to do was close her eyes and, within moments, she would drift off. On those rare occasions when sleep initially eluded her, she'd employ little tricks to render her mind blank, enabling her to fall asleep.

But reading hadn't helped. She'd gone through five chapters of the book she kept on her nightstand and was now more wide awake than ever. Silently singing the same refrain over and over again in her mind didn't work, either. Amelia felt frustrated. That self-hypnotic trick had *always* worked before.

But then, she'd never been in this position before. Never suffered through a night-before-she-was-to-meet-with-the-man-who-was-going-to-take-her-to-the-rest-of-her-life before. Because that was what it was. Carrington was coming to take her to her destiny. A destiny she neither remotely liked nor wanted.

Sitting up, Amelia unconsciously doubled her hands into fists. If she had any courage at all, she'd just turn her back on everything and run away. Go to America and avail herself of all the wondrous opportunities that existed there. America, where no one was a princess.

Except perhaps in the eyes of the man who loved her.

Something else she was never going to find out about, she thought glumly. What it felt like to be loved. Because Reginald certainly didn't love her. And she didn't love him, either. Never had. Never would.

Amelia sighed, dragging her hand through the blond hair that came cascading down about her face and pushing it back. No, running away would be the coward's way out. Cowards turned their backs on responsibilities and did what they wanted to, what was easier, what was more appealing. And above everything else, she had been raised not to be a coward. Meeting her destiny, that was what took courage. And she was going to have to dig deep to find hers.

Frowning, Amelia kicked off the covers, slid her slippers on and got off the wide, king-size bed. Because the nights in Gastonia were still cool, even though this was April, she slipped on her dressing gown,

covering the very short nightgown that she favored.
Tying it securely at her waist, she decided that she desperately needed to get some air.

More than that, she needed to walk around her
garden, even though she'd just been there hours earlier.
The time for walks in her beloved garden would soon
be behind her, but right now, she was still the Princess
of Gastonia, not yet the Queen of Silvershire. And this
was still her home.

No, Amelia corrected herself as she slipped quietly
down the back stairs, holding to the shadows and taking
care not to run into anyone, this would *always* be her
home. Nothing would ever change that.

Of the two countries, Silvershire was the bigger,
more powerful, more impressive one. But it was
Gastonia that was the more charming of the two. And
it was decidedly not as backward as she knew Prince
Reginald undoubtedly thought it was.

The strides the kingdom had taken were all due to her
father. Oh, the country still had its charming seaside
shops and internationally famous restaurants, as well as
its grand hotels and the casinos that always drew in
tourists by the droves. But Gastonia had also become
an important industrial country producing, among other
things, the very expensive, very alluring and highly
reliable Gaston, an automobile reminiscent of yesterday's romantic vehicles, with cutting-edge technology
beneath the hood that had been perfected by one of their
own engineers.

Her father was indirectly responsible for the Gaston
as well as for the country's modernization. It was he

who had raised the caliber of education within Gastonia, funding programs, bringing in men of letters and science to teach at Roman University, the institution that bore his name. Students no longer left the country in pursuit of higher degrees, they attained them here, in Gastonia. And then went on to give back what they had learned.

Amelia wondered if Gastonia's advancements were an allure for Reginald. Heaven knew the prince wasn't the type of man to be herded into an arranged marriage without feeling he was getting something out of the bargain. He probably saw his personal bank account swelling if and when he thought of the marriage at all.

The Gaston was currently all the rage in Europe. Granted, her father did not believe in the government owning the companies within its borders and to his credit, neither did Silvershire's King Weston, but she had an uneasy feeling that her future husband was not nearly so noble. He might want to change that, might want to put the money from the car company's coffers into his own pockets.

Bypassing the main hallway, Amelia pressed her lips together. It was going to be up to her to make sure that Reginald became noble. Or, at the very least, it would be up to her to ameliorate whatever black thoughts the prince might have about raping her countrymen and helping himself to the profits that were being made. Her heart felt heavy in her chest.

Opening the terrace doors, she slipped outside and hurried down the steps. Only when she reached the garden with its tall shrubs standing like silent, dark green sentries did she slow down.

She still felt as if she were running from something, because, in effect, she was, although she knew that in reality, there was no running away from what had to be.

As she began to walk the grounds, she waited for a sense of peace to embrace her. She waited in vain. Peace continued to elude her.

What were the chances that all this was merely a bad dream? That she'd wake up an ordinary person who'd just experienced an epic nightmare? Or, at the very least, that Reginald had changed his mind about marrying her, or, better still, had gotten lost forever while on some safari deep in the heart of the African jungle?

Amelia's generous mouth curved in a mocking smile. She was really beginning to sound like a desperate loon. Her fate was sealed, she might as well accept it.

She glanced back toward the palace. How had she managed to get this far from the terrace so quickly? Maybe it was time to—

Amelia stopped.

She could have sworn she'd heard something. A noise. Footsteps. Holding very still, her breath lodged in her chest, she cocked her head and listened intently.

And heard the noise again.

There was someone out here.

Her father had left that evening on business, so it wasn't him that she heard. The king had told her that he wouldn't be back until morning. When her father had left, he'd assured her that he would return well before Lord Carrington was scheduled to arrive at Gastonia's only airport.

It was a little after midnight and she felt it safe to assume that everyone who worked in the palace had retired to their own lives for the remainder of the night. Who did that leave?

She stiffened. There it was again. Rustling. Someone brushing against the shrubs that were directly on the other side of the ones she was facing. She was sure of it.

Since there was no sound of soft laughter or lowered voices exchanging endearments, Amelia knew that whoever she heard couldn't be any of the palace's younger employees sneaking a moment to share the grounds with someone special.

It had to be an intruder.

A chill ran down her back. How had he gotten past the palace security?

Her heart began to hammer quickly. Her father would have ordered her to hurry back to the palace before whoever had managed to get on the grounds saw her.

But her father had also been the one to see to it that she had extensive training in self-defense, telling her that in the end, all one had was oneself to rely on. She wasn't going to turn tail and run. This was her home, damn it, and no one was going to make her fearful while she was here.

With a rush of adrenaline, Amelia charged around the shrubs, uttering something akin to a war cry that had been designed by her trainer to help empower her and increase her adrenaline while intimidating whoever was on the receiving end.

The man who turned around to see her coming at him a second before she tackled him was tall. His muscular frame was clothed entirely in black. Like a burglar.

She'd meant to knock him down, to, at the very least, knock the wind out of him. And she succeeded.

Partially.

What she hadn't counted on was that at the last moment, the man in black would grab her wrist. When he went down, he took her with him.

The air drained out of her lungs as she was yanked down. Her head made contact with his chin. She wasn't sure who got the worst of it.

Within moments of her hastily devised attack, Amelia found herself sprawled out on top of the intruder, stars swirling through her head, her face a mere three inches away from his. If that.

If the intruder was surprised or dazed, it was for less than a heartbeat. And since hers was beating in a tempo that made "The Flight of the Bumblebee" sound like a tune being played in slow motion, the registry of the intruder's emotion came and went in something less than could be calibrated by any earthly means.

And then she heard the laugh. Deep, rich, full and completely all-encompassing. A laugh that drenched whoever heard it with liquid waves of warmth. A laugh out of her past.

Amelia blinked. She stared down at the face of the man beneath her. A man who might or might not be an intruder but who definitely was having a reaction, not to what had just transpired, but to what was happening this very moment. The very intimate contact of their bodies.

The ends of her robe were spread out on either side like the giant wings of a bird and the scrap of silk beneath seemed not to be there at all. Every inch of his rocklike body was imprinted against hers. And she was achingly aware of it.

Gastonia's cool night breeze faded instantly, all but fried in the face of the heat that was traveling up and down her body like white lightning, desperately searching for a target.

"Russell." Her voice sounded hoarse to her ears.

The smile that slipped along his lips was positively wicked. He made no effort to move or rectify the situation. "At your service, princess."

As if somewhere someone had magically snapped their fingers, Amelia scrambled to her feet, vainly trying to regain her composure. Not an easy feat when her entire body felt as if it were vibrating like a tuning fork struck against a goblet filled to the brim with subtly aged red wine.

She tugged the ends of her robe together. Her insides were still trembling, but she noticed thankfully that her hands were steady enough.

"What are you doing here?" she demanded.

Russell rose to his feet in a fluid motion she envied. "Apparently being knocked off my feet by a blazing ball of fire." He casually brushed himself off. Humor never left his lips. And his eyes never left hers.

The trembling had stopped. But she couldn't get her body to stop tingling. This was like old times, she thought. Except that instead of a water balloon, she'd been hit by Russell. Sort of.

She was a woman now, not a child. Forming coherent words should not be an insurmountable effort for her.

Taking a breath, Amelia managed to restore a measure of dignity to the moment. "I mean, you weren't due until tomorrow."

How *had* he managed to sneak into the country? Just how lax was security at the airport? She made a mental note to speak to her father.

Her father.

Her eyes widened as she remembered. "My father had a ceremony all in place to greet you at the airport."

If the information was meant to evoke remorse from the tall man before her, it failed. He gave her his trademark lopsided smile. The same one that had made her adolescent heart secretly flutter.

"Which is why," he told her, "I came in early this evening."

She knew what Reginald thought of Gastonia and the crown. Did his chief political advisor and cohort share that view? Her eyes narrowed as a wave of protectiveness passed over her. "To humiliate my father?"

He made no effort at denial. He thought her intelligent enough to know that none was needed. "To avoid attention."

Still smarting from Reginald's high-handed snub, she looked for the insult in Russell's actions. "Why? Are you ashamed to have to come to bring me back to your prince, Lord Carrington?"

She was being formal. Somehow, he hadn't expected her to be. He'd expected her, he supposed, to be exactly the way she'd been the last time he'd seen her. Sweet. Unassuming. And open.

But nothing in life, Russell reminded himself, stayed

the same. Things changed, they evolved or they died. There didn't seem to be any other choice.

He saw the way her mouth curved, saw the displeasure when she uttered Reginald's title. It was obvious that the princess was no happier about the union than Reginald was. And in her case, Russell couldn't blame her. At least Reginald was getting a beautiful woman. All Amelia was getting, beyond a treaty, was an egotistical, self-indulgent, power-hungry, spoiled brat of a man who seemed too besotted with his womanizing way of life to appreciate even marginally what he was being handed on a silver platter.

"No," he answered her question quietly, "I'm not ashamed to be the one to bring you back to Silvershire. I just don't care for any kind of unnecessary fanfare. Unlike the prince, I never really liked being in the spotlight, however briefly."

The moon was full tonight and its silvery light was caressing the man standing before her. Amelia realized that she'd stopped breathing only when her lungs began to ache. As subtly as she could, she drew in a long breath.

"Then perhaps political advisor shouldn't have been your first choice of a career, Carrington."

"It wasn't. But my father couldn't see his way clear to his only son being a beachcomber. And I liked it better when you called me Russell. No fanfare," he reminded her.

"No fanfare," she repeated with a nod, then forced her mind back on the conversation and not on the fact that somehow, during the years since she had last seen him, Russell had come into the possession of a very muscular-looking body. "Beachcomber," she echoed. "Do they still have that sort of thing?"

He laughed. The moonlight wove through her hair, turning it the color of pale wheat. He caught himself just before he began to raise his hand to touch it. He'd been sent to bring her back, not to familiarize himself with the packaging. "If I had anything to say about it, they would."

God help her, she could see him, lying on the beach, wearing the briefest of bathing suits, the tide bringing the waves just up to his toes, gently lapping his tanned skin.

She had to swallow twice to counteract the dryness in her mouth. It was a credit to her breeding and training that she could continue without dropping the thread of the conversation.

"Seriously, if you don't like the attention, *Russell*," she emphasized his name and he nodded with a smile in response, sending her pulse up another notch, "there had to be something else that you could have become."

He shook his head. He knew better. "Not with my lineage. Besides, someone needs to be there to temper the prince."

She looked at him for a long moment. There was more to the man than just practical jokes and devastating good looks. Or was he ultimately cut out of the same cloth as Reginald and just bragging?

"And you can do that?"

Russell heard the skepticism in her voice. Not that he blamed her. He had no reputation by choice. Reginald's was international.

"I have a modest success rate, but in comparison, it's still better than anyone else's." He didn't want to talk about Reginald. Not tonight. There was more than enough time for that later. He looked at her, thinking about what she had just done. "You thought I was an intruder."

"Yes, obviously." As she moved her shoulder, the robe began to slip off. She tugged it back into place, aware that he had looked at the exposed area. That he was still looking. She felt naked. And unashamed at the same time.

"Why didn't you get someone from security?" Russell asked.

Pride had her lifting her chin defiantly. She wasn't a helpless little girl anymore. "Because I could handle it myself."

She hadn't struck him as being reckless, but tackling him like that hadn't been the act of a intelligent person. "You're the princess," he pointed out. "It doesn't behoove you to take chances."

Amelia rolled her eyes. Was he like all the rest of them? Why wouldn't he be? she challenged silently. He was part of Reginald's inner circle. "Oh, please, no lectures." And then she sighed. It was a losing battle. "Or if you feel you simply must, take a number. There are a few people ahead of you."

"Such as?"

She saw his lips curving. Was he laughing at her? Having fun at her expense? Try as she might to take offense, she couldn't. There was something about his smile... But then, there always had been.

"Such as my father. His advisors. It seems these days, everyone feels they have to tell me what my duty is."

"I won't," he promised, dropping the subject for now.

And then he looked at her, compassion filling his eyes. "You're not having an easy time of it, are you, princess?"

She thought of denying it, of saying everything was fine and that she had no idea what he was talking about. But everything wasn't fine and, very possibly, never would be again. Not once she left for Silvershire and married Reginald.

With a feeling of longing wrapped in futility, she thought of the past. "Things were a lot simpler when all I had to worry about was ducking out of the way of water balloons and checking my bed half a dozen times to make sure I didn't find any surprises in it before I got in."

He laughed. He'd been a hellion back then, all right. The thing was, he couldn't really say he regretted it. Teasing Amelia was the one way he had of making her notice him. He had no crown in his arsenal, but he had been clever and he'd used his wiles to his advantage. He remembered how wide those violet eyes could get.

"These days, I'm sure the surprises in your bed are far more pleasant," he told her. "And come with less legs."

The moment the words were out, he waited for the anger to gather in her eyes, the indignation to appear on her face. Without meaning to, he'd crossed a line. But he'd always had a habit of being too frank and with Amelia, he'd felt instantly too comfortable to censor himself.

She surprised him by exhibiting no annoyance at his assumption. "The only thing my bed contains, besides sheets and blankets, is me."

The moment was recovered nicely. "The prince will be very happy to hear that."

As if she cared what made that thoughtless ape

happy, Amelia thought darkly. "Speaking of the prince, why didn't he come himself?"

He'd expected her to ask and shrugged vaguely. "He had business to attend to." If it were him, he added silently, nothing on heaven or earth would have kept him from coming for her.

Amelia laughed shortly. "What is her name? Or doesn't he know?"

Russell looked at his prince's intended bride for a long moment. For all his wealth and fame, he'd never envied Reginald. Until this moment. "You're a lot more worldly than I remember."

"You remember a thirteen-year-old girl who was afraid of her own shadow." Her eyes held his, "I'm not afraid of my shadow anymore."

He rubbed his jaw where her head had hit against it just before recognition had set in for her. For him, it had been immediate, because he'd followed the stories about her that appeared in the newspapers. Stories that were as different from the ones about Reginald as a robin was from the slug it occasionally ate. While stories about Reginald went on about his various less than tasteful escapades, hers told of her humanitarian efforts.

"I noticed," he replied with an appreciative, warm laugh.

Amelia felt the laugh traveling straight to the center of her abdomen, before it seemed to spread to regions beyond, like a sunbeam landing on a rock, then widening as the sun's intensity increased.

She cleared her throat and looked back toward the palace. It was obvious that he had to have come through there to wind up here. "How did you get into the palace?"

She watched as a smile entered his eyes, shadowing a memory. "Remember that old underground passage you once showed me?"

Amelia's eyes widened. He was referring to something that was forever burned into her memory. She'd slipped away from her nanny, leaving the poor woman to deal with Reginald, while she took it upon herself to share her secret discovery with Russell. It was the one bold incident she remembered from her childhood.

Remembered it, too, because the episode had ended in a kiss. A soft, swift, chaste kiss that Russell had stolen from her.

A kiss, Amelia thought, that she still remembered above all the others that had subsequently come in its wake.

She was glad for the moonlight, fervently hoping that it offered sufficient cover for the blush that she felt creeping up her neck and onto her cheeks.

Chapter 3

"So that's how you got in," Amelia finally said, finding her tongue.

Strangely enough, the air was not uncomfortable, but it had grown far too still between them. And she found herself feeling things. Things that, at any other time, she would have welcomed, would have enjoyed exploring, things she had never felt before, had only thought about. But feelings like this, if allowed to flourish, to unfold, would only get in the way of her obligations.

She suddenly felt a great deal older than her twenty-six years.

"That's how I got in," the tall, handsome man at her side confirmed needlessly.

They had begun to walk back to the palace, to the world where their lives were, for the most part, completely laid out for them. Where obligations constricted freedom and feelings were forced by the wayside. All that mattered were boundaries.

"I had to do a lot of stooping," Russell continued. His mouth curved as he spared her a glance. "The passageway beneath the garden to the palace is a great deal smaller than I remembered."

Amelia paused for a moment, reluctant to leave the shelter of the garden. Here, for a fleeting amount of time, she could pretend to be anyone she wanted to be.

Banking down her thoughts, Amelia began to walk again as she smiled at Russell. "You're a lot bigger than you were then." *And you've filled out,* she added silently.

"I suppose," he allowed with a self-deprecating laugh she found endearing as well as stirring. "Funny how you never really think of yourself as changing."

Moving to one side, he held the terrace door open for her. Amelia looked up into his face as she entered the palace. "Is that a warning?"

His eyebrows drew together over a nose that could only be described as perfect. Entering behind her, he closed the French doors. "I don't follow."

Amelia led the way to the rear staircase. As before, she kept her path to the shadows that pooled along the floor. The palace seemed empty, but that was just an illusion. There were more than a hundred people on the premises.

Though she sincerely doubted that Russell didn't understand her meaning, she played along. "Should I be looking over my shoulder for water balloons?"

Cupping her elbow, he escorted her up the stairs. Perfectly capable of climbing them on her own, she still enjoyed the unconscious show of chivalry, not to mention the contact. It was hard to believe that this was the same mischievous, dark-eyed youth who'd simultaneously tortured her and filled her daydreams.

"The water balloons were never over your shoulder," Russell pointed out as they came to the landing. "They were always dropped from overhead." His mouth curved a little more on the right than on the left. "I'm sorry about that."

Amelia tilted her head and looked into his eyes. They were the color of warm chocolate. How strange that she could pick up the thread so easily, as if no time had gone by at all since his last visit. As if more than twelve years had merely melted away into the mists that sometimes surrounded the island kingdom and they were children again.

"No, you're not."

She was rewarded with the rich sound of his laugh as it echoed down the long, winding hallway lined with portraits of her ancestors. They seemed to approve of him, she thought.

"All right, maybe I wasn't," Russell admitted. "Then," he quickly qualified. "But I am now." He saw her raise her delicate eyebrows in a silent query. And just for the tiniest of moments, he had an overwhelming urge to trace the arches with the tip of his finger. He squelched it. "I frightened you."

"You made me jumpy," Amelia corrected, then in case that would arouse some kind of unwanted pity, she quickly added, "You also made me strong."

He shook his head. "I don't understand."

With the grace of a princess trained at putting others at ease, Amelia slipped her arm through his and urged him down the hallway. If her heart sped up just a little bit at the contact, well, that was a secret bonus she kept to herself.

"Because of you, I became disgusted with myself. With being a mouse."

"You were thirteen."

"I was a mouse," she repeated, then added with the loftiness that befitted her station, "I resolved to be a tigress."

Russell looked at her for a long moment. "A tigress, eh?" At first, he'd thought of her as too sweet, too innocent. But there was something in her eyes, something about the way she carried herself. Maybe the image was not as far-fetched as it initially seemed.

He felt his blood stirring again and this time upbraided himself. He had no business reacting like this to his future queen.

"A tigress," she repeated with a lift of her head. "I pleaded with my father to get me trainers, not just for my mind, but for my body."

Short on water balloons, Russell sought refuge in humor. "So that you could flip intruders who crossed your path?"

Her eyes danced. "Exactly."

Another woman, he thought, might have taken insult just now. While he had his doubts about the kind of king Reginald would ultimately make, he was beginning to feel that at least Silvershire's future queen was a woman who did not take herself too seriously. That spoke of a magnanimous ruler.

He laughed softly under his breath. "Judging from the way that ended up, I'd say you need a little more training."

"I'll work on it."

They had come to a split in the hallway. Her rooms were on the far end at the right. The guest quarters were in the opposite direction, on another floor. It wouldn't seem proper for her to walk him to his room, even though she found herself wanting to. Rules, always rules, she thought impatiently, chafing inwardly.

She forced a smile to her lips. "I'll have someone show you to your quarters."

"No need. I've already settled in." Russell saw the protest rising to her lips and knew just what she was going to say. "I assumed that I would be staying in the same quarters I occupied the last time I was here."

What had been adequate for the boy was not so for the man. She was surprised that he wouldn't know that. "Actually, my father had left instructions for a suite of rooms to be prepared for you."

But Russell shook his head. "The room I'm in will do just fine. I don't need a suite of rooms," he told her. "After all, I'm only going to be here long enough for you to gather together your entourage." Since she'd been forewarned, he assumed that would only take her perhaps a day.

"My entourage," she echoed. The term made her want to laugh as she imagined traveling about with an entire tribe of ladies-in-waiting trailing after her. The very idea made her feel trapped, hemmed in. And she was experiencing enough of that already without adding to it.

"You mean Madeline." Madeline Carlyle was the

Duke of Forsythe's youngest daughter. With fiery red hair and a fiery spirit to match, Madeline was the perfect companion in her opinion. Madeline could always be counted on to tell her the truth.

Russell looked at her, mildly surprised. "Madeline? Just the one companion?"

"Just the one."

Russell paused to regard her with deepening interest. Princess Amelia was certainly different from the man she was betrothed to, he thought. Reginald never went anywhere without at least a dozen people in tow. The prince had a hunger for an accommodating, accepting audience observing his every move.

"What about a bodyguard?"

Unconsciously rocking forward on her toes, Amelia raised her eyes to his, unaware of how terribly appealing she looked. "I expect that would be you."

There was something about the way she looked at him that stirred things deep within him. It made him want to stand in the way of an oncoming bus just to protect her.

It also made him want to tell her to turn and flee before it was too late. Before Reginald had an opportunity to defile her.

But he couldn't say that. Couldn't warn her in any way. His duty, first and foremost, was to his king, to his country and to his prince. Not to a princess from another kingdom. The fact that his duty was elsewhere stuck in his throat.

After a beat he finally replied quietly, "That would be me. I suppose that means there won't be much 'gathering' involved."

"I suppose not."

Amelia tried not to think of what she was saying. Of what her words actually meant. That she was leaving Gastonia, leaving everything she loved for a man she didn't. For a man she didn't even like.

With just the faintest inclination of his head, Russell bowed. It was time to take his leave before he forgot himself and misspoke. "Until the morning, then."

"Until the morning," she echoed.

She stood there for a long moment, watching the man who had become the Duke of Carrington, who would always be the boy who reveled in ambushing her with water balloons and bugs, walk down the hall. Away from her.

She didn't know what to do with the emptiness inside.

"We can't leave."

Those were the first words Amelia uttered in greeting him the following morning as she swept into the dining room. Rather than take his breakfast in the formal dining room, Russell had chosen to take his first meal in Gastonia in the palace's informal dining room, the one that only sat twenty people instead of fifty.

Preoccupied with his thoughts, with disturbing dreams that all centered around Amelia and the marriage that was to be, Russell hadn't even heard her enter. He rose quickly to his feet now in acknowledgment of her presence. They might be friends of a sort, but there were traditions to honor and he had been trained long and well in them.

Taking a seat, Amelia waved for him to sit down

again. Since the king had yet to arrive at the palace, she sat at the head of the table. Russell was to her right. Having him there made the room seem oddly intimate, despite its size.

Instead of exchanging obligatory small talk, Russell picked up the conversation she'd started up as she'd entered the room. "By *leave,* are you referring to leaving the palace, Princess?"

"No, the country," she corrected.

He looked confused. And sweetly adorable. Did he accompany Reginald when the prince made his endless rounds at the various clubs where they knew him by sight rather than reputation? Was Russell just as eager as the prince to have women pour themselves all over him?

That's not supposed to matter, she reminded herself sternly.

But she went on wondering.

"Madeline is ill," she explained, "and I won't leave without her."

Amelia's position seemed reasonable enough to him, seeing as his assignment had been to bring back the princess and "her entourage." Curiosity prompted him to ask, "What's wrong with her?"

"Madeline has always had a passion for exotic foods." She spread the gleaming white linen napkin on her lap. "Sometimes that's not such a good thing." Madeline was up for anything; when they were children, Madeline was the one who could be counted on to swallow a bug whole to discover what it tasted like. "Something she ate yesterday didn't agree with her. From what she told me, she'd been up all night, reacquainting her knees with the tile on her bathroom floor. The doctor gave her something. Depending on how she feels, she might not be able to travel for at least two, perhaps three days." She watched his expression for signs of irritation.

But Russell took it in stride and nodded his head. "I'll inform King Weston to have the tubas put in storage for a few days," he deadpanned.

"Tubas?"

The somber expression vanished as he flashed a grin. She caught herself thinking that he had a delicious smile. "You didn't think you could enter Silvershire without a parade, did you?"

A parade. Amelia groaned inwardly. "I thought you hated the spotlight."

"I do. But it won't be shining on me," he pointed out. "The parade is for you."

She would just as soon have it canceled. But she knew that was asking for too much. Fanfare was something that was required by the people. And something, she had learned, that had to be borne with quiet, resigned dignity.

On impulse, Amelia leaned in toward him, lowering her voice even though there were only the two of them in the room, not counting the man whose duty it was to serve the meal. "I'll let you in on a secret. I don't like fanfare, either."

A breeze from somewhere brought just the subtlest whiff of her perfume to him, teasing his senses. Russell did his best to ignore it, succeeding only moderately.

"Must be hell for you, then," he commented with sympathy.

"At times," she acknowledged.

Feeling comforted by the fact that her departure was postponed for at least two days, and just a tad guilty that her unexpected boon was due to Madeline's misery, Amelia nodded toward the palace servant who stood unobtrusively at the ready. Words were not necessary. She'd had the same thing for breakfast for the last three years. Three slices of French toast. The man slipped away to bring it to her.

Feeling progressively more cheerful by the moment, Amelia let impulse continue to guide her. "Since we're not going away, I've decided to take you sightseeing."

He was surprised by the offer. And pleased. He'd assumed that he'd be left to his own devices until departure. This promised to be a great deal more entertaining than the book he'd brought along.

"Oh, you have, have you?"

The servant returned with her plate and placed it before her before deftly standing back. Amelia offered the older man a smile of thanks before continuing. "Yes, I have."

"Is that a royal decree?"

She couldn't read his expression. It was completely inscrutable. Had she been too quick to judge him so favorably? Or was he just teasing her, the way he used to? "Does it have to be?"

He thought of stretching out the moment. He liked the way her eyes widened when she seemed confused. But it wasn't fair to her and besides, he had no business placing things on anything but a respectful footing. They weren't children anymore.

Maybe that was just the problem, he thought. They

weren't children anymore. And he was having some definitely unchildlike feelings about her.

Tread lightly here, Carrington, he cautioned himself. *This is going to be your queen, not your consort.*

"No," he answered. Then, because he'd been on more than one tour during his visits here, he added, "I'd love to see your country through the eyes of an adult."

She gave her own interpretation to his answer. "Then you have given up dropping water balloons?"

Amelia slipped the fork between her lips. Finding the action arousing, Russell forced himself to look away. "Why do you keep bringing that up?"

Slim shoulders rose and then fell again in a careless motion. "Once burnt, twice shy…"

He didn't bother to suppress the laugh that rose in his throat. "As I remember it, it was a few more times than once."

That it was, she thought. "Twenty-three times to be exact."

Mild surprise highlighted his features as he looked at her. "You kept score."

"I did."

His eyes met hers. He saw humor there. "Should I be worried?"

She deliberately took a few bites of her breakfast before leaning in his direction and saying, "Be afraid, Carrington. Be very afraid."

Though neither one of them had planned it initially, they wound up spending the entire day together. Acting as his guide, Amelia took him to two museums, one devoted to art, the other to history. Though neither had ever really interested him, Russell discovered that, seen through her eyes, both had a great deal to offer. In between, she took him to one of Gastonia's many parks for an impromptu picnic lunch.

"I'm not the picnic type," he'd protested.

And she'd laughed as if he had said something really amusing and told him with a knowing look that yes, he was, and she was going to prove it.

So he ate the healthy-size sandwiches she'd produced out of a picnic basket while sitting on a maroon-colored blanket beneath the drooping shade of a weeping willow. If asked, he couldn't have said what, exactly, was between the two pieces of bread. It wasn't that it was tasteless, it was just that his attention had been completely and utterly taken by his companion.

She charmed him with her wit, with her knowledge, with her laugh…with the shape of her mouth as it pulled into a smile. Over and over again, he kept thinking that Reginald should have been there, in his place, learning to appreciate this woman who had miraculously been given to him on a platter.

And secretly he was glad that he was here instead.

Russell found himself not wanting the day to end.

And in the evening, with a myriad of stars littering the sky, they returned to the palace.

The second they came through the massive double doors, they were informed by the butler that King Roman was waiting to meet with the duke.

"I'll come with you," Amelia offered.

"Your Highness, he asked only for the duke," the butler said tactfully.

Russell expected Amelia to back away. Instead, she tossed her head and said, "But he will get a princess, as well." She looked at him. "My father will undoubtedly say something that will either concern Gastonia or me. In either case, I should know." Slipping her arm through his, she said, "This way," and brought him to the royal study, her father's favorite place.

Her father often retired to the study to contemplate matters of state and to partake of his evening brandy. More often than not, she would join him for the latter. His life centered around his country and his daughter, in that order. Amelia took no offense. It was just the way things were. But if she took no offense, she also did not take a back seat.

King Roman looked far from surprised that his daughter was accompanying his royal guest. Looking up from the book he had been casually perusing, he asked, "What's this about you creeping in like a leper, Carrington?"

"The duke doesn't care for fanfare," Amelia said, taking the liberty to answer for the man she'd taken sightseeing.

The king nodded. "Refreshing." Setting aside his book, he picked up his goblet of brandy. "This aversion of yours, I trust, does not extend to the reception I have arranged in your honor."

Russell glanced at the woman beside him. He noticed that the princess had caught her bottom lip between her teeth. Obviously, she had forgotten to tell him about that. "Reception, Your Majesty?"

"The one in the royal ballroom taking place in—" the king paused to look at the timepiece he kept in his pocket "—oh, I believe half an hour."

Having learned long ago to have nothing rattle him, Russell inclined his head. "Then I had better go and get ready. If you will excuse me?" He bowed first to the king, then to Amelia.

She was born to this, Amelia thought. To pomp and circumstance and tradition. But it still felt strange, at times, when she stood back to analyze it, to see someone bowing to her just because whimsical fate had bestowed a title on her. It could have just as easily been someone else.

Her father turned to her. He looked pleased, she thought, and not at all upset by the note she'd left in her wake informing the king on his arrival that Carrington was already here and that she had taken charge of him. "I see you two have buried the hatchet."

"There was never any hatchet, Father," she corrected gently. "Not between the duke and myself."

Roman caught the inference and looked at his daughter. "And the prince?"

"Is another story," she concluded evasively.

"Amelia," he began, his voice heavy with regret. "Amelia, you know that if there were any other way to secure Gastonia's safety against her enemies, I would do it. In these modern times, there are terrorists and countries that would take us over in an instant if not for—"

"I know." For her father's sake, because she didn't want him feeling guilty over something they both knew had to be, she forced a smile to her lips. "I'd better go and get ready for the reception. I'm afraid it completely slipped my mind."

She'd seemed unusually happy when she'd entered the room just now, the king thought. He looked after his daughter's departing figure, wondering what else might have slipped her mind today.

Chapter 4

From as far back as he could remember, Russell Southgate, III, Duke of Carrington, had been trained to keep his wits and composure about him at all times. Eventually, it had become second nature to him, like breathing. Never was it more important than during the most stressful occasions. To his late father's never-ending pride, he was considered to be a tower of strength among his peers. While others lost their heads, Russell did not. He remained calm and clear-thinking. Being rattled was not something that he could ever recall happening to him.

So it came as a complete and utter surprise to Russell that, while assuring King Roman that no disrespect was meant by either Prince Reginald or the realm of Silvershire by His Highness not coming in person to escort his bride home, he found himself stopping midword. The rest of his sentence, as well as what had come before, had simultaneously and instantly evaporated from his tongue and his mind. Everything had been eclipsed by the vision in blue he saw entering the ballroom.

He felt warm. Disoriented. And completely captivated. Only past training had him closing his mouth before his jaw slackened and drooped.

Puzzled, his back to the entrance, King Roman stared at the young duke before him, waiting for the man to continue. Turning, the king looked to see what it was that had caught the man's attention so completely, to the point of suddenly rendering him mute.

And then he saw her.

His daughter.

He saw the way Prince Reginald's more-than-able-bodied representative was looking at her. While his father's heart took pride in the fact that Amelia was a vision of loveliness that could even distract the well respected Duke of Carrington, when he viewed the moment with the eyes of the ruler of Gastonia, he was more than a little dismayed. Instincts that had allowed Roman to guide his small country from its past quaint state to what it had now become, a country devoted to both industry and the pursuit of knowledge, sent up red flags of alert and alarm.

Roman waited a moment longer. He told himself that his never-failing concern for the country's welfare, his anxiety that all go well these next few weeks, not to mention the heavy guilt he bore as a father, were responsible for his overreaction. The duke was just taken with the sight of a beautiful woman. There was nothing more to it than that.

The king fervently hoped he was right.

Forcing a smile to his lips, he leaned slightly toward the man who, until a moment earlier, had been setting his mind at ease.

"She is beautiful, isn't she?" Roman acknowledged softly.

Like a man suddenly in the grip of a hypnotic trance, his eyes never wavering from their target, Russell slowly nodded his response. And then he roused himself, regaining control over all but what he had just been saying. The subject eluded him as completely as if it had never been raised.

"But that was always understood, even when the princess was a child," he managed to murmur, hoping the king would take up this new avenue of conversation.

But the child, Russell conceded silently, did not hold a candle to the woman she had become. And even having spent almost the entire day in her presence hadn't quite prepared him for how regal, how utterly breathtaking and captivating Princess Amelia could look.

It took effort to draw his eyes away, effort he couldn't quite seem to muster, so he continued to look, telling himself he needed a moment longer just to absorb the vision that she was. Russell made a silent vow to Amelia that Reginald was never going to cause her any pain if he had anything to say about it.

Amelia walked into the room very slowly. Not because she wanted to draw out the moment, or because all eyes in the ballroom suddenly seemed to be turned in her direction, but because the heels of the shoes she wore were exceptionally high. Walking quickly could bring about a misstep. Or worse, cause her to fall down. That would not exactly be a royal moment, she mused, and she was fairly certain that if that did happen, a photographer would somehow magically pop out of the woodwork, immortalizing the moment for all time.

Making her way across the threshold, feeling as if she were moving in slow motion, a speed she was not on friendly terms with, she smiled warmly at everyone around her.

And then her eyes were drawn to the young man standing beside her father. Her heart whispered in her chest, undecided whether to beat quickly or freeze.

God, but he was handsome.

Gatherings parted, allowing her to pass unobstructed. She hardly noticed. Her destination was fixed. She could not seem to shake the feeling that all her steps up until this very moment had been designed to bring her to this man.

And with each step she took, her heart began to beat a little faster, like a drumroll growing in volume, in tempo. It seemed to swell within her chest. She was never more grateful than now for the upbringing which allowed her to keep her thoughts and reactions from showing on her face.

Otherwise, she thought, both she and Russell would be lost. Especially her.

Though she shouldered it well, she had never cared for duty. But in a way, duty was responsible for the moment. For bringing Russell here.

Despite the way she had to address him in public, always in the secret recesses of her mind, she thought of him not as the prince's cohort, not as the Duke of Carrington or by any of the titles that protocol dictated. To her, he had always been, would always be, Russell.

As she drew closer to Russell and her father, she heard the orchestra begin to play. Her mouth curved as the old familiar melody unfurled its notes through the vast room. A waltz. She might have known. Her father's favorite. The king thought she fancied them, as well. And while she liked them, she had yet to let her father know how much she enjoyed something contemporary even more.

Amelia sincerely doubted if the monarch knew that Black Eyed Peas were something other than a vegetable found on a side dish at a dinner.

Her eyes danced as she joined the two men. "I believe they're playing our song, Carrington," she teased and, to his credit, he neither looked confused nor tried to contradict her. "Dance with me." Russell glanced toward the king, who inclined his head, giving his permission. Humor curved her lips as she saw the silent exchange. "I asked you to dance with me, Carrington. You can dance with my father later."

King Roman shook his head as Russell placed a hand respectfully on her waist and took her hand in his. He watched his daughter place her other hand on the duke's shoulder. "Always outspoken," he said as the couple began to dance away. "From the moment she said her first word."

"Funny," Russell observed as their steps took them farther onto the dance floor and away from the king. "I don't remember you being outspoken when we were children." He liked the way laughter entered her eyes. Liked the way she didn't take herself too seriously.

Liked the way her waist felt beneath his hand. "You clean up well, Princess."

"So do you, Carrington." She cocked her head as if she were studying him while the music moved them about the floor. "You're almost not ugly."

"I do my best."

And his best, she thought, as the music began to swell, matching the tempo within her chest, was more than enough.

Russell had had no intention of walking the princess to her chambers. He'd had every intention that they would part company within the ballroom, or perhaps just at the door as they exited. More than anyone, he was well aware that his role in the scheme of things was to be polite, to strive not to look bored even though he would rather have been in his quarters with a good book than exchanging meaningless conversation with a collection of royals who spent the evening vying for his attention.

He would have been more than content, he silently insisted to himself, to just watch Amelia from afar. Undoubtedly he'd have been safer, too.

The problem was, the princess hadn't remained afar. She had purposely remained close to him, as if she had decided that he was her one true friend and it was his company that gave her pleasure instead of any of the others.

Toward the end of the evening, she'd almost said as much, but had stopped short before uttering the words. Her eyes had told him. That was approximately around the same time that the princess had consumed her sixth glass of very aged, very fine wine. Wine that had been expressly brought out to toast the princess's upcoming nuptials.

He had the distinct impression that rather than commemorate it, the princess was trying to blot the moment, the thought, out.

So, toward the fourth hour, as the reception was definitely winding down, when Amelia appeared to be just a hint unsteady on her feet, he'd offered to escort her to her rooms before anyone else took note of the fact that her eyes appeared just a tad too bright. His duty, he reminded himself, was to ensure the future queen's dignity.

When he made the suggestion about seeing her to her rooms, Amelia saw right through the excuse. "You're trying to help me maintain my dignity," she guessed in hushed tones, leaning her head into his. Her words ended in a small giggle he found utterly infectious and endearing.

Tact gave way to honesty. Something told him that unlike Reginald, Amelia appreciated honesty. "I'd rather not see the future Queen of Silvershire guilty of a pratfall."

She gave him no argument. Instead, she laughed, delighted. "Ah, chivalry is not dead."

"Only slightly wounded," he replied as he offered her his arm. She slipped her hand through it. Luckily. Because the next moment, the simple action was instrumental in preventing her from having a misstep end embarrassingly. She flashed him a guileless smile of thanks that was completely devoid of self-consciousness.

Carefully, he guided her from the room, thinking it best not to take his leave of his host. The king was embroiled in a heated discussion he assumed the monarch wouldn't want interrupted, and besides, he decided that perhaps it was a bit more prudent not to draw attention to the fact that he had to bring the princess upstairs because she was just this side of inebriated.

"This is very nice of you," Amelia said as they entered the hallway. The heat and the noise of the ballroom was left behind them.

Or at least the noise, she thought. The heat that came from too many bodies too close to one another seemed to linger on even though there were just the two of them. "But then, you're a very nice person, aren't you Carrington?"

He wasn't feeling all that nice right now. What he was feeling he didn't want to begin to examine. "I try to be, Princess."

"Not like Reginald," she concluded knowingly. Though her path and Reginald's had not crossed in a great many years, she kept up on the stories. And she hadn't liked what she'd read, even when she tried to view the articles in a charitable light.

She was walking slowly, Russell thought. Was that because she was afraid of falling down? He found he practically had to crawl not to outdistance her. And her words made him uncomfortable. His own personal opinion of Reginald wasn't very high, but he was nothing if not loyal to the crown. He couldn't share his feelings with her, or agree with what she was saying.

"Your Highness," he began tactfully, "I really don't think—"

She waved her free hand at him and then swayed ever so slightly. She paused to regain her composure. "Oh, please stop with the titles, Russell. I'm Amelia, just call me Amelia."

"But you are not *just* Amelia," he corrected gently. "You're the Princess of Gastonia. And the future Queen of Silvershire."

She sighed. "Yes, yes, I know." They'd come to the foot of the stairs. One hand on the banister, Amelia stopped and looked all the way up the long, winding staircase. She made no effort to take another step.

Russell looked at her, concerned. "What's the matter?"

"I don't think my feet will go." Each leg suddenly felt as if it weighed a hundred pounds apiece. It was as if the weight of her position was pressing her down.

He laughed, thinking she was joking. The expression on her face had him changing his mind. "You're serious."

She nodded. "Very." In her present state, she wasn't sure if she could negotiate the stairs wearing the shoes that she had on. Maybe if she kicked her shoes off, she thought.

But before she could act on that, she found herself being swept off the floor and into Russell's arms. He picked her up as if she weighed no more than a cast-off sweater. Holding her against him, Russell began to make his way up the staircase.

Had she been thinking a little more clearly, she might have protested, saying something about being perfectly capable of walking on her own. Except that she wasn't perfectly capable of that right now. And this was infinitely preferable to either sauntering up the stairs in tottering heels, or scampering up them barefoot.

Her body was tingling and after a moment, she allowed herself to enjoy the sensation as she laced her arms around his neck. God, but he felt muscular, she thought. Like a rock. Except that rocks were not nearly so warm.

With a slight toss of her head, she smiled up into his face. "I could get used to this. Maybe we should give you another title, Carrington. You can be the official princess carrier."

"Yes, Princess," he murmured indulgently, wishing he wasn't quite so aware of her. Wishing he didn't like the way she felt in his arms as much as he did.

She was going to hate herself in the morning, he thought. And probably him, too.

When he reached the top of the stairs, Russell looked down the hallway. It wasn't *that* far to her room, he thought. He might as well carry her all the way. That left less chance for her to stumble and possibly hurt herself.

Without a word of protest or an attempt to regain her feet, Amelia curled against him.

Warmth from her body seemed to penetrate every point of its contact with his. He found that his breathing was growing labored, more pronounced. And the climb up the stairs had had absolutely nothing to do with it.

As swiftly as he could, Russell brought her to her door, grateful that no one had crossed their path. He didn't want her to be any more embarrassed than he assumed she would be.

Shouldering open the door, he walked across the threshold, then pushed it closed again. Once inside the room, he gently released her, setting her feet back on the floor.

She made no attempt to back away, to break the connection. Her arms remained around his neck.

When he began to remove them, she whispered, "Don't leave."

Something surged inside his gut. "Princess, I have to go."

"No." Amelia rose on her toes, her arms still around his neck. He felt her breath on his lips as she spoke. "You have to stay." Her eyes searched his. "Unless you don't want to."

That was just the problem. He wanted to. In the worst way, he wanted to. And it would be for the worst if he did.

As gently as he could, Russell attempted to disengage himself from her. "Princess, you've had too much to drink."

"No," she contradicted, "I've had just enough to drink. Just enough to bank down my inhibitions." She drew her courage to her, knowing that the next steps she was going to take were right. "To give me the freedom, just for a little while, to be me."

He began to protest, to make another halfhearted attempt at doing the right thing. And then the princess caught him completely off guard by blindsiding him.

His resolve broke, like a dried twig under a heavy boot. Suddenly, he was kissing her. As heat flared through his body with the speed of a summer fire rushing through drought-withered grass, Russell closed his arms around her. Pulling her to him, he eliminated the sliver of space that had remained between them and brought her soft curves against the hard contours of his own.

Desire raced up and down his limbs, nibbling chunks out of his belly. Making him want her the way he had never wanted any other woman. The way he had never wanted anything or anyone before.

Later, when his blood had cooled and he could look back, he would know that nothing short of madness had possessed him. Because nothing short of madness would have allowed him to do this, to make love with the woman that destiny had chosen to be his queen.

Which was what she was. For one brief, shining self-contained moment in time, the Princess Amelia was his queen. Not of his country, but of his soul.

The realization throbbed through his brain that he was going to burn in hell for this. But that was tomorrow. Tonight he would gain heaven first.

Because holding Amelia in his arms like this, kissing her and losing himself within the act, was nothing short of pure heaven.

Amelia felt her insides trembling like a leaf in the wind. It was all she could do to keep the tremor from spreading to her limbs. It seemed so juvenile to do that, to tremble like some untried virgin. Never mind that she was one; she didn't want him to think of her that way, didn't want pity to enter into this.

Despite the wine that she had consumed, the wine that allowed her to be what she wanted to be, not what she *had* to be, Amelia felt amazingly clearheaded. She knew exactly what she wanted. And it was all here, standing before her in her bedroom.

She wasn't going to spoil it by telling Russell that she had been a little in love with him for what seemed like forever. Even before his lips had touched hers so fleet-ingly in that darkened passageway all those years ago, she'd been in love with him. She had always known that, despite the practical jokes and pranks, he was a protector. That she could be safe with him.

It had aroused all sorts of fantasies in her young, fertile mind. Fantasies that had had to be put aside as she grew older and came face-to-face with her destiny and duty. She was trading her dreams and her soul, allowing herself to be bartered away to secure her beloved country and she accepted that. It was just the way things had to be.

But first, she desperately wanted to be permitted a single sampling of passion, a single night of tenderness and love. The kind of night she already knew in her heart that her husband-to-be, Reginald, would never give her.

Amelia moaned as she pressed her body to his. Moaned as the kiss and her desire deepened.

He had to stop her. It was his duty to stop her, damn it, not encourage her. Not allow this to happen.

But when Russell put his hands over hers, meaning to still them as her fingers fluttered along his chest, all he could think of was how soft they felt. How delicate her skin seemed to the touch. How completely intoxicating her taste was.

And how insatiable he was for it. For her.

So, instead of applying the brakes, he pressed down on the accelerator and roared into oblivion, losing himself in the taste, the sight, the very feel of her.

He felt like kneeling before her in silent worship. He felt like ripping the clothes away from her body. She'd made him completely insane simply with one taste of her mouth.

His fingers strumming along her spine, he sought out the zipper that had been so skillfully hidden in the folds. Finding it, he tugged, even as his mouth covered hers. The beautiful shimmering blue gown that had captured his imagination slid like a sigh to the floor. Beneath it, he discovered that she was wearing undergarments in the same vivid shade of royal blue.

Stop! Stop! Unheeded commands roared through his brain. He couldn't stop, couldn't pull back. Strapped into the first car of a roller coaster that was plunging down a three-hundred-foot incline, he no longer had a choice; he was committed to the ride.

His heart hammering so hard it echoed in his ears, Russell coaxed first her bra, then the lacy thong from her smooth, firm limbs. He wasn't even aware of breathing. Maybe he had stopped breathing. Stopped, died and entered heaven without realizing it had happened.

The threads of the thong tangled in his fingers. He'd never been clumsy before. But he had never felt anything like this before, either.

"I didn't know princesses wore thongs," he said thickly. Her fingernails were digging into his arms. He could see the passion flaring in her eyes. It mirrored his own.

"And here I thought you were worldly." Her voice, her laugh, were deep, husky and caused his adrenaline to almost overflow.

She didn't want to seem overly eager, but she gave up the ruse in a little more than a single heartbeat. This was no time for games, it was a time for honesty. She *was* eager. Eager to enter this mysterious world that had been blocked from her. Eager to enter it with a guide she trusted.

It was becoming more and more difficult to catch her breath. Her lungs felt as if they were going to explode as she eagerly tore the clothes from his body. Buttons were sacrificed, as was material. She didn't care. All she wanted was for him to be as naked as she was.

Demands pounded through her body as she felt his lips on the hollow of her throat.

Wild sensations were charging through her body, centering at the very core of her.

And then they were both as naked as the moment that they had entered life, experiencing life now, perhaps, for the very first time.

Amelia pressed herself against the man she had chosen to give herself to as each pass of his mouth made the passion within her grow, made the demands become more urgent until she thought she would either explode or go out of her mind.

And then she was exploding. Exploding with delicious, wondrous sensations that rocketed through her body, making her feel as if she was inwardly scrambling for some mystical peak.

Reaching it, she discovered to her joy that the end had not come yet.

There was more. Because there was him.

Chapter 5

The trip from afterglow to aftershock was quick and stunning. The moment that his blood cooled and his sanity returned, remorse and guilt descended over Russell.

Regret did not enter into it, even though he knew it should. But as awful as he felt about betraying everything he had always held dear and in the highest esteem, Russell couldn't find it in his heart to regret the sweetest, most stirring experience of his life.

He was the future king's right-hand man and the future queen's protector. He had failed at both. In the worst possible way.

Sitting up in bed, the sheet pooling around his taut waist, Russell dropped his head into his hands in a moment of despair and shame. The crime he was guilty of committing only continued to escalate in magnitude.

He should have put a stop to this before it had gotten out of hand.

Before *he* had gotten out of hand.

Russell couldn't bring himself to face Amelia. He was afraid of the hatred and loathing he would see there. Not only had he betrayed the prince, but he had taken something very precious away from Amelia.

"You're a virgin," he finally whispered. A sigh shuddered through his perspiration-soaked body. How did he begin to apologize? "Or were."

Amelia stared at his muscular back, hardly breathing. He made it sound as if a death sentence had just been carried out. All women began as virgins. What counted was having a choice as to who would be the first. And she had made hers. She supposed it was her form of protest. She had no regrets.

Please, please don't ruin this for me, she pleaded silently.

Amelia continued to lie there, looking at his back. Her body was still humming. Was this normal? She didn't know, she had nothing to go by. All she knew was that, despite the slight moment of pain, the entire experience had felt incredibly wonderful.

"That was the unspoken part of the bargain," she finally responded, reminding him. "That Reginald receive a virgin on his wedding night." Her mouth quirked with a hint of cynicism. "I'm sure he's already had more than his share of those, as well as the tried-and-true variety."

Russell turned to look at her. He'd taken her silence to indicate loathing. At least she was talking to him. And she didn't sound as if she were angry. He searched her face for some telltale sign. He reminded himself that Amelia had always had a sweet nature.

And he had taken advantage of that.

He curtailed the impulse to run his hand along her cheek. "I had no right—"

"No," she agreed quietly, her voice low, "you didn't." She saw his shoulders tense and instantly knew what he had to be thinking. He was too honorable a man for his thoughts to be a mystery. Very lightly, she placed her fingers along his back. "Until I gave it to you."

The very touch of her fingers brought another wave of longing to the surface. He did his very best to bank it down, making an oath to himself that he wouldn't act on it, no matter what.

He looked at her over his shoulder. "I took advantage—"

"You took what I offered," she corrected firmly with the confidence of a woman who knew her own mind. "And gave me something to remember."

She was being kind, forgiving. The smile in her voice tortured him. He felt torn. Because as huge as his guilt was, as overwhelming as the burden of that act was even now proving to be, God help him, he wanted to do it again. To hold her soft, yielding body against his and lose himself in her. To make love with her until there was no air left in his lungs nor a shred of energy in his entire being.

His. Damn it all to hell, he had to stop thinking of himself, of what he needed. Of his own gratification. He needed to focus on what was best for the realm.

For Amelia. For everyone else *but* him. *That* was what was important.

She was sitting up beside him. Her hair brushed along his arm. He felt heat traveling up his flanks, curling in his belly. Goading him on.

He needed to get this out of the way first. "Princess, I don't know what to say. I—"

Moving her head slowly from side to side, Amelia pressed her fingers against his lips, trying to abort whatever disclaimer was to follow. Hearing the words would hurt too much.

She read his true feelings in his eyes and her heart warmed. "Please don't apologize. I'm not sorry it happened. A woman's first time should be memorable. It should be remembered with something other than a general sense of loathing."

Very slowly, he drew her fingers from his lips, fighting the urge to kiss each one. Holding her hand in his, he looked at her for a long moment. There were things going on inside him, things that had no place in the role fate had chosen him to play. That his king had chosen him to play.

Why this woman? Of all the women in the world, why did he find himself so strongly attracted to this one? And why hadn't he the strength not to give in?

"And was it?" he heard himself asking her.

Her mouth curved as her eyes smiled at him. "Vanity, Carrington?"

His expression was deadly serious, even if hers was not. "Concern, Princess."

"Then you don't have to be," she told him. "Not anymore. Because it was wonderful."

Her own expression grew more somber. She knew what they had done was serious. Not all that long in the past, they would have faced not just censure, but possibly death for what they had done. Even now, there was still a stigma attached to what had happened.

Knowing all that, she still wouldn't have changed anything for the world.

"You've given me something to hold on to, to remember when Reginald comes to claim what he sees as his due." She sighed, clasping her knees and bringing them up to her. "Why has the twenty-first century come to every corner of Gastonia except where it would count the most for me? I'm living a life that echoes the Middle Ages. I'm being bartered for a treaty." Forcing a smile to her lips, she ran her fingers through his thick hair. Why couldn't he have been the prince instead of Reginald? Then doing her duty would have been wonderful instead of odious. "This night may very well be the only true happiness I will ever know."

Russell shifted toward her, his heart already trapped, even before his body entered the bargain. He tugged away the sheet that she had drawn around her breasts, his blood heating as he heard her soft intake of breath.

"The night isn't over yet."

Amelia felt the pull within her instantly and made no attempt to resist it. Instead, she gave herself up to the joyous thrill that rampaged through her body.

When his mouth came down on hers, she felt all points of her body igniting again, like flares being sent up into the night sky.

This time, there would be no surprises, this time, she knew what to expect.

Or thought she did.

But there was more to lovemaking than a repetition of the motions, more than just the anticipation of release, and the first and only lover she would ever welcome to her bed spent the night introducing her to all the wondrous ways a man could make love to a woman. And during the night, Amelia proved to be an able and eager student, not merely content to absorb but to test the boundaries of her knowledge and to see what it felt like not only to be on the receiving end, but to be the one who delivered, as well.

Russell's experience was not vast. Unlike Prince Reginald, he didn't bed every woman with a pleasing face who crossed his path. He most valued not just skill, but intelligence, something to stir him beyond the physical. Amelia stirred him that way. She made love to his mind as well as his body. He ceased to be the teacher very quickly, and found himself awed and delighted to be on equal footing with her.

He discovered that Her Royal Highness, Princess Amelia, could easily make him absolutely insane. All it took was a look in her eyes, a smile on her lips, a touch of her hand along his skin.

They made love several times. More times than he had believed he was capable of. Until now.

Until her.

Russell had no idea how much time had passed. An hour, two. A week. Lost in thoughts and feelings, he had no way of reckoning. He only knew that he had never, ever felt so summarily drained and contented at the same time.

Amelia was lying beside him, curled up in the hollow of his arm, and he could not remember ever feeling as happy as he did at this moment. His heart swelled as he looked at her. Russell laughed softly to himself, his breath ruffling her hair. "I think I might never walk again."

Half asleep, she was amusing herself by playing with the hair on his arm, lightly stroking it and pretending with all her might that tomorrow did not have to come. That she never had to leave this bed, never had to know another man intimately. Only him.

"Is that a good thing?" she murmured.

"That all depends."

She half turned her face up to his, curious. "On what?"

"On whether or not the bed is on fire." He wanted to go on holding her like this, wanted somehow to make her his forever. But that was even more impossible than his sprouting wings would be.

He felt her smile against his arm as it widened. Amelia—how could he think of her as the princess after what they had just shared?—raised her head again, her eyes dancing as she looked at him. "And is it?"

"It was." He pulled her to him, settled her against his chest and felt her heart beat against his. As if they were meant to be one. If only...

"Don't take this the wrong way, Princess, but you are a natural."

She moved until she was resting her hands on his chest. Laying her head on top of them, she cocked it slightly as she studied his face. He felt the tickle of her hair as it draped along his naked skin.

"Do you think that you could find it in your heart,

for the space of what is left of this night and in light of
the fact that you have seen me as naked as the moment
I was born, to call me just Amelia?"

He loved her. The thought came to him, riding on a
thunderbolt. He loved her. And there wasn't a damn
thing he could do about it.

But right now, he could play along and pretend that
they were just two people who'd found each other. "I
could, 'just Amelia.'"

She sighed, her eyes closing again. "Good."

Raising his head, he pressed a kiss against her forehead.

It made her feel warm and wanting all over again,
even though Amelia doubted she could move. Like
him, she was utterly and entirely spent—and thrilled.
If there was guilt because she was promised to another,
because she had wantonly thrown herself at Russell,
it made no appearance tonight. Because tonight didn't
belong to her realm, and certainly not to the man she'd
been pledged to from the moment she'd drawn her
first breath.

Tonight was hers.

And Russell's.

"I wish…" Her wistful voice trailed off.

Russell looked at her, curious. "You wish what?"

She opened her eyes again for a moment. The smile
that found her mouth was soft, gentle, sad. "Just 'I
wish,'" she murmured.

"Yes, me, too," Russell whispered softly, understanding what couldn't be spoken out loud, what couldn't be.
She wished that she were someone else and that they
didn't both have duties standing in the way.

He raised himself on his elbow. "I'd better go," he began.

But she tightened her arms around him. "Not yet," she whispered. "Hold me. Just for a little while longer. Just hold me."

It wasn't in his heart to say no to her. Besides, it was unheard of for a duke to refuse a princess. Especially when he didn't want to.

So he remained where he was, holding her in his arms, saying nothing, thinking everything, until the first flicker of dawn creased the darkened sky and she fell asleep.

Then, very carefully, Russell slipped his arm from beneath her head. He held his breath as he slowly left her bed, one tiny inch at a time so as not to wake her. He watched her face the entire time for a sign that he had roused her.

Watched it, too, because he knew he would never be able to see it this way again, relaxed in soft repose, the scent of their lovemaking still on her skin as well as on his.

Russell felt a pang of longing and sorrow in his heart. Damn Reginald, anyway. Why couldn't the fool have come to get her himself? This would have never happened if Reginald hadn't allowed his appetites to dictate his behavior.

The pot calling the kettle black? a voice inside Russell's head mocked.

He was clearly no saint, but there *was* a difference between him and Reginald, he silently insisted. He sincerely doubted that the prince loved any of the women he bedded. Given a test, the Playboy Prince would probably be unable to recall the names of more than half of them. Lust was his god.

But lust hadn't been what had led Russell to give in to Amelia when she'd pressed her body so invitingly against his, he thought. He had never been one to be led around by his appetites, even as a teenager with hormones the size of boulders. Longing was what had prompted him to do what he had. To give in. Because from the first moment he'd arrived to escort her back to Silvershire, there had been something, a pull, an electrical charge, *something* that had seduced him, had whispered her name in his head and made him want her.

If they had both been free to do so, if obligations didn't bind them, Russell knew he would have proposed to her last night. Because when he had made love with Amelia, every fiber in his being had cried that it was right.

Even if it was so wrong.

Once out of her bed, Russell hastily threw on his clothing and then tiptoed to the door. He eased it open like someone waiting for a telltale squeak to give him away. None came. But he wasn't home free yet.

He needed to make his retreat without encountering anyone in the hallways until he was well clear of the princess's suite.

Russell looked furtively first in one direction, then another, before satisfying himself that no one was there to witness first-hand his leaving the princess's rooms.

Because the palace had had a modern overhaul only two years ago, there were surveillance cameras in almost every corner of the lengthy hallway. Knowing what he did about security procedures, it would be easy enough to quickly doctor the tape that could incriminate both of them. All he would need to do, once he had the tape, was create a quick time loop, for both the time that he and the princess entered her suite and then again for when he left it.

It was a relatively simple matter to erase any evidence that this had ever taken place—from everywhere but his soul. But that was his problem. What he needed to do was make sure that everyone regarded the princess above reproach.

He tried not to think about the fact that in a few short days, Reginald could be enjoying the very things that he had just had. The thought was too painful for him to examine now.

Madeline Carlyle rounded the long corridor, pleased and amazed at how quickly she had rallied. She wanted to be the first to tell Amelia that the trip to Silvershire did not have to be delayed because of her.

Rounding the corner, Madeline came to a dead stop. The smile on her appealing round face froze and then faded when she saw the tall, dark, handsome man emerging from the princess's suite. Catching her breath, Madeline melted back into the shadows, her heart hammering hard in her chest.

Her first thought was that Amelia was in danger. If that were the case, she had no business hiding. Her job was to protect the princess no matter what. But when she stepped out into the hallway again, the man she'd just seen was gone.

What had he done to Amelia?

Madeline hurried into Amelia's quarters, completely disregarding any protocol that would have her knocking on the princess's door and waiting to be allowed access. They had been friends for far too long for her to stand on protocol. Especially since Amelia would have none of it. She'd always encouraged her to treat her as if they were equals.

Rushing through the sitting room, Madeline burst into the princess's bedroom. The same room where they had played and whispered stories to one another in the dead of night when they were children.

"Amelia," she cried, "are you all right?"

But even as she asked the question, she saw that rather than looking violated, or like the victim of some sort of mistreatment, Amelia looked absolutely fine. She also looked as if she were asleep.

The sound of Madeline's breathless question elbowed its way into the dream she was having. With reluctance, Amelia opened her eyes. Dazed, disoriented, it took her a moment to pull herself together.

The fact that she was alone in bed came crashing down on her consciousness.

Her brain replayed Madeline's question as she tried to focus on the woman's concerned face. Belatedly, Amelia realized that she was still nude. As regally as she could, she gathered the sheet to herself, forced a smile to her lips and made an attempt at diversion.

"Madeline. You're better."

The redhead waved her hand, dismissing the reference to her health. All that was yesterday's news. She had very obviously stumbled across something that came under the heading of "breaking news."

And she wanted to know every last detail about it. "Never mind me, what about you?"

For a moment, Amelia avoided her best friend's eyes. She picked at the sheet, as if arranging it in a more flattering way. "What about me?"

Madeline knelt down beside the bed, her eyes searching Amelia's face for some kind of sign that would tell her if something was truly wrong. "Are you all right?"

Amelia lifted her head, tossing her hair over her shoulder. A portrait in regalness. "Yes, why shouldn't I be?"

"Because—" Madeline stopped and tried again, more coherently this time. "Amelia, I saw a man coming out of your rooms."

So, he'd only just left her now. Somehow, she found that heartening. It meant that he couldn't tear himself away. The thought made her happy. "No, you didn't."

Madeline frowned, confused. "Yes, I did, he—"

Amelia fixed the other woman with a very intent look. "No, Madeline, you didn't," she repeated, enunciating every word carefully.

Madeline returned Amelia's look, trying to gauge the princess's thoughts. "I didn't." It wasn't quite a question, nor was it completely a statement.

"No." Amelia's tone was firm and not to be argued with.

Madeline drew closer still to the woman who had her allegiance before all others. "And this man I didn't see, exactly who was he?"

They had shared everything. Intelligent, witty and blessed with a delicious sense of humor as well as irony, Madeline was the old-fashioned sort of confidante, the kind who was loyal to her very last breath. They had kept one another's secrets since before either one had understood what that meant.

Looking down on her knotted fingers, Amelia whispered, "The Duke of Carrington."

Madeline covered her mouth to keep the squeal of surprise from emerging. When her voice returned to normal, she dropped her hands and asked, "That was Russell?"

Amelia nodded. Rather than regret what, in a moment of wine-aided weakness, she had done, she found herself missing him.

"My lord." Madeline stared at Amelia, speechless.

No, he's mine, Amelia thought.

Clearing her throat, Madeline forged ahead, "Did you and he—?" And then she laughed at her own question. "Of course you did. Just look at you, you're glowing. Glowing and naked." More than slightly familiar with nights of excitement and passion herself, Madeline knew that Amelia had never been with anyone. "Was he good to you?"

"Better than good," Amelia breathed. "He was fabulous."

"If you wanted to run off with him, Amelia, I could create a diversion. I could—"

Amelia placed her hand on Madeline's, anchoring her attention. She shook her head. "No."

Madeline's shoulders slumped with disappointment.

Amelia knew Madeline had never liked the prince, had never thought of him as being good enough for her.

"No?"

"No." Amelia took both of Madeline's hands and held them in her own. "And you can never tell anyone, do you understand?"

Madeline looked into the imploring violet eyes. With reluctance, she nodded and gave Amelia her word. "I understand."

Chapter 6

King Weston sighed, closed the thick, leather-bound binders and rose from his desk. Opening the double doors at his back, he walked out onto the balcony and looked out past the light green buds of spring, past the huge expanse of greenery. From where he stood, he had a view of the ocean which soothed him.

He'd been in his office for the last hour, going over the final plans for the coronation. It seemed like only yesterday he had been awaiting his own coronation, now it was his son's he was making plans for.

His reign was coming to an end.

It was time to hand the scepter over to someone else. To Reginald. Unlike most other monarchies, it wasn't death but tradition that brought about a change in the rulers in Silvershire. According to custom, the crown had to be relinquished after thirty years—to a first-born son if there was one, to a duke if nature had been cruel and withheld heirs from the reigning ruler.

That was how he had come to his crown. He'd been the chosen one. Oh, not at first. The late King Dunford had initially favored Lord Benton Vladimir over him and it was understood that the title of king would pass to Vladimir when the time came.

However, as the crucial moment had approached, King Dunford had changed his mind. Instincts, the old king had confided to him, caused the monarch to decide that Weston rather than Vladimir would make the better ruler. Vladimir was too self-centered ever to be a good king.

He'd accepted this with a heavy heart, because he and Vladimir were cousins and friends. *Had been* friends, he amended, remembering the course of events. The friendship that had existed had died the moment the crown came between them. Just before the coronation, Vladimir had disappeared, vowing revenge.

It had been a vow that apparently was never to come to fruition. He hadn't heard from Vladimir in all these years that the crown rested on his head. No one had.

A sad smile curved his mouth. It was too bad, really, because he missed the man and the confidences they used to share.

And then there were the times that he found himself wishing that Vladimir had remained the chosen one. That it was Vladimir who wore the crown that occasionally weighed so heavily on his brow. But that, of course, was only in moments of extreme stress.

He'd tried to be a good king, to do his very level best

for the people. And they, in turn, had been there for him. It was his duty to the people that had kept him alive and had brought him back from the brink of insanity, where grief had propelled him. His beloved queen, his Alexis, had died two days after giving birth to their only child.

Reginald.

Thinking of his son now, he shook his head and did his best to bank down a mounting sorrow that entwined itself with the headache that had been his constant companion these last few weeks. The same instincts that King Dunford had once spoken of so many years ago seemed to be now tormenting him. Instincts that whispered in his ear, saying that Reginald was not fit to be a ruler.

The heart of a ruler should be centered on his people. Reginald's heart was centered on himself alone. On his pleasures, his needs. Reginald took no interest in matters of state, beyond what the state coffers could yield into his private pocket. His son's main pastime seemed to be the collection of women.

And that collection grew almost daily, if he were to believe the press. The newspapers referred to Reginald as the Playboy Prince as well as the Black Prince. The less upstanding tabloids called him something that was far worse.

And this was the head that was going to be wearing the crown of Silvershire in less than a month.

His hands on the railing, the king closed his eyes, feeling very weary and very old.

God, but he wished that his only son was more like the Duke of Carrington. His mouth curved again. Dear lord, he would have given his life if Reginald was *anything* like Russell. That was why he was constantly pushing the two together.

Close in age, Reginald and Carrington had grown up together. But they had evolved into two men who were nothing like one another, he thought sadly. The young duke was serious, focused, aside from his riotous penchant for mischief that used to prompt him to play appalling practical jokes on unsuspecting victims, such as the poor princess. But despite that bent, Carrington had a good head on his shoulders, the kind that came from more than just obtaining an excellent education. The kind that came from an innate intelligence and a inherent sensitivity to the needs of others.

For a moment, Weston watched the yachts in the harbor. They were bobbing up and down in the choppy waters like slightly inebriated dancers. He tried to remember if the forecast called for a storm. The princess was coming in today. It would be a shame if her first day on Silvershire's soil was marked with rain.

If he could have picked the perfect son, the perfect ruler, he was forced to admit, then he would have selected Carrington over his own son. What he had hoped would rub off from Carrington to Reginald had not. If anything, Reginald seemed to be even more determined to burn the candle at both ends, more determined than ever to sow his share of wild oats.

His share, Weston snorted. Reginald was sowing more wild oats than all the young men of an entire third world nation put together.

He had been much too indulgent when it came to Reginald, but that was all in the past. Reginald was thirty, he was going to have to put his reckless behavior behind him. The moment he took on the responsibility of wearing the crown, he would have to devote himself to Silvershire, not to the pursuit of his own pleasures.

And if he didn't? a small, persistent voice inside Weston's head demanded. What then?

Weston ran his hand along his aching head. He had no answer for that. All he could do was pray for a miracle, that somehow, his son would be transformed into the monarch that Silvershire needed him to be.

The king glanced at his watch. It was later than he had thought. For the moment, he tabled his thoughts of miracles and simply prayed that Reginald would show up at the airport to greet his bride. There was less than an hour to get ready. The plane that carried Carrington and Gastonia's princess would be landing soon.

If there was something in his heart that felt sorry for the young woman who was to be his daughter-in-law, he wouldn't allow himself to admit it.

The knot in her stomach wouldn't go away, no matter how much Amelia willed it to dissolve. Not only that, but she couldn't trust herself to look at Carrington, even though he sat in the seat adjacent to hers. Not yet. Not without risking having all her thoughts reveal themselves in her eyes, on her face. She couldn't afford to have anyone suspect that there was something between her and the charismatic duke.

She'd been so very sure, only two days ago, that it was better to have one shining moment of happiness than none at all. To know what real love, real pleasure was—even if she couldn't have it for more than a moment—than to endure a lifetime never having experienced it. But now she wasn't so sure. Because to know was to want. And she couldn't endanger everything she had been raised to accomplish just because of her own needs, her own desires.

Why? a voice within her demanded. Why not grasp the brass ring? Reginald has spent the whole of his adult life doing that, why not you?

But if she did that, if she indulged herself without thinking of the far-reaching consequences, then that would mean that she was just like Reginald. She wasn't. She was different. Better, she liked to think.

As Gastonia's princess, she had the people to think about. Keeping them safe, by means of an alliance with the stronger Silvershire, was her responsibility. She couldn't bow out now, no matter how much her heart longed to.

The knot in her stomach grew larger as the plane touched down on the runway. Her fingers tightened around the armrests, her knuckles turning white.

She was here. At the place that she was going to have to refer to as home for the rest of her life.

For a moment, panic flared in her veins. She desperately wanted to order the pilot to pull up the landing gear and take off again. To turn the plane around and go back to Gastonia.

Amelia pressed her lips together, keeping the words unspoken. She wished with all her heart that life had not gotten so complicated.

She should have never done what she had, Amelia

upbraided herself. But she only had herself to blame. If she had not given in to her curiosity, to her desire, she and Russell would have continued being friendly strangers, nothing more.

But now he was going to have a position of honor inside every dream she had. Almost against her will, she slanted a glance toward Russell. Their eyes met.

Her breath caught in her throat. *Breathe, Amelia, breathe.*

She looked away, only to see that Madeline was watching her. The redhead's mouth moved into a quick, comforting smile.

Madeline turned to look out the window. "We're here," she announced in a tone that the executioner might have used to tell Marie Antoinette that it was time to climb up the steps that led to the guillotine.

Aware that Carrington's eyes were still on her, Amelia lifted her chin and took on a regal bearing.

"Yes, we are."

If she sighed inwardly after the words, no one heard it. But she had a feeling that Carrington sensed it. As his eyes washed over her, she was certain she saw concern glinting in his eyes. She managed a smile that was meant to put him at his ease—and still maintain the distance between them.

As if there would ever be real distance between them, she thought ruefully. The night they had spent together had effectively burned away any kind of space that might have ever existed. Body and soul, she was his now. She always would be, even though they could never make love again. It only took that one time for the promise to be there. To be eternal.

Carrington was the first to unbuckle his seat belt. On his feet, he approached her respectfully. His voice was gentle as he said, "Princess, it's time to meet your people."

She took a deep breath, as if that would provide her with the courage that she felt ebbing away from her. She'd been to Silvershire before, but years ago and with her father. She wished he was here now, but he had made it clear that he felt she should come alone, signifying her new position. She was no longer his daughter but Reginald's intended queen. He was going to join her in a day, but her first hours on Silvershire's soil should be focused entirely on her and Reginald.

"Yes, it is," she agreed.

With slow, deliberate movements, Amelia unbuckled her seat belt and then took the hand Carrington offered to help her to her feet. She tried not to think of how that hand had felt the other night, stroking her flesh. Bringing her pleasure that she had never, in her wildest dreams, imagined existed.

Madeline popped up, flashed a smile and whispered, "It's going to be all right." Amelia returned the smile, in her heart knowing that it wouldn't be. Not while she had to be Reginald's wife.

Turning on his heel, Russell led the way to the plane's door. The steward preceded him, opening it for them before stepping back.

Russell looked at Amelia. "The people will expect to see you emerging first, Princess," he told her.

"Then we can't disappoint them, can we?" she responded gamely.

With Madeline directly behind her, Amelia stepped out onto the steps that had been brought directly before the opened door. Standing there for a moment, she raised her hand and waved to the people who had all gathered there. They didn't look unlike her own people she had left in Gastonia.

A cheer rose, enveloping her like a warm blanket as the crowd greeted her. For a moment, she remained where she was, waving, absorbing the upturned faces. There were all manner of people within the crowd. Old, young, men, women and children, they were all waving at her. All cheering for this princess they were determined to welcome into their hearts.

Waving and smiling was second nature to her. It had been required of her for as far back as Amelia could remember. It was, she thought, the meaningless side of who and what she was. The meaningful part came from lending her support, her name and her efforts to charitable foundations, to actually accomplishing things. But because of the state of turmoil that her mind was in, she welcomed this distraction. It allowed her to go on automatic pilot.

And not to dwell on the fact that Carrington was standing much too close to her, causing her body to hum. Causing her to remember the other night, when she had been alive for the very first time.

"There's King Weston." Madeline said the words against her ear as she gestured toward the monarch standing proudly with his back to the crowd as he watched Carrington and the others disembark. "But where's the prince?"

Madeline's question echoed in Amelia's brain as she scanned the area around King Weston. The tall ruler had some of his key people assembled with him. But the prince was noticeably absent.

This was entirely unacceptable, Amelia thought. It was not only thoughtless and rude, it was beyond insulting. Was he deliberately absent in order to publicly embarrass her? Was this a sign of the things that were to come? Or was he just out to show her how superior he was to her?

Amelia looked over toward Russell, her eyes reiterating Madeline's question. If anyone would know of the prince's whereabouts, it was Carrington. But she saw the duke move his head from side to side, silently telling her that he was just as much in the dark about Reginald as she was.

This was not good, Amelia thought. None of the princesses in the fairy tales she had grown up reading were ever stranded by their prince.

Maybe because he's not really your prince.

The band began to play. Amelia shut the voice in her head out. She carefully came down the narrow metal steps. Despite the din of the crowd, she could swear she heard the click of her heels as she made contact with the metal over and over again. And with each step she took, she heard the same tattoo being struck.

Run. Run. Run.

Except that there was nowhere to run to.

The king and his entourage approached, meeting her halfway. Stepping forward, Weston embraced her, then kissed her soundly first on one cheek and then the other. Finished, he stood back and beamed at her.

"Welcome, Princess."

There was warmth in the monarch's eyes, but there was something more there, she realized. There was just a hint of discomfort.

The king was embarrassed that Reginald wasn't here, Amelia thought. He was embarrassed for her and for the realm. She took heart in that.

In his mid-sixties, King Weston appeared to be in the prime of his life. Distinguished, he looked like a man at least ten years his junior. Six feet one inch tall, with a strong build, he had a full head of silver-gray hair and kind blue-gray eyes. Amelia had always liked him. She fervently wished she could have felt the same way about his son.

Stepping to the side, he gestured, presenting her to his people. "Welcome to your new home."

After a push from her mother, a little girl of no more than six approached with a huge bouquet of flowers. The little girl held it up as high as she could, offering the bouquet to her. There were carnations, perfect specimens of pink and white, mixed with several other delicate flowers that Amelia knew were native to Silvershire.

When Amelia accepted the bouquet, the little girl curtsied, then stepped back and buried her face in her mother's skirt, suddenly shy.

Amelia bent down to her level and said, "Thank you."

The little girl half turned her head toward her again and offered a small, hesitant smile.

Rising to her feet, Amelia looked at the throng that had gathered to see her. "Thank you all for coming," she said, raising her voice in order to be heard. "I'm very happy to be here."

In response, the crowd cheered and clapped. All except for a cluster of people over on the side. There was almost a militant appearance about them, even though they were all wearing civilian clothes. There was a dark-haired young man dressed in black, standing in the center. He seemed to be the rallying point around whom the others gathered. Behind him was a banner that loudly proclaimed Down With the Monarchy. Seeing it was a shock.

So, she thought, *this is not quite the paradise the king wants me to believe it is.*

It took her a moment to realize that Madeline was at her elbow. "Didn't realize you were an actress," her friend whispered to her, barely moving her lips.

"Every princess is," Amelia responded in the same low whisper. The smile she'd summoned remained on her lips as she looked out on the crowd. Turning toward the king, she nodded toward the small cluster of dissenters. "Who are they?"

"No one you need concern yourself about," Weston replied dismissively.

"That's the Union for Democracy," Russell told her. "Nikolas Donovan is their leader. He would be the one you see in front."

All she could see was Russell. But she was a princess and knew she had to conduct herself as one—as if nothing was crossing her mind but the information he was telling her, as if her pulse was not accelerating, even now. "Are they dangerous?" she wanted to know.

"Peaceful," he countered.

She nodded. "I hope they stay that way."

"I won't have them ruining this occasion," the king told her firmly. He extended his arm to her. "If you'll permit me, Princess?"

Amelia slipped her arm through his. "Of course." As he led her to the long, sleek, black limousine that was to take them back to the palace, she inclined her head toward his and asked the question she could no longer keep back. "Where is the prince?"

She felt the king stiffen, saw the smile on his lips grow just a little brittle around the edges. Clearly this was a sore point. And then she understood that by not being here, Reginald was not only insulting her, but the king, as well. He paused as they came to the limousine. "No one knows."

The driver hurriedly opened the door for them, then stood back.

"I see," she murmured, slipping into the limousine first.

The king followed, taking his seat beside her. By rights, Russell should have come next, but he stepped back, gesturing for Madeline to get into the vehicle before him. Madeline gave him a wide, appreciative grin before ducking her head and taking the seat opposite Amelia.

Manners before protocol, Amelia thought. In her heart, she knew that it would have never occurred to Reginald to surrender his position and allow Madeline to get into the vehicle before him. She could hear his young voice taunting her.

When we're grown, you'll have to mind me and do everything I say. You won't have a choice.

He'd been a dictator even then. Was he one now? Was she going to find life with him unbearable? She strove not to let depression absorb her thoughts, strove not to think beyond the moment. She should be relieved, not insulted, by Reginald's absence, she told herself.

The king's bodyguard closed the door and the vehicle began its journey to the palace, less than five miles away.

Progress was slow. People lined both sides of the streets, waving frantically even before the limousine passed them. Some held tiny Silvershire flags. A few clutched both the flags of Silvershire and Gastonia, symbolizing the merger of the two kingdoms. The mood was festive.

Everywhere but within the interior of the limousine.

Amelia sat closest to the window, waving to the faces of her new people. Though she tried not to focus on it, the significance of the prince's continued and very glaring absence from the scene weighed down on her.

This didn't bode well for the marriage, she thought, her smile never faltering. But then, she had already sensed that. Otherwise, she would have never invited Russell to her bed, no matter how drawn to him she felt.

Hers was not destined to be a fairy-tale marriage, Amelia reflected sadly, struggling to accept what she knew was her fate. Still, she continued waving and smiling at the people who wished her well and who were already, from all appearances, taking her to their hearts.

All except for the small band of dissenters.

Chapter 7

Discreet questions as to the prince's whereabouts were asked once the limousine arrived at the palace. But no one seemed to know where Reginald was. The king's anxiety continued to mount even as he prepared to attend the gala being held at the palace in honor of Princess Amelia's arrival and the young royals' upcoming wedding.

The hours slipped by. The prince was nowhere to be found.

Russell frowned to himself, returning his cell phone to his pocket. Reginald wasn't answering his personal phone. Voice mail picked up immediately, which meant that the prince had shut off his phone, something he was prone to doing whenever he was busy gratifying his sexual appetites. Dutifully, Russell informed the king that his son couldn't be reached.

On the advice of his chief counselor, King Weston changed the theme of the celebration at the last moment to center exclusively around the princess who had come to join together the two kingdoms.

Outwardly, the mood at the party was festive, but beneath the thin layer of gaiety was an underlying knot of tension. Because they cared for their king and had taken to the princess, everyone at the affair pretended that there was nothing wrong.

As he stood back and observed the guests, Russell was convinced that the prince's glaring absence was the talk of every small gathering he saw at the celebration.

At least Amelia was a hit, Russell thought fondly. But then, how could she not be? Coddling the scotch and soda he had been nursing for the last half hour, Russell smiled to himself. The change in Princess Amelia had been incredible. It was hard to believe that this was the same young girl who'd been the target of his practical jokes whenever he'd visited Gastonia.

Taking a sip from his glass, he felt the liquid spread a deep, burning sensation through his chest, warming everything in its path. It was the same sort of sensation he experienced each time he now looked in Amelia's direction.

All evening, Amelia continued to be the center of attention. At the moment Russell watched her engage several of Silvershire's leading businessmen in conversation. The perfunctory smiles on the men's faces quickly changed to looks of interest. Russell knew for a fact that the princess, in addition to being fluent in five different languages, had a business degree to her name.

The five languages put her four and a half up on Reginald, he thought with a touch of cynicism.

It seemed that there was nothing, Russell thought with more than a little pride, she couldn't accomplish if she set her mind to it.

She was charming the pants off everyone, Russell noted. God knew that she had certainly done that with him. Even before they had spent the night together.

He felt a pang stirring within him, born not of guilt but of need. It was followed by a wave of anger. The prince should be horsewhipped for standing her up this way. Reginald had known about this gala, known that it was to have celebrated their upcoming marriage. How could he *do* this to Amelia?

The very thought of the marriage, of Amelia being intimate with Reginald, made something in the pit of his stomach rise up in his throat. Russell took another sip to wash the taste of bile from his mouth.

He had no business feeling like this, no business feeling anything beyond a mild pity for whoever officially graced the prince's bed. But he couldn't help himself. This was personal. It would always be personal no matter how much he wanted to divorce himself from the situation. He realized that his hand was tightening around his glass and he forced himself to relax his grip.

Were this another time, one of intrigue and secret pacts, when daggers rather than words were used to settle matters of discord, he might have been sorely tempted…

To what? To kill Reginald?

No, Russell thought, murder wasn't his way. And it

certainly wasn't an option, even if he were the kind of person who thought nothing of killing whoever got in his way. It wasn't an option because Russell had always prided himself on his loyalty to the crown, and Reginald was the future king of Silvershire.

Which meant that he had to be loyal to Reginald, no matter what. Even though, despite all of his and the king's efforts, Reginald would undoubtedly turn out to be a bad king. But whether Reginald was or not, it was not a matter for him to take into his own hands.

Just as he shouldn't have taken Amelia into his hands, into his arms, Russell thought. That he had was his cross to bear. In silence.

He figured the almost bottomless longing he felt would make him pay for his transgression every day of his life. Even now, watching the princess as groups of men and women gathered around her, he felt himself wanting her more than he could recall ever wanting anyone before.

Hell of a cross to bear, he thought darkly, taking another drink.

"So where do you suppose he really is?"

The question came out of nowhere, as if echoing his thoughts. Glancing to his side, he saw Amelia's lady-in-waiting, Madeline. He'd been so lost in his thoughts and in observing Amelia from what he'd initially thought was a safe distance—quickly learning that there was no safe distance when it came to being around Amelia—that he hadn't heard the princess's friend approach.

From the little he had seen of her, Madeline struck him as being very honest and straightforward. By no stretch of the imagination could the lady be called shy or retiring. She was outspoken and seemed a perfect match for Amelia.

For the princess, he upbraided himself. He had to stop thinking of her by her given name and just keep reminding himself that she was the princess. And would be, in a matter of weeks, his queen. Continuing to regard her as Amelia was out of order.

He inclined his head toward Madeline, pretending he hadn't heard her. "Excuse me?"

Madeline gave him a look that said she knew that he knew what she was talking about. But for form's sake, she elaborated.

"The prince," she enunciated precisely, wishing she could grind the man between her teeth, as well. "Why isn't he here?"

Russell paused. Protocol dictated that he say something in the man's defense. That he tell this woman of less-than-royal blood that it wasn't any of her concern what the prince did, or didn't do, or where he was at any given moment. But he was far too modern in his thinking for that. And he liked the fact that Amelia had a friend to help her at a time like this. A friend who could be open.

You're her friend. Except that, because of what had happened between them, he couldn't allow himself to assume that role any longer. People would talk. He wanted nothing to sully her reputation. Nothing.

This was a very sticky situation they found themselves in, he thought ruefully.

"I don't know," he told Madeline honestly. And then,

because he felt he could trust the young woman, he added, "This behavior is pretty reckless, even for the prince."

Madeline had put her own interpretation to the prince's no-show. Or maybe it was just wishful thinking on her part. "Is this his way of saying that he won't go through with the marriage?"

That had never been in jeopardy, Russell thought sadly. "Oh, the prince'll go through with the marriage. There's too much riding on it for him not to. He might be reckless, but he's not brave enough to oppose his father in matters that really count."

Madeline frowned, taking offense for Amelia who was too kind-hearted to voice her own offense. "And not coming here doesn't count?" she wanted to know. "You know, someone other than Princess Amelia would have been humiliated."

"She's made of finer stuff than that," Russell commented, looking in Amelia's direction again.

Unintentionally, he caught Amelia's eye. For a moment, they looked at one another from across the room and he could almost feel a communion between them. But it wasn't anything that either one of them could acknowledge, even fleetingly, without consequences.

He looked away first, before anyone could see. Or so he thought.

"Yes," Madeline agreed, noting what had just happened between the duke and Amelia, even if everyone else was oblivious to it, "she is." Moving closer to Carrington, she lowered her voice. "Maybe the princess is also lucky. Maybe the prince will find that backbone every living creature is supposed to have and use it to sail away to Tahiti." She flashed a smile at him. "At least, one can hope." She ended her statement with a wink, then excused herself before drifting back over toward Amelia.

The princess's lady had winked at him. Was that supposed to mean something? Was she flirting with him, or delivering some kind of a message?

God, but he did hate complications.

Turning away to refill the drink he had finally finished, Russell all but walked into a solid wall of a man. One of the king's six bodyguards. This one was a tall, burly man who looked as uncomfortable in the tuxedo he was forced to wear as he would have been in a ballet dress fashioned with a profusion of tulle.

He gave a perfunctory nod of his head in place of a bow. "Excuse me, Your Grace, but King Weston would like to speak with you."

"The king?" Russell looked around and saw that Weston was not anywhere in the ballroom. If the royals continued to disappear like this, he mused, Nikolas Donovan and his Union for Democracy would find that winning their battle took no effort at all.

"Yes. This way, please."

They left the ballroom. Russell followed the bodyguard into the corridor and then to the king's study.

"Here he is, Your Majesty," the bodyguard announced. The moment that Russell crossed the threshold, the other man closed the doors behind him. Russell had no doubt that the man had positioned himself outside the double doors, barring anyone else's entrance until the king was finished with him.

Alone, with no prying eyes to spy on him, King Weston allowed his smiling facade to fall away. He'd known Russell since the young duke and Reginald had played together in a royal, pristine white sandbox. He felt comfortable enough with Russell not to have to maintain a pose. The man was almost like his own son.

In some ways, he actually felt *more* comfortable in Russell's presence than in Reginald's. There was an honesty to Russell that was missing in his own son.

His frown went deep, almost clear down to the bone. As did his frustration and displeasure. "Where the hell is he, Russell?"

"I don't know." He was surprised to see that the king fixed him with a long, hard, penetrating look. "I would tell you, Your Majesty, if I knew." He watched as the expression faded from Weston's face. "But I've been gone these last few days," he reminded his ruler, "bringing the princess back for the wedding."

"The wedding." Despair almost got the better of Weston as he threw up his hands.

Of late, the King had been battling the effects of what he took to be the flu. He felt feverish, at times dizzy, although he said nothing because he did not want the royal doctor fussing over him. But feeling the way he did, he was not up to Reginald's latest display of inexcusable behavior.

"The wedding is taking place in three days. No, two and a half," he amended. "Two and a half days," he repeated.

Russell truly felt sorry for what he thought the king had to be going through. Every man wanted to point to his son with pride, not frustration. "I know that, Your Majesty," he responded quietly.

"What if he decides to skip that, too, just like he skipped meeting her at the airport, just like he skipped attending the party in his and her honor?" The tension in the king's voice kept building, fueled by ever-increasing agitation. "What if he doesn't come? What am I to do then, marry the girl off to a piece of his clothing? Or to the royal sword?"

Though the situation was deadly serious, the question threatened to evoke a smile. Russell did his best to keep it at bay.

"Marriage by proxy has been done, Your Majesty," Russell allowed.

"Yes, it has. During the Crusades," the king retorted angrily. "What is he thinking?" The question was more of a lament than a demand for an answer.

Russell had been with the prince on more than one of his escapades and knew the pattern of Reginald's behavior as the evening advanced. "Right about now, Your Majesty, since the prince is missing, I don't imagine that he's thinking much of anything."

Weston's pale complexion took on color. "Because he's dead drunk?"

Russell deliberately kept his voice low, hoping to calm the king down. "That, too, I'm afraid, has been known to happen."

The king shook his head, not in despair, but in final decision. He had indulged Reginald too long and too much. He had to put a stop to it and he would. Beginning now. The prince couldn't be allowed to continue behaving like some rutting stag.

"Well, it can't," the king said with finality. "Not

anymore. He has to learn that he has to grow up. Reginald's thirty years old, for heaven's sake."

The king had begun to pace. Russell moved out of the way, giving the monarch a clear path. "Yes, I know that, too, Your Majesty."

Weston paused abruptly, as if to gather himself together. His complexion, Russell thought, was much too red. If the king was not careful, he could talk himself right into a heart attack or a stroke. He'd heard rumors, although as of yet unsubstantiated, that the king's health was not what it used to be. No doubt, Reginald and his reckless behavior had something to do with that.

The king crossed to him. They were of equal height. The king looked at him imploringly, not as a ruler but as a father. A father who had been pushed to the limit of his endurance. "I want you to find him for me, Russell."

Russell didn't want to make promises he couldn't keep. "I don't—"

The king held up his hand, not letting him finish. "You know his haunts, you know what he's capable of and with whom." A sad smile curved her lips. "Probably much more than I do. I pride myself on being informed, but there are some things a father doesn't want to know about his son." His eyes met Russell's in a silent entreaty for understanding. "So I have no idea where to send one of my bodyguards to find him. But you would know." He paused, waiting for some kind of confirmation. "Wouldn't you?"

Even though he didn't go there himself, he knew the different places that Reginald liked to frequent, some he wouldn't even repeat to the king. "There are a few places I could go to look."

"Then go. Look." The words came out like shots fired from a gun, quick, independent and lethal. "And bring the prince back, even if he orders you not to." Weston squared his broad shoulders. "You have my orders and I can still overrule the prince."

But for how long? Russell wondered. Once Weston gave up the crown to his son, Russell had more than just an uneasy feeling that there would be no safeguards that could be applied to the unruly Reginald. There would be no one to stop him, at least, not officially. Russell foresaw only turmoil in the months ahead. The way he felt about Amelia had nothing to do with his fears for the realm.

He studied his monarch's face. The king was an intelligent man. Granted he loved his son, but he had to see that Reginald wasn't really fit to take charge, no matter what his chronological age. They needed more time to make him ready to assume his responsibilities. Until now, Reginald had only been playing at being a royal. He had taken on none of the duties that went with his position.

For heaven's sake, he couldn't even show up somewhere on time.

The words burned on his tongue. Russell couldn't allow himself just to stand by and say nothing. But he knew the path was one that was lined with mines. He picked his way carefully.

"Perhaps, Your Majesty, you might reconsider the coronation ceremony," Russell suggested tactfully. "Postpone the official shift of power for a little while until such time as—"

The king wouldn't let him finish. He raised his hand, stopping Russell. "I understand what you are saying, Carrington, and believe me, I have had the same thoughts. More than once," he added heavily. "But I can't go against tradition. I can't simply break rules when it suits me and expect others not to."

Russell knew that by "others" the king was referring to the troublesome Union for Democracy. There had been efforts, ever since the group had organized five years ago, to suppress it, to try as subtly as possible to force the members to disband. But instead, it had only grown. Not by any large degree, but enough to deserve further close surveillance. They called themselves a peaceful group, but more than one so-called peaceful group had been known to become the center of violent eruptions. No one wanted to see that happen in Silvershire.

Russell found himself wondering if perhaps having the Union of Democracy take over might not, in the final analysis, be preferable to having Reginald ascend to the throne.

But he kept this to himself as he inclined his head, symbolizing his acquiescing to his ruler's wishes. "Yes, Your Majesty."

"Go find my son and tell him...tell him..." It was on the tip of Weston's tongue to instruct Russell to say to Reginald that he was a disappointment to him. But that was between him and his son. No one else, not even Russell, as familiar as he was with the scene, was allowed to be privy to that. "Just tell the prince to hurry back to the palace and live up to his responsibilities," he concluded.

"Yes, Your Majesty." Russell paused, reading between the lines. The gala was still going on, but he had no real desire to remain. He would rather be busy than standing around, left to his own thoughts. Thoughts he found difficult to deal with at the moment. "Do you want me to go this evening?"

"Yes, if you would. Now," Weston emphasized. And then he confided, "I have this dreadful feeling that every moment matters."

Russell thought of telling the king that he had no need to worry. That Reginald was just being Reginald, shallow and thoughtless and self-involved. That he was most likely in some estate, sleeping off a drinking spree, or availing himself of any one of a number of willing women who wanted to be able to boast to their friends that they had slept with an authentic prince.

But in the end, he decided that perhaps discretion was the better road to take. So he bowed and withdrew. "Yes, Your Majesty."

Russell sighed, relieved to have an excuse to go home and change out of the tuxedo that fit him like a dark glove. He didn't care that he looked good in it, it was stiff and uncomfortable. He'd never liked formal attire. His rank in life called for it, so he put up with it when it was called for, but he was far happier wearing jeans and a sweater. He had the soul of a commoner, his father used to chide him. He suspected that his father was right.

As he turned the corner on his way out of the palace, he almost walked directly into Amelia. The unexpected contact was quick and sharp, as were the pins and needles that shot all through his body.

Without thinking, he'd reached to grab for her, to steady her in case she was going to fall. Reflexes had him doing it even before he realized who it was that he had bumped into, although his body immediately recognized the familiar feel of the impact. All it took, he thought, was once, and the feel of her body had been indelibly pressed onto the pages of his memory.

God, but he was waxing poetic. At another time, it would have been enough to turn his own stomach. Was this what love did to you? Turned you into someone you wouldn't normally associate with if you had a choice? He had no answer to that. No answer to anything, except that he was being turned inside out.

Did it get better with time? He could only fervently hope so.

But something told him that he was hoping in vain.

Attempting to collect himself, he retreated to the shelter of formal decorum and released Amelia.

"I'm sorry, I shouldn't have grabbed you like that, but I was afraid you'd fall. Are you lost, Princess?" He congratulated himself on his formal tone. One never knew who might be listening in the palace and he wanted no hint of a stain upon her reputation.

She raised her eyes to his. "Yes," she answered quietly, "I'm afraid I am lost." After a beat, she added, "Very lost."

As her eyes held his, Russell knew she wasn't talking about finding her way through the palace.

Chapter 8

He was a man who prided himself on remaining cool under fire. And although standing in the hallway with the Princess of Gastonia could hardly be designated as being under fire, Russell felt himself growing more than a little warm.

As was she, he thought. Her cheeks were flushed and the temperature within the palace was moderate at best. The king liked it brisk. He maintained that it got the blood moving.

His blood, Russell thought, was having no trouble moving. Close proximity to the Princess Amelia had seen to that.

He realized that several seconds had passed and he hadn't responded to her words yet. His brain felt as if it had been taken hostage. It took effort and concentration in order to free it.

"It's a little overwhelming until you get used to it," Russell finally managed. "The palace," he added in case the princess misunderstood his meaning.

Damn, he sounded like some thick-tongued fool. He'd never possessed Reginald's silver tongue, but he'd never been a babbling idiot, either. Not until now.

But then, he'd never slept with a princess before. That changed things.

He had to put that behind him, Russell insisted silently. And what's more, they couldn't just stand in the corridor, exchanging nonsense like this. There was no telling who might see them and misconstrue things.

Or construe them correctly, he thought ruefully.

The lighting in the corridor was sufficiently bright, yet it paled in comparison to her, he thought. Everything paled in comparison to her.

He felt the long, slender fingers of temptation reaching for him. Threatening to ensnare him again. He couldn't pretend that he didn't want her; he did. All he could do was struggle for control.

But a man's control only went so far and not nearly enough time had gone by for the embers of the fire that had been lit between them to have cooled.

Not enough time had gone by for him to have cooled, either.

Just looking at her made him long for a different place, a different time. A different life.

"I just wanted to get a little air." She touched his arm as she spoke and he could literally feel the heat flaring through him. He did his best to bank it down and ignore it.

"There isn't much to be had in the corridor," he pointed out with amusement.

"More than there is in there." She nodded in the general direction of the ballroom she had just left. "Too many questions, too many people," she explained and then looked up at him. "Too many doubts."

He tried to focus on something other than her lips. On something other than the way he wanted to taste them again. "Princess—"

Second-guessing his response, she held up her hand to stop him.

"Oh, I know what my duty is," she said quickly and with resignation. "I've known what my duty was since before I could adequately understand what the word itself really meant. But the doubts I have are about the prince himself. He seems neither to know, nor to care what his obligations are as far as maintaining at least a civil relationship with his future wife." She pressed her lips together, digging deep for courage and resolve in order to get through this. "I'm not sure I can face marriage to a man who has so little regard for me that he does not even attend a ceremony meant to welcome me to his kingdom. A ceremony meant to honor us as a royal couple."

Were those tears he saw in her eyes? God, he hoped not. He had no idea what to do when faced with a woman's tears. He would much rather have spent an entire day arguing with the prince than five seconds in the company of a tearful woman.

All the more so because he was left with the odious job of having to defend the errant royal. "I'm sure he was unavoidably detained."

To his surprise, Amelia laughed shortly. "Handcuffed to a bed?"

Only supreme control kept his jaw from dropping. "Princess—"

And then she laughed, really laughed. That light, airy sound that had already won a place in his heart. The same heart that had pledged its loyalty to the crown, to the prince. He felt guilty as hell and torn in two diametrically opposed directions.

"Don't look so shocked, Carrington. I wasn't raised in an eighteenth-century cloister." She lowered her voice and seemed to draw closer, even though she didn't move a muscle. "You, more than anyone, should know that."

Was that the sound of approaching footsteps he heard? Russell looked around. He had no thought about himself, but there was the princess's honor to be concerned about. "We really shouldn't be seen talking like this—" he began to warn her.

A smattering of impatience crossed her brow. It occurred to him that Amelia was undoubtedly one of those types who looked magnificent when she was angry.

"Who shall I talk to? Madeline seems to have been charmed out of her shoes by one of the young dukes and the king is not exactly the person I can turn to with concerns about his son. The poor man looks put upon enough without having to listen to me voice my misgivings. Besides," she confided, "I haven't seen the king in more than half an hour."

"That's because he's in his study." He indicated the area just beyond the corner. "I just came from there. His Majesty requested that I find and bring back the prince." Russell saw an odd expression filter across her face. He was unable to fathom it. Had he said something wrong? "What is it?"

This, Amelia thought, had to be the definition of irony. "I find myself in a very precarious position. I don't know whether to hope that you do find him, or hope that you don't. For me, it seems to be the epitome of a lose-lose situation." But, because she was a princess and raised by her father to put her country before her own needs, Amelia rallied and then offered Russell a smile. "Of course I hope you find him. One should never misplace a prince. It's bad for the country."

As well Reginald might be, Russell couldn't help thinking. He really wished that Weston could continue as king for years to come.

And then Amelia stepped back, as if to re-enter the ballroom. "I shouldn't be detaining you, Carrington. Good luck."

The way she'd said it, he wasn't quite sure if she meant with his assignment, or something else. "With finding the prince?"

"With whatever it is you want to happen," she corrected.

With that, Amelia turned on her heel and returned to the ballroom and to the mountain of responsibilities that were waiting for her just inside the door.

* * *

It was the last place Russell would have thought to look. It was the last place he did look, because it had seemed so improbable. So tame.

For the last twelve hours, Russell had gone from one club to another, methodically working his way from the more prestigious ones down to the clubs that no one willingly admitted, at least in public, that they frequented. The ones for which the phrase *den of iniquity* had originally been fashioned.

But no matter where he went, the story always seemed to be the same. Yes, the prince had been there, but no one had seen the prince within the last two days. When he questioned the men who were often with the prince about his whereabouts, they all claimed to believe that he was at some other place, with another set of cohorts.

Russell had to bank down the intense desire to shout at the men to sober up and do something meaningful with their lives. But that, he knew, was merely displacement. The words were meant for the prince.

Russell shook his head as he left the last establishment. At the prince's present pace, Reginald would probably wind up bedding or at least propositioning every woman in Silvershire under the age of eighty by summer's end.

He got back behind the wheel of his vehicle and slammed the door. Funny, he hadn't realized how much he loathed the man until this very moment. Even animals in the wild were more monogamous than Reginald was, and he wasn't even thinking of the ones who mated for life. Reginald mated for an hour, then went on, amnesia clouding his brain.

And this was going to be their future ruler.

God had to have one hell of a sense of humor, Russell thought darkly, starting the car again.

He was out of places. Out of glitzy clubs and run-down holes-in-the-wall. He'd already checked with the airports and the harbor. The prince had not left the country by means public or private. Since Silvershire was seabound on all sides, that meant that he was here.

But where?

Deciding that when he reported to the king, he wanted to have been utterly thorough, Russell could only think of one more place to try. A place where he was fairly certain the prince wasn't: his country estate. The king had given him the deed to the property on his twenty-first birthday. When the novelty of owning a country estate had still been fresh, Reginald had thrown there more than a few of what could only be politely referred to as orgies.

He himself had begun drawing the line then, Russell recalled. The very thought of what went on there turned his stomach. But Reginald seemed to thrive on those decadent gatherings. The more participants, the better.

Angry for the princess, for the country, Russell's mood was black by the time he reached the estate.

As he'd expected, there was no one there. The only time there was any staff at the estate, aside from the gardener who was dispatched once a month and the housekeeper who cleaned on a weekly basis, was when the prince was in residence there.

He recalled that, just before he'd left for Gastonia,

Reginald had told him that he would be visiting the estate. He'd thought Reginald was joking, but this was no time to leave any stone unturned.

The estate was shrouded in silence as the last rays of late-afternoon light receded. Russell disarmed the alarm and unlocked the front door. The prince had entrusted him with the code and a key to the estate as a token of their friendship.

A friendship, Russell thought as he closed the door behind him, that had long since lost its luster—if it had ever had any to begin with.

The house absorbed darkness with the thirst of a sponge. Russell turned on the light that illuminated the foyer and hallway beyond.

"Hello, is anyone here?"

His voice echoed back, mocking him as he crossed the marble foyer. The heels of his shoes meeting the stone was the only sound he heard.

This was useless. The Black Prince was probably holed up in some woman's bedroom, waiting for his fourth or fifth wind. When it came to making love, Reginald was tireless. Too bad he wasn't like that when it came to matters of state.

Russell paused, debating going back to the palace. And then he shrugged. He was here. He might as well check the bedrooms and the kitchen. That way, he could tell the king that he had looked everywhere he could possibly think of for the prince.

"Why don't you just grow up, Reginald?" Russell said out loud in exasperation. "The princess is a beautiful woman. She'll make you happy. And you, you should drop down on your knees and thank God that you, with your black soul, were still lucky enough to get such a woman."

On the second floor, Russell marched up and down the hall, pushing open one door after another as he spoke, venting his frustration. "Your father's right. It's time for you to grow up and be a man for once in your life, not just some—"

The words caught in Russell's throat.

The bedroom wasn't empty. There was someone in the bed.

He hadn't really expected to find the prince. At best this was just an exercise in futility to cover all the bases. But there he was, in bed, stark naked from all appearances, with a sheet draped over his loins, and sound asleep as if he didn't have a care in the world.

"Damn it, Reginald," he said in the familiar voice of a man who had been a friend for more years than he should have, "how can you just lie there like that? Don't you know that everyone's been waiting for you to turn up for the last two days? You didn't come to the airport, you didn't come to the gala. You're supposed to be getting married in two days. How can you be—"

Exasperated, Russell abruptly halted what he felt was a well-deserved tirade. The prince was sleeping through it all, anyway.

With a weary sigh, Russell crossed to the bed and took hold of the prince's shoulder, shaking it. Reginald was a sounder sleeper than most, especially when he'd been drinking, so Russell shook him again. There was still no response, no indication that the prince was waking up. His expression remained unchanged.

"Sleeping the sleep of the dead?" Russell mocked with no trace of humor. "Because it certainly isn't the sleep of the just. Well, I don't care how drunk you are, the king sent me to find you and find you I did, so come on, get up. Get up and get dressed, your father's waiting. You've really done it this time with those 'wild oats' of yours and it's going to take a lot to reverse all the bad press you've been getting."

The prince remained inert.

Russell looked at him. Something wasn't right.

He could feel it in his bones. Feel it just the way he had when he had been away at school and had suddenly sensed that his father had fallen ill. That his father needed him. He had no idea how he'd known, he just had. He'd come home just in time to be at his side when his father had died.

A gut feeling had prompted him then. And now he was experiencing another one.

Russell dropped down to one knee beside the bed, staring at the prince. "Reginald?"

The prince's hand felt cold when he took it. The sensation registered the very same moment that he realized the prince's chest wasn't moving. Reginald wasn't breathing.

Adrenaline raced through his veins as Russell tried to find a pulse. There was none. As he looked more closely at the prince, he had the sickening feeling that there hadn't been a pulse for at least several hours.

Perhaps even a day. The body was not stiff, but rigor mortis was a condition that came and then receded.

He needed an expert. He needed help.

"Oh, God," Russell groaned under his breath. Rising to his feet, he took out his cell phone and quickly called the royal physician. The number was on his speed dial. The man had been summoned on a fairly regular basis for more than a decade, always to see to the prince after a lengthy spate of debauchery.

"What's the matter?" There was a hint of irritation in the doctor's voice once Russell had identified himself. "Is he hungover again?"

Russell glanced over his shoulder at the still form. "I'm afraid he's much more than that, Doctor." Rather than ask the doctor to come, he told the man what was wrong. "The prince is dead."

"Dead?" the doctor echoed in a hushed voice throbbing with disbelief. Everyone associated with Reginald had come to believe that he had a charmed life. "How did it happen?"

Russell leaned over the body. There were no telltale marks to identify the cause.

"I have no idea. He wasn't shot or stabbed and doesn't look to have been strangled. Everything is neat and as far as I can tell, in its place. There's no evidence of any kind of a struggle." These days, with the preponderance of television crime programs that came to them thanks to the Americans, everyone was an armchair crime-scene investigator, Russell thought, and that included him.

"We're going to need an autopsy." He heard rustling

on the other end. The doctor was preparing to leave. "Does the king know?"

"Not yet." There was a reason why he had delayed that call. He was afraid of what the shock of Reginald's death might do to the king. "I wanted to give you some time to reach him before I called. He's probably going to need to be sedated."

The doctor's tone indicated that he was not so sure. "Don't underestimate the old man. He's a lot tougher than you think."

"Even tough men have been known to fall apart and he hasn't been looking too good lately," Russell said quietly. "How long will it take you to get to the palace?"

The doctor didn't need any time to consider. He'd made the trip often enough, both from his home and from his office. "Fifteen minutes."

"All right. I'll wait fifteen minutes, then," Russell replied. "Once you see to the king, I need you to come here."

"Of course," the man agreed. "And here would be—?"

"The prince's country estate."

"I'm on my way," the doctor promised.

His eyes never leaving the prince's body, Russell slowly closed his cell phone and slipped it back into his pocket. A shaft of guilt pierced him. God help him, but his first thought was that Amelia wasn't going to have to go through with the wedding.

He couldn't think about that now.

There was a brocade armchair in the corner of the room beside the window. Russell dragged it over next to the bed and then lowered himself into it, his eyes never leaving Reginald's body.

What a waste. What a terrible waste.

He thought for a moment of dressing the prince, of giving him a dignity in death that Reginald had turned his back on while he'd been alive. But he knew better than to tamper with anything. Although there were indications that the prince might just have finally taken the wrong combination of alcohol and drugs, this might still be considered a crime scene. It was bad enough that he had touched first Reginald's shoulder and then the pulse at both the prince's throat and his wrist. He didn't want to compromise the scene any further.

Russell folded his hands in his lap and proceeded to wait for the longest fifteen minutes of his life. The minute hand on the ancient timepiece his grandfather had given him dragged by like a snail dipped in molasses working its way along a rough surface. It seemed almost frozen in place each time he looked at it.

Fifteen minutes took forever. But finally, the minute hand touched the sixteenth stroke. Russell flipped his cell phone open once again and called the palace.

It took several more minutes for someone find the king. He'd initially met with resistance when he refused to divulge the reason behind his call, saying only that the king was expecting it.

No father ever expected this kind of a call, Russell thought sadly.

As modern-thinking as the king was, Weston refused to carry a cell phone, feeling that it was too invasive.

When he finally came on the telephone to speak to him, Weston was on one of the palace's secured land lines.

"This is King Weston," the deep, unmistakable baritone voice echoed against his ear.

God, I wish I didn't have to tell you this. "Your Majesty, it's Carrington."

The king's voice was immediately eager. "Did you find him? Did you find the prince?"

Each word felt like molten lead as it left his tongue. "Yes, Your Majesty, I did, but—"

"What did he have to say for himself?" the monarch demanded. It was obvious that although he had been indulgent for all of Reginald's life, the king was finally coming to the end of his patience.

"Nothing." Russell stalled for a moment, still concerned about the king's health despite what the doctor had said. "Your Majesty, is the royal physician with you yet?"

"No, why should he—" There was a pause. Russell heard the sound of someone knocking and then a door being opened in the background. "Doctor, what are you doing here? Is someone ill?" the king asked, addressing the doctor.

"No, Your Majesty," Russell answered for the physician. "The doctor is there to help you."

"Help me?" the king echoed, confused. "Why would I need a doctor—?" Abruptly, a note of fear entered his voice. "Carrington, there's something wrong, isn't there?"

"I'm afraid there is, Your Majesty."

Russell could almost hear the king holding his breath. As if by not breathing, that would forestall whatever bad news was coming. "It's Reginald, isn't it?"

"Yes, Your Majesty, it is." It was as if the words refused to materialize, refuse to enter the atmosphere.

There was desperation in the king's voice. He was stalling, trying to find a reason for this melodrama that he could live with. "What kind of trouble has he gotten himself into this time?"

There was no way to say this, no way to couch the words that had to come out so that they wouldn't leave wounds, wouldn't hurt beyond measure. In his heart, Russell damned the prince for living the kind of lifestyle that had brought him to this. Most of all, he damned Reginald for making him have to say this to the king.

"Your Majesty, Prince Reginald is dead."

"No," the king cried. "No! This is a lie, a trick. You're not telling me the truth. Reginald is trying to play me, the way he always has before. So, what does he want? What does he hope to gain from all this?"

"Nothing, Your Majesty. This isn't a hoax. I'm very sorry to be the one to have to tell you this, but the prince really is dead. I found him at his country estate and he's been dead for hours, perhaps more."

He heard the receiver being dropped. And then the line on the other end went dead.

Chapter 9

Russell folded his cell phone and placed it back into his pocket. He didn't try to reach the king again. He knew that they hadn't been disconnected because of any signal that failed to get through. Undoubtedly, the king had terminated the conversation, unable to listen any longer. He couldn't blame him. He had no idea how he would have reacted in the monarch's place.

But then, he would have kept a tighter rein on Reginald than the king ever had. Maybe if safeguards had been put into place early on, if rules and a sense of moral values had been drummed into the prince's head, he wouldn't be where he was right now.

Naked and alone.

Well, almost alone, Russell amended. He shook his head, looking down at the cause of the king's grief.

"Well, you did it again, Reggie. Even in death, you've managed to disrupt everyone else's life."

And even in death, the prince had managed to be selfish, without a care for those he left behind.

Russell was worried about the king. Granted, to the passing observer, except for the last few days, the king looked to be in excellent condition, especially considering his age, but that was just the outside packaging. He knew, though it was never publicized, that the king had a number of health issues, none of them ever elaborated on, which, of course, was understandable. The public wanted an invincible ruler. If the king had a heart condition, or some sort of other malady, that would be a matter only between the king and his doctor. No one else would ever need know.

The king was by nature a private man. It physically upset him that Reginald brought so much attention to his less-than-sterling behavior. The escapades of the last few weeks had taken a toll on the monarch. His color had paled and he looked...unwell, Russell supposed was the best term for it. News of Reginald's death might cause his health to take a sudden downward spiral.

Sharp nettles of regret dragged along his conscience. Maybe he should have waited before calling the king, or better yet, left the job of breaking the news to the royal physician.

But that would have been cowardly, he upbraided himself, and he was not a coward. He did what needed to be done, regardless of the personal consequences. In all good conscience, the king had to be informed and the sooner the better. Russell knew the king. If Weston learned that he had been kept in the dark, even for his own good, he would not take the news well.

No, he'd acted accordingly, Russell decided as late-afternoon shadows began to take possession of the room. The misgivings he was having were rooted in the guilt he still felt over sleeping with the princess. In a single reckless act, he had betrayed the king, the prince, his country and his own set of values. The passage of time was not going to change the way he felt about that.

He doubted if he would ever be right with his actions, no matter how much he cared for the princess. It was something a man of honor should not have done. Despite the reasons, there was no excuse for it.

With a heavy sigh, Russell sat back in the chair, keeping vigil.

The royal physician arrived with an ambulance forty-five minutes later. To stay under the radar and not attract any unwanted attention until the matter of the prince was properly attended to, there were no sirens, no telltale indication that there was any urgency. Still, Russell had a feeling that the driver had bent all the speed limits to get to the estate in the amount of time that he had.

Russell went outside to meet the vehicle and was surprised to see a very shaken-looking King Weston emerge from the rear of the ambulance. He almost looked fragile, Russell thought. The monarch was accompanied only by the ambulance driver, the royal physician and his chief bodyguard, Bostwick, who had been with the king since he had first accepted the crown, thirty years ago.

Weston was as pale as a ghost. Russell learned later from the doctor that the king had collapsed when he'd heard that Reginald was dead and had had to be revived. But nothing would convince him not to come with the ambulance to tend to his son.

"Where is he?" Weston demanded hoarsely, striding past Russell and walking into the mansion. His voice echoed within the vaulted ceilings. "Where is my son?"

"This way, Your Majesty." Russell moved around the monarch and led him up the stairs to the bedroom where he'd found the prince.

Grimly, he stood to the side of the doorway, allowing the king to enter first. The monarch seemed to be in almost a trance as he crossed to the bed and stood over his only son.

Dr. Neubert walked in behind him. In his service for only a few years, the young physician was concerned about the toll this was having on his monarch's heart and general health.

"Your Majesty, you shouldn't—" Dr. Neubert began.

Weston waved him into silence with an impatient gesture.

From his vantage point, Russell could see the tears gathering in the king's blue-gray eyes. Protocol dictated that he hang back, that he allow the king his dignity, his moment, but Russell thought of him as a second father and as such, could not bring himself to leave the man standing so alone. He crossed to stand beside him.

"I've lived too long, Russell," the king finally said, his eyes never leaving the inert form. "No father should have to see his son dead before him." He swayed slightly and Russell was quick to lend his support, steadying him. That Weston was in a bad way became imminently clear when the king did not shrug him away but accepted his arm. For a moment, he looked very old, very worn.

"Your Majesty, please, you shouldn't have come," the doctor insisted. "You should be resting."

The king ignored him. "And this is the way you found him?" he asked Russell.

Again, Russell wished he could have done something about Reginald's appearance for the king's sake. But all he could do was nod. "Yes, Your Majesty."

Every syllable was shrouded in grief's dark colors. "Naked and dead?"

If there had been some way to excuse it, Russell would have pounced on it. But there wasn't. He knew that finding Reginald this way somehow only heightened the tragedy, the waste. "Yes, Your Majesty."

Weston sighed and shook his head. "Too long," he repeated, more to himself than to anyone else in the room. "Too long. I've lived too long."

"Your Majesty, about that sedative now—" the doctor began.

"I don't want a sedative," Weston said with such feeling that it gave Russell hope the monarch was rallying. "I want my son. I want answers. Carrington, call the constable," he ordered.

"Yes, Your Majesty." Dutifully, Russell took out his phone again.

* * *

Jonas Abernathy was the royal constable, a jovial, affable man who, when he had initially been hired twenty-two years ago, had known police procedures like the back of his hand. However, in all the years he had been in the king's service, he'd had very little chance to put his knowledge to use. His wealth of knowledge had faded until it was little more than a memory.

He and his two assistants reminded Russell of small-town officers. Though the country had its own police force, it was more for show and for parades than anything else. Crime was not a problem in Silvershire. A little theft, a few arguments that had gotten out of hand and once a jealous husband who had shot both his wife and himself, missing both times. There'd never been a murder on record in Silvershire.

As he watched the three men conducting the investigation, Russell knew that they would not be equal to the task if the prince turned out to be a victim of homicide rather than his excesses. They were going to need someone good and someone discreet to handle this.

Russell waited until they were on their way out of the mansion, following the prince's covered body as it was being taken to the ambulance, before he said anything. He stood back with the king as the driver and physician lifted the gurney into the rear of the vehicle.

"Your Majesty, perhaps you might want to employ a more sophisticated agency to look into this matter for you." When the king made no reply, he continued, "I know of an organization that is very discreet."

As if rousing himself from an unnaturally deep sleep, Weston rendered a heartfelt sigh before finally answering. "Yes, you're probably right. Abernathy and his two will never get to the bottom of this if it is the slightest bit involved." Inside the ambulance, Dr. Neubert extended his hand to him, but rather than take it, the king suddenly turned to Russell. "Where were the bodyguards while this was happening? Where are they now?" he demanded heatedly. "Where were the people who were supposed to keep my son safe?"

"That will be one of the first things that will be addressed," Russell promised. The absence of the men who usually surrounded the prince had struck him as odd from the moment he'd discovered the body.

Finally taking the hand that the doctor offered, the king climbed into the rear of the ambulance, to take a seat beside his son. To grieve over the eyes that would never again open to look at him.

He turned to look at Russell before seating himself. "All right, I leave it in your hands, Carrington. Have it looked into. Find someone to do this for me, to bring me all the answers. I need to know what happened."

Russell already knew who he would approach. There was an organization known as the Lazlo Group. It was an international agency that could be trusted to be both professional and thorough in their investigation. They did not come cheaply, but they were well worth it. The organization guaranteed results and from what he had picked up abroad, the Lazlo Group always delivered on its promise.

"Right away, Your Majesty."

Russell stood back as the driver moved to close the ambulance doors. He caught one last look at the king. For a moment, Weston was not a ruler of a small, proud country, nor a man who had helmed that country into prosperity for the last thirty years. What Russell saw was a broken man.

"Is it true?"

Russell turned away from the fireplace. April dampness had brought a need for a fire to take the chill out of the air. Or perhaps, he mused, it was the circumstances that had rendered the chill and the fire was only an illusion to keep it at bay.

He'd followed the ambulance to the palace. A clinic was maintained on the premises, where the king or the prince could be seen when they weren't feeling well without being subjected to the public's prying eyes. The royal staff came there as well to be treated for things that were not of a serious nature. But now one of the clinic's three rooms had been converted into a makeshift morgue.

Russell had left the king there and gone to the receiving room to collect his thoughts. When he saw the fire, he'd been drawn to it. He'd wanted to warm himself somehow before calling the Lazlo Group.

He hadn't expected to run into anyone, least of all the princess.

Amelia crossed to the fireplace, waiting for an answer to the question that had been burning on her tongue for a number of hours. There had been rumors that the prince was dead, that he had been killed or had taken his own life. Any one of a number of unsettling theories were making their way through the palace, not to mention the news media, and she didn't know what to think.

The only thing she did know was there was one person in the palace she could trust to tell her the truth. Russell. The moment she'd heard he was back, she'd gone looking for him. One of the palace maids had sent her here.

Russell turned away from the fire. He tried to read her expression. Fear? Joy? Relief? He couldn't tell. She had the princess thing down to a science, he couldn't help thinking. Her expression was unreadable.

"Is what true?"

A guttural sound of disgust managed to escape her lips. "Don't play the game with me, Carrington. You're the one person I'm counting on to tell me the truth. Is it true?" she repeated. "Is the prince dead?"

"Yes."

Even though she'd been the one to ask the question, it took Amelia a second to process his answer. Reginald was dead. Dreading the very idea of marriage to him, she still found it hard to wrap her mind around the concept that he was gone, that he no longer posed a threat to her independence, to her happiness.

It took her breath away.

That he was dead meant that she was free. But at the same time, it meant that her homeland would continue to be at risk because it did not have the protection of a larger country.

Mixed emotions assaulted her, each tugging her in a different direction.

"How?" She took a breath before lengthening the question. "How did he die?"

Russell almost asked if she was sure she wanted to know the details. But she was not the delicate princess of old, too sensitive to know the truth. He wasn't going to insult her by keeping her in the dark.

"Not violently. At least," he amended, "there were no bruises, no marks on his body."

But a professional assassin would know where to land blows where they might not be detected at first, Amelia thought.

"That you could see," she corrected.

The hint of a smile that curved his lips had no humor in it. "I could see a great deal." Despite everything, he found himself pausing. Even though he thought of her as capable and intelligent, he kept finding himself wanting to protect her, to shield her from the nastier side of life. "Are you sure you want me to continue?"

Her eyes darkened. "I'm not a child, Carrington. Nor was there any affection lost between the prince and myself. I think you know that." Whatever he told her wasn't going to reduce her to tears. Disdain, maybe, but not tears. He had to be aware of that.

Russell forged ahead. "I found the prince in bed. He was naked."

Somehow, that didn't surprise her. It was in keeping with Reginald's reputation. More than ever, she felt like someone who had just dodged a bullet. But for the moment, the world would see the man as her fiancé. That meant that there would be humiliation by association. "I see. Was there anyone—?"

She didn't have to finish. Russell knew what she was asking. "No, the prince was alone when I found him. Very alone," he emphasized. When she raised a quizzical brow, he added, "There wasn't anyone in the entire mansion."

That almost seemed impossible. In photographs of Reginald, he had always been surrounded by people. He had a huge entourage following him wherever he went. That they were gone could only mean one thing. "Rats leaving a sinking ship?"

Most of Reginald's hangers-on were less than savory. The ones employed by the crown were supposed to be more steadfast, but fear could send troops scattering. It all depended on what had happened in the last few hours. Russell intended to get answers. "I suppose that's as good a guess as any."

Amelia studied his face, trying to discern his thoughts. Trying not to have any of her own that were unseemly at a time like this. But then, she had never loved Reginald, hadn't even liked him. If she felt no grief at his passing, only relief, she could be excused for that. "But you don't think his death was natural."

"No, I don't," he admitted. "The prince was thirty years old and as healthy as a horse."

The prince brought another kind of animal to mind as far as she was concerned. "He also behaved like a rutting pig."

"That kind of behavior could have gotten him a knife in his back," Russell pointed out. "It wouldn't have killed him like a silent thief in the night."

Amelia paused, thinking. The prince was given to excesses of all kinds. Alcohol, women, drugs. According to more than one article she'd read, life had to be one continuous party, or Reginald was bored. "It could have been an overdose."

"Possibly." It was the first thing he'd thought of, but he wasn't satisfied with that explanation. "But I've seen the prince consume enough alcohol for two men and still remain standing. He had an incredible tolerance for both alcohol and recreational drugs." He shook his head. "Something isn't adding up."

If it turned out that natural causes hadn't taken him and he hadn't accidentally died by his own hand, then the only conclusion to be drawn was that the prince had been murdered. The thought made her uneasy. When one royal was struck down, they were all vulnerable. Unless it was personal. "Who stands to gain from his death?"

"I was thinking more of the people who actively disliked him."

She laughed softly to herself. She wasn't the only one who had dodged a bullet today. Silvershire had been spared, as well. "From what I hear, that could be most of the country. Since he was Weston's only heir, who is next in line for the crown?"

Until she asked, he hadn't even thought about the immediate consequences of Reginald's death. Or what that meant to him, personally. Since the prince had been so vibrant, the idea that Reginald might not be around to ascend the throne had never even occurred to him.

But now that it did, he found the notion appalling. He had always disliked notoriety. It had only gotten more intense as he had grown older and placed more value on his privacy. Russell's expression was grim as he replied, "I am."

Her eyes widened as she felt her heart jump. She hadn't known that. She'd had no reason to know that. "You?"

He nodded. "According to the rules of succession of Silvershire. Weston ascended the throne because King Dunford had no sons, no children of his own. There were two dukes he felt were equal to the task. Everyone felt he was leaning toward Lord Benton Vladimir. But then he suddenly changed his mind and chose Weston to be the present king."

Thoughts she didn't want to entertain began whispering along the perimeter of Amelia's brain. And if she could think them, so could others who were less charitable. Others who didn't love Russell.

Amelia pressed her lips together as she looked at him. "If the prince died under suspicious circumstances—if he was murdered—someone might think that you had something to do with it."

She thought about the night they had spent together. Had that prompted Russell to rethink his position and take matters into his own hands? Was she the reason behind what had happened to the prince? Or could Russell have conceived an elaborate plan to capture the crown and she had blindly played into his hands?

No! How could she even think that way? Amelia upbraided herself. Russell was too honorable a man to be guilty of something like that. She was willing to bet her life on that.

On what? a small voice demanded. On a man she hardly knew? On a boy who used to put bugs into her bed? She didn't really know the man who stood before her, she reminded herself. She only knew the boy he had been. A great many years had come and gone between then and now.

Amelia felt torn. Logic pointed one way, but she refused to believe that her heart would have led her astray like that. There was goodness in Russell, she could see it in his eyes, feel it in his touch. She had no answer for it; she just did.

His eyes met hers. "Do you?" He couldn't tell what she was thinking. Something froze inside him. "Do you think I had something to do with it?"

"No."

Amelia had hesitated for a moment. If she'd believed in him, she wouldn't have, he thought. "But you're not sure."

She knew that protests were useless. He could see right through her. She could only tell him the truth. "Can I swear to it in a courtroom on a stack of Bibles? No. Because I don't have any way of actually knowing where you were every moment. But do I doubt your loyalty to the crown? No. Do I think that you are a murderer? No."

His eyes held hers for a long moment as he thought of the night they'd spent together. The night that should never have happened.

"My loyalty to the crown could come under question," he reminded her quietly.

She drew her shoulders back. "That wasn't a matter of loyalty."

That was exactly a matter of loyalty, he thought. "Then what was it?"

"A matter of two kindred spirits coming together." From out of nowhere, a thought occurred to her. "Or was that out of pity?" she asked suddenly.

"What?"

Amelia shook her head. She was just being overwrought, she thought. She shouldn't have said anything. "Never mind."

But he didn't want to let it drop. "No, what did you mean by that? Was there anything that entire time that could make you suspect what happened was even remotely inspired by an emotion as condescending as pity?"

He sounded hurt, offended. She hadn't meant for any of that to happen. "No. I'm sorry. This whole situation is extremely distressing. I came here to be married to a man whose reputation I loathed—since he's gone, I don't see the point in hiding that," she said in response to the look in his eyes. "Now that he's dead, am I free of my obligation? Or am I, by default, betrothed to the next man in line?" She looked at him. "To you."

He measured out his words evenly. There seemed to be no emotion behind them. "Would that be so terrible?"

She took a breath. To his surprise she said, "That all depends."

"On what?"

"On how you feel about it."

He couldn't gauge by her voice how she felt about it herself. "How do you think I feel?"

Her temper came very close to breaking. "If I knew, would I be asking? A wondrous night of lovemaking does not automatically mean you want a lifetime of those nights. Sometimes magic is just that, magic. Meant for a hour, a night, not forever."

"So you're saying you wouldn't want to have to marry me."

Why did she suddenly feel like weeping? That wasn't like her, but she was so tired of being a pawn. "I'm saying I don't want to *have* to marry anyone, just as you don't want to be told who to marry. Marriage is a commitment that should come from the heart, not from a committee. The piece of paper involved should be a marriage certificate, not a treaty between two countries. I am a person, not a pawn." And then, like someone waking up from a bad dream, she stopped and blew out a breath. "I'm sorry, I had to get that out."

Russell inclined his head. "I understand, Princess."

She pressed her lips together again, impatience, frustration and a host of other emotions vying for control over her.

"'Princess,'" she echoed, shaking her head. "We are embroiled in intrigue, in murder and in heaven knows what else. We've slept together and might very well be married to each other before the week is out. My name is not 'Princess,' my name is Amelia."

The unexpected noise behind her sent adrenaline racing throughout her body. Amelia swung around to see that her father had entered the room and with him were several of his men. His complexion was flushed. Had he overheard her?

Chapter 10

Startled, it took Amelia a moment to rally. Since she acted as her country's representative in a great many diverse situations, her training under fire had been extensive. No one would have guessed that inside, she was still the young girl who had once tried so desperately to curry her father's favor.

Aware that the king had to have heard at least the end of her conversation with Russell and knowing that her father was far from a stupid man, she assumed he had put two and two together. But now was not the time to be upbraided for "conduct unbecoming." She was quick to throw the focus onto something that really mattered.

"Father, have you heard about the prince?"

The king's expression was grim as he nodded. "Terrible thing. Terrible thing," he repeated. "King Weston is beside himself. I tried to do what I could to comfort him, but this is a matter that will take a great deal of time for him to come to grips with. I'm told he collapsed when he received the news."

Russell felt a pang of guilt, but since the king had not addressed the remark to him, he said nothing.

"Reginald was his only son." Amelia moved so that she stood with her back to Russell, blocking him from her father's access. This was a private matter, but since it concerned Russell, she couldn't very well ask him to leave. And her father's bodyguards had been with the king for years. They were more like fixtures than men. Amelia drew herself up, asking a question she felt, in her heart, she already knew the answer to. "Will we be going home now, Father?"

Her father looked at her, a puzzled expression furrowing his brow. Behind her, she could almost feel Russell's gaze penetrating her back. "Why?"

"Because we came for a wedding and now that Reginald is dead—"

Roman cut her off. "Prince Reginald is dead," he agreed. "However, the alliance between Gastonia and Silvershire can and will still go forward." He looked at her intently, his gaze telling her she knew what was expected of her. "All that is needed for that to happen is for you to marry the next king of Silvershire."

Something inside her felt as if it was shattering. She was tired of being the good little obedient princess, tired of always doing what was expected of her. "And if that were a pig, would you have me take its cloven hoof in my hand and pledge to be faithful to the pig until the end of my days?"

Shock registered on her father's face. It echoed in the faces of his two bodyguards. She had no doubt that behind her, Russell didn't look like the picture of tranquillity, either. But she didn't care if any of them were shocked. There was a great need for her to speak her mind.

For a moment, the king looked as if he didn't know what to do with her. But when he spoke, his voice was patient. "You're overwrought, Amelia. I understand. However, nothing has really changed in the absolute sense. You have to think of the good of your people. Gastonia is a small, relatively defenseless country. Without the armed support of Silvershire, it could easily be taken over by any one of a number of countries. You are a princess, you cannot think with your heart." And then Roman looked at the tall man standing behind his daughter. "And, from what I just heard, as well as information that has been brought to me," he emphasized, "I believe a union between you two would not be entirely displeasing to either of you." He looked directly at Amelia and color crept up into her cheeks. Roman continued. "That the walls have ears is not merely an antiquated expression, my dear. I daresay that everything we do, whether we believe it's in private or not, becomes a matter of record." His meaning was quite clear as he looked from his daughter to the man he assumed would be king. "In addition to the main necessity for this marriage, for the sake of your reputation, Amelia, this marriage has to go through. Are we agreed, Carrington?"

Although his question was directed at Russell, it

was Amelia who ran interference. "It might seem a little callous to the people of Silvershire if the wedding goes ahead on schedule, only with a different groom."

Roman dismissed the idea. "Nonsense, the people love a fairy tale." His expression became serious. "What they wouldn't like is turmoil and unrest. Having the well-beloved princess marry the good Duke of Carrington will be just what they like, what they need. Gastonia will have its treaty and you will have a man you have already shown a preference for. And you, Carrington," he spared Russell a look, "will have your crown."

If the monarch only knew how little that meant to him, Russell thought. He knew the time for him to speak was now rather than later. "What if I don't want the crown?" Russell posed.

Roman looked at him as if he had just said that he had a strong desire to be flogged. "Not want the crown? How absurd. Dear boy, everyone wants the crown."

Russell had been taught to agree with royalty. To acquiesce whenever possible. But it wasn't possible. Not if there was a chance that he did not have to submit to this. He wanted a way out. Not because of a forced marriage, but because of a forced coronation.

"I don't," he said simply. "There's far too much attention attached to it. It would mean living the rest of my life in a fishbowl."

The king laughed shortly, shaking his head as if he was suffering someone who was simpleminded.

"You are already in that bowl, son. And as for not wanting the crown, I'm afraid you have no say in the matter. The rules are written," he pointed out. "And so is your destiny."

"The rules," Russell respectfully reminded him, "say that the king can change his mind."

Roman exchanged looks with his daughter. There would be no help coming from that quarter. He might as well squelch Carrington's hopes quickly, before they got out of hand.

"Right now, King Weston doesn't know his mind at all. He is in the terrible place that grief takes a man. He and I have been friends a very long time—since before you were born," he told his daughter. "In his time of grief, I know he would want me to keep things moving forward and move forward they shall." There was a note of finality in his voice as he spoke for the other monarch. "You will marry Carrington, Amelia, and Carrington will be the next king. I will hear no more about it."

So saying, King Roman swept out of the room with his bodyguards following closely behind him.

The room was very quiet for a moment. All that was heard was the sound of their breathing.

And then, because he couldn't bear the position he found himself in, couldn't bear the thoughts that were assaulting him, Russell broke the silence. "I could disappear," he offered.

Amelia stared at him, uncomprehending. This was his homeland. "Why would you do that?"

As if it wasn't written all over her face, he thought. As if her doubt wasn't palpable. "To spare you. You obviously don't want to go through with the ceremony."

Didn't he understand what he was suggesting? "If

you 'disappear,' people will think that you killed the prince and succumbed to the guilt."

"If I stay and marry you they might be inclined to think the same thing." It was damned if you do, damned if you don't, he thought. Except that until a few seconds ago, he had known which way he would have chosen to be damned. Now, he wasn't so sure and it hurt more than he was prepared for.

"Which would you rather do?" There wasn't so much as a hint in his eyes, she thought.

He shrugged his shoulders, looking away. "It doesn't seem that really matters to anyone."

How could he say that after the other night? She moved so that she was in front of him again. "It matters to me."

He wasn't sure if he truly believed that. Not after the uncertainty he'd seen in her eyes. He gave her his honest answer. "Then, Princess, I would rather marry you—and not be king."

He really meant that, she realized. That made him a unique man. "That doesn't seem to be a choice that's on the table."

"It should be." She couldn't read the expression that came over his face. "But then, if I wasn't to be king, you couldn't marry me, could you?"

Her heart froze as the thought she didn't want to entertain returned to haunt her. Could knowing that she had to marry the future king of Silvershire make Russell kill Reginald?

Oh, God, how could she think he was guilty of murder? The man she had made love with was gentle, tender. The hands that had touched her so reverently weren't the hands of a killer.

Were they?

"No," she answered quietly. "I couldn't. Not after my father had pledged my hand to the future king. But I could spare you," she went on to suggest. He looked at her quizzically. "If I were the one to run away, you couldn't marry someone you couldn't find."

Unable to resist the desire to touch her, he took her hand in his. "There's no need for you to run away. You're not the bad part of the bargain—the crown is." He brought her hand to his lips and kissed it. "And your father's right. If the public knows about us, or learns about us in the near future, then marriage to me is your only option."

Was that it? No mention of love, of desire, even of affection? Just some old-fashioned sense of duty? She pulled her hand away and tossed her head. "I don't have to safeguard my reputation, Carrington. This isn't a hundred years ago."

It wasn't all that easy to shake off the mantle of royal expectations. "Then why are you to marry the next ruler of Silvershire?" Russell asked gently.

Momentarily stumped, Amelia blew out a breath. "Point taken."

Touching her hand wasn't enough. He wanted to take her into his arms, to kiss her and make love with her. But now, of all times, they had to keep a distance between themselves. Besides, he reminded himself, she harbored suspicion in her soul. He had to remember that and not let himself be ruled by his hormones. Or his needs.

He began to back away from her, out of the room. "Princess, if you'll excuse me, I have a great many things to do."

She wanted to ask him to stay. To hold her. To tell her one last time that he had nothing to do with the prince's death. Her heart said one thing, her mind, taught to be suspicious, said another.

And she had also been taught to keep a tight rein on her emotions, so she merely inclined her head as he took his leave, saying nothing to stop him from going.

Russell had never felt more trapped in his life. He did not want to be king. Not once, in all the time that he had been growing up, had he entertained the idea of being king, even in passing or in jest. Reginald was only a year older than he was, in excellent physical health and vital and vibrant. It had never entered his mind that Reginald would not someday take the crown and be King of Silvershire.

Even though he'd felt that the prince was the wrong person for the responsibility, he had not once thought that he would make a better ruler than Reginald. He hadn't thought about being ruler at all, despite all of his schooling and qualifications, despite the fact that he cared about matters of state and Reginald wasn't interested in anything larger than the bust size of the woman he was currently with.

He, a king.

The very idea would have been laughable if it weren't so equally painful, Russell thought as he made his way down the palace corridor. What kind of a ruler would he make, anyway? He had betrayed the most sacred of trusts. Asked to bring back his future king's bride, he had slept with her instead.

Not exactly qualifications for ascending the throne.

How could he possibly be expected to lead a country if he couldn't even lead himself? If he couldn't control himself? Just now, back in that room with the princess, in the middle of it all, he had found himself thinking how beautiful she looked. How much he wanted to make love with her. Fine thoughts to be having when the prince's body was barely cold.

Damn it, this wasn't a time for angst and self-doubt. This was a time for action. The prince was dead and his first priority was finding about the circumstances that had led up to that event. His second would undoubtedly involve generating some sort of a cover-up of those circumstances, if for no other reason than to save the king public embarrassment and humiliation. The monarch had suffered enough of that already, thanks to Reginald's escapades. Enduring more of the same was not something that the king should be asked to go through.

There were intrigue and tangled webs no matter which way he turned, Russell thought. The fact that there wasn't a single living soul at the prince's estate was odd, to say the least. Reginald had always been surrounded by hangers-on and parasites. And there was the matter of the royal bodyguards. Where were they? Why hadn't they remained with the prince? He doubted very much that they had scattered of their own volition. Had Reginald ordered them away? Or had they been done away with in order to get to the prince? These and other questions begged for answers.

What had happened in the time he'd been away in Gastonia, making preparations to bring the princess back to Silvershire?

And losing his heart in the bargain, he added ruefully.

Russell sighed quietly to himself as he made his way up the spiral staircase. It was a damnable offense against all that he was raised to believe in, but in the shadowy recesses of his heart, he had to admit that he was relieved that Amelia was no longer going to have to marry Reginald for the sake of duty. The late prince would never have loved her, never have treated her with the kind of respect she deserved as a princess and as a human being.

His head throbbed. In a perfect world, he would have been able to marry Amelia with no strings attached, with no stain of doubt and suspicion attached to the union. But the world, he had learned long before he became the prince's shadow, was far from perfect. And this present situation he found himself in was apparently the best that he could hope for. To take the crown if he hoped to take the princess.

And what of the princess? Would she ever look at him without wondering if he'd had a hand in Reginald's demise? More than anything, he wanted to wipe away the suspicion shimmering in her eyes that was in danger of becoming a wall between them.

Somehow, he promised himself, he would find a way to turn everything else around and make Amelia believe that he had nothing to do with Reginald's death.

That he even had to entertain the thought hurt. She should have believed, without being told, without having it proven to her, that he was innocent.

The way to prove his innocence, he knew, was to find out exactly what had happened down to the last-minute details. He needed to learn who was with the prince in those final days and hours. And most importantly, he needed to learn if any of those people had been instrumental in having the prince killed.

His steps had brought him before the king's suite of rooms. Given a choice, he would gladly have left the monarch to his grief, but time was of the essence and they needed to get things moving. He wasn't sure if the ruler had processed what he had told him earlier about securing the operatives of the Lazlo Group. His grief and shock could have erased all memory of the suggestion.

Russell raised his hand and knocked on the finely carved oak door. In a moment, Bostwick, the head of the king's bodyguards, opened the door. The man was six feet three inches in both directions and bore a striking resemblance to a bulldog. He stood glaring at Russell, his body blocking access to the room.

Russell couldn't help thinking that it was a lucky thing he wasn't easily intimidated. Otherwise, Bostwick's scowl would have sent him running to his own room. "Bostwick, I'd like to have a word with King Weston, please."

The burly man remained unmoved. "The king is not seeing anyone," the man replied in a voice that seemed to have made the journey from the bottom of his toes.

But Russell was not about to be put off, not this time. "Bostwick—"

"Is that Carrington?" The king's voice: high, thin and reedy. He caught himself thinking that it sounded as if the monarch had aged ten years in the last hour.

"Yes, Your Majesty, it's me. Carrington." Russell raised his voice in order to be heard. "I need to speak with you."

"Let him in, Bostwick."

When Russell walked in, the first thing he noticed was the king's appearance. The strain in the man's face was incredible. He looked as if he had been to hell and back, sacrificing his soul in the process. It was difficult to believe this was the same man who had calmly gone over some plans with him just last night, before this whole business had started.

"Sit down." He gestured toward a love seat. "What is it?"

"I think we should have the prince's death looked into as soon as possible."

"You said that earlier, at the estate," the king reminded him. A sad smile played along his lips. "What? You think that I'm so grief-stricken that I've lost the use of my mind? I told you to proceed then, so by all means, proceed. Have this investigated. And when you find those who left my son in his hour of need, I want a complete accounting." He ran his hand along his forehead, as if willing back the tears that continued to gather, threatening to unman him. "Do you have anyone in particular in mind?"

He half expected the duke to mention himself. Instead, Carrington said, "I know the name of an international agency, Your Majesty. They are impartial and their track record for getting results is excellent. It's called the Lazlo Group. Corbett Lazlo has a team of highly skilled operatives who—"

Weston was vaguely familiar with the name. It was

a covert group no government publicly admitted to knowing. To his knowledge, they took care of dirty laundry.

He suddenly felt very weary. Ever since he had been told of Reginald's death, he'd felt himself tottering on the brink of abysmal despair. "Whatever you say, Carrington. I leave it to you."

Russell inclined his head. "Yes, Your Majesty." He paused for a moment, searching for a way to broach the subject delicately. There was none. He was forced to forge ahead. "Has the royal medical examiner been sent for yet, Your Majesty?"

Weston looked at him, a lost look in his eyes. The next moment, it disappeared. "What?"

"The medical examiner," Russell repeated politely. "Have you sent for her?"

The king wandered over to a window that overlooked the courtyard. In darkness, there was nothing to look at but shadows. Shadows as dark as the bottom of his soul. "No."

"I could do that for you—"

Weston turned from the window and looked at the man he had always thought of as a second son. Even as the thought crossed his mind, he felt a pang of guilt. He had no son. Not anymore. "Why?"

He and Bostwick exchanged glances. It was the first time he recalled ever seeing compassion in the latter's eyes. The man had been with the king for several decades and although it was not obvious, he grieved for his ruler. "An autopsy will have to be conducted in order to determine the exact cause of death—" Russell began as tactfully as he could.

Horror registered on Weston's regal face. "You mean cut him open?"

Russell felt as if each word were made of lead as he uttered it. "I'm afraid that's the only way, Your Majesty."

"Hasn't the prince suffered enough?" Weston demanded. His voice broke.

"I promise you, sire, the prince won't feel anything," Russell told him.

Weston sighed, coming away from the window. "But I will. I will feel every cut, every incision." The king paused, trying to compose himself. "When the queen died two days after giving birth to Reginald, I thought I could never hurt as much as I did then, losing her. I thought that I could never feel as lost as I did at the moment when her last breath left her body." He turned to look at the young man who was destined to take his son's place. "I was wrong. I'm not sure how I am going to get through this, Russell. Not sure at all."

Russell drew closer to him, silently offering him his strength, grieving not for the prince, but for the father he had left behind. "You will get through it because you are the king. And a very strong man."

A bittersweet smile played along his lips. "Not so strong, Russell. Not so strong." He looked down at the framed photograph he was holding. It was of the prince, taken on his tenth birthday. Tears gathered in the king's eyes. "I should have stopped him. When he was getting out of control, I should have stopped him. Not indulged him. But I thought, hoped, that he would outgrow this reckless behavior.

"I had a bit of a wild streak myself before I was

made the king," he confided. "The weight of the crown sobers you. Makes you humble and makes you realize that your own wishes need to take a back seat to those of your people." His voice all but drifted away as he said, "I thought that would come to him, as well."

Obligation forced Russell to say words he didn't truly believe for the king's sake. "It might have."

"But now we'll never know."

"No, sire, we won't," Russell agreed. "But we can know what happened to him. I know he would want you to find out the truth and if there is someone responsible for all this, the prince would have wanted you to bring them to justice." He paused before adding, "Even if it means cutting him open."

Weston nodded. "You're right. Call this Lazlo. Tell him I want to find out every detail, no matter how small and insignificant, of my son's last few days. Everything," he underscored.

"And the royal M.E.?" Russell prodded gently.

Weston squared his shoulders. He began to look a little like his old self. "I would like to hold off on that for a few days. Just until after the wedding day has passed. I can't explain it, I just don't want my son to be cut up into pieces on the day he should have been married, even if they do put him back together again." He looked at Russell for agreement, even though he did not expect to be contradicted.

Russell saw no reason to upset him further by pushing for a speedy autopsy. A few days shouldn't really matter, not if the events leading up to Reginald's death could be reconstructed. Reginald's autopsy could be postponed for a while and conducted at a later time.

Straightening his shoulders, Russell bowed before the king. "As you wish, Your Majesty."

"As I wish." Weston repeated the words. They rang ironically and mocked him as they drifted into oblivion. If things had gone according to his wishes, they would have arranged themselves so differently....

Pushing aside thoughts of weddings and coronations until he could better handle them, Russell quietly withdrew to place his call to Corbett Lazlo as Bostwick shut the doors.

Chapter 11

"And you suspect someone in the palace?"

The voice over the telephone was calm, resonant. It echoed slightly, the way voices over a speaker phone did. The echo did not diminish the effect. It was the same voice that had soothed distraught heads of state confronted with the kidnappings of loved ones. The same voice that had promised—and delivered—results in highly delicate government situations that the public had never even suspected.

Corbett Lazlo was a brilliant, enigmatic man very few people actually recognized. Those who did know him saw a tall, trim man with ice-blue eyes that conflicted with an almost boyish grin that even fewer were ever privy to. Some said he was an ex-CIA operative. Others claimed he was a bored genius with a love for challenges. Still others said he was the illegitimate son of a former French president and had cut his teeth on both foreign policy and espionage. No one knew for sure.

The only proven fact was that approximately twelve years ago, he had formed the Lazlo Group, an international team of highly skilled agents who specialized in, among other things, investigating the deaths of political figures.

The Lazlo Group was one of the best kept secrets of the free world. They were usually called in as a last resort, or when affairs were of such a delicate, discreet nature that no one else could be trusted to handle them.

Corbett Lazlo had no affiliation with any particular nation. He was a citizen of the world. His people did whatever was necessary to get the job done. There were never any questions asked by the party or parties who hired them. It was better that way.

The call Russell had placed to him had been rerouted several times so that Russell had no idea exactly where Corbett Lazlo was located. It was the way Corbett preferred it. Russell didn't care. Lazlo's location didn't matter. All that mattered was finding out the series of events that led up to Reginald's last day and death.

"I suspect everyone right now," Russell said, answering Lazlo's question. "Except for King Weston. And the princess," he added.

He heard what he took to be just the slightest chuckle on the other end.

"Never be too hasty in your judgment," Lazlo advised. "The princess stood to gain something from the prince's death."

Russell frowned. There had been a treaty riding on

the union. As far as he knew, there was nothing on the balance sheet if the prince died before they were married. "What?"

There was a pregnant pause on the other end, as if the man expected more of him. "Her freedom. Theirs wasn't exactly going to be a fairy-tale marriage. The prince went on whoring to the very end." He delivered the information as if he had been a witness to Reginald's behavior. Russell knew that the man kept himself informed on many fronts. "Not quite the behavior for a man who was about to be married to the woman of his dreams."

Russell could feel himself growing protective again. It had never occurred to him that Amelia might not need a champion, that she would want to fight her own battles at all times. He wouldn't hear her maligned, even theoretically. "She had nothing to do with it."

There was just a hint of indulgence in Lazlo's voice as he abandoned his point. "Nonetheless, we leave no stone unturned. My people don't come cheaply, Carrington, but they pride themselves on delivering. Everything," he emphasized. "The good and the bad."

"Money isn't a problem." He knew he spoke for the king when he made the affirmation. The monarch would have no peace until the matter of his son's death was resolved. And perhaps, sadly, not even then.

"Good. I'll be sending one of my top operatives to the palace. Her name is Lucia Cordez." Lazlo's voice was quick, staccato, leaving no room for argument as he took command of the situation. "You will invite her to the wedding. She will blend in."

About to protest that there would be no wedding,

Russell was suddenly struck by a thought. "How will I know her?"

"Trust me, you'll know her. She has the disadvantage of being stunning." A disadvantage, because he preferred his operatives to blend in rather than stand out. But he couldn't hold Lucia's beauty against her, not when she was so skilled at what she did. "Don't let her looks fool you. She's good under pressure and she is a computer expert."

That out of the way, Russell questioned the scenario that Lazlo was painting. "The wedding is canceled."

"Check your scorecard. There's been a substitution play. The wedding hasn't been canceled, just recast. Playing the part of the prince will be Russell, Duke of Carrington. Don't you pay attention to your traditions, Carrington?" When he received no response, there was a note of satisfaction in the older man's voice as he continued. "You're paying me to be informed. You're also paying me to find the truth." Again Lazlo paused, this time so that his words could sink in one at a time. "One could say that you had a great deal to gain from the prince's death."

Russell laughed to himself. Lazlo had no idea how absurd that idea was, he thought. "Feel free to investigate me."

"Thank you." His tone indicated that they would have done just that with or without permission. "We'll be in touch, Carrington."

With that, the conversation was terminated.

Russell replaced the receiver and stood for a moment, staring at the telephone, not seeing it. Not seeing anything at all in the study.

He was getting married. In less than a day if everything was held to the same schedule as before.

He had no idea how he felt about that. Other than numb.

Amelia adjusted her headpiece. The veil wasn't falling the right way. She felt tears gathering in her eyes and knew that they had nothing to do with the veil.

Tension brought the tears.

Things were happening much too fast for her. She'd never been one to enjoy life in the slow lane, but this was far more than she had bargained for. Far more than she could assimilate.

Her head felt as if it were spinning.

Less than two weeks ago, she had been in her gardens, fervently wishing that time would somehow find a way to stand still, at least for a little while. Dreading the wedding that loomed before her on the horizon like some creature that had been resurrected in a mad scientist's laboratory.

And now, despite all the changes, despite the royal tragedy of finding the prince dead in his bed, the wedding was still going to be on schedule. Only the groom had been changed.

She was marrying Russell.

Just the way, in a moment filled with passion and desire, she'd wanted to. Just the way she'd wished. Russell, who had introduced her to the world of lovemaking. Russell, who had grown into a man who was, at the core, kind and gentle and caring.

Russell, who now looked at her with distant eyes.

She knew it was because, in an unguarded moment, she'd allowed herself to tell him the truth. Tell him that, for less than a fragment of a second, she'd had doubts about him.

Dear lord, she had doubts about herself, as well. Doubts about everything right now.

But men didn't understand the emotional distress that women sometimes found themselves laboring under. Men didn't understand how women thought with their hearts as well as their heads.

Logic was the only thing that made sense to a man like Russell. And when confronted with what he thought to be the logic of her suspicions, he'd shut down. Shut her out. Grown distant.

In the last day and a half, when she'd tried to reach him, tried to get him alone just to talk to him, he had brushed her off by saying that he was too busy. He seemed to go out of his way to make himself unavailable to her.

If she didn't know any better, she would have said that he was trying to avoid her.

She adjusted the headpiece for the dozenth time. She stared at her reflection, not seeing the elaborate beadwork that had taken seamstresses weeks to complete. Maybe, she thought, she did know better.

Maybe he *was* trying to avoid her because she'd committed the sin of suspecting him. Or was it because she was right, and avoiding her until the ceremony was the only way he could handle the problem?

Was Russell involved in the prince's death?

The question kept haunting her, and every time she

thought she'd put it to rest, it insisted on rising up again, like fabled ghosts on All Hallows' Eve.

She sighed and stared blindly into the mirror, fervently wishing she could see into the future. Her future. Even if only into the next few weeks.

Amelia pressed her hand against her stomach. She hadn't eaten anything all morning. It seemed to her, as each half hour passed, that the butterflies that had taken up residence there grew a little larger.

"You are gorgeous." Amelia raised her eyes and focused. Madeline had entered the room, leaving the other bridesmaids in another room, and come up behind her. The woman paused to straighten out her train. "All except for the sad face, of course," she observed matter-of-factly. "Looking at your expression, you'd think that you were still marrying Reginald, The Black Prince, instead of Bonnie Prince Russell."

Amelia lifted her head, still keeping her face toward the mirror. Praying that Madeline couldn't see the hint of tears. "He's not a prince yet."

"Po-tay-to, po-tah-to," Madeline quipped. "Carrington is going to be king once the coronation takes place. Technically, that makes him a prince." Madeline indulged her. "Or a prince-in-waiting, if you prefer. Besides, if I remember correctly, you thought of him as your Prince Charming not all that many days ago." She shifted so that she could see Amelia's face for herself, rather than just the reflection. "Trouble in paradise already?"

Amelia shook her head. The headpiece wobbled. Madeline made a disapproving, clucking sound as she straightened it again.

"It's just too fast, that's all."

"Too fast," Madeline echoed. "Did I miss something?" she wanted to know. "Switching your emotions from loathing and dread to whoopee shouldn't be all that difficult."

It was fine for Madeline to make jokes about it. Madeline wasn't being served up on a tray named Diplomacy. "I can't shake the feeling that I'm still being used as a pawn."

Like Amelia, Madeline had grown up around politics all of her life and had made it a point to pay close heed. Unseduced by the glamour of a fairy-tale wedding, she knew exactly what was happening.

Slowly, she surveyed Amelia from all angles. The ceremony was set to begin in a few minutes. "By your father? Obviously. But since the king on the chessboard is Carrington instead of Reginald, being captured shouldn't be something to drag your feet about."

"No, I mean by Carrington. I feel, no, I mean I'm afraid," Amelia amended, "that he might be using me as a pawn."

"Carrington?" Surprise and amusement played along her face. "Amelia, think. Carrington doesn't need you to become king. He doesn't need an alliance with Gastonia to put him on the throne. But *you* need *him* to protect Gastonia from dreadful little countries like Naessa, remember?"

But the fear refused to go away. Because Russell had kept his distance, it had gotten a toehold on her and insisted on festering.

She drew Madeline close to her and lowered her

voice. "What if, after our night together, Russell decided to have the prince killed?"

Madeline's eyes met hers. Amelia couldn't tell what she was thinking. And then she saw that quirky smile she was so familiar with that lifted only one corner of her friend's mouth. The one that mocked her good-naturedly. "My, my, and don't we have the swelled head? Just how good do you think you were in bed?"

Amelia sighed, waving a hand. Madeline was right. She was overthinking this. It was just that it all seemed so surreal to her. "I guess I'm just confused."

Still looking at her in the mirror, Madeline placed her hands on her friend's shoulders and gave her a little comforting squeeze. "Honey, Carrington is crazy about you. Anyone looking at him can see that. This is a good thing, I promise." Releasing, her, Madeline stepped back. "Just this once, it looks as if your fairy godmother has really come through for you. Enjoy it. Enjoy him." Madeline's quirky smile made a return appearance. "Or if you don't want to, I will gladly become your second string and you can send me in to take your place."

The tension broke and Amelia began to laugh, really laugh. She laughed so hard that she found herself holding on to her sides. "Oh God, that felt good. What would I ever do without you, Madeline?"

Born without a single bone of conceit in her body, Madeline assured her, "You'd muddle through. It would just take you a little longer, that's all." Familiar chords began to resonate over the intercom in the vestibule. It was time. Madeline gave Amelia an encouraging smile. "I think they're playing your song, Princess."

The butterflies in her stomach made a quantum leap, butting wings against one another. Amelia's hand flew to her stomach and she pressed against it, feeling as if she was going to throw up. "Oh, God."

"Just smile and look gorgeous," Madeline advised. "And remember to say 'I do' in the right place." Bending, she shifted Amelia's train so that she could walk out of the small room. "Just remember, this could have been Reginald and thank your lucky stars that you wound up dodging that bullet."

Amelia opened the door. The other bridesmaids, a mixture of women she'd known since childhood and daughters from prominent families, all began talking at once.

The sound formed a wall of noise around her. Amelia forced a smile to her lips and froze it there as she exited the small room.

It was time to meet her destiny.

He looked so stern, Amelia thought as she approached Russell and the altar in rhythmic, measured steps, her hand resting lightly on her father's arm. Shouldn't he be smiling?

Russell stood by the minister who was officiating at the ceremony. Close beside him was the king, taking his place as the best man. She knew that the monarch had insisted on it because it made him feel closer to Reginald. Right next to Weston were the groomsmen.

All she could really see was Russell.

His face looked rigid, as if he were waiting for a battle cry instead of his bride-to-be.

Fear ran in on spiked cleats. Was this a mistake? Should she have insisted on having the ceremony canceled, or at the very least, postponed, until matters between them had been ironed out?

Until the matter of whether or not the prince had been murdered was resolved?

Any way she looked at it, this just didn't seem like the ideal time to get married. The whole country, not to mention the relationship between the two of them, was in a state of chaos. Yet here she was, approaching the altar, about to say the words that would officially join their two countries, their two destinies.

Something inside Amelia wanted her to raise her skirts, turn on her heel and run as fast as she could to the nearest exit. But she didn't do any of that, she continued approaching the altar. Approaching Russell.

Despite everything, she thought, as King Roman placed her hand in Russell's, she loved him. That much she was certain of. No matter what he might be guilty of, she loved Russell.

For better or worse.

The words had added significance to her as she heard them being said by the minister. She repeated them, cadence for cadence, glancing up only briefly at the man she said them to.

Russell's expression remained unreadable. She could feel the frost forming around her heart.

Lucia Cordez, dressed in a stunning, blue street-length dress that lovingly adhered to every supple curve her finely trimmed, martial-arts-trained body had to offer, dabbed subtly at her light blue eyes as she pretended to be moved by the ceremony she and so many others were attending.

No one had questioned her presence. With a Latin father and a mother who was half African American, half Caucasian, and blessed with model-perfect good looks, Lucia had the kind of face and bearing that easily allowed her to fit in anywhere people of quality gathered.

She'd arrived in Silvershire a little more than an hour ago, just in time to catch Carrington before he left for the church. She'd put a few pertinent questions to the duke, the most important of which was whether he knew the whereabouts of the late prince's laptop. He'd had the presence of mind to place it under lock and key within his own room.

Lucia had commended him for his action and taken possession of the key. The moment the reception got underway, she intended to make herself scarce and get started hacking into the prince's computer files. Because Reginald had been Silvershire's future king, his files had been highly secured with intricate pass codes that only he had known. She had come prepared. Cracking them could take her a matter of hours, or it could take as long as several months. Optimistically, she hoped for somewhere in between.

There was no time like the present to get started. But, for the moment, Lucia allowed herself to enjoy the wedding. It was the last word in opulence. Silvershire was not without its resources. And she had always had a fondness for pomp and ceremony. It was leagues away from her own background.

It was what she aspired to.

It felt as if the reception would never end.

Part of Amelia had nursed the hope that it wouldn't, because part of her was afraid of this moment, when the reception was on its way to becoming just a memory and she was alone in the royal bedroom with her new husband. Not afraid the way she would have been just a few short days ago, but afraid because of the issue that had sprung up between her and Russell. The issue that still remained unresolved, at least for Russell. And maybe, just in the tiniest bit, for her.

She released the breath she was holding. This was absurd. They were married now. They were a united couple before God and the world. It was time to begin acting like one.

Amelia turned around to say something to Russell, who had remained almost eerily quiet since they'd left the ballroom and entered the bedroom. She was still acutely aware that he had refrained from carrying her over the threshold.

To her surprise, she saw that her brand-new husband was crossing back to the doorway. His hand was on the doorknob and he looked as if he intended to leave. A strange chill passed over her.

"Where are you going?"

He glanced in her direction. Wished she didn't look as beautiful as she did. Wished she didn't move him the way she did. She was still in her wedding dress, looking as pure as she should have been had he not given in to his earthier instincts. "To my quarters."

She stared at him, puzzled. "Aren't these your quarters?"

He didn't think of them in that way. He'd always felt himself a visitor in the palace, no matter how many nights he'd spent here. "They're the quarters reserved for the wedding night."

Because he hadn't moved away from the door, Amelia crossed to him, taking off her headpiece and veil as she approached. She tossed them onto a wing chair as she passed it.

"Correct me if I'm wrong." Amelia began to take the pins out of her hair. "But doesn't the wedding night follow the wedding?"

He watched, unable to draw his eyes away, as her hair came cascading down like sunbeams. "Yes."

Amelia ran her fingers through her hair, loosening the last of the trapped strands. "And weren't we the bride and groom involved in the wedding?"

His mouth felt dry. She was distracting him. He had to remember why he had been so determined to walk away. It wasn't easy. "Yes."

"Then these should be our quarters," she concluded, stopping less than a hairbreadth away from him. "Jointly."

He squared his shoulders. She was making this hard. "Princess—"

"Amelia," she corrected, trying to bank down the sudden spike of frustration that shot through her. "My name is Amelia." Despite her efforts, exasperation entered her voice. "Why won't you call me that? Do I have to give you a flash card?"

She had a point. It was something he was going to have to get used to. They were supposedly equals, now. "Amelia," he repeated. "There's no need for you to act out the charade."

She didn't follow him. "What charade? That we're married?"

He struggled to maintain the distance between them. "We don't have to behave like husband and wife."

"Why? Why don't we have to behave like husband and wife? Why wouldn't we want to behave like husband and wife?" she repeated, her temper heating.

Did he have to spell it out for her? "Because the first element in a marriage is trust and you obviously don't trust me—"

She had had just about enough of this. "No," Amelia cut in tersely. "You are the one who doesn't trust me."

For a moment, she'd taken the air out of his sails. "What? I—"

She wouldn't let him continue, wouldn't let him weave rhetoric until up was down and black was white. And as she spoke, her voice rose and anger came into her eyes, making them almost shoot sparks.

"You don't trust that I have common sense. You don't trust that my heart will convince my somewhat confused mind that you are a decent, good man who could never, ever, have anything to do with the prince's death. All you can do is shoot daggers at me and growl like some wounded, unforgiving bear." As she spoke, she poked a finger into his chest, emphasizing her words.

"I had a moment, a tiny moment, of doubt, of confusion. A lapse." She held her forefinger and thumb up, to show him how tiny the occasion had actually been for her. "What does a moment count in the scheme of things? One moment in the face of a billion moments that comprise a lifetime. *Our* lifetime, if you could get off your high horse and stop looking at me like some wronged soldier who—"

She never got to finish. Her words were inflaming him. *She* was inflaming him. Unable to resist her any longer, Russell pulled her into his arms.

The next second, her mouth was covered with his.

Chapter 12

What had just happened here?

Her pulse racing faster than could be measured by any earthly instrument, Amelia drew her head back to look at Russell.

"Have I gotten to you or are you just trying to shut me up?"

"Yes, and yes," he answered, a kiss to either side of her neck separating the two affirmations.

He'd been without her too long. It felt like a lifetime, even though logically he knew that by the calendar, it had only been a matter of a few days.

His blood heated to an almost unbearable point, Russell found that he didn't want to waste any more time, not with words, not with delays. Though nothing had really been resolved to his satisfaction, though he still felt hurt by Amelia's initial flash of distrust, he couldn't resist these demands storming through him any longer.

Still kissing her, he moved his hands to the back of her dress. He had only one goal in mind: to separate the heavily beaded gown from her body as quickly as humanly possible.

His goal was thwarted almost immediately. Instead of a zipper, his fingers came in contact with what felt like a army of tiny round buttons, marching up and down the length of her back in single file. They extended from her shoulder blades to well past her waist. There had to be over a hundred of them, he thought in utter frustration as he moved his head back to look at her.

Despite the fact that her skin felt as if it were sizzling, Amelia had to bite down on her lower lip to keep from laughing. The mystified look on her new husband's face was almost too adorable to withstand.

"You're bundled up like a national treasure," he complained. And then the frown left his lips. A look entered his eyes that would have completely captured her heart—if it hadn't already been his. "In a way, I suppose that you are."

It took effort not to simply melt into his arms at that point. "The royal dresser helped get me into this," she told him. There was no way she could have fastened all the buttons on her own.

"Well, I'm not calling her to help get you out. If I can't manage this on my own, I don't deserve to be the next King of Silvershire." With desire vibrating through him, growing in urgency by the moment, he had to focus in order to hold himself in check and not to rip the gown right off her body. "Turn around," he instructed.

"Yes, Your Majesty," she curtsied, a gleam in her eyes, before she turned and offered her back to him.

"Not yet," he reminded her. "I'm not king yet." His breath teased her spine as he removed one tiny button after another from its loop. It was slow going. Far slower than he was happy about. "This is worse than a chastity belt," Russell muttered under his breath.

She felt his hands along her skin, felt her body tightening and humming in anticipation. She found it difficult to breathe. Difficult to remain where she was instead of throwing herself into his arms and kissing him with abandon.

Standing as still as she could, her hands on her waist, Amelia glanced at him over her shoulder. "And just how many chastity belts have you removed?"

Why did there have to be so many buttons? A half-dozen would have been sufficient. His fingers were growing thick and clumsy as he kept repeating the procedure over and over again. "What?"

"You just said that the buttons were worse than a chastity belt. I was just wondering how many princesses you've liberated in your time."

"You would be the first," he told her.

And, he added silently, in a way, Amelia was liberating him. Freeing his soul with her sweetness from the solitary cell where it had been confined.

Nothing had changed. He still didn't want to be crowned king, still didn't want the attention that went with this very public role he was being forced to take on, but he did want this woman. Wanted her with the last fiber of his being. Wanted her more than he had first initially realized. And if that meant enduring public scrutiny beneath a blistering spotlight, so be it. He would find some way to deal with it.

So long as he could have her. All he cared about was having her, now. He was consumed with desire, with need.

It felt as if the space of time between when they had first made love and now was several decades instead of merely several days. His body longed for her. More, his soul longed for her, for the feel of the safe haven that existed in her arms, in her kiss.

"Done," he declared with no small note of triumph as he finally pushed the last tiny button out of its confining loop.

Rather than turn her around to face him, Russell slid the dress slowly from her shoulders, down her arms. All the while he had her against him and was kissing the slope of her neck, the soft expanse of her back. He heard her moan and it only served to fuel the fire that had already begun to rage inside him.

The fire that only she could quench.

This was amazing, Amelia thought. Russell was giving her goose bumps even as he was heating her body with his oh-so-clever mouth. She felt as if she were being consumed by both fire and ice at the very same time.

How was that possible?

When he cupped her breasts, still weaving a network of kisses that ran along her back, Amelia turned within the circle of his arms so that she could face him. Face him so that she could begin removing the formal uniform that he had worn to their wedding.

He'd looked so tall and brave, standing there at the altar in his uniform. Her soldier. Now all she wanted was to have him standing there without it.

Eager, wanting, Amelia tore aside the dress sash, pushed the jacket from his shoulders and all but ripped the shirt from his body.

All the while, her body cheered her on, silently crying, "More."

"Princess," Russell teased, a wide grin on his darkly tanned face, "are you attacking me?"

"With every fiber of my being," she breathed. "And it's Amelia. Amelia," she emphasized breathlessly for what felt like the umpteenth time. When would he stop thinking of her as a title and start thinking of her as a woman? His woman.

"Amelia," he repeated, his voice low, husky with unspent passion.

She could almost feel her name dance along her skin, encased in his breath. It drove her crazy.

Everything that came after was a blur, like the events in someone else's dream.

The rest of the clothing, both hers and his, wound up in a tangled heap of brocades, silks and beads on the floor—as tangled as their bodies swiftly became.

She couldn't get enough of him.

The more excitement rose within her body in an ever-heightening crescendo, the more Amelia found herself wanting more. Wanting him. She desperately wanted the sensation he had created within her to continue forever, or as close to forever as was humanly possible.

Russell did his best to accommodate her. His pleasure in part derived from the way Amelia moved beneath him, from the moans that escaped her lips as he familiarized his hands and then his lips with every inch of her body. With swift, clever, promising movements, he brought her to climax upon climax. To joy upon joy. Joy that, only a short while ago, had been completely unimagined for both of them.

Within the shelter of an evening, she became his kindred soul. He could read or sense everything she was experiencing. He could literally see it in Amelia's face. With little effort, he wrapped himself in it, experiencing the moment vicariously with her.

He'd forgotten how almost tooth-jarring falling in love—*making* love—could be.

Finally, unable to hold back any longer, feeling as if he would burst, Russell laced his hands with hers and raised them over her head. His eyes on hers, he lowered his body slowly until the imprint of hers was indelibly pressed against it.

And then he entered her.

This time, there was no small, almost imperceptible protest at the merging. No muffled whimper of pain that she tried to keep from him. This time, there was nothing but joy—for both of them.

The island of time that they had been allowed to carve out for one another faded away all too quickly. By ten the next morning, it seemed to have occurred almost a lifetime away, even though they had made love several times during the course of the night.

With daylight came obligations and matters to see to. They both knew that.

But still, she found herself wanting to break rules, to grab up her happiness with both hands and hold it to her before something or someone made it disappear.

She watched him as he got out of bed. Though she knew it was ridiculous, a hint of loneliness whispered along the edges of her consciousness. "No one would fault us if we remained here." She raised her eyes to his. "In our own private kingdom where the rest of the world has no access."

Russell leaned over her and pressed a kiss to her forehead. "You're wrong. It does have access." Before she could protest or ask what he meant, he lightly tapped her forehead where he had just kissed it. "Right there. It barges in at the least opportune time, demanding attention."

She supposed he was right. Reluctantly, Amelia rose, tossing aside the sheet that had covered her. She felt remarkably unselfconscious about the fact that she was nude. The nightgown that her dressmaker had designed especially for last night had never seen the light of day. It was still tucked away in the bureau drawer.

No one was more surprised than she at the way she felt. But right now, there was no shame, no embarrassment after the dew of afterglow had faded. She felt at ease like this with him.

It was as things should be, Amelia thought, crossing to the closet where members of the staff had already placed any garment that she could possibly want within easy access. Opening the door, she drew a dressing gown from its hanger. Slipping it on, she purposely left the two sides hanging open as she turned around to face him.

"If I had married Reginald, we would be on our way to our honeymoon. To Hawaii, where he would undoubtedly have hit on someone even as the bellboy was checking in our luggage." She raised her head slightly, her eyes on his as she smiled. "This is much better."

He had every intention of leaving the room. Of meeting with Lucia Cordez as had been arranged when she'd arrived yesterday. But the sight of Amelia's soft, inviting curves peering out from beneath the royal-blue silk robe completely destroyed his resolve as well as his game plan.

A man was only so strong and then no more.

What would a few more minutes hurt? It wasn't as if Corbett Lazlo's computer expert was going anywhere in the immediate future. For all he knew, Lucia hadn't been able to find anything yet. The password that Reginald had implemented on his files was, perforce, a bear to break. The late prince had been gleefully proud of that.

Reginald had implemented it not to keep the enemies of Silvershire from knowing any of his private affairs, or even his own personal enemies, but to make sure that his father remained in the dark about his less-than-noble activities.

At thirty years old, Reginald had been a child to the last breath in his body.

Russell couldn't help wondering now if, for some reason, some secret piece of information on his computer could have ultimately been what had gotten Reginald killed. They might never find out.

The possibilities as to what had led to Reginald's death were endless. They could also be nonexistent. Either way, if Lucia had come up with an answer, it would keep for a few more minutes. Perhaps even for half an hour.

If he could get his fill of Amelia in that amount of time.

It amazed him, after the night they had spent together, that he still had any energy left to walk, much less to make love with her again. He knew his limitations and he had never been a machine, the way Reginald boasted that he was. But Amelia seemed to bring out a supply of hidden reserves he hadn't even been aware of possessing, he thought with a grateful smile.

"Yes," he agreed, crossing to the closet where she stood and slipping the robe from her shoulders. The garment slid from her arms to the floor. "Much better."

Amelia rose up on her bare toes, brushing her nude body against his.

Again, everything tightened in anticipation even as drumrolls sounded up and down her limbs and her loins moistened. With a soft laugh, her eyes gleaming, she threaded her arms around his neck. Her body pressed closely against his ever-hardening one.

The next half hour was lost. As was the hour that came after.

"I'm sorry I'm late," Russell apologized as he strode into the conference room where Lucia had set up her temporary office.

He had just now finished buttoning his jacket. Russell didn't have to glance at his watch to know that it was close to noon, almost two hours later than he'd originally said he would come to speak with her. His hair was still damp in places from the shower he'd taken, the one that normally would have taken him less than five minutes. It, too, had fallen behind schedule because, at the last minute, Amelia had slipped into the stall with him.

He'd never enjoyed getting clean as much as he had this time.

Lucia Cordez raised the oversized glasses she used for reading and slid them onto the top her head, giving the duke her undivided attention. She was wearing a pair of cutoff denim shorts that showed her long legs off to their best advantage and a sleeveless light pink blouse that seemed more suited to the beach than to the dark business at hand.

He noticed that there was a plate with just the barest remnants of wedding cake on it and wondered if that had been her breakfast.

Lucia smiled at him. "Actually, you're earlier than I anticipated."

He didn't see how that was possible "I said ten o'clock."

The smile on Lucia's lips told him she knew better, even if he didn't. "You were married yesterday," she reminded him. "I didn't think you meant ten o'clock in actual real time. The cake was good, by the way. I wish I could steal your chef," she added wistfully.

He looked over her shoulder at the computer monitor on the table. The binary code that covered the screen looked like some kind of decorative screen saver. "You give me something I can work with, I'll have another wedding cake made for you."

She inclined her head as if to say that sounded fair enough. "Well, as it happens, I'm still working on the prince's monarch code."

He'd thought as much. Russell groaned, running his hand through his hair. Damn it, why had Reginald enjoyed that part of it so much? Was it because it made him feel as if he were acting his age instead of behaving like the eternal juvenile he always seemed to be?

"However," Lucia went on, "there is some good news, so to speak."

"And that would be—?" he asked, gesturing for her to continue.

"In looking for the encryption code, I stumbled across a sealed file on his computer." A small, triumphant smile crossed her lips. "It only took about half an hour to crack the password. When I opened the file, I saw that it contained a batch of personal e-mails." Lucia leaned back in her chair to look at him. She needed to see his face in order to gauge whether or not he was hiding something. It wasn't unheard of to have the client not altogether forthcoming when it came to an investigation. "Are you aware that Prince Reginald was being blackmailed?"

"Blackmailed?" Russell echoed, confused. That didn't make any sense. "What could they possibly have to blackmail him with? The photographers followed him everywhere. Everything about his sordid life was a matter of record."

"Apparently not everything, because the prince was making regular withdrawals from his private account. That usually means that regular payments were going somewhere. In addition, there's mention of several meetings, all coinciding with withdrawals. The sender also threatens to 'expose' the prince several times in case he was thinking of going to the authorities."

Russell began to wonder if there was anyone on Reginald's side. The list of people who had something against the man kept growing. He almost felt sorry for the late prince. "Do you have any idea who was blackmailing him?"

Lucia shook her head. "That I haven't found out yet. I haven't been able to trace the source of the e-mails—yet," she emphasized the word. "But I've only been at this for less than a day," she reminded him with the confidence of one who had had eventually met every single technological challenge she'd encountered.

By the expression on her face, Russell surmised that Lazlo's operative was not in the habit of making excuses or feeling that she needed to.

"Anything else?" he asked before leaving her to her work. He really didn't expect her to answer in the affirmative.

"Yes." He stopped in his tracks and looked at her. "Possibly there's a little Reginald out there somewhere."

Russell stiffened. "What?"

The depth of Reginald's stupidity never ceased to amaze him. Or maybe it was just the prince's incredible ego that had allowed him to think that he could leave traces of his indiscretion right there, in his computer. This after he had gone through all the trouble, at Reginald's behest, of tracking the woman down to pay her off.

He did his best to appear surprised.

Strange how things turned out. Reginald's vanity could very well prove to be his saving grace. Reginald's unborn child was the natural heir to the throne. That could easily take him off the hook. With any luck, Weston could act as regent on behalf of the child until such time as the child was of an age to rule on his own. Anything was preferable to his having to be crowned, Russell thought.

And probably preferable to Reginald having taken the crown, he added as an afterthought. He had no doubts that, barring some miracle, Reginald would have made a terrible monarch.

Feigning surprise, he asked, "Who's the child's mother?"

"Strictly speaking, there is no child yet," Lucia informed him. "But the woman is pregnant. From all indications, by several months."

"And she claims that Reginald is the father." It wasn't exactly a question, but a statement that begged for a response.

"From what I saw in the e-mail, she's certain. Her name's Sydney Connor." She hit several keys on the laptop, then turned it around so that Russell could see the screen. "I was able to trace her e-mails to a computer back in Naessa."

"Naessa," he echoed.

Things were beginning to fall into place. Relations between the two countries were less than amicable. If he were to draw up a list of potential suspects who would have wanted to cause chaos within Silvershire by eliminating Reginald, the rival kingdom would be near the top. There were factions within Naessa, dangerous factions, that had aligned themselves with terrorist groups which had struck at Silvershire before and undoubtedly would again.

Was this woman working in conjunction with one of the terrorist groups? he wondered. "Do you know anything about this Sydney Connor?"

"Not yet," Lucia freely admitted. "But the day is still young. Give me a little time." She grinned. "A little bit of sugar wouldn't be out of line, either." Her grin broadened. "I run on sugar and coffee, in case you're interested."

"I'll have some coffee and pastries sent in immediately," he promised. "Would you prefer doughnuts, coffee cake or French pastries?"

"Yes," was her only response. Lucia turned her attention back to the laptop.

With a diet like that, he wondered how the woman managed to remain in the shape she was in. "I'll have them bring you a selection," he told her as he let himself out.

An heir. Reginald's "mistake" might now very well prove to be his own salvation. An heir meant that he wouldn't have to go through with the coronation.

He felt like a man who had just crawled out from beneath the crushing weight of a boulder. The relief was immeasurable.

Russell began to whistle while he walked.

Chapter 13

Russell stopped whistling.

He had realized, as he headed back to his quarters, that if there were an heir to the throne, if this woman, Sydney Connor, really was pregnant with Reginald's baby and if she could be found, then his coronation need not take place.

But, it suddenly occurred to him, if it didn't, what then would become of his union with Amelia? Would it be terminated, annulled, rescinded, as if it had never happened?

It was obvious that the only reason their wedding had gone off on the preset schedule, without missing so much as a beat, was because King Roman was anxious to have the treaty between their two countries go forward.

In that light, things had not changed all that much since ancient times. Countries still needed to forge alliances in order to survive. The strong protected the weak, not of out any sense of altruism, but because of the stakes involved. Two countries together were stronger than either country was on its own.

If an heir suddenly surfaced, and the line was restored to King Weston's house, then how would he, Russell, figure into all this? What would his role be? Would he even have a role, beyond that of political advisor? Since he would not be king, would Amelia's father call for an annulment and have her—what, pledged to a child? he wondered cynically.

Or would King Roman place pressure on his old friend and have Weston take Amelia as his wife? That was a possibility he hadn't even thought of until this moment. Weston had been without a queen these thirty years. The thought of having a beautiful young bride might be very appealing. It would go a long way to healing the wounds he now felt.

And where would Amelia weigh in on all this? Would she dutifully go along with whatever her father decided to do, for the "good of the kingdom?" Or would she ask her father to change his mind? To withdraw his negotiations? Would she demand not to be the pawn that she'd told him she felt herself to be in all of this?

He'd like to believe that she would, but he couldn't in all honesty be sure.

They had spent a wonderful night together that had seemed even better, if that were possible, than their first night had been. But that had to do with attraction, with chemistry, with emotions, none of which mattered when it came to the ultimate matters of state.

Russell shook his head. There were too many possibilities, too many uncertain elements. Too many "ifs" crowding his brain.

His good mood faded.

He held off saying anything to anyone about Lucia's findings for two days. And two nights. Two nights in which time and life were suspended as he found a perfect haven in the bed that had once been intended for Prince Reginald and his bride. The bed that was now his and Amelia's. He made love with her as if he was savoring a very precious, very fragile gift, never once telling Amelia that all this might be fleeting.

And then, on the morning of the third day, he couldn't put it off any longer. Slipping out of bed quietly in order not to wake Amelia, he quickly got dressed and left to see about business.

After first checking with Lucia to see if she had come up with anything further—she hadn't—he went to see the king. It was time Weston was apprised of the situation. Once Weston knew, the situation would be, more or less, taken out of Russell's hands.

His first loyalty had to be with the crown, Russell told himself, not with any feelings he might have. His was not to pick and choose, but to serve. If, after everything, it turned out that it was his destiny to be king, then so be it. But that eventuality might not ever take place.

And if that wound up costing him the woman that he had come to love with all his heart, that, too, was a matter of destiny.

Bracing himself for whatever the future had in store for him, Russell knocked on the door to the king's private quarters.

"They can't possibly think that we're actually responsible for this."

The protest, uttered in disgust, came from Nikolas Donovan. He was sitting on his small balcony that overlooked the sea, having breakfast alone. Only seagulls heard his words as he threw down the newspaper. A breeze ruffled the pages that came to rest on the round glass-top table. He hardly noticed.

The article that had stirred his ire dealt with the prince's resent death. It was the fifth in as many days. His death filled all the papers. Articles examining his life, his foibles and addictions, his lineage, abounded everywhere. Ad nauseum. Even if he'd liked the man, which he vehemently didn't, he would have been sick of him by now.

The article that had gotten to him dealt with speculation as to whether or not the cause of the prince's final curtain call from life was the result of an accident, or intentional. And if it was the latter, whose intention had been followed? The prince's or someone else's? Had the prince, the article demanded self-righteously, been the victim of some kind of plot?

If it was the latter, the article went on to say, then perhaps attention might be well drawn to the Union for Democracy.

Slate gray eyes had grown dangerously dark as Nikolas struggled with his temper. Rising, he shoved his hands into his pants and stared out at the sea.

Nikolas Donovan was the head of the Union for Democracy, an anti-monarchy organization that had been in existence only a short amount of time, about five years. But in that time, he was proud of the fact that no one had resorted to any kind of actual violence.

Unlike the monarchy, he thought darkly.

It was because Silvershire was not a democratic state that his own parents had been killed when he was a baby. Killed by the man who now sat on the throne, he'd been told by his uncle. Uncle Silas, his father's brother, had raised him from the time he was a baby. It had been Silas who had drummed into his head, for as long as he could remember, that power belonged to the people, not to one person solely because of the accident of birth. Silas advocated a complete overthrow of the monarchy.

For his part, Nikolas was working to have a gradual change come about. If nothing else, his group wanted to get a stronger voice in the government. So that self-absorbed narcissists like the late Prince Reginald did not pose a threat to the common man.

His handsome features became almost dark as Nikolas's thoughts turned to the late prince. He'd known Reginald personally. They were the same age and had, Reginald by privilege and he by the sweat of his brow, attended the same schools together. Their paths at Eton and Oxford had crossed on occasion. But for the most part, he was absorbed in his studies and Reginald had been too busy bedding anything that moved.

Even back then, he had been a man with a mission. That mission had been, and still was, to bring a better form of government to his country.

However, that mission hadn't included killing the present-day crown prince, no matter how much he personally loathed and despised the man.

That the prince was dead evoked no sense of sorrow from him. Nikolas was certain that, had Reginald ascended to the throne, he would have abused his power, just as he had abused it as a young man at Oxford. There was no question in his mind that the country was definitely better off without him.

Russell, Duke of Carrington, the man who stood next in line, whose marriage to the Princess Amelia of Gastonia earlier this week had all but solidified the man's position in the scheme of things, was a better choice from what he knew of him, but still not the ideal one. The ideal choice would have been no king at all, because Silvershire deserved to be a democracy. A democracy where the people had a say in the government that ruled them.

He would go to his grave believing that.

In the last year, he had pulled out all the stops, urging anyone who would listen to join the movement, to make it bigger, stronger. A voice to be reckoned with. Presently, it was mostly comprised of people his own age and younger. The generation that had come before, ironically, his parents generation had they lived, believed in tradition, in maintaining the status quo. But they did not have as much at stake, as much to lose, as the younger generation did.

As he did, Nikolas thought. His generation was not complacent, would not go gentle into that good night like obedient sheep. Moreover, it was his dearest, heartfelt, fervent desire to avenge the death of his parents and make King Weston step down.

And have no man of royal blood step up to take his place.

He and his organization had stirred things up when they could, making people aware that they should demand a voice, a choice. The Union for Democracy had caused disruptions whenever they could to wake people up. But killing was another matter. He would have thought that had been made abundantly clear to anyone who knew of the group.

That the rumors even hinted that he and his followers were behind the prince's death was ridiculous. But he knew how these things spread. Knew, too, that it didn't take much to set people off against one another.

Though he didn't like the idea, he knew that he and his followers were going to have to be prepared for the worst.

Nikolas left the rest of his breakfast untouched as he went inside to see about getting together with his key people and making sure that the word went out that the Union for Democracy had nothing to do with the prince's death. Though he always advocated the mind over the sword, there was no place for martyrs in his plans. They had to be ready to fight if it came down to that.

In another town, the man whose neighbors knew him as Silas Donovan smiled to himself as he read the same article. It had begun. The unrest, the discord he'd hoped for, had plotted for and nurtured, was beginning.

He'd waited a very long time for this. Forever, it seemed. But revenge was finally taking form. Revenge against the man who had ruined his life. Who had taken his birthright. And the instrument he would use to bring it all about was a very personal one. When all was revealed, the significance would not be lost on Weston.

He could hardly wait.

Weston was grieving now. The so-called monarch would grieve even more very soon.

Silas Donovan began to laugh to himself. Anyone who would have heard him would have shivered from the malevolent sound.

King Weston looked at the young man before him for a long moment before finally responding. Grieving, still saying goodbye and unable to make himself give the order that would allow the autopsy to take place, the monarch was having trouble processing the information he had just been given.

It meant that he didn't have to say goodbye to his son. Not completely.

"A child, you say?"

Russell had begun to think that perhaps the monarch hadn't heard him. Since Reginald's death, Weston had withdrawn into himself to the point that there were times when he seemed to shut out the rest of the world entirely. He was a changed man, changed completely from the genial ruler he had been.

"Yes."

Weston took a breath, as if he'd been holding it, waiting for the right answer. "And it's Reginald's?"

Russell wanted to be completely honest with the king. That meant not giving the man any undue false hopes. "We're not sure of that yet. Ms. Cordez has managed to find only a handful of e-mails from the woman. It's going to take some time to put all the pieces of the puzzle together. And then, of course, there'll have to be DNA testing to substantiate her claim."

"Of course." Weston nodded. But the look in his eyes had become eager. It gave him a shred of hope, of something to hang on to. "Does anyone know who and where this woman is?"

"We know who, or at least the name she was using." The king looked at him, waiting. "Sydney Connor," he told the monarch. "But as to her whereabouts, again, we're not sure."

"Find her," Weston ordered.

The directive "immediately" was understood. Russell began to withdraw from the suite. "Yes, Your Majesty."

"Wait." Already at the door, Russell obediently turned around and waited for the king to speak. "You said something about 'the name she was using.'" The king furrowed his brow, concern marking his features. "Why wouldn't she be using her own name? Do you think this might be some kind of deception?"

The question struck Russell as odd. The king was usually sharper than this. "Your Majesty knows that royalty has always been the center of intrigue. Nothing is ever what it seems."

Eyes that were red-rimmed from tears met his. "You are."

Russell smiled. In all his years of service, and in the years that had come before that, when he had been Reginald's "chosen friend," he had not once ever lied, not once tried to present anything but the truth. "Thank you, Your Majesty, but I am the exception."

The king laughed at the simple remark. And then his features sobered until they bordered on grave. The monarch looked at him. "You realize that if there is a child and it is Reginald's and a male, then you won't be the next ruler of Silvershire."

Again, Russell inclined his head. The smile that was on his lips was not forced. It rose of its own volition. "Yes, I know."

A man completely devoid of ambition was rare. "And that would be all right with you?"

That would be perfect with him, Russell thought. Aloud, he said, "You might recall, Your Majesty, I never wanted to be king."

Weston was aware of that, but circumstances bring about changes, and desires flourish even in desert terrain.

"That is not what I am asking." The king paused. "Thirty years ago, I didn't want to be king, either. Not with as much resistance as I witnessed you originally display, but I had made peace with the fact that Vladimir would be king once King Dunford passed on the crown. Even though I didn't feel that Vladimir had the best interests of the people at heart, he would have had my allegiance.

"However, after my protests had been overridden and King Dunford gave the crown to me, I discovered that I liked being the king. Liked having the reins of the country in my hand. Liked the thought that perhaps I was helping the people I was serving. I knew in my heart that Vladimir would abuse his power, place himself first instead of in the service of his people, so initially I took it as my obligation."

For a moment, Weston allowed his thoughts drift to another time, a time when his hair was dark and his body firmer. When there had been a wife by his side and anything was possible.

"And eventually," he continued, looking at Russell, "I was glad I did. Eventually, I came to enjoy my lofty position. It is seductive in its own right, being king," he confided. "Now things are in place for your coronation and I want to know, if this child does exist and we do find it, how are you going to feel?" When Russell said nothing, Weston supplied a word for him. "Cheated?"

"Relieved," Russell finally countered after a moment had passed. "I have never in my life wanted to be the center of attention. I always did much better when I was allowed to work off to the side."

But the king heard only one thing. "There's hesitation in your voice, Carrington."

He couldn't dispute that. But he wasn't hesitating because he wanted the crown. Not for its own sake at any rate. "I was wondering…"

"Yes?"

There was no delicate way to broach this. Russell felt almost transparent as he asked, "If I am not to be king, will my union with the princess be annulled?"

The question caught Weston by surprise. "I hadn't thought of that. Under the circumstances, I don't believe so, but it would have to be discussed with King Roman." And then the thoughtful frown disappeared, to be replaced with a tickled laugh. "Forgive me, Carrington, but this is placing the horse before the cart. If there is a cart. If there is a horse," he added with a hopeful note.

To Russell's surprise, the king let out a long, soulful sigh. "I still cannot make myself believe that Reginald is actually gone. I miss him, Russell," he confided, his voice lowering to almost an intimate whisper. "Miss the thought of him, actually. Our paths did not really cross all that often these last few years." The king waved his hand vaguely about. "I was always involved in matters of state and he was always out, doing some-thing," Weston's mouth twisted in an indulgent smile, "*unstatesmanlike* I suppose would be the best description of what he got himself into."

Russell felt for the man, but he knew that they had to move the investigation forward on all fronts. And the king had stymied one avenue. He began as gently as he could. "Your Majesty, about the autopsy—"

Momentarily lost in thought, in the possibility that Reginald had left behind a piece of himself, it took Weston a second to realize that Russell had allowed his voice to trail off. "Yes? What about it?"

Several people had put the question to him, asking him when the funeral was going to be held. The funeral couldn't be arranged until after the autopsy was per-formed. "I think we need to attend to that."

Weston looked away, gazed out the window, saw the years that had passed. "We will."

"Sooner rather than later, sire," Russell urged. "Ar-rangements need to be made for the funeral. I can handle that for you if you wish, but first—"

"I know, I know, the autopsy. Yes, you are correct, of

course. I'll give instructions about that presently, I give you my word." Turning from the window, he looked at Russell again. "A baby, you say?"

Russell smiled indulgently, knowing that he would not be leaving soon. "Yes, sire, a baby."

When Russell finally left the king's quarters some twenty minutes later, he was concerned about Weston's state of mind as well as the monarch's general health. The king, always so robust, so vibrant-looking, suddenly seemed to be wearing his years heavily. Russell knew it was the shock of the prince's death on top of his concerns about the state of unrest that was presently rocking Silvershire. The actions of the Union for Democracy had stepped up. Rumors of it coming to a head had been heard. He'd half expected something to take place during the wedding. The king had called in extra security around the palace just in case.

It seemed too much for one man to handle.

Reginald's autopsy was the immediate matter that really needed to be seen to, but there was no way to overrule the king. At first the delay had been because he had wanted his son's body to remain whole until after the wedding. Then the excuse was that he only wanted the royal medical examiner to perform the autopsy. Away on a short vacation, the doctor had turned around immediately and taken a flight back, only to be caught up in a temporary quarantine because two of the passengers on her return flight came down with a mysterious ailment. But she was here now, and still the autopsy was being delayed. He could only hope that the king's common sense would finally prevail.

Maybe news of the baby would finally get the king to move forward. Thank God Lazlo's operative was making some headway. The woman felt she was getting close to cracking the prince's code, which would open up the rest of the files to them and perhaps give them a better insight as to who might have wanted not merely to threaten the prince, but to actually carry out that threat.

And then there was the matter of the blackmail. Who and what was behind that?

He had a dozen questions and so far, no answers. He reminded himself that patience was a virtue, but he wasn't feeling very virtuous right now.

Amelia heard him before he even had a chance to enter the informal dining area within their quarters.

Her mouth curved. Strange how quickly she had gotten in tune with the sound of his steps. Her smile widened, its tributaries spreading out all through her.

Ironic, wasn't it? This was the first time that she was actually happy to be the princess of Gastonia. Not that she didn't love her country, but she could have loved it just as much if she'd been a commoner. But being the princess, with a princess's obligations, had, thanks to a twist of fate, allowed her to marry the man she had always secretly loved. Even despite all those strange little bugs that had come crawling out of her bed and the water balloons that had come flying almost out of nowhere during his visits.

She felt just a fleeting pinch of guilt at being happy

over Reginald's death, but then, she had to be realistic. The man would have made an awful ruler. His personality, that of a self-absorbed hedonist, was cast and set. There was absolutely no reason to believe that ascending the throne would have made Reginald behave in any other manner than he always had.

On the contrary, it might even have made him worse. No one in Silvershire would have been happy, least of all her.

Well, no one, she amended silently, but the women Reginald took to his bed and rewarded with trinkets for their favors.

"Good afternoon, my husband. It's about time you made a little time for me," she joked as she turned around.

The smile on her face froze when she saw the somber expression on Russell's face.

Chapter 14

"What's the matter?" The words slipped from her lips in slow motion as nerves began to knit themselves together and tighten.

Something was wrong, Amelia thought, looking at Russell. Something had changed since last night when, like all the other nights since the wedding, they had found a haven in each other's arms. Her mind stretched itself in several directions at the same time, searching for a reason for the somber expression on her husband's face.

Had he found out something more about Reginald's death? Had someone else been killed? Was there some kind of further trouble or intrigue brewing against the crown?

The burden of leadership weighed heavily on her shoulders. Concerns about subversive organizations and the havoc they could wreak were never all that far from her mind and especially now that she had become the wife of a man who was about to ascend the throne of Silvershire.

Heads of state were given to dark thoughts, even if they tried to maintain a light, gentle touch, she thought sadly, wishing it were otherwise. She had only to look to her father to know that.

Had her father's thoughts been lighter, more optimistic in nature, she knew that he would have not felt the need to forestall a possible and entirely theoretical attack from Naessa by marrying her off to the future king of a stronger, more powerful country. Within reason and adhering to the proper boundaries of the social world into which she had been born, Amelia felt that she might have been left to her own devices in choosing a mate. Possibly allowed to even follow her heart instead of an international game plan.

And she would have wound up exactly where she was, she thought, married to Russell, who was the man of her heart's choice.

Sometimes life arranged itself in mysterious ways, she mused.

Russell wasn't sure just how to say what he had to say. Never glib, he'd still been thought of as being diplomatic. It had always been his job to exercise damage control after Reginald had had one of his escapades. But when it came to matters that concerned him, his tongue felt as if it were bundled up in an overcoat that was two sizes too large.

So he picked his way slowly through what was suddenly a potential minefield to him. "Amelia, certain things have come to light."

She'd never seen him look like that before, as if *hope* were only a word to be found in a dictionary. Her heart felt like a solid lump of coal in her chest.

"Things?" she repeated, bracing herself for the worst. "What things? And why do you look as if you're about to tell me that my pardon has been revoked and that I am about to face a firing squad?"

He nearly smiled. Incredible how her exaggeration had almost hit the nail on the head. At least, as far as his own situation was concerned. She, of course, might have feelings of an entirely different nature if this baby did turn out to be Reginald's heir. If that caused their union to be rendered null and void, Amelia might not greet the news with a heavy heart. She might even, it occurred to him, be relieved.

He was quiet. More so than usual. This was a bad sign. Amelia tried not to let her imagination run away with her, but it wasn't easy. And there were no clues that she could discern in his eyes.

When she'd woken up this morning to find Russell gone, she'd just assumed that the new king-in-waiting was going about some sort of royal business. Taking the crown over from Weston required a great deal of transfer of information. And there was the coronation looming before them. The date had been changed, but still, it couldn't be in the too-distant future. There was a great deal that had to be attended to between then and now in order for Russell to become prepared for that auspicious occasion.

Unlike her, she thought ruefully. Her role in the upcoming coronation was merely decorative. Her only job was either to stand or to sit beside Russell and look proud, which she knew she could handle without being required to resort to any acting on her part, because she was proud, very proud. Proud of the man she had taken to her heart. Proud of the man that she knew he was. Russell was everything that Reginald had never been and, had he lived, she was fairly certain he would never have become. Honest, kind, loyal, Russell was the kind of man who was concerned about leaving the world a better place than when he had first entered it.

But the dark look on his face probably had nothing to do with the coronation.

Or did it? she suddenly wondered.

Talk to me, she all but screamed mentally. Out loud, she felt she had to prod him along. "Is this about Reginald?"

"In a way, yes." And then, in the light of the repercussions that would follow Reginald's thoughtless act, Russell amended his statement. "In a very large way, actually."

She didn't like the sound of that. Had she been alone, she might have sat down, braced herself before hearing more. But she had always prided herself on meeting adversity head-on, on "hanging tough" before a world that was quick to judge. And Russell, she reminded herself, had never seen her in action. She couldn't give in to weaker elements and show him that she was unnerved. He had to think of her as strong.

"Is he alive?" she finally asked in a hushed, disbelieving voice.

Had there been some mistake made earlier? Had the body that Russell found in Reginald's bed only resembled Reginald marginally? Was that what he was so obviously wrestling with telling her now?

Oh God, please don't let it be that. Don't let me have to marry Reginald, after all.

She'd hang tough, she promised herself. A marriage was a marriage and there was no way she was ever going to leave her marriage bed, no matter what Russell was about to tell her.

Stunned by the question, Russell looked at her incredulously. "You mean did he suddenly rise up from the dead? Reginald was many things in his lifetime, but a vampire was never one of them." Although, more than once, he'd heard the late prince referred to as a blood-sucking ghoul.

She cleared her throat, feeling a little foolish for being so skittish. "No, I just thought that maybe a mistake had been made in identifying the body."

"I was the one who found the body," he reminded her. "It was Reginald. No mistakes were made."

Outside, a cloud passed over the sun, suddenly making the room seem dark. She fervently hoped it wasn't an omen. Amelia drew her courage to her and demanded, "Then what is it that you're talking about? What has this to do with Reginald?"

He looked at her for a long moment, wondering what her reaction might be. Despite her words, did becoming a queen outweigh everything else for her? There was only one way to find out. "There might be an heir."

Confusion narrowed her eyes. "An heir?"

He felt a twinge of guilt for having kept this from her, but it hadn't been for long.

"The computer expert that was sent from the Lazlo Group discovered some personal correspondence on

Reginald's laptop from a woman claiming that she was pregnant with his baby." Russell couched his words carefully. "It could be a hoax—"

"Or, it could be true," Amelia countered pragmatically.

Very honestly, she was surprised that this was the first paternity claim to be made, and that there was only one. Reginald had gone around scattering his seed with abandon since he'd been in his teens. That this was the first so-called bastard that had surfaced was rather incredible.

Amelia paused for a moment, looking at Russell. He spoke to her as if she were his equal in this, instead of some hanger-on to be kept in the dark. She liked that.

She hadn't been wrong about him, she thought. Her heart had picked the right man to love.

"And if it is true," Russell continued, "if she does give birth and the child turns out to be a boy—" He paused, studying her face as he waited for the significance of what he was saying to set in.

It didn't take much to know where Russell was going with this, Amelia thought. "You're thinking he could be next in line, rather than you."

"Yes."

When she was a young girl, everything about her life seemed to be cast in stone. Things were fixed according to her father's word or to the traditions that seemed to rule so much of her life. Now, with this news, it felt as if everything was in flux and what she thought was stone was merely plaster of Paris, easily cracked. Easily shattered.

The crown was not yet on Russell's head and, if certain things came to pass, it might never be. She looked at Russell, trying to gauge what he was thinking. The man could play poker with the best of them, she decided. Had her kingdom's only income still been garnered from the casinos, he would have made a perfect symbol of the successful gambler.

"How does that make you feel?" she finally asked.

He answered her honestly. "Relieved—except..." Unable to finish, he looked at her.

"Except?" she prompted.

He was not one to wear his heart on his sleeve, but when it came to her, he found that he couldn't quite help himself. "Except for the fact that if this does come to light, your father might call for an annulment of our marriage."

"An annulment?" For the first time since Russell had entered the suite, she found herself laughing. Laughing so hard that her next few words were shaky as she uttered them. "Annulments are granted if the marriage isn't consummated. I think it's a little too late to call off the marriage using that as the excuse on record," she quipped. "We've 'consummated' this marriage a great many times as I recall." She put her hand on his shoulder to steady herself. "I'm afraid an annulment is out of the question, Russell."

He took her hand, about to brush it off. He found himself holding it instead. Wondering if he'd been a fool, thinking that he would be allowed to face eternity with her at his side.

"This isn't a laughing matter, Amelia. You know what I mean."

Amelia took a breath, doing her best to steady herself. But her cheeks refused to pull themselves into a serious expression no matter how much she told herself they should.

"Yes, I know what you mean and I beg to differ, Carrington. The day we cease to laugh is the day we begin to die. This most certainly is a laughing matter because, in case you hadn't noticed, I got the last laugh, so to speak." When he looked at her quizzically, she explained. "I didn't have to marry that horrible hedonist."

And then she stopped abruptly. Russell was looking at her as if he was trying to assess something. As if he was seeing her for the first time. Because she was so incredibly attuned to him, she suddenly realized what he had to be thinking. It hit her squarely in the pit of her stomach.

She might have been affronted, Amelia thought, if the thought wasn't so completely absurd, so foreign from anything she might have entertained.

Because she always tried to put the best possible face on everything, even an insult, she decided to take Russell's unwarranted suspicion, however fleeting, as a compliment to her ability to take care of herself.

"No, Russell, I didn't have Reginald killed, if that's what you're thinking. I would have had to take a number and I have never liked having to stand in line. My father once said that if I had to stand in line to get into heaven, I'd probably decide to go to hell instead." She cocked her head, studying his face. This wasn't all. "What else is bothering you?"

The thought that she might have had a hand in Reginald's demise had been a fleeting one at best. Though she didn't strike him as being a pushover, he knew she wasn't capable of coldly ordering someone's death.

He might as well get through all of it, he thought. "Our union only took place because your father believed I was the man Weston was selecting for the crown. If that crown goes to someone else, what then?"

She didn't see what the problem was, at least, not for them. Her father wouldn't be happy that the marriage did not back up their countries' alliance, but things did not always work themselves out perfectly no matter how much effort went into arrangements.

"Then you pledge your allegiance to the baby or whoever King Weston chooses and we return home to Gastonia to live happily ever after."

That didn't satisfy him. Hers was not the last word on the matter. "Won't your father want you to marry whoever is king here?"

Her laugh was soft, indulgent. She touched his face affectionately. "Not even my father would marry me to someone after I'd just been married before God and the good citizens of Silvershire, not to mention Madeline," she added with a broad smile. "That would be ludicrous."

"But the marriage was to reinforce the treaty," he insisted.

He was worried about that, she suddenly realized. Her heart grew warm. He was afraid she would have to walk out on him. As if that could ever be possible.

"My father's not that small a man," she assured him softly. "Having his daughter married to the Duke of Carrington, the king's right-hand political adviser, carries weight to it," she assured him, then added, "Especially when he sees how happy his daughter is—in direct contrast to how very unhappy he knew she would have been if Reginald had lived and he had become her husband."

A small wave of relief finally came. Russell allowed himself a small, affectionate smile. "You're referring to yourself in the third person."

Amelia pretended to toss her head. "All us royal types do that." And then she laughed and winked.

He put his hands on her waist, holding her for a moment, thinking how quickly he had gotten used to having her in his arms.

Again, his expression became somber as concern nibbled away at him. "But if it came to that, if your father decided that Gastonia's needs were immediate and urgent and since the heir to Silvershire's throne was an infant, perhaps a more suitable match for the matter of security could be made with the prince of another kingdom—" There were still a few kingdoms that could come into play when it came to making treaties, kingdoms that knew safety lay in alliances.

She didn't want to play this game. It was tiring and pointless. What he was suggesting wasn't going to happen. Amelia placed her finger to his lips, stilling them. "Don't borrow trouble, Your Highness. I'm your wife and I'm going to remain that way."

She'd called him "Your Highness," as if he were a prince. It was in jest, but he couldn't divorce himself from the thought that that was what she wanted from the man she was wed to. The promise of a crown.

His eyes searched her face as he asked, "Would it bother you if I wasn't king?"

"It wasn't your crown that drew me to you in the first

place," she reminded him, lacing her arms around his neck. She sighed as her body came in contact with his. "It won't be your crown that will make me want to remain."

"Oh?" The weightier matters of Reginald's death and the state of the country took a back seat to what was happening here, in this section of the palace. He felt his mouth curving into a smile, felt his body following suit. "And what will?"

Her arms still around his neck, Amelia pressed her body tightly up against his. Her eyes were dancing as she said, "Guess."

She could make him forget everything else in a heartbeat. He'd never met another woman like her and was grateful that somehow, fate had arranged for her to be his. "I had no idea that you were this lusty, Princess."

"Neither did I, Carrington," she teased, amusement highlighting her features. "See what you've done?"

"I?" he asked innocently.

"Yes, you." She raised herself up on her toes, bringing her mouth up close to his. "You've made a wanton woman out of me." She could feel love exuding from every pore of her body. It was incredible what a difference a few weeks made. Just a month ago, she'd seen her life—certainly her happiness—ending. And now, she could honestly say she had never been happier. All because she was married to Russell. "And then an honest one."

"I had nothing to do with that," he reminded her. "That was the king's choice. And, as for the first matter, as I remember the series of events, you were the one who chose me, not the other way around."

With a laugh filled with pleasure, she kissed him. She did it quickly, then did it again before drawing away, savoring the masculine taste of his lips. She could feel her blood singing.

"If they don't make you king, you could always become the royal lawyer," Amelia quipped. He reached for her, but she playfully took a step back, lacing her fingers through his hand. "Now, tell me everything. Just who is this woman who says she's having Reginald's baby? Do you know her? Do I?"

He drew her over to the sofa and sat down, pulling her onto his lap. She settled in, lacing her arms around his neck as she listened.

"No to both," he told her. "Unless it's an alias of some kind. According to what Lucia found out, the woman's name is Sydney Connor. The e-mail was tracked back to Naessa."

"Naessa," Amelia echoed incredulously. She banked down a shiver. There had been threats made against her father from several terrorist factions whose roots, it was discovered, ran deep in Naessa. "Nothing good ever comes from Naessa."

"Not so," he contradicted. When she looked at him quizzically, he said, "If this woman is on the level, then the future king of Silvershire might well be coming from there. If Sydney Connor is a native of Naessa, then Silvershire's new king would be half Naessian."

Amelia frowned as she turned the idea over in her head. There had been too much bad blood in the past between their two countries and Naessa.

"I don't think that's going to go over very well with

the people of Silvershire. Or with the people of Gastonia, for that matter," she added.

Russell nodded. She had a point, he supposed. For the sake of peace in the kingdom, Weston might not want to recognize a bastard's claim to the throne. It might set off too many diverse factions.

For the moment, his ascent to the throne seemed inevitable again.

"And it might just set off Nikolas Donovan and his little band of merrymakers," he commented dryly.

He could almost hear what the Union for Democracy would have to say about placing Reginald's illegitimate son on the throne. They could use the country's unrest to demand that the entire sum of governing power be turned over to the people.

Amelia put into words what he hadn't said. "And unless Reginald secretly married this woman, which I sincerely doubt, the fact that the baby is a bastard might make a great many people unwilling to accept that child as their king. For that matter, the king might chose not to recognize the baby, either," she added. "In any event, Weston still has the right to choose whomever he wants to be king since he no longer has a living son to take the crown."

Amelia smiled at him, her eyes encouraging. "I'm afraid that you are going to be king of Silvershire whether you like the idea or not, my sweet." She curled up in his lap. "Just think of me as your consolation prize."

"I think of you as the *only* prize," he answered just before he kissed her.

The kiss, meant to be fleeting as he stood up to take

his leave, took on a life of its own, growing and flowering until it threatened to overwhelm them both, blotting out the room, the palace and everything that was beyond the very small circle created by the two of them.

She heated his blood the way no other woman ever had before her. An eagerness went galloping through his veins, causing him mentally to discard the rest of the things he had intended on seeing to in the next few hours.

Nothing was nearly as important, nearly as pressing, as allowing himself to make love with this woman he had had the great fortune to have bestowed on him as his bride.

"Don't you have somewhere to be?" Amelia breathed against his mouth as he began to remove her clothing with the speed and dexterity of a finely skilled magician. Not to be outdone, she began separating him from his own garments almost as quickly as he was peeling her out of hers.

"Yes." His own breath was growing shorter and shorter just as his anticipation was steadily growing greater and greater. "I do. Right here," he told her. "Right now."

"Can't argue with that," she laughed softly.

And she didn't. Not for the next few hours.

Chapter 15

Russell turned his head toward the woman who somehow still managed to be a complete revelation to him. Amelia was in bed beside him. He had things he had to tend to. He knew they both did. But right now, nothing seemed to be as important to him as savoring this moment, lying here next to her.

"But you would be all right with that?" he asked, still wondering what he had ever done to deserve to be so lucky. "With the possibility of my not becoming the next King of Silvershire?"

Amelia turned so that her body was tucked against his. She smiled up into Russell's face, the warm glow of lovemaking still very tightly wrapped around her. They had already settled the matter, she thought. For all intents and purposes, it looked as if he were going to be the next king. But if he wasn't, she didn't care. Perhaps, she mused, she even liked it better that way. Because then they could go home.

"You're king of my heart, Russell, that's all that really matters to me." And then her smile faded just a little as a thought occurred to her.

Russell propped himself up on his elbow. He didn't like the way her brow furrowed. *Was* there an obstacle after all? "What?"

She picked her words carefully. The male ego, she knew, was a very fragile thing. Would his be bruised if the scenario he suggested really did play itself out? "If this does come about, if you're not crowned the King of Silvershire, would my being Queen of Gastonia some day bother you?"

Russell pressed his lips together, not to think, but to suppress the smile that rose to his lips. Titles had never mattered to him and he was comfortable enough in his own skin not to feel threatened by any she had. As long as she loved him. "You mean would it bother me to be a kept man?"

In her experience, men such as the ones he referred to idled away their time in vapid pursuits. That wasn't Russell.

"The only thing you would be 'kept' at is busy. Being the prince consort requires a great deal of work. You would be involved in guiding Gastonia, in keeping it safe. I don't intend to rule my country alone," she informed him. Amelia stroked his cheek lightly, feeling excitement taking hold again. "We are partners, you and I. Partners in everything that we do. Nothing would make my heart happier than returning to Gastonia. But I will not go without you," she added quietly. "And I will not remain there without you."

Russell turned his body until he was leaning over her again. He slipped his hand along her face, tracing its features slowly with his fingertips.

Amelia sighed just as her new husband brought his lips down to a breath away from hers. "I never believed in fairy tales," she told him. "Until now."

"Stick with me, Princess," he murmured. "The best is yet to be."

But the knock on the outer suite door, at first respectful, then louder, told them that whatever was to follow would have to wait. At least until they sent whoever was at the door away.

"Princess, are you in there?" There was no mistaking the urgency in Madeline's voice. It rang out, loud and clear. Her friend's tone gave no indication that she was about to go away.

Amelia exchanged glances with Russell. "Your lady-in-waiting apparently doesn't seem to want to live up to her title," he quipped.

Feeling protective of her friend, as well as somewhat frustrated, Amelia said, "Madeline has always had a mind of her own," just before she raised her voice so that Madeline could hear her through the door. "Yes, what is it, Madeline?" She glanced at Russell and smiled. He pressed a kiss to her throat, making her pulse jump. Oh, but she loved this man. "I'm…a little…busy…right now."

"Princess, the king is looking for your husband. I thought maybe he'd be in there with you." The smile that was in Madeline's voice said she knew exactly what was going on behind the closed doors. "King Weston requests that both of you meet with him at the royal clinic as soon as humanly possible."

At the mention of the clinic, Russell sat bolt upright, concerned. Thoughts of sharing another round of pleasure with Amelia were temporarily shelved. He reached for his clothing.

"Is the king ill?" he asked, raising his voice.

"I wouldn't know, Your Grace," Madeline answered. "He does not appear to be. But I'm just the messenger. One of several he requested look for you," she added.

Amelia scrambled out of bed. Russell paused a moment to let his eyes drift over her appreciatively. Rousing himself, he cleared his throat.

"Tell His Majesty that we'll be right there," he instructed. He allowed himself only a moment to fleetingly brush his lips over hers. "To be continued," he promised in a whisper.

"I will hold you to that," Amelia responded as she hurried into her clothes.

They lost no time in getting to the clinic. When they arrived, they found the king sitting in the corridor right before the entrance. The expression on his face was grave.

His complexion was far from viable, Russell noted. And the monarch's hands were clutching the chair's arms, his knuckles almost white from the effort.

"Is everything all right, Your Majesty?" Russell asked before Amelia had a chance to.

Apparently lost in thought, Weston raised his head

like one coming out of a deep trance. The monarch
looked at him as if surprised to see that there was anyone
else there. When he became aware of Amelia, he attempted a dignified smile to greet her.

"Hello, my dear." Weston shifted his eyes toward
Russell. "And no, everything is not all right." A sigh
escaped his lips. "My only son is being cut up." He
struggled for strength to continue, to face the pain that
seemed to be looming everywhere, waiting to ensnare
him, to take him captive. "I've finally given permission
for the autopsy to be done. You were right, of course,"
he told Russell without preamble. "We need to move
forward, to get answers if we can. And to finally bury
Prince Reginald the way he deserves to be buried."

Relief whispered through Russell. He was seriously
beginning to worry about the king's mental state, afraid
that the monarch was withdrawing more and more into
himself. Since Reginald's death, he'd caught the king
talking to himself on more than one occasion. In
addition, he was concerned that the monarch might just
decide to go ahead and hold the funeral, burying the
prince without having the autopsy performed.

He knew that, from the king's standpoint, Reginald
was dead and that discovering that his death had
occurred naturally or at his own or another man's hand
did not change the end result. Reginald was gone. He
had feared that Weston would be overwhelmed with
that glaring reality and that it would cause him to lose
sight of the fact that they needed to know how.

"When did it begin? The autopsy," Amelia added
gently, kneeling down beside the man who, even a few

days earlier, had looked so dynamic, so bold, and who now seemed to be a shadow of his former self.

Grief had done that, she thought. Grief had hollowed him out until he appeared brittle and frail.

"Less than half an hour ago. I thought you should be here for the outcome," he murmured to Russell.

"We'll stay with you." Russell's eyes met Amelia's and she gave him a small, imperceptible nod in response. "Until it's over."

Gratitude came over the monarch's features. "I would be in debt to you for that," he told them, looking from one to the other. A little of his former self was restored, at least for the moment. "I know I should be strong enough to remain here, waiting to be told the results. But the image." His eyes looked haunted as he envisioned what was going on a few short feet from where he sat. "I can't get the image out of my head—" He swept his long fingers along his temples, as if trying to banish what he saw in his mind's eye, as if he felt an almost unbearable pounding. The king was suffering from headaches that were growing greater in number and more intense each time.

"We have nowhere else to be, Your Majesty," Amelia assured him gently. Smiling into his eyes, she laced her fingers through his. Weston looked at her as if seeing her for the first time. The gratitude in his eyes was all the thanks she needed.

The hands on the antique grandfather clock that stood a little way down the lavishly decorated corridor seemed to move at an inordinately slow pace. Russell wanted this to be over with, to have the autopsy completed and the king's son sewn back together again, to be a whole person again rather than the sum of parts that had been weighed, calibrated and measured.

Granted, he had been the one to lobby the king the hardest to have the autopsy performed, and they needed the answers that the autopsy would provide, but he had no idea he would be here, only a few feet away from the actual autopsy room, while the royal medical examiner performed her duties. Somehow, that seemed rather ghoulish to him.

A necessary evil, he told himself, glancing over toward the princess. He didn't have the right to complain, even silently. Just look at the hand that fate had dealt him.

Amelia had been carrying on a steady stream of conversation the entire time they'd been waiting, bless her, he thought. She seemed to know a little about everything. Right now, he and the king were being given a verbal tour of the factory where the Gaston, the car that had firmly placed Gastonia on the map as something other than just another collection of casinos, was manufactured. The king actually seemed mildly distracted, which he knew was Amelia's main, most likely only, goal.

And then, after what seemed like hours, the door opened and Dr. Abby Burnett came out. There was a grim expression on the physician's usually amiable, plain face.

Weston was on his feet immediately. The chair almost fell backwards from his momentum. "Well?" he asked eagerly. "Is the prince...?"

"Yes," Dr. Burnett told him. "I've just now finished stitching him back up." She pressed her lips together, obviously wrestling with something. She nodded at the chair behind him. "Your Majesty, perhaps you'd like to sit down."

Weston frowned, dismissing the suggestion. "I *have* been sitting down. Sitting down so long that I'm fairly certain I have permanently flattened your cushions." He drew his shoulders back, momentarily looking like the formidable ruler he had always been. "Now, out with it. What have you discovered?"

There was a wealth of information to dispense. The doctor picked her way through it carefully. "That your son did not die a natural death. That he didn't even die accidentally by his own hand."

"There was no drug overdose?" Weston made no effort to cover his eagerness for the confirmation. This, at least, would take his son out of the realm of being just another careless drug abuser. He didn't want that to be Reginald's legacy, that he'd died accidentally while seeking an artificial rush.

"Unless, of course," the medical examiner added dryly, "Prince Reginald intended to 'accidentally' poison himself."

"Poison?" Amelia echoed, trying to process the information.

She knew of the adult Reginald predominantly through what she had read in the newspapers and magazine. Even the most charitable, conservative accountings made the man out to be difficult to deal with. How many toes had Reginald stepped on, how many people had secretly plotted getting their revenge against him? It looked as if one of them had finally succeeded. But who?

Amelia glanced at her husband and wondered if they would ever get to the bottom of it or if this was destined to remain one of those unsolved mysteries that teased armchair detectives from time to time.

"Poison," the medical examiner repeated. Her tone left no room for argument.

"What kind of poison?" Russell wanted to know. If they knew what kind and its strength, maybe they could track down its purchase and with that, perhaps discover the name of the killer.

"Did he suffer?" Weston wanted to know before the medical examiner could answer Russell's question.

The look in the doctor's eyes told Russell that Dr. Burnett was torn. Torn between ethics and empathy. Between telling the king the truth and allowing the monarch to seek solace within a comforting lie.

But then the medical examiner raised her head as if she had made up her mind. Her expression told him that she was going with the truth. Lying, even for the best of reasons, would only undercut her ultimate value to the king. He had to be able to trust her. To know that he could believe what she told him.

The king was not a stupid man. Once the pain of hearing what she had to tell him had worked its way into the tapestry of his life, King Weston would realize that no one simply fell asleep after ingesting poison. That before death claimed the despairing soul seeking an end, there came the feeling of being strangled, of suddenly realizing that you were about to die and that there was nothing that could be done to avoid the inevitable.

Dr. Burnett placed a comforting hand on the monarch's shoulder. "Somewhat, I'm afraid."

Amelia slipped her hand into Weston's, pretending not to see the tears gathering in the man's eyes. "I'm so sorry, Your Majesty," she whispered.

"But there is something more."

Dr. Burnett's words sliced through the pain winding itself around his heart. Weston stared at her.

"More? The word no longer has any meaning to me, doctor. There is no 'more.' I've lost my son, my only son. For me, there is only less, not more."

"Well, Your Majesty," the medical examiner went on almost wearily, as if bracing herself for a very steep uphill climb, "that's just it."

"What's just it?" Russell asked, cutting in. He exchanged confused glances with Amelia, who shook her head, indicating that she had no more of a clue about what was going on than he did.

"It doesn't look as if you've really lost your only son," Dr. Burnett went on, only to have the king interrupt her again.

"What are you talking about?" Weston demanded. "You just dissected him in your clinic. You just came from there." He gestured toward the clinic's doors.

Dr. Burnett slipped her slender hands deep into the pockets of the lab coat she had thrown over her operating livery. "I dissected someone," she agreed, "but it wasn't your son."

Amelia was trying to make sense out of what was being told to them. "Someone switched the bodies?" she guessed incredulously.

Dr. Burnett's eyes shifted toward her. "Yes, but not right now."

"I don't understand," Russell interrupted. What she was suggesting wasn't possible. The clinic had been secured. The palace was always secured and never more so than now. No one short of a magician could have come in and switched the bodies before the autopsy. Besides, there was also the fact that Weston had just been with Reginald earlier today, paying his final respects. The doctor had to have made some mistake. "When could this so-called 'switch' have taken place?" he challenged.

Her answer floored them all. "My guess is thirty years ago. At the hospital right after the queen gave birth."

For the first time in days, color rose to the king's cheeks. "What are you talking about?" he demanded heatedly. "That isn't possible."

"I'm afraid that it is," Dr. Burnett said calmly. "That it has to be. There is no other explanation."

The calmer she sounded the more agitated Weston grew. "No other explanation for what?"

The medical examiner took a deep breath and began. "Your Majesty, as a matter of course, a blood panel and tox screen were performed on the sample of blood I took from the dead man."

"My son," Weston interjected sternly.

She nodded politely and went on. "For whatever reason, someone in the lab accidentally did blood typing, as well. The man on my autopsy table had type O negative blood. You and your late queen were both AB positive. There is no way that man in my clinic is a product of a union between you and the queen."

"Someone made a mistake," Weston insisted.

"No mistake, Your Majesty. I ran the second test myself." Dr. Burnett looked to Russell and Amelia for support before turning her attention back to the king. She remained unshakable in her conviction of the findings. "I have no idea why this was done or who was behind it, that's not my job. What I do know is that the man I performed an autopsy on wasn't your natural son and that if there was a switch—"

Russell cut in, as the full import of what the medical examiner was saying hit him, "Then the Prince of Silvershire is still out there somewhere."

"I have a son? Another son?" Weston looked like a man shell-shocked as the question dribbled from his lips in slow motion, just the same way his gaze drifted from the doctor to Russell. It was clear that he didn't know whether to be overjoyed or shattered by the news.

"No, not another son," the medical examiner corrected. "Your *only* son. I don't know who the man on my autopsy table actually is or was, but the fact remains that he couldn't have been your son."

"You're right," Amelia cut in, trying to come to grips with what the doctor had just told them. "If a switch was made, it had to have been done in the hospital. Most likely as soon as the newborn baby was taken from the queen to be cleaned up."

It all sounded so far-fetched, so unreal. "Why? Who?" Weston cried, stunned. He looked at Russell,

wanting something logical to hold on to. Feeling like
a man who had just been given hope and had his soul
condemned at the same time, with the very same
words.

The real prince was still alive. This meant that he
couldn't take the crown, Russell realized. The thought
brought with it a wave of energy that filled his heart. He
didn't have to be king, didn't have to suffer through the
kind of life that was examined and reexamined on a
daily basis. The relief he felt was incredible.

"We don't know why or who yet," Russell told him,
"but we *are* going to find out." He looked at the sover-
eign. "I promise you that, Your Majesty. We'll find out
who he is and why he was taken. And why we haven't
heard anything about it until now."

It would seem to him that if there was a royal abduc-
tion, whoever had done it would have tried to take advantage of the situation. Yet in thirty years, there hadn't
been a single word about it. Not a demand for ransom
or even a hint that it was done. Why?

He couldn't shake the feeling that something dire was
about to happen.

Reginald's poisoning took on a different perspec-
tive. Perhaps it hadn't been done for some personal
wrong. Perhaps poisoning the prince had been the first
step in the present reign's undoing.

"Your Majesty?" Amelia prodded when the king
made no reply. She slanted a glance toward Russell,
concerned about the monarch's state of health. "Would
you like to lie down?"

Very slowly, Weston turned his head toward her, as if unable to move his eyes independently. "I—I—"

He couldn't go on, couldn't force any more words from his lips. There was no air with which to move them. His heart was hammering too hard for him to catch his breath. What there was of it was quickly fading from him. And his head, his head was doing very strange things. Lights were winking in and out, blurring his vision, making him see things out of his past. Things that were not there.

A baby. His wife. Both appeared to him in flashes and then were gone. And all the while, there was this pounding in his brain. A pounding that grew ever louder.

Weston's knees gave way, failing him.

Like a crumpled doll, the king collapsed. He would have hit the floor had Russell's reflexes not been so keen. He grabbed the monarch just before the latter hit the floor.

Propping him up, Russell looked at the king. "Your Majesty, can you hear me?" Russell cried. Weston's eyes rolled back in his head.

Dr. Burnett was at his side immediately. "Bring him in here!" she ordered, leading the way into the clinic. Russell picked the unconscious man up in his arms and followed her. Amelia was right beside him.

An alarm was sounded. Instantly, there were technicians and equipment materializing from all over the fully stocked clinic. Russell placed the king down on the gurney that had been brought over, then stepped back. Amelia shadowed his movements, her eyes never leaving the king's crumpled body.

"Is he—?" She couldn't get herself to finish the question.

"He's still alive," Russell told her.

The staff did what they could. The defibrillator paddles were not necessary. The king's heart went on beating, but despite all their best efforts, the king remained unconscious.

Maybe it was better that way, Russell thought, watching as the king was taken to a private room. Everything that had happened in the last few minutes had been too much for the monarch to process. The man needed his rest. His body needed to fight its way back to health. To grow strong enough to handle the adverse situation it found itself in.

"Inform whoever needs to be told that the king is staying here tonight," Dr. Burnett told Russell.

"Do you think a hospital might be better for him?" Amelia suggested.

"The king has been fighting off the effects of the flu," the doctor told her. "We're running some tests, but perhaps all he needs is a little rest. We can tell more in the morning."

Russell nodded. In the meantime, he thought, he had answers to find and a potential king to track down.

"We're not going to Gastonia just yet," he told Amelia.

Gastonia's princess threaded her fingers through her husband's as the doctor drew a curtain around the king's bed. They would be going home soon enough, she promised herself. Right now, Russell needed to be here. Needed to stand by his king and help him. His sense of duty and responsibility were among the things she loved about him.

"I know," she murmured. Her tone told him he had her full support.

A man could not ask for more. Not even if he were a king.

* * * * *

THE PRINCESS'S
SECRET SCANDAL

BY
KAREN WHIDDON

THE PRINCESS'S
SECRET SCANDAL

Karen Whiddon started weaving fanciful tales for her younger brothers at the age of eleven. Amidst the Catskill Mountains of New York, then the Rocky Mountains of Colorado, she fuelled her imagination with the natural beauty of the rugged peaks and spun stories of love that captivated her family's attention.

Karen now lives in North Texas, where she shares her life with her very own hero of a husband and three doting dogs. Also an entrepreneur, she divides her time between the business she runs with her husband and writing the contemporary romantic suspense and paranormal romances that readers enjoy. You can e-mail Karen at KWhiddon1@aol.com or write to her at PO Box 820807, Fort Worth, TX 76182. Fans of her writing can also check out her website at www.KarenWhiddon.com.

As always, to my lover and best friend,
the man whom I model all the heroes after—
my husband, Lonnie.

Chapter 1

"Are you sure she's—?" Chase Savage broke off, stifling a curse.

A horn honked. Traffic inched slowly forward. He pressed the cell phone against his ear with one hand, keeping the other on the steering wheel while he negotiated the heavy downtown Silverton traffic.

"Yes, of course." His caller chuckled. "Isn't it obvious?"

Though he hated to do so, especially to his boss, as head of the royal publicity department Chase felt he must point out the obvious. "She's avoiding the reporters."

The all-important press. Couldn't live with them, couldn't live without them.

His Grace, Russell Southgate, III, Duke of Carrington, and Chase's employer, made a rude sound. "For now. She's holding out. You know how the game is played. You've dealt with her kind before."

Chase sighed. At the ripe age of twenty-nine, he really *had* seen it all. There seemed to be an endless supply of royal groupies and hangers-on, all wanting something for nothing. Some craved sex, most sought money or a slight slice of fame. Royal fame. Which he knew could often be a royal pain in the ass.

"Are you certain Reginald didn't—" Chase began.

"*His Highness* might be difficult, but he's still next in line for the throne. And this is not just any groupie. Even if she is from the wrong side of the blanket, she's still daughter to Prince Kerwin of Naessa. You know that."

"She doesn't move in the usual circles. I've never met her."

"I know." Carrington sighed again. "Maybe that's what intrigued Reginald. Who knows? Though Reginald is denying everything this time, his mistake could have an enormous impact. Not just Silvershire is affected. The woman says she's pregnant, for God's sake. If this is not handled properly, the situation could become a political disaster." The Duke muttered a particularly un-royal curse, making Chase grin. Unlike most of the royals he spent his time protecting, when Carrington let down his guard, he could be a regular guy. Almost.

"Get to her before she talks to the press. The damage she could do…" Chase could hear the other man shudder, even over the phone line.

"So you want me to 'handle' her?" As a huge, blue SUV cut him off, Chase lay on his horn. "How?"

"With style and class, as usual. Offer her money to take her child and disappear. You can do it, the way only you know how. I have confidence you'll do splendidly, as usual."

The rare compliment, coming from Carrington, told

Chase more than anything how important this was. In the six years since Chase had moved up the ranks from royal bodyguard to publicist, Carrington had been a good employer and a fair boss. He'd been instrumental in Chase's career, taking an interest in the younger man and helping him navigate the sometime intricate maze that comprised royal life.

Effortlessly and tirelessly making the royals look good had earned Chase a promotion to head of public relations. The Wizard of PR, his staff called him. He sort of liked the name.

"I'm on my way to the Hotel Royale now." Chase consulted his watch, a Rolex, which had been an expensive holiday gift Prince Reginald had given half the palace staff. "I should be there in, oh, thirty minutes or less."

Traffic slowed to a stop, forcing Chase to hit his brakes, hard. Rush hour sucked. Most times he managed to avoid the snarl of cars by working late at the palace. Not today. Today he had to hightail it over to the plush hotel in downtown Silverton and intercept this woman before she checked out. Best to confront her in her room, to make the offer in private. Timing was everything in his business.

"You'll handle this." It wasn't a question. Carrington rarely asked. He expected or demanded. And what he wanted, he got.

"Yes, I'll handle it. Never fear." Chase closed his cell phone and turned up the volume on the radio. He'd down loaded and burned a new CD of classic American rock last night. Aerosmith blasted over the speakers, making him grin. Stuck in traffic was as good a time as any to enjoy his favorite tunes.

He saw no need to plot a strategy—groupies were

groupies. Once he started talking money to this woman, he anticipated a quick resolution.

Reaching the hotel, he eschewed the valet parking and drove into the parking garage himself. With the ever-vigilant press always on the lookout for a story, he didn't want to risk being seen.

The Hotel Royale had a back entrance and he used it now. Carrington had given him the woman's room number, so he took the service elevator to the sixth floor. He encountered no one, not even hotel staff. Shifts were changing, and he anticipated another ten or fifteen minutes of privacy.

Moving silently on the plush carpeting, he found her room and shook his head. Her door was ajar, the deadbolt turned out to keep the heavy door from closing. Since maids often did this when cleaning the rooms, he wondered if he'd arrived too late.

Pulling the door open, he saw he was not. With her back to him, a slender woman with shoulder-length, cinnamon-colored hair was loading clothes into an open suitcase she'd placed on the bed.

"Not much of a princess," he drawled. "Where's your entourage? Sydney Conner, I presume?"

Her head snapped up. When she met his gaze, he felt an involuntary tightening low in his gut. Damn. She was heart-stoppingly gorgeous. He'd expected that. They all were.

But this woman was no flashy blonde, Prince Reginald's usual type. Her wealth of thick, silky hair framed a delicate, oval face. With her generous mouth, high cheekbones, and dark blue eyes, she had a serene, quiet sort of beauty, not at all what Chase would have expected from one of Prince Reginald's lovers.

Instant desire—fierce, intense, savage—made him draw a harsh, ragged breath.

Staring at him with wide eyes, she reached for the phone. Calling hotel security, no doubt.

"Wait." He held up his ID. "I'm with the palace."

Her full lips thinned. "Let me see."

He tossed it, surprised when she caught the laminated badge with one elegant, perfectly manicured hand. After she ascertained he really was whom he'd said he was, she replaced the phone in the cradle and narrowed her amazing eyes.

"I locked my door. How did you get in here?"

He gave her a slow smile, his PR smile. "Actually, your door was open. Rather careless, don't you think?"

That caught her off guard. Glancing at the door, she blinked, then frowned. "What can I do for you, Mr.…" She studied the badge again, her lush lips curving in a rueful smile. "Savage? I'm on my way out, so this will have to be quick."

Again when she looked at him, he felt that punch to the gut. This time, a flare of anger lanced through his lust.

She was good, he admitted grudgingly. Her every movement was elegant, sensual. Her appearance, from the cut of her expensive, designer clothing to the pampered, creamy glow of her skin, spoke of wealth and breeding. Not your usual palace hanger-on at all.

But then, she *was* a princess.

"Where are you going?"

"That's none of your business," she told him, matching his cool tone. "Since I have little to do with the royal family of Silvershire these days, I don't understand why you're here. What do you want?"

He flashed her a hard look, belatedly remembering at the last moment to soften it with another smile. "As you saw from my ID, I'm with the royal publicity department. His Grace, the Duke of Carrington, sent me."

She stared, her emotions flashing across her mobile face, hope, disbelief and a tentative joy chief among them. She read the badge one last time before handing it back to him.

"Reginald spoke to the duke?" she asked. "He told him about our baby?"

Hearing the raw emotion in her voice, Chase felt a flash of pity. The look she gave him told him she'd seen and hated both that and the fact she'd let her guard down enough to show her feelings to a total stranger.

Chase narrowed his eyes. "I wasn't informed how Lord Carrington learned of your claim."

"But Reginald—" She bit her lip.

"Reginald what?"

One hand instinctively went to her belly. *Protective.* He noted this and filed it away for future reference. "What do you and/or Lord Carrington want with me?"

She was sleek and beautiful and sexy as hell. Chase could think of a thousand ways to answer that question, though he'd say none of them. He had a job to do.

He lifted his briefcase. "I've been authorized to offer you—"

The window exploded in a shower of glass.

"Get down!" He leapt at her.

Too stunned to react when he pushed her down, Sydney fell heavily, the man on top of her. Panicked, terrified the fall had hurt her unborn child, she fought to get up.

"Stay down," he snarled. "That was a gunshot."

"A gunshot? Why would someone shoot at me?"

When he looked at her, she saw a different man. Gone was the affable, smiling stranger. This man wore a grim face, a hard face, the kind of face she'd seen on her mother's bodyguards, hired mercenaries for the most part. Dangerous men who played by their own set of rules.

"Who are you, really?" She whispered, still cradling her abdomen. "You might be in public relations now, but I'm thinking you might have another job title, as well."

He looked away, climbing off her, still keeping low to the ground.

Another shot rang out, taking out what was left of the window.

He cursed. "That window—what's it face?"

Confused, she shook her head. "I'm not sure. I'm on the sixth floor. No view. All that's out there is the roof of one of the lower buildings." Then she realized what that meant. If she were to climb out her window, she'd be able to step without much discomfort onto the other roof.

The shooter was that close! She had to protect her baby.

"We've got to get out of here." He grabbed her hand, yanking her to her feet. "Stay low and follow me."

He started for the door.

She grabbed her purse. "I need my passport."

"Come on." Once they reached the hall, he turned left.

"The elevator's that way." She pointed right.

"We're taking the stairs. Hurry."

They hustled all the way down. Their footsteps clattered on the metal edges, echoing in the narrow stairway.

"Let's go, through here." Tone low and urgent, he shepherded her out a door marked as an emergency exit, instantly setting off the hotel alarm. "Good, a distraction," he shouted over the clanging bell and whirring siren.

Outside, momentarily disoriented, Sydney stumbled, squinting into the bright sunlight. He gave her arm another tug, urging her on, past the line of parked cars on the curb.

"My cello." She suddenly remembered her beloved instrument. "I can't leave it. Go back and get it, please?"

"No. I'll buy you another."

"You don't understand. It's a Stradivarius, one of only sixty left in the world." She attempted in vain to pull herself free, knowing she personally couldn't go back after it. She had to protect her baby at all costs, even if that meant she lost Lady Swister, her cello. "Please," she repeated. "It will only take a moment."

Grim-faced, he stared, sending a chill of foreboding up her spine. "You want me to risk my life for an instrument?"

"A three-million-dollar instrument. Please." She gestured again. "We've obviously lost the shooter."

"For now." A muscle worked in his jaw. "How the hell did you get a three-million-dollar cello?"

"Reginald gave it to me. I—"

They both heard the sharp report of another shot. Seemingly at the same time, the side window of the car behind them shattered.

"Go. Now!" Not hesitating, he yanked her after him.

They took off at a run, across the deserted street and into a narrow alley.

"But my cello…!"

"Forget the cello. This way."

"My rental car's closer." She pointed at the cute red Gaston Mini, parked near the corner. "Right there." Fishing the remote out of her purse, she punched the unlock button.

A second later, the car exploded.

The force of the blast knocked them both to the ground.

An instant and then Chase yanked her to her feet. Dazed, she could only stare at the roaring inferno that, seconds before, had been her car.

"Are you all right?"

She blinked, looked down at her torn slacks and bloody knees. "I…I think so."

Sirens drowned out even the still-clanging hotel alarm. Any minute now, police, ambulance and fire trucks should careen around the corner.

"Good." He tugged at her arm. "Come on then. Run!"

Another gunshot, uncomfortably close, took out another windshield.

"Come on."

They took off running. Several glances over her shoulder and she still couldn't see the gunman, or anyone in pursuit.

Still, she had to protect her baby.

"Don't look back. Just run!" He led her left, then right and left again into a concrete parking garage. Their footsteps echoed as they ran toward a low-slung, black Mercedes.

By the time he bundled her into the car, she was out of breath and panting. Another quick look assured her they hadn't been followed. "So far so good."

"They found your room and anticipated the door we'd exit," he muttered. "It's only a matter of time until they find us. We're not waiting around until they do."

Starting the engine without sparing her a second glance, he shoved the gearshift into reverse, backing so fast his tires squealed. Then he gunned the car forward. The powerful motor roared as they shot into the street. They careened around the corner, barreling toward the main thoroughfare.

Suddenly, she felt every cut, every bruise. Worse than

that, her lower back hurt. Alarm flared through her. Had she injured her baby? Sydney cradled her abdomen, trying to regain her breath, her mind whirling.

"What?" Now he looked at her, his hazel eyes missing nothing. "Are you hurt?"

"No. Yes. I—I don't know." She bit her lip, both hands covering her still-flat abdomen. "I'm pregnant. I'm worried about my baby."

"You don't look pregnant." One hand on the steering wheel, he issued this observation in a bland, bored tone, as if he dealt every day with shootouts and chases. For all she knew, maybe he did.

"I'm barely eight weeks." Stiffening, she refused to look at him again, glancing out the window as she finally took notice of her surroundings. They were heading away from downtown, toward the Silvershire International Airport. "Look, Mr. Savage…"

"Call me Chase."

She ignored him. "Mr. Savage. Where are we going?"

Instead of answering, he gave her another hard look. "Any idea who was shooting at you? And why?"

"No. I think it's more likely we got caught in the middle of someone else's troubles."

"Troubles?"

She waved her hand. "You know. Gang war or something. We were in the wrong place at the wrong time."

"Princess—"

"My name is Sydney."

"Sydney, then. They shot at you. No one else. You. Your car exploded. Of course this was aimed at you."

Lifting her chin, she considered his words. He was right. "Why? Why would anyone want to harm me?"

Keeping an eye on the rearview mirror, he took the exit that led to the airport. "You claim to be carrying the crown prince's child. You know there's a political firestorm going on now with those democracy advocates. That'd put you right in the middle of it."

"True. But Reginald and I aren't married. My baby is no threat to anyone."

"Yet," he said.

"Ever." Closing her mouth before she said too much more, Sydney caught sight of the Welcome to Silvershire International Airport sign. "Where are you taking me? Why the airport?"

For the first time since appearing in her doorway, he looked surprised. As though she should have known. "The royal jet is waiting."

"The royal jet?" A tentative spark of hope filled her. "Has he asked you to bring me to him?"

"Who?"

Impatient, she shifted in her seat. "Reginald, of course. My baby's father. Are you taking me to see him?"

There was no pity in the hard glance he shot her now.

"No," he said. Nothing more.

But then, what else could he say? Reginald had made it plain he didn't want her or the unplanned baby she carried. She'd even learned he'd gotten engaged to a beautiful princess from Gastonia. He'd moved quickly, proving his words of love had been nothing but lies.

The knowledge shouldn't hurt so much, but it did. Mostly, she thought with a wry smile, because she'd unintentionally done the one thing she'd always sworn not to. She'd inadvertently mimicked her mother's life.

When she looked up she realized Chase watched her and

most likely had misinterpreted her smile. No matter, she was going home to Naessa soon. Then what he or anyone else in the country of Silvershire thought wouldn't matter a whit. Not at all.

She'd managed to do as her mother had done, but unlike her mother, she wouldn't ever call her baby a mistake. From now on, Sydney had a child to think of. From now on, her baby would always come first.

A quick glance at the handsome man beside her told her nothing. Chase Savage had protected her, but what were his real intentions?

They pulled up to an iron gate marked Private. Chase pushed a button on his console and the barricade swung open. Driving slowly through the rows of hangars, he punched in a number on his cell phone, a razor-thin model which looked like something out of a James Bond movie. He spoke a few terse words—not enough for her to glean the gist of the conversation, and snapped the metal phone closed.

"All settled," he said cheerfully. "I've gotten us emergency clearance." They turned right, into the airport's private section. Sydney had flown out of here before, as most of her friends' families were wealthy. Here, in various hangars, the rich kept their personal jets. No doubt the royal family had several.

"Emergency clearance for what?" she asked, as they pulled up in front of a nondescript, gray metal hangar. "If Reginald—" she swallowed tightly as she spoke the name "—didn't send for me, then why'd you bring me here at all?"

He frowned. "I had to take you somewhere safe."

"Not really." Studying him, she wished she could read his closed expression. "I'm not your responsibility. As a matter of fact, why are you—head of Silvershire's public relations department—here to begin with?"

For the first time since he'd appeared in her hotel room, cool, confident Chase Savage appeared at a loss for words.

She pressed her advantage. "You started to say something earlier, before the shooting started. You said you'd been authorized to do something. What was it?"

"Not now." He shook his head. "We'll discuss that later, once we're in the air."

"In the air to…?"

"I'm taking you home, to Naessa. You'll be safer there than here."

"Home?" Exactly where she wanted to go. Except… "I need my cello." The Strad could never be replaced.

"I'll send someone after your instrument," he promised. "The police should be there by now. They won't let anyone mess with it."

"I need to see a doctor and make sure everything is all right with the baby."

"You can do that once you get home. It's only a forty-five-minute flight to Naessa."

Something still bothered her, though she wasn't sure what. He'd addressed her every concern smoothly. Too smoothly. Maybe that was the problem.

She glanced around them. "This doesn't look like the royal hangar. Where's the Silvershire crest?"

Expression implacable, he shrugged. "The king won't allow that because of the danger from terrorists. The royal crest could act as a huge bull's-eye for undesirables."

He had a point, though she hated the word he'd used. *Undesirables.* In Naessa, as the king's unacknowledged daughter, she'd been called that and a lot worse. *Bastard* had been her mother's particular favorite. For a while Frances had adopted it almost as a nickname, referring to Sydney as her bastard spawn, reminding her at an early age how she'd ruined her mother's life.

Sydney vowed her child—son or daughter, whichever—would only enrich hers.

Chase got out of the car and crossed around the front to Sydney's side, opening her door and holding out his hand. She slipped her hand into his larger one, noting the calluses on his long, elegant fingers, and allowed him to help her from the low-slung car.

Staring up at his rugged face, Sydney wondered about his ancestry. Though he wore a well-cut, conservative suit, his shaggy hair and hawklike features made him appear dangerous. She wouldn't be surprised to learn he had a trace of pirate in him.

As if he'd read her thoughts, he smiled, stunning her. He really was, she noted abstractly, struggling to find her breath, quite beautiful. In a hard, rugged, utterly masculine way.

She reminded herself that beautiful men were bad news. Reginald had provided her with living proof of that.

Once Chase had closed the door behind her with a quiet thunk, she had another round of misgivings and tugged her hand free. While private jet was always more comfortable than commercial, she barely knew this man.

"We don't have time for this." He consulted his Rolex, shooting her a look of pure male exasperation.

The watch looked familiar. Ah, yes. Reginald had gifted all his staff with similar watches for Christmas.

"Shall we go?"

Finally she nodded.

Up the steps into the waiting jet they went. A short,

blond man greeted them. Evidently, he was one of the pilots. He pulled the door closed before disappearing into the cockpit.

Sydney had time to note the jet's plush interior before one side of the hangar opened like a giant, automatic garage door.

Chase barely glanced at her. "Buckle your seat belt."

His cell phone chirped. Immediately, he answered, turning away from her to try and conduct his business with a measure of privacy.

The plane began to taxi forward.

Chase closed his phone and then powered off. When he looked at her, the dangerous mercenary had returned, full-force.

"What is it?" she asked. Something, some wild suspicion, an absurdly ridiculous hope, made her ask. "Was that call from Reginald?"

His hazel gaze touched on her coolly. "Is that why you came to Silvershire? To see the prince?"

"Of course. I wanted him to look me in the face and tell me..."

"Tell you what?"

"Never mind." No way was she admitting to this man, this stranger, the depth of her shame. Reginald had pretended to love her. And now, when she carried his child, a baby they'd made together, he pretended he didn't know her. She sighed. "Forget I asked that. It was foolish of me."

Chase watched her a heartbeat longer, then he dipped his head, his hazel eyes shuttered.

Another thought occurred to her. "Is this plan to remove me from your country carried out at Reginald's direction?"

"No." He gave her a long, hard look. "This is entirely

spur-of-the-moment. Not planned. After what happened back at the hotel, I had no choice. It's not safe for you in Silvershire. Especially now."

That caught her attention. "Especially now?"

"That phone call…Things have changed," Chase said softly, as though his words could hurt her.

"Why? What's happened?" She searched his hard, rugged face. "What are you not telling me?"

He took her hand and leaned forward, compassion turning his hazel eyes dark. "That phone call I just got? It was the Duke of Carrington, my boss. I'm sorry to have to tell you this, but Prince Reginald, the father of your unborn child, is dead."

Chapter 2

"Dead?"

Her amazing eyes widened as she took in his words. Shock and disbelief flashed across her face. *She hadn't known.* Russell had been so certain, but he'd been wrong.

Sydney Conner was hearing the news for the first time. Chase would bet his life on that.

"Dead?" She repeated, bewilderment echoing in her husky voice. "Reginald? Are you sure?"

Still watching her closely, he nodded. Unbelievably, he had a random urge to touch her, to stroke her creamy skin and soothe the grief from her face. Instead, he clenched his jaw and kept his hands to himself.

"When?" Her husky voice vibrated with sadness.

"He died last night, at his country estate. We—that is, the royal public relations department—have a press conference scheduled for—" he glanced at his watch "—right about now."

"A press conference?" She said the words as though they were foreign. Again her sapphire gaze searched his face. "You're telling the truth? Reginald…is…really… dead?"

"Yes." He kept his own face expressionless. "You'll see it in the papers tomorrow."

Though her hands shook, she felt no immediate sense of loss. She'd already lost Reginald the day he'd walked away from her and the child they'd created. He'd made it plain he wanted nothing further to do with the woman he'd once courted so ardently.

The foolish woman, a bitter smile curved her lips, *who'd trusted his words of love.* "I can't believe it."

He said nothing, merely continuing to hold her hand and watch her.

Reginald. Dead. Now her baby would never have a chance to know its father. Even though Reginald had refused to acknowledge her pregnancy, she'd had hopes he would change once the child was born.

Even though her own sire hadn't.

"Was there an accident? How…how did he die?"

"No accident. There's some speculation it was a drug overdose. Other than that, I don't know. They haven't begun the autopsy. I'm sure I'll be notified—as will the press—when they know anything."

"Overdose?"

"You didn't know he did drugs?"

Slowly, she shook her head. Pulling her hand free, she pressed herself into the seat. Tension began to build in her shoulders. For an instant, she longed for Camille, her talented, personal masseuse back home in Naessa, and she rubbed her aching neck. The beginnings of a headache started behind her eyes. Damn it. She felt vaguely guilty, though she knew her wishing him dead had nothing to do with what had actually happened.

Though he'd dumped her and scorned their child, Reginald didn't deserve to die.

"Are you all right?"

She'd been so lost in her own thoughts she'd managed almost to forget he was there. *Almost* being the key word. She doubted people often forgot a man like Chase Savage. Even sitting still, he dominated the cabin space.

"I'm fine," she murmured. "I think."

For a moment she thought she saw compassion in his hazel eyes. Because she didn't want that, she swallowed and lifted her chin. "Did you know Reginald well?"

"*Prince* Reginald?" He raised his brows. "He was a bit out of my stratosphere."

What could she say to that? "He was out of everyone's stratosphere."

"What about you?" he asked. "How'd you meet him?"

"After a performance." A thousand bittersweet memories rushed back to her. He'd sent her flowers the first night. And every night after that, in every city in which the symphony had performed. He'd come backstage every single time, charming her fellow performers, his dark and hooded gaze focused on her. Only on her.

Afraid, she'd refused his invitation to dinner. Again and again. Her refusals never seemed to faze him, for he'd continued to ask until finally, wearily, she gave in. After all, as he'd pointed out, it was merely a simple meal. What objections could she have to eating?

That dinner had been the beginning of her downfall.

"Reliving the excitement?" Though his tone was kind, he gave her a mocking smile.

Without thinking, she shook her head. "Just remembering," she told him softly. "Reginald was a charismatic man." She wouldn't tell him the rest. "His death will be felt by many."

"Perhaps." Chase gave her an odd look. "But then, of course, you must have seen a different side of him."

Before Reginald's betrayal, Sydney could have talked about him for hours, and cherished every word. She'd believed he'd loved her, she who'd been so patently unloved her entire life. She'd bloomed under his attention. Now that she knew the truth, that she'd merely been a flavor of the month to him, she felt foolish. What she'd mistaken for love on her own part was mere infatuation. But she'd refused to retreat into her safe little shell. For her baby's sake, she'd pursued Reginald back to his own country, determined to give her child what she herself had never had. A father.

Staring blindly out her window, she realized the light-colored fog had changed, darkened.

She took a deep breath. "You still haven't told me why you're here. In view of what's happened, I think I should know."

After a moment, he nodded. "As you know, I'm head of public relations for Silvershire. Prince Reginald forwarded the e-mails you sent him to the duke, who dispatched me to handle you."

"Handle me?" As though she was some royal hanger-on who now presented a problem.

"Yes. I was sent to check you out." His gaze swept over her, making her insides tighten.

"Now it no longer matters. Reginald is dead. My baby will never know its father now."

"No longer matters?" He watched her closely. "You aren't going to try and claim rights to the throne?"

After a startled moment, she could only shake her head. "I have no reason to do that. If King Weston wants my child to be named heir, then I would consider it."

"Your child has royal blood. Not just Reginald's but yours. You're Prince Kerwin's daughter."

"Bastard daughter." She smiled, a pro at hiding the hurt. "There's a world of difference between the two. Believe me. That's why I find it difficult to believe that someone wants to kill me. I'm important to no one, especially my sire."

Hearing her own words, she winced. She hadn't meant to reveal so much to this employee of Silvershire's royal family.

"I still think the attack was because you're carrying Reginald's baby."

"Why would that matter? Reginald and I were not married. My child," she swallowed, forcing herself to say the hateful words, "is illegitimate." Like her. "A bastard child can never be heir. Believe me, I should know that better than anyone."

"True, but the playing field has changed. The prince is dead. Your child is the last of the royal bloodline."

"I care little about that. Being a princess has only brought me discomfort and unwanted attention."

"Unwanted?" He still watched her closely. "Is that why you haven't gone to the newspapers or granted a television interview?"

He sounded incredulous, but then he was in public relations. Nothing would be more important to him than the press.

She couldn't tell him she didn't want to be like her own mother, who seemed to spend much of her life courting reporters, while Sydney had been, until Reginald, able to skirt the edges of their radar. She'd like to return to her former quiet life, if possible. "I'd prefer to avoid notoriety."

His incredulous expression told her he didn't believe her. "You're saying you'd actually shun the limelight? You're an illegitimate princess who's been largely overlooked. Until now. I know how this works. You'll bask in your fifteen minutes of fame, just like anyone else."

Like any other groupie, he meant. As her mother had been. Still was, as far as she knew. Sydney no longer spoke to her mother. "I repeat, I'd prefer a quiet life."

"You could make a lot of money exploiting this."

"I have plenty of money," she said stiffly. "My sire set up a trust fund for me. And, as I'm sure you know, I play cello with the Naessa Royal Symphony."

"True, but now you'll have a child to support. One can always use more money."

She looked out the window instead of attempting to dignify his comments with a response. They'd flown into dark clouds. Lightning flashed to the west, and rain splattered the jet's windows.

Inhaling, exhaling, she willed herself calm. Years of yoga, breathing exercises and even hypnosis had helped conquer her unreasonable terror of storms.

The jet banked sharply to the right.

An involuntary gasp escaped her.

Chase smiled reassuringly. "Don't worry. I think it's just

one of those sudden spring thunderstorms. If it had been forecast, we wouldn't have flown anywhere near it. I'm sure we'll go around. Franco's flown this jet a hundred times or more, and Dell's been his copilot for years."

Before he finished speaking, the jet dropped, a rapid bounce, pushing Sydney up and against the confines of her seat belt before she bounced back. "What the—?"

"Turbulence."

Since Chase's implacable face showed no signs of alarm, Sydney took his words at face value. His very serenity was soothing, though she found herself wondering if the man was ever alarmed at anything.

The rain began to pound them. Thunder boomed. Lightning flashed stronger and more often. It looked as though they'd flown right into the middle of the worst part of the storm.

"I thought you said he'd take us around?"

"I'm sure he's trying. We're climbing, can't you feel it? This must be a large storm, so he's probably trying to get above it instead of going around."

All logical and competent-sounding. Still, Sydney's gut instinct was sounding multiple alarms. Her absolute fear of storms came roaring back, intensified by the fact she was being tossed around in a small jet.

She took a deep, shaky breath. "It's green outside."

For the first time, Chase frowned. "That's not good."

Her stomach plummeted. Was that the understatement of the year? She gripped her seat, closed her eyes, and muttered a prayer. When she opened her eyes, she immediately looked to Chase. He watched her intently.

"You're absolutely terrified." He sounded surprised.

Wordless with fear, she jerked her head in a nod.

"It's going to be all right. Look." He pointed out the window. "We're still climbing. Soon we should be above the storm."

Even as he spoke, the first hail hit them. Small, round balls of ice began battering the wings. Next came what sounded like a series of pops in rapid succession. Outside, the ice balls grew larger, more numerous, pummeling the wings. The jet veered left, then right.

"We've got to give Franco and Dell credit." Admiration sounded in Chase's clear tone. "They're still climbing."

The air outside her window became all ice balls, so many it appeared to be a blizzard of ice.

Bam. Sydney jumped, gripping the sides of her seat so tightly her hands ached. "That sounded like a small explosion." She'd barely finished the words when the jet plummeted again. Muttering another quick prayer under her breath, she bit her lip to stifle a scream, unable to resist glancing at Chase for reassurance.

Though expressionless, the tight set of his jaw told her he was worried, too.

The dive lasted longer this time. It seemed, she thought, fighting the first edges of panic, to go on forever.

Were they about to crash into the ocean? Or worse, into the mountainous edge of Silvershire? She had no idea where they were or what might be below them.

Then again, if they crashed at this speed, what they hit wouldn't really matter.

Finally the plane leveled.

Sydney exhaled in relief.

"Despite his attempt to climb, I think we've lost a lot of altitude." Chase sounded calm, matter-of-fact, as though none of this worried him. "I'd better go talk to Franco." He pushed himself out of his seat and the plane lurched, then took another violent drop.

He lost his balance and stumbled toward Sydney.

Wide-eyed, she reacted instinctively, throwing up her arms. He stopped with his face inches from her breasts.

God help her, she could feel her face heating.

Slowly, he raised his head to meet her gaze. She could have sworn she saw a flicker of amusement in his hazel eyes before he climbed back to his feet. "My apologies."

Tongue-tied, she dipped her head in acknowledgment.

"Wait here," he ordered, making his way to the cockpit.

As if she planned on going anywhere! She grimaced as the jet pitched and bobbed. If she had a parachute, she'd definitely consider jumping. She flexed her shoulders, feeling tension knots as she stared at the closed cockpit door.

A moment later, Chase returned. His expression looked even grimmer, if such a thing was possible.

She straightened, her aches forgotten. "What? What's wrong?"

"Not good. We've lost an engine. The hail must have damaged it."

Her heart stopped. "What now?"

"Franco and Dell are good. They're searching for a place to make an emergency landing. They'll get us down safely."

"With one engine?"

"Yes. We'll be fine."

Swallowing, she pushed back her panic. She'd traveled a lot with the symphony, and knew this wasn't great, but it wasn't lethal.

Thunder boomed again, so loudly the jet shook. A jagged bolt of lightning flashed so close she wondered how it had missed them. Though the hail had tapered off and was mixed with driving rain, the storm's fury scared her almost as much as the possibility of crashing.

"Talk to me." Not caring that her desperation showed in her voice, she touched his arm. "I need a distraction."

Another man might have made light of her fear. But Chase took one look at her and nodded. "Tell me about your family."

She had no family. "I'd rather hear about yours. Do you have brothers and sisters?"

"I have two brothers and two sisters." He smiled fondly. "We're a noisy, affectionate bunch. They're all married now, and their spouses are part of the family, as well."

"But you've never been married?" Gripping her seat, she wondered why she'd asked, but as the plane did another hop-and-skip movement and she felt her stomach come up in her throat, she realized she didn't care.

"No," he said, his expression closed. For a moment she could have sworn she saw a flash of anger and hurt in his eyes, and she wondered.

Then she remembered. She'd read about him a few years back. Chase might work at keeping the royal family out of the news, but that meant his own life was up for public scrutiny, as well.

"You were engaged," she said slowly. "To the daughter of an earl. I remember now. And there was some sort of scandal, involving another—"

"Yes." His harsh voice cut at her like a knife. "I was engaged. It didn't work out. No need to rehash all the details."

There had been a baby, Sydney remembered. Another man's child, though the woman had tried to pass it off as his to get him to marry her. The wedding ceremony had actually started when the woman's lover, a high-ranking duke from Gastonia, had interrupted, claiming both the woman and the baby as his rather than Chase's. While flashbulbs popped and cameras whirled, Chase had learned the truth. In front of the entire world, he'd been jilted.

The repercussions had nearly cost him his job. Though he'd presented a stone face to any and all questions, and had since cut a wide swath through Silvershire's female population, Sydney knew how badly he must have been hurting.

After all, she could certainly relate.

"Did you love her?" she asked softly.

Instead of answering, he narrowed his eyes. "Did you love Reginald? Did you truly believe he was the one you'd spend the rest of your life loving?"

Throat tight, she nodded.

Emotion flashed in his gaze. Rage or torment, she couldn't tell which. "Then I think we're about equal, aren't we? We both know what it's like to be played for a fool."

As she opened her mouth to apologize, a dark-haired man appeared in the doorway of the cockpit. The copilot, Dell. All the color seemed to have drained from his face.

"Chase." One word, then he went back to his controls.

Instantly, Chase unbuckled and took off for the front of the plane. While he was gone, though the jet seemed steadier, she could have sworn they now descended rather than climbed.

An eternity seemed to pass before he returned.

His expression hard, he stood staring at her for a moment before dropping down into his seat and refastening the seat belt.

"Chase?" She touched his arm. "What did he want?"

"To give me bad news." The gaze that met hers was

bleak. "If you're a praying person, you'd better start now. Though he's bringing us down to try and land, the other engine has sustained damage, too. Franco doesn't know how much longer it will last."

She stared at him, a stranger until that very morning, and twice the bearer of bad news. "We're going to crash?"

A muscle worked in his jaw. "It certainly looks that way."

God help her, she didn't want to die the same way she'd lived her life—alone. But she wasn't alone, she had her baby. Her unborn child.

Once, music had been enough. She'd thought her art was her life, her reason for existence, her sole, all-consuming passion. The weight and solid feel of her cello, the pure, smooth sound of her gleaming horsehair bow gliding across the strings, had been her everything. Until now.

Now her baby mattered more than anything.

She had to live so her child could be born. Grabbing Chase's hand, she gripped his fingers. "I can't believe this. I'm not ready."

He unhooked his seat belt. "Come here."

"What?" She stared blankly. "What do you mean?"

His expression compassionate, he pushed the buckle and freed her from her own restraint. "Come here."

Still she resisted. "But isn't it safer to stay buckled in?"

"Maybe. Maybe not. But there's no way in hell either of us need to go through this alone. Now come here."

He pulled her out of her seat and into his arms.

At first, she held herself stiffly. But the human need for contact and comfort outweighed any other considerations and she relaxed. Chase was bigger than she'd expected, and the lean hardness of his body felt reassuring.

Heart pounding, she let her shoulder rest against his chest. Once she'd settled in, arms around his neck, his around her waist, he refastened his seat belt so they were secured together.

"Okay?" he asked.

She nodded, trying to keep her breathing even, resisting the impulse to gulp air, knowing if she started hyperventilating, she'd pass out. And she didn't want that. If there was a way to save herself and her baby, she needed to stay awake and take it.

The plane bucked and, once again, straightened itself out. Sydney released a breath she hadn't even been aware of holding, and a tremor shook her.

"Steady." His deep voice rumbled from his chest. Under her ear, his heartbeat pounded.

She looked up at him, a stranger, a rugged, beautiful man, and caught herself wishing she'd met him earlier, at another time and place. "I don't want to die."

"Me neither. I'm just hoping Franco and Dell can bring us down safely."

"Isn't there anything else we can do?"

"Yeah." A ghost of a grim smile crossed his face. "Pray."

The plane took another odd skip and it seemed their descent had become a plunge.

Sydney shuddered.

Chase smoothed her hair with his tanned hand. "Take it easy. They've still got it under control."

The lights winked out. The interior of the cabin went black.

Chapter 3

Something burning…smoke. Sydney tossed her head restlessly, sure she was dreaming, but wondering why she hurt so badly.

Experimentally, she moved. And groaned. She ached, she hurt and she felt as if she'd been pummeled senseless by an angry giant with a hard fist.

Her baby! Opening her eyes, she found she was lying on craggy rocks, too close to the gently lapping waves for comfort. Smoke billowed from a cluster of trees nearby, and she smelled the acrid scent of aviation gas.

Jet fuel.

She was soaked, as though she'd been in the water and somehow made her way to the shore. Since she had no conscious memory of doing so, she was lucky she hadn't drowned.

Lifting her head, she winced as pain lanced through

her. She touched her aching shoulder. Her hand came away sticky with blood. Blinking, she stared at her red fingers, and bit back a sob. What on earth…?

A piece of metal looked as though it had been stabbed into the ground nearby.

The plane crash!

Though it hurt, she turned her head again, toward the smoke, looking for Chase. Was he there, near the fire?

"Chase?" She tried to yell, but her voice would only croak. She had to get up, get over there, and see if she could help rescue him or Franco and Dell.

Swallowing, wincing as even that small movement hurt, Sydney told herself she had to get up, move away from the ever-encroaching waves and find Chase.

She couldn't make her body move. She lifted her head, trying to see the rest of her, to ascertain whether she'd been injured worse than she knew. Apart from her aching head and stiff neck, and the now-throbbing cut on her side, she felt no other actual pains.

Then why couldn't she push herself to her feet?

A small explosion rocked the beach. More smoke billowed out from behind the row of trees. The jet, most likely. She should be glad she'd been thrown farther away.

Thrown. All at once, the staggering truth of what had happened hit her. Miraculously, she'd survived a plane crash.

So far.

She refused to think anything negative. She was alive. That counted for a lot. From the looks of things, it appeared she might be the only one who had survived. She and the tiny, precious life growing inside her. She could only pray her unborn child was all right. At least she had no cuts on her abdomen, no aches or bloodstains to indicate she'd miscarried.

Her baby *had* to be all right. More than anything, she prayed her unborn child had not been injured.

She finally struggled to her feet. Standing, weaving, she licked her lip and tasted blood and salt and sweat. Thirsty, so thirsty. She swayed, her vision blurry, and then forced herself to focus. Focus. Live.

A blur moved toward her, moving fast in the blinding sunlight. An animal? No, a man. Running toward her. Shielding her eyes against the sun, she squinted as she tried to make him out.

Chase? Her heart rate tripled. Could it be? She rubbed her blurry eyes and again attempted to focus. Yes, Chase. Moving toward her. Whole. Unhurt.

Glancing down at herself, she winced at her bloody, torn blouse. She swayed again, dropping to her knees. Damn, her head hurt. She might be injured there, too.

"Sydney!" Chase. Blinking, she lifted her head and attempted a feeble wave.

He ran toward her. His lips moved, but she couldn't understand his words. She stared at him, resisting the urge to reach out her hand and sob in relief. He'd made it through the crash in even better shape than she. Except for a still-bleeding, jagged cut on his leg, he appeared to be unhurt.

Good. Then maybe he could help her, until rescue arrived.

Her last conscious memory was of Chase scooping her up in his strong arms.

When the plane went down, damned if Chase's first thought wasn't for the woman. Maybe it was the part of him that would always be a bodyguard, but he'd known he needed to shelter her, protect her and keep her safe, even if it took his own life to do so.

Then everything went black as they'd hit.

When he'd come to in the midst of the smoking wreckage, smelling jet fuel and feeling the searing heat of the fire, Sydney was nowhere to be found. He'd known he had to get out of there before the whole thing blew, but first, he'd looked for the others.

Franco and Dell were dead. After swiftly ascertaining there was no hope for them, Chase knew he didn't have time to drag their bodies from the smoldering wreckage. He needed to get out quickly, aware an explosion was imminent.

He saw no sign of Sydney.

He crawled from the battered jet and, after looking around once more, Chase took off at a run. He made it a hundred yards before the thing exploded, knocking him to the sand.

On all fours, he said a quick prayer for the two dead men. Then he stood and brushed dirt and gravel from his legs. Most of his cuts and scratches appeared to be minor. One wound on his knee bled but he felt no pain.

He began by searching the immediate area around the wreckage. They'd come down in a hilly area, clipping the tops of the massive trees before crashing near the rocky beach.

Sydney—or her body—had to be here somewhere. They'd been strapped in together. How they'd been separated in the final moments, he couldn't begin to speculate.

She wasn't anywhere near the wreckage. Next, he expanded the search area, more and more worried when he still couldn't locate her. The forest area was thick and wild;

still he searched through the dense foliage with no luck. While searching, he came across a spring-fed pond and noted its location. A source of drinkable water would be vital to their survival if they weren't rescued quickly.

As he ranged the perimeter of the woods, pushing aside thorns and vines and undergrowth, he drew closer and closer to the rocky shoreline. As he began to scan the rocks near the water, he heard a hoarse cry up the beach.

There—past the larger boulders, too close to the gently pounding surf, Sydney! When she attempted to rise and sank back down to all fours, his heart stuttered.

"I'm coming!" he yelled, taking off at a run toward the ocean. When he reached her, she tried again to stand.

Bleeding from her wounds and weak, she fainted in his arms.

But she was alive. That was all that mattered.

Carrying her back to the shade of the forest, he lowered her gently to a pile of leaves. Lifting her torn blouse, he ran his hands over her, searching for broken bones and finding none. If she had internal injuries, that would be another matter and much more difficult to detect.

She moaned, shifting fitfully. She had a nasty cut on her shoulder, another on the back of her head, though it looked worse than it was due to the way head wounds bled.

If she had a concussion, which seemed highly likely, he couldn't let her remain unconscious.

"Sydney, wake up."

No response.

Chase heaved a sigh and lifted her to her feet. Her deep-blue eyes opened, cloudy with confusion.

"Come on, we've got to walk." Still bearing the brunt of her weight, he half dragged, half carried her into the forest, toward the pond he'd found earlier. If he could get Sydney there, they could wash off the blood, making it easier to judge the true extent of her wounds.

"Walk?" She shook her head, trying to drop back to the ground. She would have succeeded, but he kept his arm around her waist. "No. I want to sleep."

"No can do." He let her lean on him while they pressed through the undergrowth, and he did a rapid assessment of the situation.

Plane down, two survivors. No working radio; at least, the one in the jet had blown with it. His cell phone had disappeared in the crash—with his luck it had fallen into the ocean. And, though they'd filed a flight plan when they'd left Silvershire, he didn't know if the storm had taken them off course or how far.

They were on some sort of island. Though small, it appeared hospitable. The place was most likely some rich bastard's private getaway, though the area where the plane had gone down didn't appear cultivated. Chase resolved to explore it later, especially if rescue took some time.

All their hope would be on the jet's emergency beacon. Even if it had been damaged or destroyed in the fire, a signal should have already gone out to lead rescuers to them.

Or the bad guys, assuming they had someone on the inside. They had to be extremely careful.

Chase cursed again. He felt as though he was once again in Special Forces, on some kind of covert mission, rather than the head of Silvershire's Department of Public Relations. More than anything, he wanted a working cell phone. He needed to get in touch with the office and fill them in.

He could only imagine the public relations nightmare going on back home. Since Reginald had died, he'd bet things had gone to hell in a handbasket. With so much going on, Chase needed to be back in Silvershire *now.*

He lived for his work. Except for the brief derailment when he'd thought he'd fallen in love with Kayla Bright, he'd focused his entire life on his job. Always had, always would.

Now, stranded on an island with the one woman the press would be salivating over, he'd been rendered virtually useless. Public relations was difficult to manage when one had no contact with the public.

As he thought of the press, circling like sharks in search of a meal, he realized he'd now become a potential story. Once the reporters realized he and the beautiful woman who carried the prince's son were lost together, they'd be fabricating the stories as fast as the papers could print them.

Christ. Carrington would be furious; he might even feel betrayed. After what had happened with Kayla… Chase shuddered. He'd thought he'd loved her enough to ask her to become his wife. When she'd tricked him into believing another man's baby was his and then jilted him publicly, his own personal anguish had been splashed all over the papers. His infatuation with Kayla had nearly cost him his job once. Only Carrington's interference had saved him and his tattered reputation.

Never again.

This situation had too many common denominators.

Such publicity, even if unwarranted, was exactly the kind of derailment Chase's career didn't need.

He shook his head. Silvershire—and his job—seemed thousands of miles away. Now, stuck for God knows how long on this deserted island, staying alive took precedence over anything else.

Sydney stumbled and nearly fell. The wound on her neck had started bleeding again. Her expensive outfit, torn and dirty and bloodstained, was ruined. Since she had nothing else to wear, all he could do was see what parts of it were salvageable. Either that, or else she'd have to run around using leaves to cover herself, like Eve outside the Garden of Eden. A sudden mental image of Sydney, her sleek curves glistening in the sunlight, nearly had him staggering.

Luckily, he was able to regain his balance.

Finally, they reached the pond. At the edge of the water, he stopped. Sydney looked up at him, her dazed expression telling him she might be going into shock.

"Are you all right?" he asked, his tone gentle.

She licked her lips and tried twice before finally answering. "I think so."

"We're going to get into the water here and get cleaned up. I'll hold on to you, I promise." He took the first step forward, pleased when she moved with him.

The first step took them in up to her waist.

She gasped and began shivering. "Cold!"

"Not really." He knew he had to hurry, because victims of shock had to be kept warm. "Hold still and let me clean you off."

Teeth chattering, she did as he asked. He told himself as he swept his hands over her wet skin, that his touch was impersonal. Nevertheless, his hands on the curve of her hips, her flat belly, felt as if they were touching forbidden fruit. When he accidentally brushed her full breasts and felt her nipples hard against his palm, his body responded, despite the cool water temperature.

He concentrated on cleaning her up and ignored his libido's bad timing.

"I need you to put your head under the water," he said. "Do you want me to dunk you or can you do it yourself?"

Though she still shivered violently, when she looked at him he saw her gaze had cleared. "I can do it, if you hold on to me."

At his nod, she gulped air and dropped under. When she resurfaced, slicking her hair back from her face, his breath caught in his throat. Damned if she didn't look like some primitive nymph, sleek skin gleaming in the dappled sunlight. The shreds of her wet clothing clung to her body and outlined every hollow, every curve.

He was so hard he hurt.

Self-directed anger made him gruff. "Good enough." Helping her up onto the bank, he tried to ignore the way his hand cupped her rounded bottom. Once he was certain she'd be okay, he dived under himself, swimming with powerful strokes to the middle of the pond. Here, he trod water, reminding himself to come back later and explore the depth.

As soon as he had his body under control again, he emerged. Sydney sat, huddled into a wet ball, shivering.

"Let's get you back into the sunlight to warm you."

Docilely, she allowed him to lead her back to the beach area, where he sat her on a huge boulder in full sun.

Now, he needed to see what he could do to make them shelter.

A large side section of the jet had landed on the rocky beach. It would make a decent roof, much better than any primitive thatch thing he might attempt to construct from leaves and sticks.

He grabbed the section of metal and started dragging it toward the trees. It was heavier than he'd realized.

As he moved it inch by inch, dragging it over rocky ground, he wondered how long they'd have to wait until rescue arrived. He refused to consider the possibility that someone else might get here first.

Sydney opened her eyes to find Chase watching her closely, his hazel gaze unreadable. She licked her lips and he handed her a tin cup of water. "The cup is left from what remains of the jet's galley. I found several of them—and a spring-fed pond—near the interior of this island."

She sipped gratefully, her throat still raw. "My baby…"

He looked away, obviously ill at ease. Instead of answering a question that could not be answered, he tried to distract her. "I found your purse, too." He held up the black Fendi. "Remarkably intact. Not even a scratch."

Throat aching, chest tight, she nodded. She really didn't care about the purse, other than being glad to have her passport. She had more important matters to think about. Until she could get to a hospital, she had no idea if her baby was all right. "How long have I been out?"

"You drifted in and out all of last night. I've been keeping watch. When you finally fell into a real sleep, I slept some. Now it's morning." Again he glanced at his wrist, then gave a wry smile. "Though I don't know the exact time. Your watch is gone, too."

"That's okay." She sat up, waiting for dizziness and felt absurdly pleased when the earth didn't spin. They were in some kind of small shelter, made of bits and pieces of the crashed jet. He'd piled sticks and branches near one side, no doubt for when they needed to build a fire. "Where are the pilots?"

"They're both dead. When the cockpit exploded, they

burned." A shadow crossed Chase's rugged face. He had a good five-o'clock-shadow going, which had the effect of making him look even more dangerously masculine. He was so beautiful, looking at him made her chest hurt.

Sydney shook her head. She'd survived a plane crash, minor injuries, and felt like her insides had been scrambled. Had the bump on her head permanently addled her wits? She focused instead on his words, remembering the blond man who'd flown the jet. "I'm sorry."

Chase looked away. "I wanted to bury them, but I couldn't get them out in time." His low voice was tight, controlled, but she thought she could detect an undercurrent of grief.

Wincing, she nodded. "How long before someone comes for us?"

Chase raised his head and met her gaze again. "I don't know. The jet's radio was broken. My cell phone's gone. I have no way to contact anyone. All I can hope is the plane's emergency beacon did its job."

Still woozy, she pushed to her feet, waving him away when he tried to steady her. "We can stand up in here." The shelter he'd improvised for them was nothing short of amazing. He'd anchored pieces of metal from the jet between three trees, using the middle one as a brace. It looked, she thought, quite sturdy, considering.

He saw her looking and shrugged. "It'll do until we're rescued."

She seized on his words, allowing them to give her hope. "I'm sure it will," she told him. "Provided rescue comes soon."

She stepped out from under the shelter to brilliant sunshine. Shading her eyes with her hand, she glanced toward the beach, noting the way the sun reflected off the sea. "So we have water, but what about food? Would it be too much to hope some food survived the crash?"

"A few packets of crackers. That's it. But I've seen some small game in the woods. And of course, there are fish."

"Can you hunt?"

He gave her a supremely male look of arrogance. "Of course I can hunt. I fish, too. We won't starve, if it comes to that." He coughed. "But my cooking is abysmal."

"Cooking's no problem. I can cook." Pushing her hair back from her face, she busied herself organizing the wood in a neat stack. "That is, if you can figure out a way to make a fire."

"You can cook?"

"Yes." She raised her head to look at him. "Why do you sound so surprised?"

"I don't know. Maybe Naessa is different than Silvershire. I would have thought you had your own army of chefs, ready to make whatever exotic dish you fancied."

"Not in my household. I live alone, and like it that way."

"Hmmm." The sound he made told her he didn't believe her. "I watch the news, read the papers. You grew up with every luxury money can buy. Your run with the elite upper crust."

"That was college." She smiled, trying to pretend she cherished the memory. "We've lost touch since then." The truth of the matter was, none of the wealthy friends who'd permitted her to hang with them could relate to her life now. Playing cello for the symphony was, as one jet-setting type had put it, boring. Endless practices and performances left no time for partying.

"Still," he persisted. "Your mother is in the news quite

often. You grew up with chefs, maids and butlers. I find it surprising you know how to cook."

"Even cooks get a day or two off. My mother liked to keep me busy. Until she packed me off to boarding school, I was my mother's personal chef." The instant she'd finished speaking, she realized what she'd said. More than she'd revealed to anyone about her childhood, ever. Including Reginald. Especially Reginald.

So why now? Why Chase, who was still a virtual stranger?

He cocked his head, regarding her with a speculative look. "Still, you're quite wealthy. You mentioned a trust fund earlier. Did your father set you up with that?"

Common knowledge, especially for someone in public relations. "Yes."

"But according to the press, you and your father aren't close."

"True." She dipped her chin. "The trust fund is the only thing my sire ever did for me. He has other children, by his wife. I don't know them."

"You never refer to him as father, always sire. Why?"

"He never was a father to me."

"Yet you're still his child, still the daughter of a prince. You must have something in common."

"Illegitimate daughter." She tried to keep the bitterness from her voice. "There's a big difference. Actually, I've never even met the man."

Then, because talking about it still hurt, even after all these years, she took a hesitant step forward. When her legs held, she tried another. Gaining confidence, she moved out from under their shelter and crashed off through the underbrush into the shadowy forest.

"Where are you going?" he called after her.

"To gather more firewood." She tossed the lie over her shoulder.

After a moment, Chase followed. "Sydney, I—"

"Seriously, I'd rather be alone. Shouldn't you be fishing or hunting or something?"

He came up alongside her, moving so swiftly and quietly he startled her. He grabbed her arm. Annoyed, she stopped and glared up at him. He'd moved so fast she hadn't been able to avoid him. His face was in shadow, making it difficult to read his expression.

"You're right. I should be fishing or hunting." But he made no move to go.

Absurdly, she wanted to hurl herself into his arms and let him hold her while she cried. She looked at him, tried to speak, and found herself sobbing.

He made the move to gather her close. "Shh."

Stiffly, she let him hold her while she cried. Would being in a man's arms always be her salvation? She wasn't her mother.

At that thought, she pushed herself away from him. But he wouldn't let her go.

"It's all right. We've survived a plane crash. I know you're worried about your baby." His voice sounded calm, but she could hear his pounding heartbeat under her ear. His chest rose and fell with each breath, and she realized his arousal mirrored her own dawning awareness of him as a man.

"I…" Lifting her head, she saw desire blazing in his eyes, need harsh in his handsome face.

"Chase?" She froze.

"Adrenaline," he ground out the word. "Natural reaction. We're alive, after all, and we only feel the need to prove it."

Was he trying to convince her, or himself?

But he was right. Primitive, fierce desire shook her. Irrational, maybe, but she wanted him. Boldly, she skimmed her hands up his muscular chest. He responded with a sharp intake of breath. Moving closer, as though she'd climb inside him if she could, she felt his arousal against her belly and shuddered.

Standing on tiptoe, she pressed a whispery kiss against his throat, tasting the salt of his sweat on his skin.

"Sydney?" He sounded like a man in torment. "Be careful what you start."

But she couldn't think, couldn't rationalize. Urgency driving her, she tilted her head back and looked up at him, letting him read her own need in her face. "Kiss me, Chase. Now."

With a half groan, half oath, he complied. Demanding, he covered her mouth with his, using his tongue to force her lips apart so he could enter.

Her arousal grew as his pirate's kiss plundered her mouth.

Lost in a fog of desire, at first she didn't react when he pushed her away, holding her at arm's length.

"If we do this now, we'll be sorry for it later." His dark look told her he already regretted things had gone so far. But his body—his magnificent, fully aroused body—told her differently.

She swallowed hard, her chest rising and falling with each jagged breath. Part of her wanted to fling herself at him, knowing he wouldn't be able to resist a second time.

But luckily, rationality conquered desire, and she nodded. "You can let me go," she said, her voice tight and controlled, though her body still tingled. "I promise I won't touch you again."

His pulse beat in his throat. He held her gaze for a long moment, his hands still on her arms, so close she could feel the heat radiate from his body.

"Don't make promises you can't keep." With that, he released her, striding off toward the shoreline. For one absurd moment she thought of chasing after him. Instead, she stayed in the shadowy woods, watching him with her heart in her throat and wondered what had happened to her pride.

Chapter 4

Sydney gathered as many sticks as she could find, knowing they could always use more firewood, while keeping her eye out for berries or anything recognizably edible.

She wanted to go home, to her townhouse in Tice, on Naessa's western shore. She wanted her own doctor, a thorough examination, then a huge dinner of pasta and bread.

Since none of those things were immediately forthcoming, she concentrated on what she could have. A meal of freshly caught fish or wild game. A way to get through an uncomfortable evening with a man who both despised and desired her.

And she felt the same, God only knew why.

Shaking her head, she continued gathering wood and prayed rescue would come soon, before she disgraced herself even further.

Later, when he returned with two dead rabbits dangling

from his hands, she eyed the poor things and nearly gagged. It was one thing to think about eating wild game and another thing entirely to have to actually do it.

Something must have shown on her face.

"Remember, you have to eat. After all, you're eating for two," he said.

"I know." She pointed to her impressive pile of sticks. "How are you at starting fires?"

He frowned. "I don't think rubbing two sticks together will work without flint. Or," he reached in his pocket with his free hand, "I can use this." He held up a silver lighter, flashing a grin.

After a moment of stunned amazement—he was so damn beautiful when he smiled—Sydney shook her head and chuckled, too. "I didn't know you smoked."

"I don't. I found this near the wreckage. It must have belonged to Franco or Dell."

Soon he had a small fire going. Despite her initial misgivings, the wild hare tasted better than she'd expected, and she finished hers quickly, licking the remaining fat from her fingers.

They sat in companionable silence, watching the bright orange sun sink toward the horizon. Clouds were gathering to the west, dark ominous clouds, making her shiver.

"There's a storm brewing out over the ocean." Chase must have seen her looking. "We can only hope it will miss us."

A storm. Sydney shivered. Already she could smell the scent of rain in the air. The atmosphere fairly buzzed with electricity. *Great.* She'd promised not to touch him again, and all she could think was how much safer she'd feel in his arms.

Chase Savage. A man she barely knew.

A quick glance at him, relaxing on his elbows by their

small fire, told her he was completely unaware of her irrational fear. She studied his muscular arms and long legs, and pushed away a stab of desire.

In the distance, thunder rumbled.

Heart pounding, she jumped to her feet.

He looked up in surprise. "Where're you going?"

Carefully, she avoided looking at him. "For a walk, I think."

"Don't be gone too long." He went back to watching the fire. "That storm will be here in less than an hour."

Hesitating, she thought about telling him of her fear, the sharp terror that overtook her in the midst of a storm. But knowing he'd believe the worst of her no matter what she said, she held her tongue and moved off down the beach. Skimming rocks into the waves, she watched the storm march closer across the sky and trembled, trying to conquer her anxiety

Scooping up a flat stone, she aimed and flipped her wrist. Another rock hit the ocean with a plop. She hadn't ever gotten the hang of skimming them across the water either.

Dry-eyed, chest aching, she looked over her shoulder at the small fire. In the dim light of dusk, she could just barely make out his silhouette, now sitting upright, adding sticks to the flames.

Alone.

To paraphrase one of her mother's favorite country and western songs, she felt so lonesome she could cry.

She shouldn't feel like this—after all, she was used to being by herself. Solitary. When she'd been a child, her own mother had refused to hold her. Sydney had gotten what comfort she could from an endless parade of nannies. After losing one too many beloved nannies, she had retreated into her own newfound shell. Comfortable there, she'd believed she'd made a good life, a safe life, insulated from hurt. She'd believed she was happy.

Until Prince Reginald had come along. Then, with his honeyed words and silken touch, he'd made her realize there was more to life than simply existing. A few months of his false adoration, and the walls she'd so carefully constructed around herself had crumbled, allowing a surprisingly passionate woman to emerge from the ruins.

Now, in the process of learning to rebuild those damned walls, just for tonight she longed to rip them away and toss them into the ocean.

None of this made sense.

So she walked and tossed rocks and, as the sky darkened and the sound of thunder grew louder, trembled and tried to figure out what she was going to do.

Chase waited until it was nearly dark to go look for her. Then, irritation fueled by frustration, he went after her.

For a woman who'd been Prince Reginald's plaything, passion certainly appeared to surprise Sydney Conner. Of course, this could all be a game to her, a way to amuse herself until they were rescued and she could return to her manicures and designer clothing. Chase's experience had taught him beautiful women were like that.

But Sydney seemed…different. More innocent, somehow. Shaking his head, Chase snorted. Kayla had convinced him she was different, too, once upon another life. He'd even believed her when she'd told him the baby she'd carried was his. He'd vowed to be careful whom he trusted after he'd learned Kayla had lied.

Careful? Once again, he burned for a woman. He desired Sydney Conner. Plain and simple. Even knowing she'd been the prince's lover and carried Reginald's baby, he wanted her.

He kept to the shelter of the trees, and the first raindrops splattered the leaves as the outer edge of the storm reached the island. Lightning flashed and thunder rumbled across the dark sky, briefly reminding him of the horrific moments before the royal jet had crashed.

Where was Sydney?

The next flash of lightning illuminated her, running toward the forest over the rocky beach. The rain began to pelt him in earnest as he took off for her. They met halfway, which told him she'd seen him at the same time he'd seen her.

Some old television commercial with two people leaping into each other's arms flashed into his mind. Damn, he had it bad. He forced himself to slow his pace.

Drenched, they skidded to a stop in front of each other. Eyes wide and haunted, she pushed her soaked hair away from her face and wrapped her arms around her thin waist.

Chase cleared his throat. "Are you all right?"

She nodded. "Yes, I think so. I have this thing about storms."

"Follow me." He had to shout to be heard over the roar of the downpour.

They ran through the deluge, lightning flashing all around them. The wind drove the rain in sheets, making it difficult to see. When they reached the shelter, he was relieved to see it still stood, despite the storm's fury.

At the entrance, she hesitated, glancing back at him while water ran down her face in rivulets. "I—"

"Come on." Hand in the small of her back, he helped her inside. Out of the rain, the small space felt warmer.

"How long do you think this storm will last?" The tremor in her voice could have been because she was cold.

"It's huge. This is just the leading edge. I think the waves will surge, so it's a good thing we're sheltered up here, away from the beach."

Still as a statue, she stood motionless in the dark, dripping and shivering. Only a few feet separated them. He wanted to wrap her in his arms and let their combined body heat warm them, but hesitated. "Are you all right?"

"We're surrounded by metal," she said, teeth chattering. "Is it safe to be here while there's lightning?"

The rain beat steadily on the metal roof, but the rough structure held. "Safer than outside in that storm."

He could have sworn he heard her whimper low in her throat. "Sydney?"

Pulling his lighter from his pocket, he clicked it on. In the second of light the flame provided, he saw her pale, pinched face, the terror in her dilated eyes. "You're really frightened."

She made a strangled sound of assent.

He fought the urge to take her in his arms. "Don't be afraid."

"I have a thing about storms," she told him, her voice shaking. "Once, when I was a child, I was in a sailboat during a storm. The boat capsized. I almost drowned. Since then, I've always been terrified of them."

Ah, damn. One step closed the distance between them. Telling himself he would offer only comfort, he gathered her close. Violent tremors shook her and, soaked and be-draggled, her sleek skin felt like ice.

"It's all right," he murmured, sinking to the ground, his arms full of drenched woman, trying to warm her the only way he could.

Her shivers had become great shudders. She clung to him with a desperation that touched him, despite all he knew about her.

"I'm sorry." Her apology was low, her voice full of shame. "I'm so damn cold…"

He began to try and warm her in earnest, though he imagined the touch of his callused fingers felt downright sacrilegious as he rubbed them over her soft skin. The silky softness of her wet body, the curve and perfection of her form, told how far out of his league he was with a woman like her.

But she needed him now and, no matter what else he might have become, he would always have some bodyguard in him.

He prayed she wasn't aware of how much she turned him on.

Apparently not. Oblivious, head against his chest, she continued to tremble and clutch at him, gasping out loud when another crack of thunder and flash of lightning shook the earth.

"Shh." Attempting to soothe her, he continued to try and thaw her, to rub warmth back into her frozen limbs, while ignoring the heat that rose in him at the feel of her wrapped around him.

Disgusted with himself, he grabbed the lap blanket he'd salvaged from the wreckage and handed it to her.

"Get out of your wet clothes." His voice sounded like rusty nails. He prayed she wouldn't notice.

"Now? Here?" Her shocked tone made him smile, glad she couldn't see him in the darkness.

Gently, he eased her from his lap, and shifted to lessen the pressure brought on by his growing arousal. "Yes, here. Use the blanket to dry off. Then wrap up in it."

"Good idea." A moment later, the sound of her unzipping her ragged slacks had him gritting his teeth. Images of Sydney, sleek and naked in his arms, tormented him, adding to his physical discomfort.

Feeling like a voyeur, he listened as she peeled off her wet blouse, and held his breath as he imagined her unhooking her bra and freeing her lush breasts. He ached to reach out and cup them, so he clenched his hands into fists to keep from doing exactly that.

"There," she said, and sighed. "You're right. This blanket feels good. Much warmer."

He couldn't find his voice to answer, so he said nothing, listening to the storm, his heartbeat drumming in his ears, and the harsh sound of his uneven breathing.

Another crack of thunder, and the rain began to batter them. The accompanying flash of lightning showed Sydney, wrapped in the blanket and standing, body rigid, her eyes wide with silent terror.

Chase clenched his jaw. If he made it through this night without touching her, he should be awarded a medal.

"Come here," he told her, shifting to shield her from his raging erection. "Lie down and let me hold you."

"Thank you." She settled on the ground next to him.

Then, touching her with only his upper body, he wrapped his arm around her slender, blanket-wrapped shoulders, and wondered how the hell he was going to get any sleep.

Sydney opened her eyes, drowsy and comfortably warm. Outside, the storm still raged, but wrapped in Chase's muscular arms, her fear had vanished. The dim light told her morning had arrived.

And she was naked, curled up against his equally bare body. Instantly, she came awake, her heartbeat tripling.

Chase still slept, his chest rising with his deep and even breathing. With one arm, he kept her close to him, tucked spoonlike against him. Twisting slowly in his arms, she lay on her back and studied him. Even asleep, he was beautiful. The stubble on his chin made him look even more masculine, even more sexy.

She had no urge to move, nowhere to go. Content to watch him, she tried to figure out her own admittedly skewed logic. She and Chase. A man she barely knew, who'd made it quite plain what he thought of her.

If it weren't so damn pitiful, she'd laugh. Chalk one up to feeling extremely vulnerable. Not only did she consider her and her unborn baby's survival a miracle, but her companion on this deserted island was a drop-dead-gorgeous and sexy-as-hell man.

Another woman might have found this heaven. Sydney tried to decide if she was in hell. The last thing she—or her child—needed was another disastrous relationship.

It might have been better if she'd demanded he make her another shelter, but the truth of the matter was that she didn't want to be alone.

No, if she was being totally honest, the simple reality was she craved his kiss, his touch, his smile.

Chase.

When he touched her she felt like the most desirable woman on earth.

She was an idiot: lying here naked while her clothes, surely dry by now, lay within arm's reach of their makeshift bed.

But berating herself did little good. She was only human after all. Every time he shifted his body, she felt the movement vibrate along her nerve endings, straight to the inner core of her. The storm-moist air caressed her bare skin, and she felt hypersensitive. Everything—the rustle of the leaves underneath them, the rise and fall of his chest, his masculine scent, the way his tousled blond hair fell across his forehead—aroused her as she'd never been before.

He turned, still sleeping, and muttered something, too low for her to understand at first. A name? While she tried to puzzle that, he snuggled against her, his perfectly formed body pressed against the full length of hers. For an instant, she forgot to breathe.

Good Lord, how she wanted this man!

Tentatively, she stretched, rubbing herself against him like a starving cat. Her entire body tingled. Her breasts were tender and aching, and her pulse beat hot and heavy in places she'd never known it could.

Ah, temptation. One heartbeat away from continuing to move her body against him while he slept, she tried desperately to remember the reasons she shouldn't. But all she could think about was how badly she wanted to stroke him, caress him, and take him beyond the bounds of his control before he woke and rationality set in. A veritable feast of man sprawled out before her, Chase unknowingly lured her to do things she'd never before done, even with Reginald. She'd placed her hand against his chest and begun to trace it lower before she realized she'd moved.

Horrified, she froze. What was wrong with her? Yes, she was attracted to him. He was the most beautiful man she'd ever seen. What red-blooded woman wouldn't be?

But she wasn't like this. Sydney had always been different. Once, only once, had she given in to impulse and let Reginald's lies persuade her to his bed. And now she carried his child, the baby of another beautiful man who'd broken her heart.

Had she learned nothing from her mistake? Having been a fool once, was she doomed to act foolishly forever?

"Sydney?"

Her breath caught. With a gasp, she removed her hand from him. "Yes?"

"You're awake," he said, his voice husky with sleep or, she shivered, desire. His hazel eyes roamed over her, reminding her she was still naked, stretched out seductively, as if she'd been waiting for him to wake and make love to her.

In a way, she had.

Feeling her face heat, she rolled away and grabbed for her clothes. The tattered shorts, once her favorite pair of slacks, were still damp. She pulled them on anyway.

"Yes. The storm woke me," she said, struggling to yank her mostly dry blouse over her head.

Never taking his eyes from her, he sat up, dragging his hand through his hair. One corner of his mouth quirked in a smile. "Some storm. I'm glad this shelter held."

Even fully clothed, her heart still raced like a runaway rabbit. She cleared her throat. "So far, so good. Not even a single leak."

His gaze dropped lower, to her breasts, where her nipples pushed rebelliously against her ragged shirt. He gave a harsh intake of breath, his eyes darkening.

She couldn't help but wonder if he was as turned on as she.

No way was she finding out. Knowing how volatile the situation could become, she climbed to her feet and crossed her arms.

He tilted his head, squinting up at her. "Are you all right?"

"I'm fine." Her need still pulsed within her, making her ache. She tucked a wayward strand of hair behind her ear, wishing she could think of something to say, something to diffuse the fierce sexual tension making the air feel so heavy.

Chase sat up, drawing the blanket close and carefully wrapping it around him.

"Sydney, don't." Though husky, his voice sounded tight, controlled, much like the man himself most of the time. If not for the hunger in his eyes, she'd think him unaffected. "Don't try to seduce me."

Seduce him? If he only knew how badly she wanted to and how hard she'd tried to resist him. She swallowed. "I'm not."

Narrowing his gaze, he raked his hand through his hair. He looked away and cursed. "I don't know what it is about you. I even see the promise of sex in your smile."

"Sex in my smile?" Though she tossed his words back at him, a thrill ran through her at his words. "That sounds lovely, but it's ridiculous. I've done nothing to entice you. I wouldn't know how! I've never tried to seduce anyone in my life."

He clenched his jaw and got to his feet, keeping the damn blanket snug around his waist. "But you have. Maybe you don't realize it, but everything about you is a seduction. The way you move, the way you toss your head. Your smile, your voice…" Cursing under his breath, he took a step toward her and stopped, hands clenched at his sides. "You'd tempt a dead man straight into hell."

"I—"

"I'm not finished. When I first saw you, I wondered. You weren't Reginald's usual type. But now I can better understand what the prince saw in you."

Reginald. Hearing that name was like a dash of cold

water. If Chase had wanted to hurt her, he'd succeeded admirably. Together, she and Reginald had created another life, and he'd spurned her. Not just her, but all of it. The man hadn't wanted his own child. Exactly as her sire hadn't wanted her.

She should be used to rejection, honestly. But that didn't stop it from hurting. Hot tears stung the back of her throat. Damn hormones. She turned away, fist to her mouth.

Behind her, Chase snarled. "One mention of Reginald and that's enough to bring you to tears? Did you truly care for him that much?"

He sounded furious. And hurt. Which was impossible. Either way, Sydney knew she shouldn't care. Didn't care. Hell, she *wouldn't* care.

The rain had picked up again, mirroring her mood. On the edge of losing her fragile grip on self-control, she didn't answer. Couldn't answer, when it came right down to it.

"Who are you, Sydney Conner?" His hoarse voice told her he'd moved up behind her. He touched her shoulder, his hand impossibly gentle, and turned her to face him, pulling her close to his chest. Though she didn't resist, she let him hold her, keeping herself rigid. Silently, he stroked her hair, while she fought back tears that came for no good reason.

"Go ahead and cry."

Those four words, muttered against her hair by a man she suspected would rather miss every target on the firing range than soothe a weeping woman, pushed her over the edge.

She cried while he held her, this stranger who wasn't a stranger, not any longer. Nearly dying in a plane crash and being stuck together on a deserted island had made him feel familiar. Intimately.

Her tears soaked his bare chest. Bare, muscular, hard

chest. Dimly, this registered and, as her weeping subsided, she found herself longing to move the hand pressed against him. To splay her fingers, to stroke him slowly, to allow herself to indulge in all that masculinity right there under her fingertips.

His comment about seduction hadn't been that far off the mark.

Good Lord! Had she truly become her mother? Gone totally over the edge? Though she'd already made one mistake her mother had made, she vowed she wouldn't make another. If her affair with Reginald had made her this way, she needed to get back to the woman she'd been before.

This didn't make her desire for him disappear, or even lessen. She still craved his touch, somehow addicted to something she'd never even had.

Hah! If he'd thought she'd been trying to seduce him before, what would he think if she gave in to her irrational need to caress him?

She wouldn't. She'd made enough mistakes to last her entire twenty-four years, Reginald chief among them. She didn't need to make one more.

Hiccuping, she sniffed and pushed herself away. "Sorry about that." She wouldn't look at him, her feminine vanity not wanting him to see her no doubt bright-red nose and swollen eyes.

He muttered something that sounded like "That's okay."

Though she waited, he made no move to leave, even though the drumming of the rain had all but stopped.

Wiping at her eyes, she managed a watery smile and gave the doorway a pointed look. "I don't know about you, but I'm starving. The rain's letting up. How about we go outside and forage for some breakfast?"

"What?" he stared at her as if he thought she'd lost her mind. "It's barely dawn."

"I'm pregnant," she said crossly, then smiled to soften the sting of her tone. "Not only am I changing the subject, but I really am hungry."

Crossing his arms, he swallowed. "You know, I keep forgetting you're pregnant."

One deep breath, then another. Soon, maybe her erratic heartbeat would slow down to normal. "It's too soon for me to show." Patting her still-flat abdomen, she grimaced. "Give it a few months. I've had so little time to actually enjoy my pregnancy. Every little girl dreams of the day when she'll be pregnant and become a mommy."

"Even a princess?"

She could see him relaxing in stages. "Yes, even a princess. I wanted to be able to luxuriate in it, wallow in it, you know? Instead, I'm trapped on an island with little food and no—"

"Luxuries." He sounded so hard and so certain, she blinked.

"That's not what I was going to say. I was thinking more of people. Friends that care."

The look he gave her was skeptical. "Don't tell me you don't miss the life you had in Naessa. You made the papers often, you know. Your lifestyle was no secret. I saw your townhouse on the coast on that TV show. You lived like royalty."

If only he knew. She'd filled her home with beautiful things, trying to fill the emptiness inside her. She'd been lonely more often than not, especially when she wasn't traveling with the symphony.

But he didn't know that. No one did. "I confess to missing some of it, yes."

"What?" His voice was fierce, and his hazel eyes darkened. "Which do you miss most? The Egyptian cotton sheets? The fine restaurants? Or the chance to have Frost and French design your maternity clothes?"

"You know about them?"

"I'm in public relations. I have to keep up with the trends. Answer my question. Which do you miss the most?" He took a step closer, his face intent.

Heart caught in her throat, she stared at him.

He leaned close, and for one heart-stopping moment she thought he was going to kiss her. Worse, she knew if he did, this time she wouldn't pull away.

Chapter 5

Luckily for both of them, he caught himself in time.

Clearing her throat, she searched desperately for something to say to pretend she hadn't noticed. Outside, the rain had slowed to a light patter on their metal roof.

"I really do miss my friends," she said, inanely. "What about you?"

He shrugged.

"Since your business takes you out and about, I imagine you must have a large circle of friends."

"Not really." He rolled his shoulders before snagging his own shirt and slipping it on. Apparently he was as eager as she to act as if nothing had happened. "My job consumes most of my day. I have little time to maintain friendships outside of my work. However, my coworkers and I get along well, and of course, there's always my family. Your turn."

For a second she didn't understand, eyeing him blankly.

"Are you close to your family?" He stepped into his shorts.

Her mouth went dry. Averting her eyes, she attempted to swallow while listening to the rasp of the denim. "My family?"

"Yes."

"No." She shook her head, trying to focus on the question. The only family she had was her mother, which equaled no family at all. "I'm not. I assume you are?"

"Oh, yeah. My parents live near the west coast of Silvershire, in their dream retirement home. My brothers and sisters are all married and have children. We all get together several times a year."

Finally, she regained her senses, though the entire conversation still seemed surreal. "I always wished for a big family."

"I read you're an only child."

"Yes." Since her mother had felt having Sydney had ruined her life, the woman had taken steps to ensure she didn't have any more children. "But I made a lot of friends in the symphony."

At her mention of her job, Chase grimaced. "I bet you're glad now that you left your cello in the hotel. That thing wouldn't have survived the crash. At least this way, you have a chance of getting it back."

"True. If it's still there."

"That was a five-star hotel. I'm sure they have your instrument in their lost and found department."

"As long as no one realizes it's a Strad, it's probably okay. Otherwise, they'd sell it on the black market." She gave him a tentative smile, finally feeling normal. "Right about now I should be back in Naessa, getting ready for Silvershire's Founder's Day celebration. We rehearse every night for a month. This will be my third performance for your king."

At the mention of the celebration, Chase frowned. "Given the bad blood between your father and King Weston, I'm surprised Naessa's symphony was invited this year."

Lifting her chin, she forced her mouth to curve in what she hoped resembled a smile. "I've always heard the fish bite better at dawn. Is there any truth to that?"

"Changing the subject?"

"Yes," she said, her voice mild. "I'm still hungry."

He gave a half bow. "Which would you prefer? Fish or rabbit?"

"*Do* the fish bite better at dawn?"

"Maybe. I guess I'll go out there and find out. I take it you'd like fish for breakfast?"

Her lower back ached. Absently, she rubbed it while she pondered his question. "We had rabbit last night." She had to smile at her words.

"What?" Chase caught the smile.

"Listen to us, talking about eating wild game as though discussing the menu at Chez Niablo." She sighed. "I need protein, lots of it, for the baby. I feel the need for fish."

"Then fish it is. Catch." He tossed her the lighter. "Why don't you see about making a fire while I get our breakfast?" Then, without a backward glance, he left.

Surprised she'd caught the lighter since she'd lifted her hand in reflex, Sydney closed her fist over it. The silver metal felt both foreign and reassuringly normal. She turned to the small pile of wood he'd brought inside the shelter and gathered an armful before stepping cautiously outside.

Though still overcast, the sky looked considerably brighter. With the light mist and soft breeze, the still-dripping forest smelled earthy and fresh. The storm had gone. Shrouded in clouds, the small hill they'd dubbed Haystack Mountain could be seen clearly.

Three tries and Sydney finally had a respectable fire going. She fed the flames dry wood, and glanced toward the beach, trying to catch a glimpse of Chase in the waves.

While she watched the fire and waited, she thought of how drastically her life had changed in a few days. Now, with her existence pared down to survival, simple pleasures like the warmth of a fire or the feel of a man's rough stubble against her cheek seemed more precious than diamonds.

Finally, Chase returned, carrying not only two large fish, but what looked like a battered backpack.

"I went poking through more of the wreckage." He placed the backpack on the ground. "I found this. It must have belonged to one of the pilots."

She noticed he avoided saying their names and realized that must be his way of dealing with his grief. So instead of commenting, she focused on the fish.

"How long will that take to cook?"

He smiled. "I thought you said you knew how."

Unembarrassed, she shrugged. "I learned how to cook gourmet meals using an oven. If cooking over an open fire is similar, then I'm good to go."

"Let me show you." Using the same rig he'd made to cook the rabbits, he spread the fish over the fire.

They watched in companionable silence while their breakfast cooked. Every so often, he turned the spit.

Finally, he gave her a satisfied look. "I think it's done."

Removing the fish from the fire, he split each in half, using a triangular rock as a cutting implement. Then he transferred her portion to a piece of bark and handed it to her.

"You're pretty handy with nature," she commented.

"I trained at a pretty elite bodyguard school in Carring-tonshire." Taking a bite of his fish, he pointed to hers. "Now eat."

Aching again, Sydney complied. "It's good."

"You sound surprised." He'd wolfed down his portion before she'd even finished chewing.

"I guess I am." Chewing slowly, she savored the flavor. "Even without the benefit of seasonings or spices, this is wonderful. It's flaky and moist." Though she'd eaten at gourmet restaurants in both their countries, she thought she'd never tasted anything so delicious.

"It's fresh."

It took her a moment to realize he was teasing her. She eyed him, his rugged face relaxed, and replied in kind. "It'd be even better if I didn't have to pick out the bones."

Chase grinned. "Tough," he told her. "There are some things you have to do on your own."

Finishing her portion, she licked her fingers to get every bit of meat. When she looked up again, Chase's light-hearted expression had vanished. His look burned her all the way to her core.

"Chase—"

"No." He jumped to his feet and took her bark from her, dumping the fish bones in the fire. Then, without a backward look, he strode off into the forest.

After a moment of hesitation, she ran after him. "Where are you going?"

He cast a dark look over his shoulder. "In lieu of a cold shower, I'm going to take a bath in the pond."

She practically had to jog to keep up with him. "I'd kill for some soap."

Hefting the backpack, he kept going. "I found some."

"Soap?" She felt like Eve, being lured with a different kind of apple. "Is there enough for both of us?"

"I'd prefer to bathe alone, thank you." He gave her another hard look. "I'll bring back the soap so you can have a turn."

She stopped, letting him continue on alone. He was right. Thoughts of him emerging naked from the pond with rivulets of water caressing his muscular body was way more temptation than she was up to resisting.

And resist she must. Because, unless their rescuers made an appearance, they'd spend another night sleeping side by side in the small shelter. She had to stop thinking of him that way before they both did something they'd later regret.

On the way back to the camp, she took a detour and found a patch of early strawberries. Going back for the tin cups Chase had found earlier, she returned to fill them with strawberries.

Bare-chested, hair damp from his swim, Chase returned and handed her the soap. "I'll see you later."

Resolutely, she kept her gaze on his face. "Where are you going?"

He seemed just as determined to avoid looking below her chin. "I thought I'd climb Haystack Mountain and see if I could get a better visual on this island."

Though it was on the tip of her tongue to ask to go, she didn't. Instead, she nodded and took off for the pond and her own bath. She didn't turn around to see if he watched her leave.

That night, he brought them a small wild pig. She'd gathered more wood, spreading it in the sun to dry before hauling a short stack inside the shelter in case of more rain. While he dressed the meat, she built up the fire. Though she hadn't seen him all day, she kept her distance while he cooked their dinner on another stick-made spit.

The scent of roasting pork made her mouth water and finally, she went closer. "That smells wonderful."

He nodded. "I re-explored the wreckage hoping to find a working cell phone or radio or something. Instead, I found the remains of the galley." He held up two forks. "I brought back these and those plastic food trays to use as plates."

Feeling absurdly tongue-tied, she looked away.

"I also found an underground route to some caves." He brushed back his hair from his face.

"Caves?"

"This is an interesting island. Below the pond is a lot of volcanic rock. There were a couple of large caves, accessible only by water. When I get more time, I'll explore them." He fed another stick to the fire. "What'd you do while I was gone?"

"I picked a bunch of berries and gathered firewood." She sighed. "I also took a nap. I've been really tired today."

"Isn't that normal?" Turning the spit while he watched her, his expression was unreadable.

"For pregnant women, yes."

"I climbed Haystack and got a better view of this place." He gestured toward the beach. "It's not a huge island, and I didn't see any signs of habitation. I did find a sandy beach on the other side, rather than this rocky one we're near. The wildlife is abundant—even with me crashing around in broad daylight I saw a lot." His teeth flashed white. "Not a bad place to build a vacation home. I haven't figured out why the owner hasn't yet."

Sydney nodded. Just looking at him made her ache. His blond hair was sun-streaked, though she wondered how much time he spent in the sun, back in Silvershire. With his darkened tan and his stubble, he looked even more dangerous than he had before.

And more sexy.

Her stomach growled, bringing her thoughts back to food. "How much longer?"

"I think it's about done." Moving the cooked pig to a rock, he made good use of a steak knife to cut up their meat. Handing her a plate, he filled his and retreated to the other side of the fire to eat.

Sydney felt as though he was drawing a battle line.

Instead of worrying about that, she concentrated on her food. They ate in silence.

When they'd finished, eating almost all of the small pig, Chase dug a hole and buried the remains.

Once he'd finished, he returned to his side of the fire.

Night fell suddenly. Stars flickered above in the velvet-black sky. Across from her, separated by the dancing flames, Chase used the steak knife to carve another stick to use as a spit.

Sydney tried to enjoy the quiet, listening to the night sounds of the forest as the myriad creatures emerged to hunt and play. All her life, she'd been so excruciatingly lonely that silence had been intolerable to her. Until she'd learned to play the cello. After that, she'd always managed to fill the quiet with her music.

Now, without her cello, once again she sat alone. On the outside looking in. Only when she played with the symphony did she feel part of something larger, no longer solitary in her insulated little world.

Sitting across the fire from this hard man, she felt even more alone than when Reginald's gaze had slid dismissively over her in a crowded restaurant. Reginald, once so blatant in his adoration, had pretended not to know her.

Chase made no such pretense. He simply preferred not to talk.

She recognized this. Years and years of living on the outside of the "inside" people, had trained her for it. How not to interfere or intrude. How to make certain her existence didn't impede or alter their lives in any unpleasant way.

Her mother had taught her well.

But this wasn't Naessa and she wasn't a child. So—she took a deep breath—she wouldn't put up with it again. Not here. Not now. Not ever again. She spoke.

"Do you think someone will find us?"

Barely pausing in his carving, he turned those amazing hazel eyes of his to hers. "Yes."

"Why do you sound unhappy about that?"

He stabbed the knife into the ground. "Do I? I'm not, not at all. I'm hoping the right people find us first."

"The right people?"

"The ones who are on our side."

She hadn't thought of that until now. Cradling her stomach and the growing life within, she tried to picture these people and shook her head. She still wasn't sure if they were a figment of Chase's imagination, or real, nameless, faceless enemies. There had been the shooting, certainly, but nothing had ever happened to her until Chase had shown up. They could be his enemies more than hers.

Except *her* car had been blown up. Hers, not his.

If there was someone out there gunning for them, it would seem it was really her they were after.

But why? Did they hate her merely because she carried Reginald's child? Or was it because of her ties to

Prince Kerwin of Naessa? Perhaps they were unaware her sire had never acknowledged her, though how they could be when it'd been trumpeted from every tabloid, she had no idea.

Even a few months ago, when the largest one had done a feature on her and Reginald, her bastard status had been mentioned, along with the speculation about whether, if she and Reginald were to wed, her father might consent to legitimize her.

The same paper had been the first to report on Reginald's intentions to honor his long-term betrothal to Princess Amelia Victoria DuPont of Gastonia. It seemed they'd been betrothed as toddlers in a secret agreement between King Weston of Silvershire and King Roman of Gastonia, a betrothal Reginald had conveniently forgotten to mention to Sydney. He planned to marry the princess during his coronation ceremony, which he'd ordered to be the most lavish the people of Silvershire had ever seen.

The same morning the story broke, Sydney had learned she was pregnant with Reginald's child.

"Surely it won't come to that. We've been missing, what, three days? Your duke must be looking for us."

"I'm sure he is. But then, so are they."

She glanced back at their small shelter. "We don't have any weapons."

"Not a one."

"Maybe we'd better find another place to hide."

"That's why I went up the mountain. If the wrong people show up, we'll need somewhere to ambush them."

His words only served to remind her how precious life could be and how abruptly it could be cut short.

Unable to bear the isolation any longer, Sydney rose.

Hugging herself, she moved around the fire and dropped to the ground next to Chase.

His mouth tightened, but he made no comment. The look he gave her was sharp and, for nameless reasons, touched a place deep inside her. But then, the way he affected her had nothing to do with reason.

Averting his face, he continued to work at whittling the stick. She studied him, memorizing his features, knowing that even once she returned to her normal life, she'd never forget a single detail of his face.

Reginald's good looks had been more patrician, elegant. More remote. She'd thought she'd loved him, but she realized now what she'd mistaken for love had been gratitude for attention. She'd been so hungry for affection that she'd turned a blind eye to all Reginald's failings. Knowing his reputation, she'd believed her love had changed him.

Loving Reginald had been her biggest mistake. Until now. Looking at Chase, at the stubborn set of his chin and his deliberate unawareness of her, she knew she was about to make another.

The fire crackled and popped. Around them, she could hear the night sounds of the forest, and the soft scratch Chase's knife made on the wood.

Soon, they'd let the fire burn down and retire for the evening. Soon, they'd lie side by side in their small shelter and try to pretend to be unaware of each other.

She was tired of resisting, tired of existing half-alive and so achingly alone. She wanted him. And he wanted her. After they were rescued, she'd go home to Naessa and never see him again. Until then, for however long they were stranded here, they only had each other.

Heart hammering in her chest, she took a deep breath

for courage. She touched his arm, bringing the heat of his shadowed gaze to her face. "Chase, I need to ask you something." Swallowing, she wished her voice wouldn't tremble so, or sound quite as breathy.

The knife stilled. Waiting for her to continue, he raised one golden brow.

Now or never. She felt as though she was diving, head-first, into a bottomless pool.

"Last night, when you held me, I felt better than I have in months. Less afraid, more secure. I liked feeling that way. A lot."

Ignoring his harsh intake of breath, she continued. "I want to sleep in your arms again tonight. Will you hold me through the night?"

Chapter 6

Did she know what she was asking of him? Chase couldn't believe what he was hearing. As Sydney stared at him, her slender fingers pale on his tanned arm, desire slammed into him like a punch to the gut. Gritting his teeth, he used every ounce of willpower to keep from yanking her hard against him, and covering her mouth with his.

Sydney had become an obsession.

Earlier, the way she'd watched him had been bad enough. He'd felt the touch of her luminous gaze like a silky caress, teasing his nerves to an aching awareness.

"Chase?" She scooted closer, filling his nostrils with the scent of warm, fragrant woman. He clenched his jaw. God help him if she were to move her hand from his arm and splay her fingers across his chest. She'd feel his heart thudding like a wild thing as he fought to keep himself under control.

She had no idea how much he wanted her. Wanted to

tangle his fingers in her hair and tilt her face to him. Wanted to feel her lush curves, full against him, without even small scraps of clothing acting as a barrier between them. Wanted to bury himself deep inside her and bring her to a ragged, shuddering completion as they moved together in a rhythm as old as time.

Ever since she'd turned that midnight-blue stare of hers on him, Chase had been battling himself. Now, with her so close, her lush mouth slightly parted, her long-lashed blue eyes dark with a desire that matched his own, he found her all but impossible to resist. His body quickened and he fought to keep from losing control.

Then her words penetrated his fogged brain.

She wanted to be held.

She'd asked in the way of one human asking another for comfort, not someone craving hot, wild sex.

Chase knew if he touched her, he'd do a lot more than hold her. He suspected Sydney realized this, as well.

Think of Kayla, he told himself savagely. Kayla had used his lust to blind him to her lies. And she hadn't had one-tenth the effect on him as Sydney.

Sydney. How he wanted her. Being around her made him feel as if a potent aphrodisiac had spread with lightning speed through his blood.

His control slipping, Chase tried to remember how Sydney had planned to use Reginald. Though Chase hadn't liked the man and even thought he'd deserved to pay the consequences for his actions, Sydney had to have known what she was getting into. No one was that naive. Or that successful.

Chase, like Reginald, knew a lion's share of gorgeous, sexy women. None could hold a candle to her.

Sydney Conner was sex on wheels.

But the question remained, what did she want from him?

Though she acted as though it was simple, human comfort, he knew better. She was beautiful, like Kayla. He had to believe beautiful women always had an agenda.

"Chase?" Even her voice, husky and sensual, seduced him. The mere act of hearing her say his name made him take an unthinking step toward her. "What is it? What's wrong?"

He had to stop this. Get a grip on his famous iron control. He could do this. He was a pro at handling sexy, beautiful women. With all his experiences, he hadn't lived the life of a monk after all. Resisting even the most sensual woman, while difficult, was doable.

Then he made the mistake of looking at her.

Sydney continued to stare up at him, her heart-shaped face breathtakingly vulnerable, her eyes so dark, pupil and iris appeared to have blended. He searched her expression for the particular confidence sexy women had, that innate knowledge that they could wrap a man, any man, around their little fingers. But either Sydney was different, or she was a damn fine actress. He saw nothing in her delicate features but a hint of sorrow, of pain, and a stark, lonely hunger that matched his own urgent need.

She wanted, he reminded himself savagely, to be held. So damn it, he'd hold her.

Somehow, without being conscious of moving, he found his hands on her, sliding across her soft skin, slipping up her arms. She made a sound, not of protest, not exactly, more of welcome, and he answered low in his throat.

Need, raw and sharp, clawed at him. Still, he made a heroic effort to keep himself from taking her, though she felt warm and supple and willing in his arms.

Willing. With a hoarse cry, he covered her mouth with

his. She met him halfway, lips parted, tongue mating. As before, the taste of her was sweet, like a nearly ripe peach.

When he pulled back, she made a soft mew of protest, pressing her body against him in a wordless plea. She touched her lips to his throat and he burned.

He heard another sound, realizing with a curious detachment it was the harsh, uneven rhythm of his own breathing. Or was it hers?

Was he crazy? Had he lost his mind? She was everything he ran from, everything Kayla had been and more.

And, as Kayla had been, she was pregnant with another man's child.

He gave himself a mental shake, which did nothing to lessen the heat in his blood. She reared back as his body stirred against her, her eyes wide and dark and her face clear, no artifice in her expression, just a sensual, womanly awareness. Awareness of the way her simple, quiet femininity called to him? Awareness of his body's raging hunger for her, only her?

Was she like Kayla had been, well aware that the lure she'd cast had reeled in yet another masculine conquest?

A second later he chastised himself for reading too much into her response. Sydney wasn't Kayla. She had her own motivations, her own needs. Perhaps she was only tired of being alone, apart, separate. Maybe, like him, she longed to touch, to make contact, to feel.

Maybe, she really needed him.

Him.

He knew a moment of wonder, then his innate cynicism set in. He was reacting to her like a sex-starved soldier, newly returned from the battlefield. Perhaps the sunlight had scrambled his brains. Or more likely it was the feel of her, all soft skin and womanly curves, but he tugged her closer, trying to be gentle when he wanted to be rough, comforting when he wanted the raw rhythm of hot, mindless sex.

She'd asked him merely to hold her, not make love to her. Was he reading too much into her words?

Yet she came to him, pressing herself against him for a moment, and as her curves molded to his body he knew he could take her there, on the ground near their fire, and slake his thirst deep inside her.

Hard, aching, he couldn't think, could barely stop himself from pushing against her, from laying her down and peeling off her clothes. He wanted to nuzzle her breasts, take her nipples into his mouth and taste her.

She made a soft sound and he found himself looking down at her. Her beautiful eyes were full of passion.

"Sydney?" Their gazes locked for the space of a heart-beat, and another. Without consciously willing it, Chase found himself claiming her mouth again.

The instant their lips touched, fire flared between them once more. He broke away, breathing hard, cursing his lack of willpower. She whimpered, and his body surged against her. She felt it, too, the infinitesimal change in his body as he fought to keep his raging arousal under control.

"What is it about you?" he growled, unable to make himself push her away. "Why are you doing this?"

With heavy-lidded eyes she looked up at him, her expression serious. He saw no hint of a tease or the simpering coquettishness he'd come to associate with the women who followed the royals, wanting sex. Rather, as she worried her bottom lip between her teeth, she looked as troubled as he felt.

Around them, the sound of surf pounding the rocks blended with his heartbeat.

Finally, she spoke. "I want you," she said. "But before I do, there's something you need to understand."

When he would have moved toward her, she held up her hand. "Reginald was my first."

Uncomprehending, he stared. "What?"

"I was a virgin before him. I've never been with anyone else. I thought he loved me, but he didn't. Now I'm pregnant."

Something inside him splintered. At her words he felt the rage leave him, an icy chill spreading through him instead. What he knew of Reginald's depravations could fill a book. For her first experience at lovemaking to have been at the hands of that...

Even for Reginald, this was a new low. Seduce a virgin, an illegitimate princess, impregnate her, then dump her to go off and marry a legitimate one. Though she gave no signs of knowing it, Sydney Conner was the most sexy, desirable woman Chase had ever met.

The possibility that she might be lying didn't make him feel any better.

"Sydney, I—" Oddly enough, her innocence only made him want her more.

He started toward her.

"Wait." She held up a hand, her delicate features remote. "I didn't tell you that to make you feel sorry for me. Actually, I'm not sure why I told you at all."

"I'm glad you did." He touched her shoulder and she looked up at him, her eyes full of unshed tears. All his resolve flew out the window. "I want you, Sydney. How I want you."

Her expression softened and she held out her arms.

"Then make love to me, Chase. Erase what he did to me from my memory. Make love to me."

Make love to me. He groaned. Despite his longing and the red-hot fantasies which haunted him, Chase knew he should back away.

Instead, he pulled her into his arms, slanting his mouth across hers. She met him halfway. He touched her, letting his hands roam over her curves freely, as he'd been aching to do. Her answering cry was a heady invitation.

Squirming against him, each movement acerbated the fierceness of his arousal, pushing him closer and closer to the edge of his ragged control.

"Chase," she spoke his name in a broken murmur, her lips against his throat. She trailed kisses there, making him shudder.

She didn't protest when he pulled off her blouse, nor when his fingers fumbled with the clasp of her bra. Then, when her breasts were free, he cupped them in his hands and suckled her, rolling each rosy nipple between his lips.

Arching her back, she moaned. Together, they sank to the ground. She found the waistband of his shorts and pulled the snap apart, finding him hard and swollen and spilling from his undershorts.

When she wrapped her hand around him and stroked, the movement brought pleasure and agony.

"Stop," he ground out. "You'll have me losing control too soon, too fast."

He pushed her back onto the sand, throbbing, hard, ready. With his finger he entered her, finding her wet and tight. She groaned. He readied himself between her legs, about to push into her, when a roaring sound filled the air.

"Chase?" She raised her head, a look of horror filling her face as she came to the same realization as he did.

Listening, he lifted himself up and cursed. "That's a chopper, landing on the beach. We need to hide until we know who it is."

In one swift motion he rolled off her, yanking up his shorts and helping her up and into her bra and T-shirt. "We're either about to be rescued or attacked."

Chapter 7

Together, they watched the chopper land on the rocky beach near where they'd buried the pig carcass. Before the whirring blades had even slowed, a tall, dark-haired man climbed out, followed by two others. Not only did the chopper look military, but the men appeared dangerous. All wore sunglasses, and she could see they were all armed with pistols. All of them were large men with the build of bodyguards.

"They look like bad guys." Sydney turned to Chase, still trying to adjust her clothing.

"Nope, they're not. We're in luck," Chase said, relief lightening the harshness in his eyes. "Those are my men, they work for me."

"Hell of a PR department you've got going." She eyed the weapons glinting in the sunlight. "Do you guys double as covert ops or something?"

Immediately, his expression shut down. "What we do—
or don't do—in Silvershire has nothing to do with Naessa."

Once again, he reminded her she was an outsider.

"I understand." She matched his cool tone.

His gaze locked with hers. Another time, she might
have found it amusing that Chase looked away first. Now,
she felt only an awful ache spreading inside her heart.
Despite that, when he held out his hand, she took it.

Fingers laced together, they ran across the sand, Chase
shouting out one of the other men's names as they ran.

Twenty minutes later, the pilot put the chopper down at
a place she didn't recognize.

The airstrip appeared to be private, with the helicopter's
landing pad clearly marked.

Chase stayed by Sydney's side, helping her climb out
from the chopper. A white Hummer limousine waited.
With the other men leading the way, they bypassed this,
heading for a small, unimpressive brick building. Inside,
they stepped into an empty room furnished only with a
single desk and a folding metal chair. A door marked
Women was at one end; Men was at the other.

"Here you'll find showers and all the necessities, as
well as some new clothing." The husky man Chase had introduced as William pointed to two suitcases. One, a small
Gucci looked familiar, her favorite traveling bag.

"That's mine," she said. "Where did you get that?"

"Before his death, Prince Reginald had given us all the
things you'd left at his flat, asking that we return them to you."

"Us?"

William looked at Chase. Gaze locked on Sydney,
Chase nodded slowly. "Go ahead."

William flashed her an impersonal smile. "The royal public relations department. Us. We took the liberty of bringing your clothing, as well as of purchasing a few new items for your stay."

Alarm bells went off. "Stay?"

This time they all looked at Chase. He murmured, "Why don't you get cleaned up, then we'll talk."

Talk? About what? "I need to see a doctor before I do anything," she insisted.

Expressionless, he surveyed her. "Clean up first. Then we'll take you to a specialist for a thorough examination."

"But—"

"There's no doctor here, Sydney." Chase touched her arm. "Get cleaned up, change your clothes and we'll go. You'll feel a lot better if you do."

"What about my cello?"

He held up a finger. "Later, okay?"

Slowly, she nodded.

"I'll be right there if you need anything." He pointed to the other door. "William, Carlos and Jim will stand guard outside."

Stand guard? Didn't anyone else find it odd that Silvershire had a PR department made up of bodyguards? Shaking her head, she grabbed her suitcase and entered the women's room, locking the door behind her. With a sigh, she peeled off her tattered clothing, dropping it in the trash bin. Then, crossing to the mirror, she studied her image. Nothing had changed. Sydney Conner, cellist, stared back at her. Other than the sunburn and the disheveled mop of hair, she looked much the same as the woman who'd stayed at the Hotel Royale a few days before. She caught sight of her ragged fingernails and grimaced.

Though externally she could see little signs of the ordeal she'd lived through, inside, her entire world had shifted. It would take more than a simple shower to make her feel normal again.

Her thoughts wandered to Chase. He seemed to have no problem reverting to the person he'd been before the crash. But then, he didn't have a baby to worry over.

Turning the tap on full blast, she stepped into the shower, fighting the urge to hurry so she could get to the doctor. Despite her niggling worry, the soap and shampoo and hot water felt wonderful.

After toweling off, she eyed her still-flat stomach and wondered. She'd feel it if something were wrong, wouldn't she? Combing out her wet hair, she muttered a quick prayer for her unborn child, then opened her door to find Chase and the others waiting.

The sight of him, clean and in a black, Armani T-shirt and pressed khakis, made her mouth go dry. He'd shaved and tied his damp blond hair in a casual ponytail, which made him even more rakishly and elegantly handsome.

"There you are." He smiled at her, but his smile didn't touch his eyes. With a dip of his chin, he gave a signal, and the other men moved to flank them.

"Ready?"

She nodded. "I can't wait to get to a doctor."

They stepped outside into the bright sunlight and approached the limo with an almost military precision. William held the back door open. As Sydney climbed inside, Chase got in next to her. William and the other two men took the opposite seat.

The last time Sydney had ridden in a limo had been the night Reginald had broken up with her. He'd arrived for their date, flowers in hand, though this time instead of the usual red roses, he'd brought her pure white. He'd been unusually quiet, his aristocratic features reflecting his nervousness. He'd fidgeted in the plush seat, while the car took them to downtown Silverton's finest restaurant.

That night had felt mystical, magical. Sydney had actually suspected Reginald was going to propose. Instead, over aperitifs, he'd told her their relationship was over and he could no longer see her.

While the car glided silently along the curving streets, William filled them in on how they'd been located.

"The plane's emergency beacon was still working," he said. "We were surprised to learn you'd crashed on Chawder Island."

"Why?"

"You filed a flight plan to Naessa. Chawder Island is several hundred miles west of the correct route."

Chase's brows rose. "The storm must have blown Franco off course. He and Dell tried to land us safely. They were good men and damn fine pilots." He shifted restlessly. "This Chawder Island, who does it belong to?"

"The Lazlo Group is looking into that. Ownership is registered to a corporation whose existence appears to be a front for someone else."

Watching the scenery outside the car, Sydney knew a growing feeling of alarm. "This doesn't look like the road into Silverton. In fact, I'd swear we weren't even in Silvershire. Where are we?"

Chase glanced at William. The other man gave her a reassuring smile. "Carringtonshire."

Carringtonshire? That was in the northwestern part of Silvershire, a part of the country she'd never visited. The twisting road seemed to be in the remote countryside. Nothing but trees and hills could be seen, no matter how far she looked.

"Why?" She stared at William, then Chase.

William tapped his laptop case. "We're headed for the royal vacation lodge on Lake Lodan."

"Vacation lodge?" She turned on Chase. "You promised me a doctor. I want to see a doctor immediately. Before anything else, take me to a hospital."

Chase smoothed a wayward hair from her face, tucking it behind her ear. "Calm down. It's all been taken care of."

William nodded. "Yes, Miss Conner. I've taken care of everything. We should arrive at the lodge in twenty minutes, and I've arranged to have a top-notch ob-gyn meet us there."

"Top-notch?" She squinted at him suspiciously. "This Carringtonshire looks like a country area to me. How'd you manage to find a doctor like that out here in the sticks?"

"Luckily, Dr. Kallan was on holiday nearby. He's excellent." William's professional tone spoke of one used to making arrangements for others. He regarded her expectantly, making her smile faintly. If not for his beefed-up appearance, he'd be a perfect personal secretary.

She sighed. "That's a start, but honestly, I'm going to need more than just an examination. I'll need blood work and a sonogram. I need a hospital. Then I want to go home to Naessa."

William looked at Chase. So did Carlos and Jim.

"In good time, Sydney. First, we're going to Lake Lodan." Chase's cool, calculating look no longer fooled her. "After that, we'll take things one at a time."

"I don't understand." She crossed her arms. The plush

interior of the limo was starting to feel like a prison. "No more of this nonsense. Once I've seen the doctor and had my tests at a hospital, I want to go home. You can drop me at Silvershire International as soon as possible. I can arrange my own flight."

Chase's expression was closed, remote. "One step at a time, Sydney. One step at a time."

Ever-helpful William leaned forward. "Chase thought, in view of the situation, it'd be best to keep you hidden here in Carringtonshire for a little while."

"Situation? Hidden?"

The other men exchanged a look as she stared at them. Chase touched her arm. She was so angry she jerked away, glaring at him. "I think you'd better explain."

"You know someone is trying to kill you. Until we learn who and why, better safe than sorry."

She took a deep breath, letting it out slowly. "That's not your problem."

"But it is," he said smoothly. "You are carrying the prince's baby. Our employer, the Duke of Carrington, has asked us keep you safe."

"Are we back to that again? You were taking me home when—" She inhaled sharply as a horrible thought occurred to her. "You don't think the plane crash—?"

"We're looking into that, ma'am." William didn't even glance at her as he spoke. He was too preoccupied downloading information into the smallest, sleekest laptop she'd ever seen.

"If they caused the jet to crash, they killed those two pilots."

"True." Chase touched her arm lightly. "But I'm thinking hail brought it on. It was an accident."

William looked up from his screen. "Do you seriously believe that? It seems awfully convenient."

"I was there." Chase's sharp voice contained a rebuke. "Besides, no one could have known Sydney would be on that jet."

"You filed a flight plan." One of the other men spoke up, earning a sharp glance from William.

"True." Chase gave the other man a thoughtful look. "But if the jet was sabotaged, that would mean it's someone on the inside."

All three men shifted uneasily. Chase folded his arms. "Any thoughts?"

The more these men talked, the less they sounded like public relations workers. She could easily picture any of them in Silvershire's secret service.

None of the others had any answers. But they all agreed Sydney was still in grave danger.

"Right now," Chase said, his gaze intense, "whoever they are, they're probably searching frantically for you."

"Not to mention the press. They've been going wild since the princess disappeared. No one knows about the crash. We've managed to keep a lid on that." William's wry smile and quick shake of his head told her he had his doubts as to the truth of that statement.

"The press?" Sydney fought the urge to rub her aching lower back. The sooner she could talk to that doctor, the better. "Why would the press care what I do? Since they publicized Reginald's and my breakup, they've left me alone."

"You're in the news again." William swallowed, looking from her to Chase. "Reporters are scouring the streets trying to hunt you down. In the meantime, they've dug up every detail about you they could find."

"Why?" Chase's voice was cold. "Because she was Reginald's last lover before he died? I wouldn't think that's newsworthy now."

"That's only part of it. Someone leaked information to them about the pregnancy. We know it wasn't you—" he jabbed a finger in Sydney's direction "—since you were on Chawder Island when the story broke."

They all looked at Sydney.

She lifted her shoulders in a shrug. "I didn't do it. I avoid the press like the plague."

"Then who?" Chase barked, glaring at his employees. "If there's a leak at the palace, I want it found, now!"

"Understood, sir. We're looking into it."

"Who's in charge of damage control?"

William shrugged. "I'm not sure. Melody has been running the department in your absence."

"Damage control?" Sydney crossed her arms and resisted the urge to tap her feet. "Why would you even need such a thing? So I'm pregnant, and Reginald and I weren't married. Things like that happen occasionally, even in Silvershire. What's the big deal?"

"For one, you are Prince Kerwin's daughter." Chase bit out the words.

William cleared his throat, looking nervous. "There's more, and it's worse. The press is reporting you and Reginald *were* wed and that the child you carry is heir to the throne. They're citing a reliable source."

"What?" Both Chase and Sydney erupted at the same time. "It's only been four days since Reginald died."

"The papers claim you and Reginald married in a secret ceremony last month. One of them even says they have explicit photos."

Chase narrowed his gaze. "Is that so?"

Sydney gave in and rubbed her throbbing temples, then moved her hands to her lower back. "Well, they're lying. Reginald and I were never married. The only truth in all that is that I am pregnant. And—" she leaned forward, looking from one man to the other "—I really don't care what the reporters say. It doesn't matter to me. I'm pregnant, I want to rest. I just want to see a doctor and then go home."

Chase shook his head. "It's not safe."

"I don't think these people, whoever they are, will follow me back to Naessa."

"They will."

"Fine." She gave up and let herself sink back into the plush leather seat. "We'll talk about this later, after my examination."

When Chase didn't reply, she turned her attention to the scenery. Lined by granite boulders and an occasional cliff, the winding road curved through massive oaks and towering pines. Finally, Lake Lodan came into view, sunlight glinting off the water.

"It's beautiful," she said.

"The royal family's lodge is on the western side of the lake." Chase watched her intently, as though he expected her to bolt as soon as the car stopped. Not a bad idea, but hardly likely. He must have forgotten she'd seen how fast he could run.

One more sweeping curve brought them close to the lake. The wind stirred the sparkling water into choppy waves, sending them crashing against the stone cliffs. Sydney sighed, thinking of Chawder Island. Though their stay there had been brief, she'd felt as though they'd existed in another world, a cocoon filled only with her and Chase. Surreal. No wonder she felt different.

"Are we climbing?"

Chase answered with a short nod.

William looked up from his laptop. "We're nearly there."

The road became steeper. More cliffs, rocky and studded with trees, rose on one side. On the other, the lake spread out like a glistening blue jewel.

"Christ!" The driver swore. Directly ahead of them, a car swung wide around a sharp curve. Moving fast, the other driver headed directly toward them on the wrong side of the road.

"Hold on." The limo driver wrenched the wheel. The large vehicle, not made for precise turns, swung and began to skid toward the rocky cliffs. If they went over, they'd be killed.

At the last instant the other car switched lanes, again coming directly at them.

"He's trying to hit us!" William screamed, one second before the other vehicle slammed into them.

The impact spun the limo the other way. Luckily for them their rear fender barely touched the guardrail, not enough to slow their reverse sideways motion.

The other car, having hit them in the rear quarter panel, ricocheted the opposite way. It took out the guardrail, hanging on the edge for one awful moment before vanishing over the side of the cliff.

After careening left, then right, and hitting a huge boulder, the limo came to a stop. They all looked at each other. Chase held Sydney in place, while the other men shot out of the car, guns drawn.

"All clear," William said.

"Come on." Chase got out first, extending his hand to Sydney. Shakily, she climbed from the backseat.

"That was no random accident," Chase shook his head, his expression grim. "I'm thinking that was another attempt to take you out of the picture."

"No way," she scoffed. "It had to be an accident, a drunk driver or something. First off, how would they even know where we are? Second, I still don't know why anyone would want to kill me."

"You're carrying the prince's only child." He caught her arm. "That might be reason enough for some people."

William and the other two men peered over the rail. The limo driver was on his cell phone, no doubt calling in the accident.

"I want to see." Sydney shook off his hand and went to the edge of the cliff. The other car had come to rest at the bottom of the rock wall, a crumpled heap of twisted metal. "I hope you called for an ambulance," she told William.

"I called the police. They'll dispatch medical assistance."

"If they survived." Again, Chase spoke almost in her ear. Still dazed, Sydney fought the urge to turn her face into his chest for comfort.

Looking shaken, their driver walked over. His short, black hair was mussed, as if he'd run his fingers through it in agitation. His face drained of color, he shook his head. "They were either drunk or…"

"Something," Chase put in smoothly. The warning look he gave Sydney let her know he didn't want his speculation about the near miss revealed to the driver, a man not in his employ.

Lights flashing, the police arrived, along with a fire truck and an ambulance. Because of the wreck's location, only one police cruiser stayed to take the report; the others drove back the way they'd come. There was a public swimming area further north that would give them access to the crash if they drove up the beach.

Once they'd finished supplying the remaining officer with details, and determined the limousine was still drivable, they climbed back in to resume their journey.

A few more miles and several more curves in the road later, they pulled up to massive iron gates. Worked into the iron was the royal coat of arms. She sighed, watching as the gates swung slowly open. The Royal Family of Silvershire's private lake lodge, one of their many vacation hideaways. This particular one she'd never heard of, though the press had reported on many others. In such a remote location, with no easy access, it seemed even the press hadn't been able to infiltrate these gated walls. No doubt this was why Chase had chosen it as a hiding place for her.

After the accident that might not have been an accident, she was beginning to think Chase wasn't so far from the mark. Until those crazy people were caught, maybe staying here with protection was the best option.

Inhaling deeply, still shaky, she tried for calm. None of their party had been hurt, but if the other car had merely made a blunder, she felt horrible for them.

"Chase?"

He looked at her, his hazel eyes serious. "Yes?"

"Can we call and check on those people back there? You know, whether they lived or…"

"Died? We can check with the police department later." His serious expression told her he was just as affected by what had happened as she.

"Miss Conner?" William leaned forward. "I think you'll

like it here. The royal family maintains a very sumptuous lifestyle, even at this lake lodge. We have a full-service salon, a masseuse and personal trainer, as well as a fully equipped gym and indoor pool." He smiled, too brightly, as though he was trying to erase the last hour with his words. "What more could you ask for?"

What more indeed? A clean bill of health for the baby.

She turned to look at Chase, startled to find him watching her intently.

"What?" She asked.

He shook his head and looked away without answering.

As the limo drove through, the gates closed behind them with a clank. Sydney let her head sink back against the plush leather and briefly closed her eyes. Deciding to stay was a relief of sorts. She was exhausted and could use a few days of rest and relaxation, especially in such lavish surroundings. No doubt this place had the kind of luxury she rarely got to enjoy anymore, especially when traveling with the symphony.

But she couldn't relax until she'd received a clean bill of health both for herself and for her baby. She sat up, eager to see the physician and begin the tests which would, she hoped, relieve all her worries.

William stowed his laptop and the two other men put away their Palm Pilots. Briefly, she considered asking if the royal PR department issued the devices as standard equipment. Then she caught sight of the "lodge" and forgot all that.

Perched on the cliff like some massive cedar hawk overlooking the lake, the building looked large enough to easily accommodate one hundred or more guests. Through the two-story window over the door, she could see a wall of windows on the waterside, filling the house with light and a breathtaking view.

The limo coasted to a stop. The driver got out and opened the door for Sydney. When she stepped into the blinding sunlight, she stumbled. Instantly, Chase was there, offering his arm.

At first, she wanted to snub him, to show him she was perfectly capable of walking in on her own. But when she saw the massive double doors open and a footman wearing royal livery emerge, she changed her mind.

Though she might carry the blood of a princess, and, as a child, had often longed to meet her sire, Reginald had been her only exposure to royalty. Quite frankly, she found the prospect intimidating.

"Come on." Keeping her arm in his, Chase led her up the stone steps, through the great doors and into the foyer. Their footsteps echoed on the green marble floor.

He released her arm as the doors closed behind them. Turning slowly, Sydney tried to take it all in, but couldn't.

Gleaming floors, walls and ceiling crafted of warm oak, she had an impression of granite and wood and steel, skillfully melded into a welcoming warmth that could have won design awards. This place was the stuff of glossy magazines, reminding her of her mother's penthouse condo.

As she took it all in, she spied a familiar black instrument case leaning against one wall.

"My cello!" She crossed the room, trailing her fingers over the black case reverently. "How did you locate it?"

"We had it flown in." William smiled as both she and Chase turned to stare at him in surprise. "Rest assured, it wasn't damaged in the shooting. The hotel was holding it in their lost-and-found department, along with your suitcase full of clothing. We've put that in your room."

Chase shot her a look that said *I told you so.*

No matter. Sydney sighed with pleasure. Now all she needed was a clean bill of health for her baby and a way home. Then her life would be just about perfect. Even if her baby would never have a father.

A man who could have only been the butler cleared his throat. "May I show you to your room?"

She swung round to eye Chase. "I'd prefer to see the doctor first."

"Get settled and freshen up." Despite his size, or maybe because of it, Chase looked at home in the deliberately rugged yet opulent surroundings. He stood out from the other men like a rare coin among wooden currency. "I'll send someone for you when the doctor is ready."

Nodding, she turned to follow the butler and realized her misgivings were because she didn't want to leave Chase— proving once again that she wasn't herself since the plane crash. Despite feeling mortified, she couldn't stop herself from looking at him over her shoulder.

"You'll be fine." The kindness in his voice told her that somehow he must have understood.

Her room was, like the rest of the lodge, luxuriously comfortable. Everything, from the oversized bed covered with a cream-colored, exquisitely soft, down comforter, to the well-made, gleaming oak furniture, was of the highest quality. The room had the feel of an ultraprivate, ultraluxurious, resort for the very pampered ultrarich.

Feet sinking into the thick carpet, Sydney padded over to the windows and pulled the heavy lined drapes open.

She gasped out loud at the view. Her room overlooked the lake. It spread out below her like a liquid sapphire, shimmering in the sunlight. Whitecap waves dotted the surface, along with sailboats and the occasional yacht. She could make out other homes dotting the countryside, all large and luxurious, though none matched this one for sheer magnificence.

Since she'd showered earlier, she had nothing to do but wait.

"The doctor's here."

Startled, Sydney turned to find a smiling young woman in a maid's uniform hovering in the doorway. Evidently, she'd once again forgotten to close her door.

"If you'll follow me, please?"

Eagerness warring with nervousness, Sydney went.

Chapter 8

Once the examination was complete, Sydney waited, her heartbeat booming in her ears. Dr. Kallan had confirmed Sydney's suspicion that only an ultrasound examination and a complete blood workup would tell if her baby was all right. The equipment to do this test was, of course, only available at a hospital. The nearest facility was in the next town inland, a good thirty-minute drive on winding roads. Dr. Kallan had gone to tell Chase and the others.

A moment later, the doctor returned. He smiled reassuringly as he patted Sydney's hand. "They've agreed to take you into town. The car is being brought around now. I'll meet you at the emergency room there."

A grim-faced Chase and his three stooges waited for her in the great room.

"Ready?" His cool gaze gave away nothing.

Schooling her own expression to match his, Sydney nodded.

Though they left by unmarked car, someone must have tipped off the reporters. When their black Mercedes pulled up to the emergency-room entrance, a cluster of photographers eagerly awaited their arrival.

"Keep driving," Chase instructed the driver. "This isn't an emergency. Go around to the back."

"They've probably got people stationed there, as well." Sydney kept her tone calm. "If so, take me back to the emergency room. Dr. Kallan said he'd be waiting for me there."

"It doesn't look like we're going to be able to avoid the reporters." William sounded energized.

"I'll be fine." Sydney sighed. "I've been dealing with them off and on for most of my life."

"Don't speak to the press." Chase met her gaze. "Let us handle them."

"Don't worry. I have nothing to say to them."

Scowling, he glared at her. "They think you married the prince."

"I know."

"Wishing it was true?"

She only shrugged off his sharp-edged question. At least if she had, her baby would be acknowledged. Legitimate.

On the other hand, her child would be heir to the throne. He or she would never have a normal life. Thinking of her half-brothers and -sisters and the rarefied air they lived in, she'd already decided she didn't want that for her own child, not if she could help it. She'd planned to discuss alternatives with Reginald.

But since he'd refused even to speak to her, that talk

had never happened. Now it was all up to her to take care of her baby.

Chase eyed her, his sharp gaze missing nothing. "I've got people setting up an official press conference for you this afternoon, so you can set the record straight. Once it's known you're not carrying the next official heir, maybe the death threats will cease."

She sighed. "I was hoping hiding out here would take care of that."

"Until we know more about that car that tried to run us off the road, I'm taking no chances. Plus, with all the reporters here," he gestured at the waiting crowd, "whoever is after you will know exactly where you are."

She peered through the tinted glass, eyeing the eager faces, the microphones and cameras. Somehow, without intending to, she'd managed to achieve what her mother had always craved. She was in the spotlight.

All Sydney wanted to do was return home to Naessa and her life of relative anonymity. She wanted to lick her wounds in private and prepare for the upcoming birth of her child.

"Coming here might have been a big mistake." William leaned forward. "They'll make the connection between this town and the royal lodge. Before long they'll be camped outside the gates."

"I needed to have tests run." Sydney kept her tone firm. "So I had to come here whether you like it or not. Plus, you can't keep me hidden forever." Unbidden, thoughts of Chawder Island intruded. She couldn't help but speculate on what would have happened if they'd stayed longer. She'd never experienced anything quite like the explosiveness of nearly making love with Chase. She wondered what the real thing would be like.

The heat in Chase's gaze told her he shared her thoughts.

Embarrassed, she looked away, back out her window to where the vultures circled with their flashbulbs and their video cameras.

The car slowly circled the building. Clusters of reporters were gathered around each entrance.

"They're unbelievable." Sydney had gotten her first experience with paparazzi early. As a young girl, her mother had enjoyed taking her out in public dressed in outlandishly expensive outfits. Someone had always been around to snap a picture of the illegitimate princess and her lovely mother for the tabloids.

Her mother had considered it amusing. She'd preened for the cameras, thriving on the notoriety. Sydney had always been the opposite. As she'd grown, she'd begun to see the press as stalkers and her mother as a panderer.

Once grown, she'd done her best to live in a way designed not to draw attention. The more quietly she lived her life, the less the press hounded her. Lack of flash and bling made for boring pictures. Soon, the press all but ignored her. A cello-playing, illegitimate princess who never partied wasn't considered newsworthy.

Until the Crown Prince of Silvershire had taken a shine to her. Dating Reginald had changed all that. She grimaced at the thought. Like her mother, the prince had seemed to enjoy the attention. Sydney had been content to leave him the limelight. She'd preferred to remain in the shadows.

Damned if she was going to let them hound her baby.

"Take us back to the emergency room," Chase ordered the driver. "Pull up as close to the door as possible. I'll take her in there."

The instant she and Chase stepped from the car, they were surrounded. Flashbulbs popped and microphones were thrust in her face while the reporters shouted questions. Stone-faced, Chase shouldered his way through while Sydney clung to his back.

Each time someone shoved a mike in front of him, he repeated four words. "Press conference later today."

Once inside, they found the brazen press had followed.

"There." Chase pointed. A nurse held a door open for them, letting them bypass the check-in desk. One of the perks of being attached to royalty, Sydney supposed.

"Wait here." Her shoes squeaking on the linoleum, the nurse indicated two hard plastic chairs. "Dr. Kallan is on his way."

Sydney sat. Chase remained standing, his hands crammed in his pockets.

"What's wrong?" she asked softly.

Instead of answering, he responded with a question. "You really don't like the spotlight, do you?"

So that was it. Of course. He was head of public relations. Dealing with reporters was his job and, she suspected, his life.

"I told you I didn't. Why? Was there something wrong with the way I avoided them?"

Though she'd meant the question as sort of a joke, he regarded her with a serious expression. "Do you really want the picture they splash all over the newspapers to be one of you with your face burrowed into my chest?"

She shrugged. "Honestly, I don't really care. All I was thinking about at the time was getting through the crowd, not how I'd look in the news."

"But—"

"Miss Conner?" The nurse was back. "If you'll follow me."

Chase started to rise, too, but Sydney stopped him with a look. "You can wait here."

The muscle that worked in his jaw was the only sign he gave of how he felt about her request. But he did as she'd asked. As the automatic doors closed behind her, Sydney felt a stab of regret, which she automatically suppressed. Her baby's welfare had nothing to do with Chase and wanting his support was only more foolishness on her part. Plus, all the water she'd had to drink in preparation made her uncomfortable.

The sonogram was done with quiet efficiency, the warmed gel and the gentle motions of the technician soothing. After they'd finished and cleaned her up, she was taken to another room where a different nurse drew blood.

Barely forty-five minutes had passed before Sydney rejoined Chase in the private waiting room.

"All done?" Chase's hooded gaze spoke of a simmering anger. Since he had no reason to be angry, Sydney pretended not to notice.

"It'll be a little while until I get the results." Despite her best efforts to sound cool, calm and collected, her voice caught.

"Don't worry." He touched her arm. "Everything will be all right." He held her gaze for the space of a heartbeat before he looked away.

Because she hoped he was right, she said nothing. Instead, she studied his chiseled profile. Perversely, she wished he wasn't so damn beautiful. If he weren't, she might find it easier to hate him, if it came to that when all this ended.

She could deal with that, she told herself, as long as she

didn't lose her heart. And God knew, she would never be that foolish again.

The nurse emerged, causing them both to look up. "If you'll follow me?"

This time, when Chase followed, Sydney let him.

They were led down a long hall to a small office. Two high-backed leather chairs faced a mahogany desk.

"The doctor will be with you shortly," the nurse said.

Sydney stared at the chair, her rapid heartbeat feeling as though it were in her throat.

"Sit."

"I don't know if I can."

His smile was a flash of white. "Of course you can. What else are you going to do? You can't pace in such a tiny room."

He had a point. Sydney sat.

When he lowered himself into the chair next to her and then took her hand, she froze. He squeezed her fingers and she decided to take the comfort he offered.

A moment later, Dr. Kallan bustled into the room, smiling broadly. "I have good news. You're absolutely fine and your baby is developing normally."

Sydney released her breath. Clutching Chase's hand, she turned to him, her eyes filling. "Thank God."

Chase's hard expression softened. "Congratulations."

Impulsively, she leaned over and kissed him before jumping to her feet and hugging the doctor. "You don't know what a relief it is to hear that."

The gray-haired doctor smiled back. "You're about eight weeks along. Everything looks good."

"Could you tell the baby's sex from this sonogram?"

He shook his head. "Not yet. It's too early. We can

usually determine the sex of the fetus accurately by sixteen to eighteen weeks using ultrasound or fifteen to sixteen weeks with an amniocentesis. Or, if you'd like to come back in two weeks, we can do a CVS, chorionic villus sampling. That's usually reliable at ten or eleven weeks."

"I won't be here then."

At her words, Chase stiffened.

The doctor smiled. "Then I'm afraid you'll have to guess a bit longer." He stood and held out his hand.

After she shook it, he inclined his head. "If you need anything else, have your people give me a call."

Once in the hallway, Sydney headed for the doors under the sign marked Exit. Chase stopped her.

"We need to discuss a strategy."

"A strategy for what?"

"Dealing with the press."

She sighed. "What's to discuss? We'll just do the same thing we did before. Breeze through them with a bunch of 'No comments.'"

"We can't. We can get away with ignoring them once. If we do it twice, they'll speculate."

"So? Let them." She tried to pull away, but his hand on her shoulder prevented her. "Let me go."

"Do you want to read a story in the morning about how you got rid of your baby?"

Shocked, she stared up at him. "What do you mean?"

"You know how some of them can be, especially the tabloids. Lacking truth to report, they'll simply make something up."

"I would never do such a thing."

"They don't know that. The general public doesn't either."

"You can tell you're in public relations." She couldn't keep the bitterness from her voice.

Stoically, he watched her.

"Fine. We'll make a statement. What do you want me to say?" Despite her anger, her emotions were perilously close to the surface. The back of her throat stung, and she blinked away tears.

"Sydney—" With a curse, he crushed her to him, covering her mouth with his in a hard, possessive kiss.

Neither heard the doors silently swing open.

A flashbulb popped. Then another. Suddenly, reporters with camcorders and cameras surrounded them.

Jaw clenched tightly, Chase released her.

She turned in time to see the cameraman flash a thumbs-up sign. She recognized the reporter standing next to him as Chris Endov, one of the beat reporters for the *Daily Press,* Silforshire's main paper.

"What do you want, Endov?" Chase asked. Though he sounded pleasant enough, Sydney recognized the thread of steel underlying his tone.

"I have a few questions." Endov came closer. "For you, Miss Conner. First you're hot and heavy with the prince, and now that he's dead, you're with his royal publicist? Any particular reason for that?"

Chase answered before Sydney could even open her mouth. "No comment." Arm around her waist, he began shepherding her away.

The reporters followed, shouting questions.

"Are you still pregnant?"

Sydney tensed. Without even looking at them, Chase tossed off a quick, "No comment."

"No, wait." Sydney stopped, turning to face the restless

throng. "I want to answer that. Yes, I definitely am still pregnant. I came here to have a routine checkup."

More flashbulbs. Several of the camcorders were rolling. Sydney tried to look a dignified as possible, memories of her mother's simpering pandering haunting her.

"Do you know your baby's sex?" someone shouted.

She forced a smile. "No, it's too early for that."

"Were you and Prince Reginald secretly married?"

Without waiting for her answer, another reporter followed up. "Now that the prince is dead, are you planning to step forward and proclaim your unborn child heir to the throne?"

She stood straight and tall, the afternoon breeze lifting her hair. "Absolutely not."

"Then," someone else called out, "you're saying your baby will be born unwanted and illegitimate, like you?"

Someone gasped. The rowdy reporters fell silent, one by one. Chase cursed.

For Sydney, time seemed to stand still. She blanched, turning her face away from the crowd, toward Chase, longing for the comfort of his broad chest.

He took a step toward her and stopped, his expression dark. When she raised her gaze to him, she knew she wasn't strong enough or quick enough to hide her stark pain.

"Old wound," she said, striving for lightness but sounding instead as though she'd taken a blow to the solar plexus. She kept her eyes fixed on Chase while she spoke, using him as an anchor.

Something dark, something haunted, crossed his face. She noticed how he fisted his hands, though he kept them at his sides while he searched the crowd to try and find out who'd spoken.

She didn't want to know.

Someone cleared their throat.

"Who asked that?" Voice deadly calm, Chase searched their faces. No one stepped forward.

"Then we're done here," he said, taking Sydney's arm to lead her off.

"I have one more question." A woman wearing too much makeup and an overloud orange dress raised her hand.

Chase sighed. "Go ahead."

"Miss Conner, you never answered the question." Her broad face had the determination of a bulldog. "Is there any truth to the rumor that you and Prince Reginald were married before his death?"

His expression furious, Chase shook his head.

"She's engaged to me," he said.

Several in the crowd gasped audibly, but none louder than Sydney.

Once said, Chase wanted to call those words back. He had no idea what had come over him. The declaration had just popped out. From nowhere. He knew better. What he'd said was not only foolish, but improbable, implausible and highly suspect. Yet now, having said them, he realized he'd have to make them work—somehow, until something could be done to rectify his mistake.

Sydney gazed up at him, her eyes wide and impossibly blue. "Engaged? We are so not—"

"Talking about this now," Chase put in smoothly. Then, partly because she had a mutinous set to her chin, and partly because her open mouth just looked so damn inviting, he kissed her again.

As before, the moment his mouth covered hers, he was lost in a tidal wave of desire and need. Standing stiffly, she sighed into his mouth. Then, as lust all but consumed him, she brought her arms up around his neck, tangled her free hand in his hair, and held him in place. Her tongue stroked and tempted and teased and either she was the best damn actress he'd ever met, or she craved him as badly as he wanted her.

He almost forgot they were standing in a hospital surrounded by reporters. His desire for Sydney filled him, and any other time, any other place, they would have made hot, urgent love.

Out of the question. He lifted his head, breathing raggedly, and fought to regain his shattered control.

Now though, the ultimate PR professional had a pressing problem. With her wild kisses and her body melded so close to his, she'd aroused the hell out of him. They had a crowd of spectators. If he turned to face the reporters now, they'd know exactly how much he wanted Sydney, his brand new fiancée.

Her breathing as ragged as his, she hid her face against his chest, her color high.

The reporters all shouted questions—and ribald comments—at once. Dimly he became aware of flashbulbs popping. Damn. He had to hand it to her. Sydney had succeeded in making him do what he'd never done in his entire career in public relations—lose control in front of the press. *Hell,* he thought ruefully, hanging on to the last shreds of his tattered restraint as he eyed the news cameras, in this case, *in front of the entire world.*

Still, he couldn't help longing to finish what he'd inadvertently started. *Another time, another place…*

Regretfully, he took a deep breath and, keeping Sydney tight against him, turned partially to face them. Ignoring the upraised hands, the videocams, the shouts, he forced his expression into an indulgent smile. "Ladies, gentlemen. May we have a little privacy, please?" A foolish request. He knew it, they knew it, but by simply asking, he'd guaranteed himself a bit more time to get his unruly hormones under control.

As he'd expected, this caused a good-natured uproar. Most laughed and shouted ribald jokes. A few loudly protested. While they argued among themselves, Chase tried to think of playing golf, which was the most calming, unsexy thing he could think of.

He had to give Sydney credit. Though one look at her dilated pupils and unsteady breathing told him she was just as affected as he, she smoothed her hair with one hand, her shirt with the other, and straightened. When she did look toward the crowd, her serene expression gave nothing away.

She wore, he thought with grudging respect, the face of someone used to dealing with the press. In his line of work, he had to admire that. Royals like her made his job that much easier.

Together they ignored the reporters. Thirty seconds later, feeling almost normal, he removed his arm from Sydney's shoulders.

"So are you aiming to move up in the palace hierarchy, Mr. Savage?"

He answered smoothly, though he knew what they meant. "Not possible. I don't have royal blood. You should know better than that."

"But she does." A woman with short dark hair, dressed casually in faded jeans and hiking boots, pointed at Sydney. "She's a princess of Naessa. What does this bode for the two countries' continued relations?"

Political implications. Not good. Carrington hadn't briefed him on the official palace response.

While he searched for a suitable nonanswer, Sydney straightened and lifted her chin. With his hand still on her shoulder, he could feel her tension—she all but vibrated with it.

Her blue eyes were cool as she measured the other woman. "No, as someone else so succinctly pointed out earlier, I'm illegitimate. I have no real title. I'm certain there are quite a few of Prince Kerwin's by-blows running around Naessa. My actions carry neither political clout nor connotations."

This brought another round of shouted queries.

Sydney held up her hand. "You know and I know that I have no real claim to fame. I live a quiet life, not bothering anyone. And no one, including the press, bothers me. Most importantly, I don't think any of this makes me particularly newsworthy."

"You were seen quite frequently with Prince Reginald, before he died."

She sighed. "He was a great fan of the symphony."

The dryness of her tone made a few of them chuckle.

"Were you two lovers while she was sleeping with the Prince?" Paul Seacrist, of *Silvershire Inquisitor* fame, stepped forward. The tabloid, known as *The Quiz,* bore the logo of a large, all-seeing eye. Which often felt particularly appropriate, since their cameramen seemed to be everywhere.

Sydney gasped. Chase squeezed her shoulder, letting her know he intended to handle this one himself.

At the smug knowing leer on the man's pinched face, a stab of anger went through Chase, sharp as a knife. If he gave in to impulse and punched the guy out, there'd be hell to pay. What a field day they'd have with that!

He took a deep breath. He hadn't gotten to his position as head of PR by losing control.

Quieting, all the reporters watched them, waiting for a reaction, cameras ready.

Suddenly, Chase realized he recognized the voice. It had been Seacrist who earlier had hurt Sydney by calling her illegitimate and unwanted. He took a step forward.

Seacrist continued to wait expectantly. Something in his expression told Chase he knew if Chase touched him, not only would he have the story of the year, but a million-dollar lawsuit, as well.

Damn it!

It took all of his training and skill, but Chase kept his head. "You've just insulted me, Miss Conner and the deceased prince. I expect an apology. Now."

"Apology?" The other man looked disappointed. "I was only asking a simple question. I meant no insult."

Chase inclined his head, accepting the reporter's words, since he could do little else.

There were more questions, all routine. Chase fielded two or three about the baby, answering in such generalities that he told them absolutely nothing. He'd developed a knack for this sort of thing, appearing to be utterly forthright while revealing little of the truth.

Doing what he was paid to do, he should be in his element. But he was not. For the first time in his career, Chase felt as if he were watching the reporters who vied for his attention from a distance. Instead of feeling energized, he felt annoyed and irritated.

Through all this, Sydney held herself regally, gazing at

the reporters defiantly. Her cinnamon hair glowed, even in the harsh, artificial light, and her eyes stood out starkly in her pale, pale face. While trying to hide her hurt, she was absolutely beautiful. Watching her, he felt a clenching low in his stomach.

God help him, he still longed for her. Even now, he wanted to kiss the side of her long, creamy throat, tangle his hands in her lustrous hair. Instead, he leaned closer, inhaling her scent, and whispered in her ear. "Are you ready?"

"For what?" she mouthed.

"To make a run for it. After all we've given them, we should be home free."

She rolled her eyes. "Do you really think they'll let us go?"

"That's why we're going to make a run for it. We'll leave them no choice."

She nodded. "Then let's go. But this time, I'm going first." Taking a deep breath, she plunged through the crowd for the doorway. Amused, he followed.

Like sharks moving in for the kill, the press surrounded her, blocking her path, still calling out questions.

Undeterred, she continued to push forward.

Following behind her, Chase gave them all a rueful smile. "What, no privacy?"

The ones closest to him laughed.

Finally, they reached the exit and squeezed through the doors, heading for the car. Once he'd seen Sydney safely inside he turned to face the reporters, one hand on the door handle.

"Come on, people. Settle down." He heaved a loud, mock sigh, and waited. Once they'd quieted, he gave them an impersonal smile. "I'd planned to hold a press conference later, but now I see no need. You have had more information than I ever intended you to have."

There were several collective groans. Finally, he held up his hand, and they quieted. "I think that's all, folks. We just gave you all a fantastic story, announcing our engagement. So it seems to me you'd take that and run with it and allow us some small measure of privacy. We'd like to celebrate— just not in front of a crowd."

This time, he spoke a partial truth. He wanted to be alone with Sydney, to explain why he'd said what he had.

One last, diehard newshound stepped forward. "What about the baby? How does it make you feel, Mr. Savage, knowing your wife-to-be is pregnant with another man's child? Not just any other man, but Prince Reginald, your boss?"

Even the casual mention of Reginald in the same context as Sydney grated on Chase's nerves. And the reminder she was pregnant by another man was much-needed. It served to remind him why he couldn't allow his desire for her to cloud his judgment any further. Put that way, his sudden urge to help Sydney seemed stupid—something he already knew.

Not since he'd been left at the altar by Kayla, then publicly humiliated by her announcement that the baby he'd thought was his belonged to another man, had he allowed his emotions to rule him. His attempt to take some of the heat off her had just guaranteed that the press would continue to speculate. And to hound them.

Chapter 9

William and the others regarded them curiously as they got settled. Sydney didn't speak, not even after Chase had climbed in beside her and pulled the door closed behind him. She waited until the car pulled out and the other men were once again involved with their electronic gadgets.

"Chase?"

With an effort, he made himself look at her, steeling himself for what he knew was to come. Based on his experience with other women, he expected theatrics, shouting and tears and possibly even curses.

He'd forgotten he was dealing with a princess by blood, even if she didn't carry the official title.

Her regal bearing and the simmering anger in her husky voice were the only signs she was upset.

And all he could think about was how badly he wanted to kiss her again.

Leaning forward, she looked him in the eye. "What exactly happened back there?"

Feeling reckless, Chase let a slow smile spread across his face. "I think we just got engaged."

William looked up so sharply he nearly popped his neck. One of the other men dropped his Palm Pilot, fumbling, his seat belt still clasped, to retrieve it.

"What was that? What did you say?"

"I said that Miss Conner and I have just become engaged."

"You're kidding!" William exploded. "There's no way—"

Maybe because his raw emotions simmered too close to the surface for him to control, Chase felt his cool facade slip. He let it show in his eyes as he looked at the other man. "Why is that, William?"

Taking the hint, William closed his mouth and sat back in his seat. He grabbed his own Palm Pilot and began fumbling with it. "Never mind," he mumbled. "Don't know what I was thinking. Congratulations, sir. Ma'am."

Sydney made a rude sound, causing William to raise his head in surprise. A sharp glare from Chase made him look away again.

"Well?"

He looked down into her upturned face and sighed. Even after all that, after knowing he'd messed up big-time and would have to find a way to correct it, he wanted to kiss her. "Can we talk about this later?" he grumbled.

She glanced at the others, trying to pretend not to listen and doing a poor job of it, and sighed. "Certainly. Though it will be at my convenience, not yours. Agreed?"

"Agreed."

When she looked away, Chase set his jaw and stared

straight ahead. He could feel Sydney's resentment, and he couldn't really blame her. Aware the others were sneaking quick glances at him, he ignored them, hyperaware of the press of her thigh against his. He couldn't help but wonder what it was about Sydney, how even now his desire for her was such that all he could think about was pulling her onto his lap and kissing her thoroughly.

He shifted in the seat, trying to make space where there was none. Since he wasn't able to do so, Sydney took care of the problem for him. Scrunching up so close to the door she must have been uncomfortable, she moved so that no part of her body touched him. At all.

He felt this absence of touch a thousand times more sharply than he should have.

When they pulled up to the royal lodge, everyone scrambled to exit the car. Except Sydney. Shoulders stiff, she climbed out and shot him a look over her shoulder. Her eyes the color of a storm-tossed sea, she shook her head. By the time he recovered enough to go after her, she'd disappeared into the house.

Practically running, Sydney barreled up the stairs and turned right when she should have turned left. The hallway looked the same, but she found herself in a large library instead of the bedroom she'd been assigned.

Curious, she eyed the floor-to-ceiling bookshelves with a dawning sense of wonder. Inspecting a shelf, then another, she saw classics and current bestsellers, research material and picture books. Whoever had collected these books had been a person of vast and varying interests.

So engrossed was she in taking in this smorgasbord of

reading material, she nearly missed the huge portrait of Reginald hanging over the antique writing desk.

Her breath caught. Feet sinking in the plush carpet, she moved slowly closer, taking in his blond hair and blue eyes. Would her child look like this, or would there be a combination of both their features, hair color and eyes?

The father of her baby. Crown Prince Reginald, now dead. Studying his patrician features, she waited for the familiar anguished feeling, but felt nothing but a sort of distant sorrow.

"Missing your lover?" Chase's voice, harsh and low, sent shivers of warning along her spine.

She didn't answer; instead she continued to examine the portrait. Remarkably lifelike—and life-sized—the painting had to have been made fairly recently.

Chase moved to stand beside her. "Cold-looking bastard, wasn't he?"

With a gasp, she turned to face him. Contempt and an icy sort of rage filled his face. But he was looking at the painting, not at her.

"Chase," she began.

"I know. I shouldn't speak ill of the dead."

With a nod, she turned to go, her heart heavy.

"Sydney…" The anguish in his deep voice stopped her, made her turn to face him.

"What was he to you?" He jabbed his finger toward the portrait. "I can't reconcile the idea of you with him."

"I thought he loved me."

He looked at her, hunger blazing from his eyes, but did not touch her. "And you," he asked. "Did you love him back?"

Feeling as though she was suffocating, she stepped back, away from the man who'd inexplicably made her realize what she'd felt for Reginald hadn't been love. Not by a long shot. "I thought I did." She choked out her reply and then, because she was afraid of what else she might say, brushed past him and out the door. Hoping she could remember the way to her room, she made her way down the hallway, telling herself she was glad when he didn't follow.

Though she wanted an explanation for his bizarre announcement, that'd have to wait until later. Right now, her emotions were too raw, her feelings about him too conflicted. What he'd told the press at the hospital had shocked her. She didn't know if Chase really thought he was helping her by announcing a fictitious engagement, or if he was mocking her.

Or, she sighed as a third possibility occurred to her, he might be trying yet another ploy to get her to remain at Lake Lodan.

Quite honestly, she didn't know what to think, how to feel, where to go. The only thing she knew for certain was she needed time to figure things out.

What was wrong with her? Covering her face with her hands, she couldn't decide whether to laugh or cry.

She'd come to crave Chase Savage. When he entered the room, everyone else ceased to exist. When he moved, the masculine grace of his muscular body made her catch her breath. One look from him and her throat went dry.

And the explosive passion when they touched haunted her dreams. His kisses, his touch, the way his hard body felt under her exploring fingers, made her quiver. Even now.

She'd begun to wonder how colorless her life would seem once Chase was no longer part of it. Such an admission, even to herself, shook her to the core.

Knowing her hormones were out of whack due to her pregnancy didn't help either. She could only blame hormones for so much emotional upheaval.

The only thing she knew for certain was when he kissed her, she forgot all reason. Merely seeing his hard profile made her long to soften his expression with kisses.

Something in him called to her. If she'd met him before Reginald, before she carried another man's child, she might have taken a chance on him.

Now, she couldn't afford to take a chance on anything.

She located her room without further incident. Once inside, she changed into a comfortable pair of jeans and sneakers. She felt confined, trapped in a twenty-five-thousand-square-foot mansion with iron gates on one side and cliffs and a lake on the other.

Then she spied her cello. With a relieved sigh, she lifted the case and headed back for the library, praying she didn't run into Chase. With its rich oak floors, walls and ceilings, the acoustics should be wonderful. She padded down the hall, trying to fill her mind with the notes she'd play.

The cello had always been her salvation in the past. It would save her now, as well. She'd lose herself in the music and forget all about her problems, even if her solution was only temporary.

Once she reached her destination, she grabbed a comfortable, French-style chair and began setting up her instrument.

Reverently, she popped open the case. Unharmed, the maple gleamed as softly as if she'd just polished it. Lovingly, she removed the cello and, holding the neck lightly with one hand, she reached for the bow. She was startled to notice her fingers shook.

This bow, despite its origins, was her favorite bow ever. Reginald had ordered it custom-made for her. He'd allowed her to choose her own horsehair and she'd selected the finest, whitest hair herself. Some cellists preferred a darker hair, believing it "grabbed" better, but she liked her bow to glide across the strings. She preferred a clean, pure sound.

Once she had everything ready, she gave the cello one final check and began to play.

After Sydney had left, Chase had studied the portrait of the man who now felt like an enemy, and wondered. What had Sydney seen in the man? His features reflected his arrogance, his disdain for anything not directed at him, his comfort, his pleasure. Reginald had been dissolute, a player and a wastrel. Seeing Sydney mooning over his likeness had made fury twist in Chase's gut.

He didn't want to try and analyze the reasons for this, so he'd left the library and stormed off to his own room, glad it was far from hers.

Once there, he'd dropped onto the bed and tried to call Carrington on the new cell phone William had given him. When he'd reached the duke's voice mail, he'd left a message, planning to ask for a reassignment back in Silverton. Then, in urgent need of distraction, he'd just decided to wander downstairs to the great room and indulge in some hundred-year-old Scotch, when he heard an unusual noise.

A note.

The sound was haunting, like ghosts teasing the wind. Chase listened, not sure what he was hearing, only knowing it was a different kind of music than he'd ever heard before.

Skittering across his skin, the sound teased, taunted. Led him to take a step forward, feeling as though he'd been bewitched by some ancient spell.

He went looking for the source of the sound, knowing it could be only one thing. At the door to the library he paused, listening as his amazement grew. He'd known she was talented, but classical music had never been his thing. Until now.

Then he saw her, red hair ablaze in the muted light. Sydney. Her music called to him, true. But *she* called to him even more.

Transfixed, he stood, and watched her play.

The polished maple of her cello glowed softly. Eyes closed, she appeared lost in coaxing the sound from her instrument. Oblivious to him or anyone else, her elegant hand led her bow across the strings in swift, yet sensuous gliding. Rapid, then slow, each sweep brought forth a haunting sound, as though the cello wept.

This music was as different from classic rock as day was from night. Normally, not at all his cup of tea.

But somehow, he was charmed. Enthralled. He longed to touch her, to kiss her pulse where it jumped at the hollow of her throat. Instead, he stood in the shadows and listened and watched.

The notes glided and climbed. The tempo grew faster. Sydney's bow flew, her face flushed, eyes still closed.

When the last note died off, she opened her eyes in a sudden flash of blue.

His heart caught in his chest.

Desire clawed at him. Lust and need and yearning propelled him toward her without even thinking.

He wanted her. Now.

Gaze still locked with his, she hurriedly set the cello and bow aside, and lifted herself up to meet him halfway. His hard, fierce kiss swallowed her soft cry.

Finally, Chase let himself do what he'd longed to do each and every time he saw her. Feeling as if he were a blind man who'd thus far been denied the power of touch, he drew his hands over her, savoring each lush curve, each satin hollow, memorizing her shape and scent and feel.

Body arching toward his hands, she matched the urgency of his caresses with her own. Her long, elegant fingers stroked him, until he was shaking with a need so intense he felt violent.

Their clothing was an unwanted barrier for each of them.

"The door," she managed, no doubt fearing a servant would wander in.

He crossed to the doorway and with one swift motion, tugged the door closed. Then, impatient for her once more, he returned and kissed her. The long, sensual kiss had them both breathing hard.

Shaking, he managed to undo the buttons of her blouse without tearing it. She tried to do the same to his shirt and could not. When she looked at him, her eyes wild and so dark they were nearly black, he moved her hands and ripped his own shirt off his chest.

The remainder of their clothing swiftly followed, until they faced each other with nothing covering their skin.

"Let me look at you," he said hoarsely. And she, with a soft, hesitant smile, let her arms drop to her sides and faced him.

The sight of her, so perfectly formed, nearly brought him to his knees.

Then, her soft smile widening, she took a step forward. "I'd like to do the same."

For a moment he didn't understand her whispered request. Then, when he realized she wanted to look at him as badly as he'd wanted to see her, he bit back a groan.

She came closer, circling him. When she pressed her naked breasts into his back, he shuddered. She kissed his neck and, with a savage cry, he turned so that his chest and hers, hard and soft, touched.

"Not yet," he told her. "I want to kiss you, here."

She began trembling as he tasted each taut nipple, and her moan of ecstasy nearly undid him. When she began stroking him, tentatively at first, then growing bolder, he burned under the feel of her hands on him.

He touched her, too, the sweet honey of her body more temptation than he could bear.

The couch seemed impossibly distant, but, half carrying her, he tumbled onto it. She sank into the buttery-soft leather as he buried himself in her.

Finally.

They fitted together perfectly.

Utterly and completely right.

Maybe now, he told himself with the last shred of coherence remaining to him, once he'd slaked his hunger, he'd stop burning.

She kissed him again, her open mouth and the movement of her body a heady invitation as they moved together. He started to close his eyes, but then opened them. He wanted to watch her beautiful face, see the expression in her eyes as they danced together to the music she'd played for them both.

He burned, she shattered. As she did, he felt his own release begin and realized an awful truth. Rather than easing the way he burned for her, the fire had spread. She'd managed to enflame not only his body, but his heart and soul, as well.

He was, Chase thought, as he cradled her in his arms, in big trouble. The kind of trouble he not only didn't need, but after the fiasco with Kayla, had vowed never to let happen to him again.

* * *

The next morning, Chase went down to get coffee, leaving Sydney still asleep in his bed. He smiled when he remembered how they'd hastily dressed after the first time they'd made love, and then headed from the library to his room. He'd felt giddy, like a young kid. Giggling, she'd been the same. They'd whispered and exchanged breathless kisses while they'd slunk down the long hall.

Once they'd reached his room, she'd laughed so hard she'd fallen back onto his bed. He'd dived on top of her and they'd ended up in each other's arms again.

The laughter had changed to kisses, the kisses had led to caresses, and before long he was buried deep inside her, while she moved seductively under him.

She hadn't intended to stay the night; he hadn't intended to let her. They'd cuddled and he'd thought their lovemaking over, but a short while later, her tentative touches had him fully aroused again.

Amazing. Astounding. And absolutely, perfectly, fulfilling.

After a third marathon session in each other's arms, they'd both fallen deeply asleep. When he'd wakened to an armful of still-slumbering Sydney, he'd felt more content than he'd ever felt in his life.

Content? Fulfilled? Such feelings horrified him, especially since he knew how quickly they could disappear and how badly he'd hurt afterwards.

So when he'd woken to find her cuddled in his arms, and realized he wanted to stay that way indefinitely, he'd slid from his bed without waking her, stumbled to the bathroom where he'd brushed his teeth and dragged a brush through his hair. Then he'd hurriedly dressed and left her sleeping in his bed.

The kitchen was crowded; the other men appeared to have just finished their breakfast. Bright sunlight streamed in through the window over the sink. Outside, he could see the lake, bluer than the cloudless sky, with only a few boats marring its perfect surface.

Sydney would like—no. Heading for the coffeepot, Chase ordered himself to stop thinking of Sydney. But the mere thought of her brought to mind how badly he wanted to return to his room and join her, naked under the covers.

"What's up with you?" William regarded him curiously, peering out from behind the morning paper. "You look unusually content this morning."

The other two men eyed Chase, as well.

Carlos broke into a grin. "No, he looks like a well-fed lion who's just brought down a gazelle. I'm betting this has something to do with the beauticious Ms. Conner."

Ignoring the dark-haired man, Chase looked at William, who shrugged and went back to his newspaper. Sitting next to him, Jim wisely kept his mouth shut, though his bemused expression told Chase exactly what he was thinking.

His contentment showed in his face. Damn it. Sydney had somehow softened him. He wasn't sure he could afford to be so weak.

Sydney. Again he could see her, long, silky legs tangled in the sheets. In his mind's eye, she stretched, her full breasts outthrust, begging for the touch of his hand, or mouth.

Hell, he had it bad.

"There he goes again," Carlos commented. "He has the look of a man in lo—"

"Don't even say it," Chase snapped. Despite his irritation, or maybe because of it, he caught himself longing for Chawder Island. At least it had been deserted.

He eyed the three men and shook his head. "You know, it seems like it should be about time for you guys to head back to the palace, don't you think?"

Again glancing up from his newspaper, William shrugged. "Look, Savage, we'd all like to get back to the excitement of the palace. But we can't. When Lord Carrington orders it, we'll go. Until then, we have orders to stay."

"Yeah," Carlos put in, his mouth full of muffin. "Even with things so messed up back in Silverton, they want us to stay here in the sticks. Can you imagine?"

Jim nodded glumly. "With all that's going on, you'd think our entire department would be on call."

"What's going on?" Chase asked.

With a grimace, Carlos pointed at the paper William was reading. "The newspapers are going crazy. Rumors about the prince's death are flying, varying from a drug overdose to suicide. The king is supposedly dying, Sydney is rumored to have wed Reginald, and some reports are speculating she'll take over instead of the duke."

"Which papers?"

Carlos named two or three, ending with their nemesis, *The Quiz*.

"Anything about my engagement?" He crossed his arms.

William answered. "Not yet. Maybe that'll make tomorrow's papers. And the next issue of *The Quiz* isn't out until Thursday."

Carlos drummed his fingers on the table. "I don't understand how the PR department let things get so out of hand in our absence."

Cursing, Chase raked his hand through his hair. He couldn't help but hear the unspoken implication in the other man's voice. He was head of public relations.

Because he wasn't there to head up damage control, the other men thought he was letting the department down. Hell, he couldn't blame them.

"I don't understand why Carrington didn't call me in." Eyeing a particularly lurid headline that stated Reginald was really alive and hiding out in China, he shook his head.

"You mean you don't have a choice?" William sounded skeptical. "I thought you were here because you wanted to be."

"I'm here because I was sent here. Like you. Don't you think I'd rather be back in the thick of things?" Even as he spoke, he wondered. Would he? If going back meant leaving Sydney behind, how would he feel?

Jim spoke up finally, leaning his elbows on the table. "What are you hearing from the inside?"

"Not much." William's grim look matched Chase's gut feeling. "Our coworkers are being unusually tight-lipped." Which meant Chase had trained them well. "But then, I'm not in the loop. The upper brass only tells us what they think we need to know, which is precious little."

The upper brass. That could only mean Carrington.

As if on cue, William's cell phone chirped. Answering, he spoke a few words before handing it to Chase. "His Grace wishes to speak with you."

Ah, talk about serendipity. Now he would get answers.

Carrington's first words were to ask if Chase was alone.

"I can be." He motioned for William and the others to leave the room. The other men obeyed immediately, muttering about the secretive upper brass and not bothering to hide their interest in the phone call.

When the door closed behind them, Chase stepped out onto the patio for extra privacy. He stood looking over the lake, cell phone in hand, and had a premonition his life was about to change. "Now I am. Go ahead."

"Chase, the news is not good." Since the duke was always straightforward in his communications, Chase wondered at the amount of stress his boss was under.

"I understand," he said.

The duke sighed. "In the short time you've been gone, things have gone from bad to worse. Momentously worse."

Since Carrington was the original optimist, known for his dry humor, this was unlike him.

His mind raced. Such pessimistic urgency meant something big was about to erupt, something the royal PR department needed to handle. Chase was a master at putting a good spin on just about anything. He gripped the cell phone, feeling his adrenaline surge. This was why he worked in PR. At times like this, he loved his job. He was needed and he was ready. "What is it?"

"Reginald was murdered." Carrington took a deep breath. "The autopsy revealed high levels of cocaine in his blood. As you know, he was a regular party animal. I told you that at first we thought he'd died of a drug overdose. But the digitalis indicated otherwise."

"Digitalis?"

"The cocaine was laced with it. It's a drug that strengthens the contraction of the heart muscle, slows the heart and helps eliminate fluid from body tissues. It's used to treat congestive heart failure."

"Did Reginald have a heart condition?"

"Not at all. The doctor said there have been several documented cases of it being used as a poison, but that's rare. The use of it is known mostly to physicians."

"Someone wanted it to look like an overdose." Chase's thoughts raced. Reginald's excesses had been well-known and well-documented, even if the king had turned a blind eye to them. "The killer must have hoped the cocaine would blind us to anything else."

"Exactly. And the toxicology reports show this was not pharmacy-grade digitalis. It can be extracted from a plant called foxglove. Not easy, according to the doctor, but it can be done. Someone deliberately poisoned him."

"So the consensus is that he was murdered?" Chase shouldn't have been so surprised. Reginald had made many enemies over the years. Add drugs and you were asking for trouble. "Any suspects?"

"Several. We've got people working on narrowing it down."

By *people*, Chase knew Carrington meant the Lazlo Group. Headed by Corbett Lazlo, a brilliant, enigmatic man few had actually seen, the Lazlo Group was an international team of highly skilled agents who specialized in handling delicate government situations. Their cases included locating and rescuing kidnapped royals, investigating "deaths" of political figures, and reacquiring stolen information and artifacts. The duke had recently hired them, with King Weston's permission.

"There's more." The weighty silence following this statement caused anxiety to knot in Chase's stomach. He cleared his throat and waited, wondering what could possibly be worse than murder.

Chapter 10

When Carrington spoke again, he sounded weary. "King Weston collapsed when they broke this news to us. He's been unconscious for over twenty-four hours now."

Chase swallowed. "Is it serious?"

"He's in a coma. Dr. Zara Smith, the topflight neurologist, has been called in. We're hoping it's not a brain tumor."

"Press conference?"

"Not on this. None of this can be leaked to the general public."

"Of course not." Chase understood what the duke wasn't saying. With the king out of commission and no heir to the throne, they needed to do all they could to keep chaos from erupting in Silvershire.

Damage control. His specialty. He needed to go back to Silverton and handle the PR. There would be press conferences, releases. There were a thousand things that would need immediate handling. They needed him. He was good. No, he thought without a trace of humility. He was the best.

"I can handle this. Send a plane for me. I'll be back as soon as—"

"No."

"No?" Chase couldn't believe what he was hearing. "I'm sorry? You don't want me back to handle the fallout?"

"No. We've got it handled."

Stunned, Chase couldn't find his voice for a moment. Finally, he cleared his throat. "All of it?"

"You stay there. You're needed to deal with that particular delicate situation. The last thing we need is war to erupt between Silvershire and Naessa."

"War?" Dumbfounded, Chase forced himself to relax his grip on the cell phone. If he squeezed it much harder, the damn thing would probably break. "Sir, with all due respect, Sydney is illegitimate. Her father's never publicly claimed her."

"Ah, but that's not to say he won't suddenly declare her his beloved daughter. It's happened. You'd be surprised at the things people in positions of power can view as expedient."

Chase tried again. "But I've seen the papers. You need me."

"Chase," Carrington chided. "You can stay in close conact with your staff. They can handle this, as long as you check in with them once in a while. Tell them to call you if anything major erupts that they can't handle."

After the latest fiasco because of his absence, Chase didn't want to take a chance. In times of disaster, times like this, a pro was needed. *He* was needed.

But his employer didn't seem to think so.

"I don't understand." He felt as though he were being

fired. "Send someone else to handle Sydney Conner. I really think—"

"No. You don't understand. I need you there, with her. In addition to what we've already discussed, we've found more e-mails on Reginald's computer. Mixed in with Sydney Conner's attempts to contact the prince about their baby, we've found other, more threatening e-mails. We're not sure who sent them, and they weren't from the same e-mail address Sydney used earlier, but they were attempting to blackmail the prince. Lucia Cordez is sorting them out now."

Threatening? Blackmail? Chase blinked. Sydney? No way. "Determining the e-mail address should be relatively simple."

"They're working on it."

"Surely you don't think Sydney…"

Again, Carrington sighed. "We don't know, but it's a distinct possibility. But only that, until we have more to go on. This entire situation with her has the potential for disaster."

Chase closed his eyes and bit back another curse. How would his boss feel when he learned what Chase had done? He knew he had no choice but to tell him; the story would hit the papers soon, if it hadn't already.

"Chase?" Carrington's voice brought him back to the telephone. "Are you there?"

"I am." He took a deep breath. "There's something I'd better tell you before it hits the papers." As quickly and succinctly as possible, Chase outlined his and Sydney's pretend engagement as of the day before.

"You did what?" The duke's voice reflected his shock. "I read that in one of the tabloids, but thought it was the usual lies. My God, Chase. I know you take your job seriously, but this is going a bit too far."

"It'll help take the heat off her for now. Once all this blows over, I'll announce we broke it off."

"What made you do it?"

"I don't know." But he did know. He'd seen the stark pain in her eyes at the reporter's words. Not good. Sympathy and public relations weren't a good combination.

"Well then," Carrington sounded positively gleeful, "you should have no problem getting her to stay at Lake Lodan."

Restless, Chase began to pace. He hated feeling out of the loop, cut off from the heart of the action. Away from the palace. "She wants to go home."

"To Naessa? Not possible."

"True, but I'm running out of reasons to make her stay. She's not a prisoner, and she hasn't been charged with any crime. I can't hold her against her will."

"Charm her. As long as I've known you, women have been climbing all over you."

The vivid imagery conjured by the duke's words made Chase break out in a light sweat. Just thinking of last night and the woman who still slept in his bed, made him feel in need of an ice-cold shower. The burning, desperate passion that had flared between him and Sydney had seared him. He'd never felt anything like it.

Carrington spoke again. "Chase? Are you there? Is there a problem with you charming the girl? I'd think you two would be rather close now, especially after your ordeal together."

Charming the girl? Earlier, when he'd believed Sydney a groupie, Chase would have had no problem doing just that. Now…he didn't know. Especially since she'd totally freaked when he'd announced their pretend engagement.

"I don't think she likes me very much." His excuse sounded lame, even to his own ears. But it was the truth, though their bodies had reacted to each other like moths to a flame.

Carrington chuckled. "Right. You're engaged. After all, you forget how well I know you. Since when has a woman, any woman, not liked you? Come on, man. Where's that legendary charisma? You've been a player since I've known you, and that's a long time."

"She's…different." That was as close as he could come to explaining her effect on him.

"Different?" The duke's chuckles became an outright guffaw. "I've seen pictures of her. The woman's hot. You can deal with it. I have faith in you."

The words made Chase smile grimly. So far his orders were clear. Stay with Sydney, keep a watchful eye on her while keeping her safe and away from the press. A tall order, especially since he now had to worry about keeping her safe from himself.

Speaking of keeping her safe, he still had one very important question for the duke. "Speaking of Sydney, have the Lazlos learned who's trying to kill her?"

The duke was silent for so long, Chase wasn't sure he'd understood. When he finally spoke, he sounded pensive. "They're exploring various avenues."

"Not good enough," Chase snapped, before he caught himself. "Sorry."

Carrington accepted his apology with a quiet, "That's all right."

"Is there anything else you can tell me?"

"No, not really. I can't elaborate yet. Just as with Reginald, there are several factions who might have good reason to want her—and the baby she carries—dead. That's why your engagement, even if it's pretend, is a risky move." A trace of humor colored Carrington's voice, as though he had his own suspicions about why Chase had done such a thing.

"Oh? How so?"

"If there is someone out there gunning for Sydney Conner, you've just linked yourself with her. You could be a target now."

"Why Carrington," Chase used his most droll tone. "I didn't know you cared."

The duke ignored the feeble attempt at humor. "Of course I care, you big idiot. You're a great PR guy—and an even better friend."

Chase had to swallow to get past the lump in his throat. "Don't forget, I was a bodyguard. I know how to handle threats. Still, I'd be interested to see what the Lazlo Group turns up."

"I'll call you as soon as I learn anything. But for now, I want you to keep an eye on her, charm her, befriend her, do whatever you have to to keep her there, out of the spotlight, away from the media. Once all is said and done, if she's innocent of nothing worse than sleeping with Reginald, we'll give her the same settlement we originally intended."

The settlement he now carried in his wallet. A certified bank check made out in the amount of seven hundred and fifty thousand pounds.

Pay her to go away. That's what Chase had been sent to do in the beginning, when someone had started shooting at them. The amount of money he'd been given to bribe her was staggering to him, but would Sydney, with her trust fund, find it so?

"Chase?"

Blinking, he cleared his throat. "Got it."

"Fantastic. Until then, watch your back." With that final warning, Carrington rang off.

Chase knew he'd have to watch more than his back. He had to make sure his heart wasn't involved.

Sydney woke alone in Chase's bed. Outside the open window, she heard the sound of a child's laughter. Smiling, certain she'd imagined the cheery noise, she yawned, wondering why her body felt so sore.

Then the truth hit her.

She'd slept with Chase. Actually, they'd done very little sleeping. She'd finally given in to her craving and made love with him.

What had she done? Hand to her throat, she trembled. Their coming together had been unlike anything she'd ever experienced before. Worse, merely thinking of his kiss, his touch, and she longed for him again.

Stretching, she winced. Despite feeling as though she glowed from within, she ached in places she'd never ached before. Her entire body blushed when she thought of the sensual way they'd devoured each other.

Chase Savage, sent by the royal family to deal with a "problem." Her. Now, being with him was a bittersweet reminder that she didn't learn from her mistakes. First Reginald, and now Chase.

Ah, but Chase... Before, she'd only wondered how she'd live without him once she went home. Now, she knew. Nothing would ever be the same. And the worst part of it all—she wished her baby's father had been Chase instead of Reginald.

Sitting up and combing her hair with her fingers, she wondered if mistakes, like bad luck, came in threes. If so, she could only wonder what her third blunder would be.

Sighing, she tossed back the covers and located her clothes. Once dressed, she made her way back to her room and her shower.

Later, clean and wearing her favorite pair of faded jeans, Sydney made her way to the kitchen. At the sound of Chase's deep voice, she froze and, her face heating, changed direction. Though her stomach felt hollow, she'd get something to break her fast later, when the kitchen was deserted.

Outside, the sunlight looked warm and welcoming. She slipped out into the side garden and found a worn, wooden bench next to the rose arbor, partly in the morning sun. With a pleased sigh, she sat down, leaned back and closed her eyes.

"When the sun hits it just right, your hair looks like it's on fire."

Sydney opened her eyes to see a slender, dark-haired child studying her with solemn eyes. Five or six years old, she clutched a battered stuffed animal to her thin chest.

"Hello. What's your name?" She squatted so she was at the child's level.

"Martha." Trusting, the little girl stepped forward and held out her hand. "May I touch your hair?"

Sydney laughed. "Of course you can." Once Martha had finished patting her head, Sydney stood. "What are you doing here?"

With a bright smile, Martha pointed toward the door. "My babysitter's sick, so I came to work with my mama."

Giggling, she ran to the rosebush and sniffed a flower. "I'd rather stay outside and play than stay with her."

Sydney got up and took the child's hand. "Does your mother know you're out here?"

The little girl only shrugged. Then, frowning, she pointed to the sky. "Look, it's going to rain!"

Dark storm clouds were indeed rolling in. Even as Sydney watched, they overtook the sun, plunging Martha and her into shadows.

Despite her terror of storms, Sydney refused to be distracted. "Where is your mother, Martha?"

Martha sighed. Her little nose wrinkled. "In the kitchen, helping the cook. That's where she works. But it's really hot in there. I like it way better out here. Especially now," she sniffed the air like a curious puppy. "It smells like rain. I love to play in the rain."

And all Sydney could think about was how badly she wanted to hide. "I know you like it out here." The wind had picked up, whipping Sydney's hair around her face.

Martha lifted her arms to the sky and twirled. "Don't you?"

"Not really." Sydney tugged her forward, toward the house. "Tell you what. Let's go find your mom. If she says it's okay for you to be with me, I'll see if I can find a book to read you. They have a huge library here."

"Really?"

Because the child sounded so amazed, Sydney chuckled. "Really."

"But I want to play outside."

Shivering in earnest, Sydney shook her head. "Not if there's a bad storm. Coming outside wouldn't be safe then."

"Are you scared?"

Sydney couldn't lie to the child. "Yes, I am." Cocking her head, Martha studied her, small mouth pursed with fascination. "A little."

In the distance, thunder sounded. Sydney shuddered. "A lot. I don't like storms." She held out her hand. Martha took it, still studying Sydney's face.

"Why?"

"I nearly drowned once. A storm came up when I was on a sailboat. The boat turned over." She wouldn't tell the child she'd been trapped underneath the sail, nor that her mother had made no effort to save her. If not for a shift in the wind and the man who'd been her mother's paramour of the moment, Sydney had no doubt she would have drowned.

As if she understood, Martha nodded. Clutching Sydney's hand, she went along docilely, as though she didn't mind going inside.

Instead, as soon as Sydney reached for the door, Martha pulled her hand loose and took off running, giggling as she ran. "My mommy says the best way to deal with a fear is to face it." As she ran, lightning flashed above them and the sky darkened to the color of pre-dawn.

Stunned, at first Sydney simply stood frozen, one hand on the door. Then, as the little girl dashed out of sight, she took off after her, pushing away her instinctive terror to the back of her mind.

Martha wanted to play and clearly did not understand the danger. Because she was the only adult around, Sydney thought, as she chased the little girl out into the wide-open expanse of lawn on the north side of the property, she had a responsibility to bring the child to safety.

When she caught up with Martha, she'd reached the end of the yard. Holding on to the tall, iron fence with one hand,

Martha grinned up at her as Sydney came running up. Heart pounding, all Sydney could think of was how metal attracted lightning.

Still, she knew she couldn't reveal the extent of her terror to the little girl.

"Hey, you," Sydney gasped, out of breath. "I caught you." She reached to pry Martha's hand away from the fence. If she had to, she'd drag her kicking and screaming inside.

The first spatters of rain hit her face.

"Oh goody! It's going to pour!" Martha took off again. Grabbing for her arm, Sydney narrowly missed.

Thunder boomed. Instinctively, Sydney cringed, cursing. The precious second allowed Martha to gain ground. For a second she appeared to be considering a headlong dash in the opposite direction, back toward the house. Then, staring down at the lake below, she seemed to change her mind, skidding to a stop.

Not wanting to spook her, Sydney slowed to a walk, moving closer, hoping to grab Martha while the girl's attention was elsewhere.

"Look!" Martha pointed.

Closer, Sydney pretended to have seen. "I see that." She was nearly there.

"No, you don't." Martha danced away. "You've got to look."

"Fine." Shading her eyes with her hand, Sydney tried to see what had caught the child's attention. "I'm looking. Look at what?"

"That bird." Pointing, the little girl scrunched up her face. "I want to touch it."

Following the direction of Martha's finger, Sydney saw

a small white swan swimming near the shore below them. "It's pretty, isn't it?"

"I want to touch it," Martha repeated.

Closer. Ten feet. Eight. "Well, you can't. First off, there's no way down there. Secondly, it would probably swim away if you got near—"

Before Sydney could finish the sentence, Martha took off, disappearing over the edge of the cliff.

For a second Sydney's heart stopped. She stared, disbelieving. Then, as her heart resumed pumping, she rushed to the edge and saw a narrow, worn path twisting down the cliff to the lakeshore. Moving with the utter carefree carelessness of the very young, Martha was about a third of the way down.

Thunder boomed. A millisecond later, another bolt of lightning flashed, lighting up the sky. The rain came in sheets, driven by the wind.

Below, Martha screamed in terror. She lost her footing and began to slide, shrieking as she tried to grab hold of something to stop her rapid decent. But she couldn't and Sydney caught a glimpse of her terrified little face as she plunged down, then hit the lake with a splash. She bobbed up, then disappeared under the water as a jagged bolt of lightning flashed above them.

With no choice, Sydney went after her.

Chapter 11

There were days when Lake Lodan looked like a postcard from paradise, all sparkling, calm water and clear, robin's-egg skies. Days when the sun enticed, the breeze beckoned, and the sailboats presented a picture of serenity and ease.

Today, Chase reflected, was not one of those days. He walked as close to the cliff's edge as he dared and stared out at the now-deserted lake. Above, the sky darkened as storm clouds gathered, roiling black and gray, and the wind carried the threat of more than mere rain. A wicked storm was brewing, and there'd be nothing subtle about this one.

Standing on the edge of the cliff, Chase thrilled to the electric feeling in the air. Unlike Sydney, he'd always loved storms. Even when he'd been a child, his mother'd had to drag him inside, away from both thunderstorms and blizzards. The savagery of nature's fury fascinated him. Today, with his insides in as much turmoil as the weather, the coming storm would be a welcome distraction.

The sound of the choppy waves slamming against the rocks mirrored the sky. With the barometric pressure dropping and his nerve endings tingling from the electricity in the air, all he could see was Sydney's face.

Remembering her terror of storms, he wondered if he should go to her. Without a shadow of a doubt, he knew she'd be inside, trying to hide her fear. He could imagine wrapping her in his arms for comfort and stealing one kiss. Vivid images of what that kiss would lead to had him shifting restlessly.

Better to avoid her, let her deal with the weather in her own way. He needed to clear his head.

Though he'd known her less than a month, he couldn't stop thinking about her. Aching for her, wanting her, craving her. Prince Reginald's discarded mistress.

Sydney.

Leaning heavily on the wooden railing, he peered glumly at the restless lake and released a shuddering breath. What was it about this woman that affected him so? How was she different from the dozens of others, equally beautiful, equally sexy, he'd known?

He had no answer. He only knew she was. Everything about her, from the top of her fiery head to the delicate shape of her perfect toes, enticed him. After their one night of passion, he'd thought his hunger for her would be slaked, and therefore lessened. Instead, this one night had given him all the more reason to burn for her.

They fitted together like a hand in a glove. A very soft, very snug, leather glove, he thought. When they'd been together, he'd felt more than lust. When they'd reached the peak of release, he'd felt more than sexual fulfillment. Much more. Too much more.

Damn it. He tightened his hand around the smooth iron rail. This one woman, Sydney Conner, had him dreaming again of the possibility of enjoying a life like his parents. He thought of his mother and father, of their obvious affection for each other, the love they shared, passed out indiscriminately to each of their boisterous brood.

Each of his siblings had found love, married and they were raising their own children. Of all the Savage brood, Chase was the only one who'd chosen to devote his life to a career rather than domestic contentment.

Because of Kayla. When she'd shown him his foolish dreams weren't possible, he'd thrown himself into his work with all the passion he would have brought to their marriage.

And never, not once, had he ever questioned his choice. Until now. Now he could swear he saw nothing but a gnawing emptiness stretching out before him.

Until he'd met Sydney and contemplated an existence without her, he'd never felt alone.

Now, the prospect of returning home each night to his professionally decorated and very empty apartment in downtown Silverton seemed too high a price to pay, even for a job he loved.

Chase was, he knew, indulging in foolishness. Foolish dreams were for other men, not him. No doubt he'd feel more like himself once he got back in his familiar environment.

Not wanting to examine his new emotions any closer, he shook his head and lifted his face to the moist wind. Here came the storm. He waited for the familiar excitement to fill him, but worry for Sydney superceded it.

Once, he'd been a bodyguard. Protecting others was ingrained in him. Even now as head of PR, finally on the right track career-wise, he seemed poised to take a wrong turn, an unnecessary detour back in time.

And he couldn't seem to stop, to resist Sydney's potent lure. He felt like a man drowning.

Startled out of his musing by a strange sound, he cocked his head and listened again. Below, the noise came again, a child's shrill shriek. He peered down at the shore, trying to locate the source of the cry.

There, below, near the choppy water's edge. In disbelief, he watched a small black-headed girl slide down the cliff, arms flailing as she tried to regain her balance. A second later, her high-pitched scream was cut off as she slipped and the water swallowed her.

He started forward, running. When he'd inspected the grounds at their arrival, he'd spotted an old path on the other side of the house. He ran for that now, keeping an eye on the water below, desperately praying the child would reappear.

Thunder crackled. Lightning flashed. The sky opened up.

Below, Sydney appeared; running, stumbling down the rocky beach. Reaching the spot where the girl had gone under, she climbed up onto a rock. Then, without hesitation, she jumped into the wind-tossed waves after the little girl.

Chase's heart stopped. There—the path. As he scrabbled down the rocky cliff side, he could only pray he wasn't too late to save them both.

Sydney emerged from the water just as he reached the cliff bottom. He moved as fast as he could to her, careful on the slippery rocks. When she spotted him, she tried to hand him the water-soaked little girl and failed.

Around them, the storm reached a crescendo of fury.

He jumped in, took the child from Sydney's arms, and made his way over the rocks to a grassy area on the shore. Laying the little girl down, he turned to go back for Sydney and saw she'd climbed out after him.

The rain lashed at him as Chase turned his attention to the small girl. He began CPR until she coughed, a heaving, hacking sound, and all the water she'd taken in came up.

Lightning illuminated her tiny, limp body.

"She's breathing," Sydney said, her teeth chattering. "Martha's breathing."

"Sydney?" He spared her a glance. She'd wrapped her arms around herself as though she could conjure a towel. Huge shudders shook her and she looked on the verge of shock.

"Y-y-yes?"

"Run for the house and call for an ambulance. We need to get Martha to a hospital as soon as possible."

Before he'd finished, Sydney took off. A moment later, Chase lifted the unconscious child and began the arduous climb to the house.

Later, as the storm moved away and the paramedics wheeled the now-alert child out, followed by her grateful mother, Chase looked for Sydney. He found her, damp clothes clinging to her, staring out the window at the lingering rain.

Without a sound, he slipped up behind her and wrapped her tightly in his arms. Motionless, she accepted his wordless comfort, laying her head against his chest. Together they stood and watched the remainder of the storm batter the lake.

He felt a sense of completion, of fulfillment, more different and exhilarating than he'd ever felt with a woman before. Once again, he ignored the doubt raising its ugly head, and chose to live in the moment.

She shivered. He kissed her neck.

"That was really brave."

"Not really. Anyone would have done the same." Though her tone was unremarkable, when she looked at him, he saw remembered terror stark in her eyes.

"Brave," he insisted, nuzzling under her ear. She turned into him, hiding her face. "For you even to be out there, with your thing about storms, is remarkable. And that little girl owes you her life."

"No. Not me. You saved her. You brought her up out of the water and did CPR." Shuddering again, she shook her head and held on to him as though her life depended on it. In turn, he wrapped his arms around her and found himself wishing he never had to let her go.

That night, Chase visited Sydney's room. Awake as though waiting for him, she welcomed him with a sleepy smile and open arms.

After another blissful night filled with sensual pleasures, chest tight, he lay and watched her sleeping. Finally, he rose and returned to his own room, leaving her alone in her bed.

The next morning, a newspaper had been slid under his door. Several more had been stacked neatly in the hall. Curious, Chase retrieved them, opening each one to see, with little surprise, that his and Sydney's engagement had made the front pages of them all. Most were guardedly optimistic, though several took a unique spin on what should have been a happy event.

Illegitimate Princess's Newest Scandal, *The Quiz*'s

headline screamed. A few other tabloids picked up similar themes, many accusing Sydney of lying about her baby belonging to the prince when she had obviously gotten pregnant with Chase.

He sighed. From the moment he'd opened his mouth, he'd expected no less. Now he had to deal with the consequences of his impulsive actions.

A cold shower helped him think more clearly. He'd barely finished drying off when his mother called. She'd seen the headlines.

"Why didn't you tell us?" She sounded hurt. In the background he could hear his sisters chattering, laughing, and scolding their kids.

"Mom, I was going to call." As soon as he figured out what to say. He supposed he ought to tell his family the truth, but he couldn't risk someone slipping up. As far as the press and the rest of the world needed to know, he and Sydney really were engaged.

"When did this happen? How long have you been seeing this girl?" She fired questions, one after the other, without even giving him time to answer. To her credit, she didn't mention Kayla, or how he'd been left standing at the altar the very day of his planned wedding.

When his mother paused to take a breath, he interjected. "It was a sudden thing. Impulsive."

"Impulsive? Marriage should never be done on impulse. It's a lifelong commitment." Her rebuke was soft, but no less heartfelt. She and his father had been married forty years this past autumn.

Knowing she was right, he pushed away a stab of guilt. It was only an engagement, after all. It wasn't as if he'd actually married Sydney under false pretenses.

"When are we going to meet her?"

"When?" He glanced at his watch. "I don't know. Things are hectic at work right now. But soon, okay?"

His mother sighed. "Hold on. Your sister wants to talk to you."

Chase tensed. Which sister? His eldest sister had taken on the role of official family spokesperson. This couldn't be good.

When his older sister, Sarah, came on, he knew he was in for it.

"I'm concerned." She began without preamble. Her tone was sharp. "We're all worried about you. This woman was sleeping with the prince right up until he died."

What could he say? "I know, but it's complicated."

"Complicated?" She snorted. "I've seen pictures of her. Are you thinking clearly, or not thinking at all?"

As he tried to collect his thoughts, there was a soft knock at his door.

Thanking the interruption, he murmured his apologies and, along with a promise to phone back later, disconnected the call, much to his sister's irritation. "Come in."

"Good morning." Sydney peeked her head around the door. Her bright smile faded when she saw all the papers. "What's going on?"

"Take a look." He handed her the *Inquisitor*. "Might as well start with the worst one first."

"And we had the misfortune of making this week's issue." She shook her head, a tiny frown appearing between her eyebrows as she began reading.

When she'd finished, she worried her lower lip. "I don't like this."

"I know." He suppressed the urge to hold her, knowing

if he touched her they'd end up right back in bed. "Don't worry. This won't last long. If we stay out of their radar, they'll lose interest and hound someone else."

"I know." With a grimace, she tossed the papers back onto his bed.

"Sydney?"

"Hmmm?" She looked up expectantly.

"Let's talk about you and Reginald."

Just like that, her expression shut down. "Why?"

"Because I knew him," he said. "He was a partier and a player. Between the booze and the drugs, not to mention his harem, I'm trying to understand how someone like you ended up with someone like him."

Moving as though each of his words had been cuts, she crossed the room and took a seat on the edge of his bed. "He said my love had changed him." She sounded disgusted. "I know—oldest line in the book, and I believed it. Looking back now, I think I was dazzled."

"Because of who he was?"

Before he'd even finished, she shook her head. "No, not because of that. Though you might find this hard to believe, I've never cared about such things. My sire still pays for my mother's house and her lavish lifestyle, but he never paid me a visit. Reginald dazzled me with attention. I thought—" she swallowed, looking away for a moment before her bright-blue gaze found his "—he really cared. Of course, he didn't."

Her bitter voice increased his longing to hold her. She'd said the last sentence in a way that told him she didn't believe she was worthy of Reginald's love.

Reginald hadn't been worthy to touch the hem of her skirt.

Oblivious to his rage, Sydney shook her head and continued. "Now, I realize I never truly knew him."

Chase bit back the retort on his tongue and watched her, trying to keep his distance, trying not to feel. If he closed his eyes, all he could see was the prince with his hands on her soft, silky skin. Furious, Chase fought the urge to touch her, to purge the image from his mind.

Instead, he crossed his arms and fought himself. The need to protect her warred with his desire to understand.

Then, though he really didn't want to know, he asked. "Tell me how you met."

Watching him with shuttered eyes, she sighed. "You must have read the papers. Sometimes I think Reginald staged the entire thing. He came backstage when the symphony played in Silverton for a month. He brought red roses and clever promises. I told him no. He came again the next night. And the next, and the one after that. Always with the roses and the honeyed words. Each time, he grew more and more extravagant. I found him amusing, at first. But he was a prince, like my sire. I should have known better."

"What changed?" Chase heard the harshness in his voice and made an effort to soften his tone. "You were a virgin, untouched. How could you let a man like that—" He swallowed, bit back his words. Then, when he thought he had himself under control again, he continued. "What did he do to make you agree to become his lover?"

She gave him a sharp look. "Nothing happened overnight. He kept it up for weeks, Chase. Weeks. When our stay in Silverton ended and the symphony moved on, he came, too. He traveled from city to city, wherever we played. And finally, one night when he asked me to dinner, I went. I remember thinking at the time how it was only a simple meal. How much harm could it possibly cause?" She bit her lip and gave a self-conscious laugh. "Little did I know."

Did she sound wistful, or sad? Suddenly, he realized he didn't want to hear any more. The intimate details of Sydney and Reginald's affair were none of his business, none of his concern. The fact that hearing about them made him want to punch the wall was another reason.

She had him tied up in knots. Like Kayla, he told himself. Best if he remembered how that had ended.

Ah, but Sydney was still talking.

"We started having dinner together two, maybe three times a week. Then he showed up on my day off and wanted to take me on a picnic."

"No shopping? I thought guys like that bought their lady friends lots of bling."

"He tried to give me jewelry. But I didn't want to ever be like my mother, so I refused to accept his gifts. But I'd come to enjoy his company. Reginald can—" She stopped herself, swallowed and continued. "Could, I mean. Reginald could be a very charming man when he wanted to. When we had our picnic, he brought a basket with cheese and crackers and pâté and wine. He spread a blanket on the ground for me to sit on. And then—"

He saw red, but couldn't keep himself from asking. "Then what? You had sex?"

"No, Chase. He kissed me. I enjoyed the kiss. We went on this way for a month."

Why the hell did this feel like a betrayal? As though she'd cheated on him? Disgusted, Chase tried to catch his breath, to calm himself. He hadn't even known her then. And worse, she didn't seem to realize what she was saying, how every word cut him and made him desire her more for her naive need.

The prince had been notorious for his rapid conquests.

The mere fact that she'd been able to resist him had no doubt fueled his interest.

"Men always seem to want the one thing they can't have."

He wasn't aware he'd spoken out loud until Sydney answered him. "And then once they've obtained it, they don't want it anymore." She clasped and unclasped her hands. "I thought he cared, Chase. Shows you how incredibly stupid I was. When he got tired of me, he moved right on to the next woman."

The words she didn't say echoed in his mind. Leaving her pregnant with his baby.

"What kind of man doesn't care about his own child?" Her anguish was palpable. "I couldn't believe it when he pretended not to know me. He deleted my e-mails, refused delivery of my certified letter. He didn't want to hear that I was pregnant. He wanted me to go away."

He couldn't take any more. With an oath, he crossed the room and pulled her into his arms. "I'm sorry, Sydney. I shouldn't have asked."

"I—"

"Shh." He kissed the top of her head, promising himself he'd keep things chaste. But she turned in his arms and, facing him, pushed herself to her knees. Dragging his face down to hers, she kissed him, desperately using her tongue and her lips to drive all thoughts of her with the other man out of his head.

The only other words she said before they sank in a tangle of covers and sheets and skin was to comment, "How very convenient we're on your bed."

Then he kissed her again and neither spoke for a very long time.

* * *

The sound of alarms going off woke them. Chase opened his eyes, shifting Sydney from on top of him. She sat up, her glorious hair tangled, blinking in confusion.

"What's wrong? Is there a fire?"

"I don't know." He tugged her to her feet, feeling his door for heat before opening it. "I need to get you outside." Yanking open the door, he pulled her, stumbling, into the smoke-filled hallway. "Come on."

"But what about William, Jim and Carlos? We need to find them."

Still dragging her, he cursed. "No, *I* need to find them, once I'm sure you're safe."

Just then, William came running up, motioning frantically. "This way. We need to get outside."

Single-file, they held on to each other as they made their way blindly down the hall. Chase kept Sydney in front of him, close.

"What about the others?" he asked.

"I sent Carlos and Jim to round up the servants. They should already be out."

"Good. I don't want to lose anyone."

"We shouldn't. The alarms warned us in time."

Sydney coughed, her eyes watering in the thick smoke. Chase yanked off his black Armani T-shirt. "Take this. Hold it over your face."

Her gaze searched his. "But what about you?"

"I'll be fine." He pushed her gently. "Now move."

They reached the back door a few seconds later. William shoved it open and they all stumbled outside, gasping in the fresh air. Sydney rubbed her eyes and her hands came away black with soot.

Keeping one arm around her, Chase faced the other man. "Have you seen the fire?"

"No," William admitted. "Just a lot of smoke. The fire department's on its way. I've called for the police, as well."

A few minutes later, the fire engine pulled up, lights flashing, sirens wailing. A police cruiser accompanied it, though the officers remained outside while the firefighters did their job.

Afterward the fire captain emerged with something in his hand, motioning to the policemen. Chase went, too. Sydney followed.

"No fire. Someone set off a couple of these." He held up a blackened, empty metal tube.

"What is it?" Chase asked.

"Smoke bombs." Both the fire captain and the police officer spoke at the same time. "Homemade, from the looks of them. Potassium nitrate and sugar, mainly. Cook it and stuff these tubes with it, add a safety fuse and, voila—you get a ton of thick smoke."

"Why?" Sydney had meant to stay quiet, but the instant she blurted the question, they all turned to look at her. "Why would they want to smoke us out?"

The policeman shook his head. "I don't know."

Chase blanched. "To get you outside. Damn, we've been played for fools." Ignoring the uncomprehending looks on the other's faces, he herded Sydney toward the gardening shed and greenhouse, shielding her with his body. While they moved fast, he constantly watched, searching the area for anything out of the ordinary. William, Jim and Carlos were right behind him.

Scratching his head, the uniformed officer followed.

Once they reached the greenhouse, Chase tried the door.

It was locked. With a hard shove of his shoulder, he rammed it. The thin wood gave way, splintering.

"Come on." Chase led Sydney inside. "Though they can see you through the glass, this offers some protection. William, Jim, Carlos—form a circle around Sydney. We'll protect her with our bodies. Anyone wanting to take a shot at her will have to go through us first."

"Sir?" The cop stood in the doorway, peering at them in the murky light. "Would you care to clarify that comment?"

Chase measured the shorter man with a quick, hard look. "Not just yet. But if I have need of your services, officer, I'll let you know."

As the officer was about to speak, someone from the group still assembled on the back lawn screamed.

Chapter 12

The cop spun and sprinted for the crowd. Sydney started forward, but Chase grabbed her and pulled her back into the shadowy humidity of the greenhouse. Leafy ferns sheltered them. "No," he growled. "Don't move."

William and the other two men hadn't budged. Sydney fought the urge to push at them and make them get out of the way.

"We need to go see what happened. That sounded like someone was hurt."

"Let the cops deal with it. We're staying here. If there's a sniper with his weapon trained on the crowd, who do you think he's looking for?"

She stared, the color draining from her already pale face. "Here? Inside the gate?"

Without answering her rhetorical question, he turned to

look at the other men. "William, Carlos, check out the house. Jim, stay with me. We need to keep Sydney between us."

William and Carlos disappeared inside. Jim stepped closer, keeping his back to Sydney while he scanned their surroundings. The cop never returned.

A few minutes later, they heard another siren.

"Ambulance," Chase told her. "That's a good sign. If whoever got shot was dead, they wouldn't bother to call an ambulance."

Sydney glanced at her watch. "What's keeping William and Carlos? Surely they could have checked out the house by now."

Jim and Chase exchanged a look. When Chase glanced down at Sydney, he was smiling. "They're very thorough. They won't be back until they're a hundred-percent positive the house is safe."

Nodding, Jim grinned at them both. "You trained them well, sir."

"If you have a moment, I'd like to talk to all of you." The police officer had returned, looking grim. "There's been a shooting. The woman is en route to the hospital."

"Was she badly hurt?" Sydney tried to step around Chase, but he moved enough to make that impossible.

The cop looked from one to the other, his expression hard. "She was shot in the back. They were able to get her stabilized. Other than that, I couldn't say."

"Did she have red hair?"

Instead of answering, the police officer jerked his thumb toward the house. "Let's go inside. I have a few questions for you. All of you."

William and Carlos stepped through the door. The small greenhouse was becoming quite crowded.

"All safe," William said.

"Let's take her in now." Chase didn't even have to ask them before the other two men stepped around the cop to flank Sydney.

Seeing this, the policeman moved to block the doorway. "What's going on here?"

Chase merely looked at him.

"Answer the question!"

"You didn't answer mine. In case you didn't hear me, I'll repeat it. Did the woman who was shot have red hair?"

"Yes," the cop growled. "She was one of the cooks or maids. Are you saying the shooter might have been aiming for her?" He jerked his thumb at Sydney.

Heaving a sigh, Chase glanced at the house before looking the officer full in the face. "Yes. We think someone is targeting my fiancée."

From the way he referred to her, Sydney deduced he knew all of this would make the news. She inhaled softly, but kept quiet while Chase finished.

"From the back, someone might have thought the staff member resembled the princess. Now, will you get out of our way so we can get her in the house?"

Finally, the cop stepped aside. He followed them as they moved in a tight knot of bodies and opened the door for them when they reached the house.

Once inside, Chase politely answered his questions. Watching, Sydney noticed how he used his public relations training to put his own spin on the truth.

Finally, she could take no more. "Sir?"

They all looked at her.

"We'd like to keep this out of the media, if possible."

Though Chase and his men shook their heads, smiling,

the policeman took her seriously. "I can promise you those reporters won't learn anything from me, ma'am." He closed his notepad and stepped back. "Looks like I'm done here. The crime-scene guys will be a while wrapping things up outside."

Chase nodded. "My man will show you to the door."

"What about protection?" the cop asked. "I'll request beefed-up patrols of the area."

"Good. Palace security will be called in, as well." This seemed to satisfy the officer. Still grim-faced, he left.

"Now." Chase looked at his men. "We need a security detail on the premises. Call the duke and arrange it."

Without another word, William hurried away.

Exhausted, Sydney couldn't think. Couldn't move, couldn't speak. Chase was right. Someone really *was* trying to kill her. She sank down on the sofa and leaned her head back, wishing she dared to close her eyes.

A moment later, William returned. "I left the duke a message to call me back."

"At least I kept all this from the media," Sydney told them.

All the men laughed.

"I doubt that." Still chuckling, Chase dropped on to the couch beside her.

"But he promised…"

"Just wait. First time someone waves a television camera in his face, he'll spill his guts. I've seen it happen a hundred times."

"But—"

The doorbell rang. They all froze.

Sydney clung to Chase. Firmly, he pried her fingers off his arm. "Stay here."

Pushing himself off the couch, he went to the front

door and stood to the side while he looked through the peephole. "I don't see anything." He reached for the door handle to open it.

"Don't." Sydney jumped up and started forward. "Chase, please."

"Get back. If there's someone watching out there, he'll be gunning for you." Something glinted in his hand. A gun. A weapon she hadn't even known he had.

Slowly he opened the front door.

Martha, the little daughter of the cook's helper, stood shivering on the doorstep. As soon as she saw Chase, she burst into tears.

Quickly, he drew her inside. She ran to Sydney, still sobbing. "That was my mama the bad man shot. They took her to the hospital and wouldn't let me go with her."

Sydney held her, smoothing back her hair. "I'm sure she'll be all right." She wasn't sure of anything at this point.

"I want to see my mother," Martha wailed. "Why'd they take her away?"

"To make her well, honey."

With sniffles and hiccups, Martha began to take notice of the others in the room. She straightened. "There's lots of people here."

Sydney smiled at Chase over the child's dark head. "Yes, there are."

"Policemen and firemen and ambulance drivers." Wiping at her eyes, Martha sniffed. "And the bad man."

Chase froze. "The bad man?"

Vigorously, the little girl nodded. She lifted one chubby hand to reveal a crumpled paper clenched in her fist. "He gave me this to give to you, Princess Sydney."

Heart racing, Sydney took it, smoothing the paper

against the arm of her chair. Keeping one arm around the little girl, she digested the words silently, before handing it to Chase.

He read it out loud. "'Watch your back and look for the way out. Or your bastard won't live long enough to claim the throne.'"

William frowned. "That doesn't sound like a threat. More like a warning." Chase agreed.

"But from whom? And why? I have no aspiration to the throne." Sydney glanced around the room, noting all the windows. Then Martha began weeping again, and Sydney busied herself calming her. Finally, the cook, who turned out to be Martha's aunt, came to take the little girl and put her down for a much-needed nap. Chase made a mental note to ask her later, when she'd calmed, what the bad man looked like and how she knew he was bad.

The rest of that afternoon, every random sound startled Sydney. The simple cry of a crow, the gentle clunk of the air conditioner when it kicked on, the lake breeze sending a tree branch scraping against the window, all became a reason to suspect someone was out there lurking. Stalking her.

Her fear was mostly for her unborn baby. More than anything else, she wished Reginald had not been the father. If he hadn't, no one would be after her.

"Would you like to come with me?" Chase, sensing her unease, squeezed her shoulder. "We're going to review the security videos."

"Yes." She hadn't even realized there were security cameras. Of course there were. This was the royal lake house after all.

But this time the expensive surveillance equipment hadn't done its work.

"The front-door camera went dead for fifty-eight seconds." Chase shook his head. "Not good."

"Blank tape. Nothing," the head of security said. A large, rawboned man of sixty-odd years, he had the look of a former police officer. "Same as the ones that were focused on the front gates."

"The fire, the shooting, then what?" wondered Chase. "When he realized he'd shot the wrong woman, he came back to give the little girl a note?"

"Maybe he stuck around," William suggested. "This place has a ton of servants."

"Or," Carlos put in, "maybe there's two of them."

"Two of them." Chase appeared to be mulling over this theory. "One bad guy, one good?"

"Maybe one bad guy, one not so bad." Carlos indicated the note in Chase's hand. "I still think whoever gave that note to little Martha is trying to warn Sydney."

"A lot of good the gates and cameras were."

"It was a breach, plain and simple." Nearly bouncing in place, Carlos's excess energy told of his agitation. "Whether there is one guy or two, the whole thing is pretty brazen, what with the police swarming around the grounds."

"We'll need to report this to royal security." William sounded glum. "They won't be happy."

"*I'm* not happy!" Chase exploded. "First the sniper, then this."

Despite her churning stomach, Sydney felt unnaturally calm. "This person, or people, have just upped the threat. They got awfully close this time. Closer than the car trying to run us off the road."

They all stared at her.

"Sydney—" Chase began.

"No. I'm not safe here. They were inside the gate, disabled the cameras, set smoke bombs and shot a poor servant, just because she has the same color hair as me. I need to go somewhere else. Someplace safe."

"They found you here," Jim spoke up. "How do you know they won't find you again if we move you?"

Sydney crossed her arms. "Has anyone thought to wonder *how* they found me?"

Grim-faced, Chase nodded. "I'm afraid there's someone on the inside, communicating your moves. That's the only explanation."

"But who?" Carlos asked.

"We're actively trying to find out. But the fact remains that this person, or people, knows enough about the royal lodge to breach its defenses. This is a problem." He looked at each of them, his expression only softening when he reached Sydney. "And as Carlos said, they're bold as hell. Any ideas, anyone?"

No one spoke at first. Finally, Carlos stepped forward. "I think we need to request extra guards from Silverton if we're going to stay here much longer. I agree with Sydney. This is no longer a safe environment. Personally, I'd recommend we head out."

"I'm inclined to agree with you." Pulling Sydney to him, Chase kept his arm around her shoulders. She didn't even attempt to pull away. Having his strength so close made her feel better, even if it was only temporary.

"You'll need to check with the duke," Jim reminded him.

"I will." Chase's voice was hard. "But no matter what, we need to move Sydney."

The telephone rang, startling them. William answered, listened and then hung up. "At lease we've received one bit of good news. That was the hospital. That woman who was shot has been moved from critical condition to stable. The doctor anticipates a full recovery."

Though Sydney forced a smile, genuinely glad, even that bit of information didn't help dispel her overwhelming foreboding. She had to keep pushing back an edge of panic, wanting to grab her suitcase and her cello and run.

When they exited the security room, she felt even more vulnerable.

As though he sensed this, Chase stayed by her side. But he was clearly distracted, not saying much, waiting for the duke to phone.

Finally, she sent him away with some nonsense about needing to take a nap herself.

But she couldn't go to her room. There she felt trapped. If the killer knew enough about the estate to disable the security cameras without sending out an alarm, they no doubt knew where she slept.

So she drifted around the house like a ghost, staying away from windows, as the day lengthened. Though William, Jim and Carlos watched her, they kept their distance. Restless and frustrated, she wondered if her worries were communicating themselves to her baby. For his or her sake, she hoped not.

Dusk came and she refused to turn on any lights, or allow anyone else to illuminate the rooms she occupied. Eventually, Chase found her, took one look at her face and led her into the room which housed the indoor pool, giving the other men a glare that clearly said they weren't to be disturbed. Pulling the blinds closed on all the windows, he locked the door behind them.

"Did you hear from the duke?"

"Yes. He's got the Lazlo Group working on another safe spot for us."

She nodded. "All of us? Can we plan a way to split up temporarily, so this stalker won't find us?"

"It will be just you and I."

Staring, she studied his shuttered expression. "Why?"

"I don't know who to trust. So you and I will be leaving without telling any of the others."

"I don't know about that. I…"

"I do." He held out his hand. "Come here."

Without a word, she moved into his arms. He kissed the side of her neck and she trembled, wishing she could stop feeling as though she were trying to wake from a long, endless sleep full of nightmares.

"It's going to be all right." He kissed her again, trailing his mouth to her ear, grazing her earlobe before moving along her cheek and finally capturing her lips.

She closed her eyes, swaying against him. Mouth lingering, the gentleness of his kiss challenged her. The slow exploration of his tongue drove her fears from her. Burning…there was only him. She drank him in, welcomed him.

Though his breathing sounded harsh, he undressed her with such reverence that her knees went weak. Standing naked before him, she kept her gaze locked on his, her mouth going dry as he began to remove his own clothing.

Then she went to him. He met her halfway.

They fell onto a nearby chaise longue, pushing away the stack of clean, white towels. The warmth of the heated water, combined with the sharp scent of chlorine were barely noticed, so intent were they on each other.

When he entered her, she shuddered. And when his lips

again claimed hers, she admitted to herself how much he mattered to her. This man, his touch, had become her everything.

The last thought she had before she gave herself over to sensation, was how much she wished they could become a family. Chase, herself and her unborn baby.

Afterwards, Sydney couldn't sleep. Chase didn't seem to have the same problem. At her insistence, they'd remained in the poolroom, bunking down on the cushioned chaises.

Lying beside him listening to his deep, even breathing made her feel even more restless. She eased herself from the chair, standing on shaky legs, and slid into the pool.

The water felt cool and soothing.

Taking a deep breath, she began to swim laps. Maybe if she continued until she could move no more, she might be able to sleep.

The splash of her inelegant breaststroke woke Chase.

"Sydney?" Chase sat up, dragging his hand through his hair. "What's wrong?"

She swam to the side and rested her elbows on the edge. "I'm working off my frustration and fear. How long do you think it'll be before we can leave this place?"

"Tomorrow." His eyes gleaming in the dim light, he rose and slipped into the water next to her. He ran his hands down her side, making her shiver. "You feel good."

"Not inside. I'm scared to death. We've got to get away from here."

He kissed the side of her neck. "I agree. And we will. But not tonight. Carrington's promised to call me first thing in the morning."

She shifted restlessly in his arms. "There's no way I can sleep tonight."

One more kiss, moving from her neck to her lips. This one was long and deep and drugging. When he pulled back, she was breathless.

"Who said anything about sleeping?"

The next morning, the sun streaming in through the poolroom skylights woke them. Despite her worries, Sydney had finally drifted to sleep in Chase's arms.

"Good morning." While he watched, she stretched. He felt a stab of desire. As though they hadn't made love twice in the night, he craved her. He wanted her again, right here, right now.

As he pushed himself to his feet to clear his head, his cell phone rang. Carrington. He glanced at Sydney.

Watching him, she gave a half-awake smile and shrugged. "Go ahead and take your call. I'm going to have a nice hot shower." Blowing him a quick kiss, she climbed out of the chaise. He glimpsed long legs and creamy skin before she slipped out of the poolroom, closing the door behind her.

He flipped open the phone. "Savage here."

"Chase, while I was checking on options for you, I got more bad news," Carrington began without preamble, highly unusual for him. "The Lazlo Group has put Sydney high on their list of suspects in Reginald's murder. That might even be the real reason someone wants to kill her. You might be trying to protect a murderess."

Stunned, Chase froze. He couldn't move, couldn't speak. Though the duke never spoke rashly or without just cause, this time he was way off base. Sydney? No way.

Chase spoke carefully. "What are they basing this on?"

"A woman matching her description was seen with the prince the night he died. She would have had a good reason."

"A good reason? Numerous women are scorned by the men who got them pregnant. That's not reason enough to kill."

"Not reason enough? For killing Reginald? Come on, man. You knew the prince." It was the first time Chase had ever heard Carrington disparage his relative, though all knew there'd been no love lost between them.

"True." Chase had to work on keeping his tone even. "But if she killed Reginald, who's trying to kill her?"

"Who knows? There are hundreds of possible reasons. Maybe she's part of a larger plot. Her country—Naessa itself—could be involved. Maybe someone is trying to silence her so she can never confess."

Chase ran a hand through his hair. "I'm not believing this. Are there any other suspects besides her?"

"The Lazlo Group is looking into numerous leads, including a terrorist cell that might be affiliated with Sheik Kadir Al-Nuri. But right now, more evidence points to Sydney Conner than to anyone else."

Grimly, Chase tried to picture Sydney killing. Doing so was a stretch of the imagination he couldn't quite manage. "No hard evidence though, right?"

"True. It's speculation at this point. But I can promise you we'll get to the bottom of this." Carrington sounded optimistic. "If it *was* her, she'll have made a mistake and they'll find a clue. The Lazlos are good."

They were more than good, they were legendary. In any battle, Chase wanted them on his side. Too bad he couldn't enlist their services to find out who was after Sydney. But they were focused on trying to prove she'd killed the prince.

Sydney a killer. No way. Carrington didn't know her the

way he did. "I know they're good, but they must have more to go on than someone saying they saw her with him. She carries his child. I still don't understand what she'd accomplish by killing him."

There was silence while Carrington considered. That was one thing Chase had always liked about his boss; the duke was not given to rash or impulsive actions.

"Maybe she wasn't thinking clearly," Carrington finally said. "Both Reginald's e-mails and his actions made it clear he wanted nothing to do with her or her baby. You know what they say about a woman scorned. It's possible she went to him, they made love, and she tried one last time to get him to accept responsibility for his actions."

Even now, the mention of Sydney making love with Reginald made Chase wince. "You think when Reginald refused…"

"She decided to kill him."

"That doesn't sound like Sydney. Believe me, I know her. She wouldn't do something like that."

Again the duke fell silent. When he spoke again, his tone was sharp. "Chase, you sound as if you're becoming far too involved with this woman. Last time we spoke, I asked you to be careful."

"I—" Swallowing hard, he bit back any retort. "I'm fine. What about us moving? Have you found us a place?"

Carrington went silent. "I've had a change of heart."

"What?" Chase's heart sank. "What do you mean? She's got to be moved."

"Oh, I agree. But the Lazlo Group wants to question her about the murder."

Chase's pulse began to pound. "What are you saying?"

"I'm ordering you back immediately. With Sydney."

For the first time since starting to work for Carrington, Chase questioned an order. "Sir, with all due respect, I don't think that's a good idea. There's someone working on the inside. If I bring her back to Silvershire, she'll be a sitting duck."

"Bring William and the rest of your men to help you guard her. There's no help for it. We've got to find the prince's killer. If she did it, she's going to prison."

"Sydney Conner is not a killer."

The duke ignored him. "Notify everyone to get ready. The chopper is being dispatched within the hour."

Closing the cell phone, Chase felt numb. All along, he'd asked to be allowed to go back to Silvershire, back in the thick of things, in his element. He'd wanted to be allowed to do his real job, rather than acting as some overblown bodyguard to a pregnant princess.

But that was before he'd come to know Sydney. He couldn't take her back to Silvershire. Protecting her would be damn near impossible. She'd view this as a betrayal. And rightly so, as he'd promised to keep her safe.

Safe. Hell, he didn't even trust his own men. How could he protect her once she was at court?

Yet if he didn't take her back, he'd be allying himself with her, in the duke's eyes. He'd lose his job. Carrington would never forgive him for disobeying a direct order and choosing a possible murderess over him.

Mind in turmoil, he took a deep breath and went down to the gym to work out. Maybe after a good thirty minutes and some well-deserved sweat, he might be able to figure another way out.

When he'd lifted enough weights to make his muscles

ache and pummeled the punching bag until even his teeth hurt, Chase stepped into the shower. How well did he know Sydney, after all? He'd known Kayla a lot better, or so he'd thought, and she'd left him at the altar for another man with more money and a better title.

But this was Sydney. Whether or not they made a future together, her life was in danger. She needed him, perhaps even more as a bodyguard than a mate.

His job had once mattered more to him than anything else, including Sydney Conner. And now? He was no longer certain.

Toweling off, he knew what he had to do. Though he didn't want to admit it, he'd already made a tentative decision.

Now all that remained was one final test.

Chapter 13

Following the sound of childish laughter, Chase found Sydney and Martha in one of the indoor gardens, tossing a brightly colored ball back and forth over the well-tended grass.

As usual, the sight of Sydney made his breath catch in his throat. Skylights provided sunlight, and the golden glow made her creamy skin appear even silkier. She wore shorts and a halter top. For the first time, he detected a bit of roundness in her stomach. Laughing with Martha, intent on tossing the ball, she hadn't noticed him yet.

Watching her play, he felt another kind of ache. Though he'd never been an imaginative man, he thought he might have been given a glimpse five years into the future. She'd frolic with her own child in much the same way, gathering him or her up in a quick hug, before she bestowed a loving kiss.

He wished the baby she carried was his. Stunned, he looked away, before finding his gaze drawn right back to her, waiting for her to see him.

Martha noticed him first, her exuberant smile fading as she took in his serious expression.

"Sydney?"

Her own smile faltering at his tone, she gazed up at him, searching his face with her impossibly blue eyes. "Chase? What's up?"

"I need to talk to you." He kept his voice neutral.

Sydney tilted her head and looked at him, the glorious fire of her hair mussed as though a lover had just run his fingers through it during lovemaking.

His body instantly responded. Damn.

Her sapphire eyes were clear and guileless. "Now?"

"Yes" His gruff tone spoke of his inner turmoil. The chopper would be here shortly. "We don't have much time."

Instantly alert, she nodded. "Let me take Martha back to the kitchen so her aunt can keep an eye on her."

Without a backward glance, she walked over to the little girl, who'd become entranced by a jewel-colored butterfly. She sat with her hand outstretched, the fragile creature perched on her finger, fluttering its brilliant wings.

Chase watched as Sydney bent and spoke quietly to the child, then helped her flutter her tiny fingers, setting the butterfly free. She led Martha by the hand, attempting to skirt Chase, but Martha pulled free and ran barreling at him, throwing herself at his legs so hard he staggered.

"Whoa, there."

She slid to the ground and peered up at him. "My mama says you saved my life."

"Sydney did," he told her, smiling despite his inner turmoil. "I only helped."

"Mama says I should thank you." She blew him a delicate kiss. "Thank you."

Touched, Chase blew her kiss back. "You're welcome. Now go with Miss Conner. She has something she needs to do."

"Something impor…im…portant?" She grinned as she struggled with the word.

"Yes. Very important." Sydney scooped Martha up in her arms, swinging the giggling child high before setting her on her feet. "Let's go, you." She led the little girl off, shooting one last smiling look at Chase over her shoulder.

Chase felt that look in the depths of his stomach. He was in far too deep. That made it even more necessary for him to be absolutely certain.

He'd offer her the check for seven hundred and fifty thousand pounds. If her amazing blue eyes lit up with excitement and she grabbed at the money with a promise to run, he'd know. Then he'd go back to Silverton, to the duke and his job and leave her to her own devices.

If not…he felt dizzy thinking of the possibilities.

Waiting, he paced until she returned.

"Chase?" She walked up to him, still smiling. She'd gathered her unruly hair into a ponytail. He itched again to run his fingers through it, freeing the auburn strands to caress her face and shoulders.

Wincing, he pushed that thought away.

"What's wrong?" She came closer, bringing with her the light floral scent she wore. "Why do you look so grim? What did the duke have to say?"

"I have a lot to tell you in a very short time. He took a

deep, shuddering breath. "First off, they've discovered Reginald didn't die from a cocaine overdose as they'd originally thought."

She frowned. "Cocaine? That's odd. He never used the stuff around me. I'd heard the rumors, of course. But actions speak louder than words, and since I never saw him take, smoke or snort anything, I figured they weren't true."

"They were," he told her, keeping his voice as level as possible. "But that's not what killed him."

She waited, her open expression expectant.

He took a deep breath. "Reginald was murdered. Someone poisoned him."

Sydney reacted exactly as he'd expected, the way an innocent person would. With shock. "Murdered? Why? Who? Are you sure?"

"I'm just repeating what I was told. They don't have a suspect yet." He told the lie casually, still intent on her reaction.

"What about us moving? Where does he want us to go?"

"That's just it. He won't authorize a move." Another lie, but no way was he letting her know he was willing to give up his job for her until he was certain.

She gasped. "Won't authorize a move? But it's not safe here. You know that! What are we supposed to do?"

His heart gave a foolish leap at the way she said *we*. Ruthless, he quashed it. "Sydney, you have a choice. When I found you at the Hotel Royale, I brought a check with me. A certified bank check for seven hundred and fifty thousand pounds."

Crossing her arms, she waited, her expression puzzled.

"I was authorized to offer it to you. They wanted me to offer you the money to disappear, right away."

Silence. She just looked at him. When she finally spoke, he couldn't discern any hint of emotion in her voice.

"Where to?" Her face was blank, her eyes so dark he couldn't read them.

His heartbeat a painful thud in his chest, he took a deep, shuddering breath. "I don't know. America, perhaps? South Africa? Australia? There are several places you could go. All of them far away, all of them much safer."

"So you want me to take your money—excuse me—the crown's money, and make myself and my baby disappear. Do I have that correct?"

"No." He held himself absolutely still, afraid if he moved he'd shatter into a thousand pieces. "That's not what I want. But what I want doesn't matter. This is about you—what do you want to do?"

Again silence, this time stretching out for so long he fought the urge to pace. Or hit something, which had him thinking fleetingly of how badly he needed to make another trip to the gym. A few more rounds with the punching bag might help.

Her gaze searched his face. It wasn't bright, nor expectant, but wounded and hurt. When she finally spoke, her voice was clear and cold. "I'm not willing to do that." She regarded him as if she didn't know him.

He ached to hold her, but knew she wouldn't permit that, not until he explained.

"Sydney, I didn't think you would, but I wanted you to know everything, every option you had available." Quickly he outlined his conversation with Carrington.

She shook her head, the disgust in her voice making him smile. "They really think I killed him?"

"You're a suspect, no more. I know better. You no more

killed Reginald than I did." If he had more time, he could hold her and tell her how he felt. But that would have to come later, once they were safe.

"Hurry and get your things. We've got to go before the chopper gets here. I'll meet you at your room."

"What about William, Carlos and Jim?"

"I don't trust anyone from now on. It's just you and me." Allowing himself one quick kiss, he sent her off with a promise to meet her in ten minutes.

Then he went to gather his own things.

Practically running when she reached her room, Sydney began throwing her clothing into a suitcase. Without even attempting neatness, she stuffed designer shirts and skirts and jeans all together in a wrinkle-inducing blob. Unlike her. But then, her behavior ever since she'd met Chase Savage had been unlike her.

While she packed, she thought about the bribe. Honestly, she was surprised that Silvershire had believed they could buy her off. Had they truly thought she'd take their damn money and gratefully disappear? But then, they didn't know her at all. Didn't know how many times as a child she had wished her own mother would confront Prince Kerwin and demand he acknowledge his daughter. Instead her mother had eagerly taken the money he'd continued to give her, unwilling to rock the boat and endanger her precious silver spoon.

For money, Frances Conner had ensured her daughter would be considered a bastard her entire life.

Though Sydney could do nothing about her child's legitimacy, especially with Reginald dead, she'd never take money from anyone to make herself and her baby disappear. Her child deserved better than that.

Once she'd crammed everything into her suitcase, she slammed the lid, pushing until the locks clicked. Then she turned her attention to her cello. Though she hated to leave her beloved instrument behind, she had no alternative. Carrying a cello would not only identify her to anyone watching, but slow them down. She could only hope they'd return it to her later, after all this was over.

Just in case, she put her hair up into a tight bun and wrapped a gray scarf around her head. Huge dangling earrings and large sunglasses finished her costume.

Surveying herself in the mirror, she managed a smile. She looked nothing like Sydney Conner, cellist with the symphony. She was ready. Chase should be here any minute.

A tap on her door made her smile.

"Come in."

The door swung open. Jim stepped inside.

"Sydney?"

Remembering Chase had said he didn't even trust his own men, she moved in front of her suitcase, blocking it from view. She couldn't do anything about her appearance. Maybe he would just think she was in a weird mood. "Yes, Jim?"

He looked apologetic as he closed the door behind him.

"I'm sorry to have to do this, but they paid me an awful lot of money." Before she could react, he grabbed her and shoved a cloth over her mouth. The sickeningly sweet scent of chloroform was the last thing she knew.

Moving swiftly, Chase tossed his things in his duffel and weighed his options. He'd have no choice but to borrow one of the cars belonging to the estate. After that, he'd take her to his buddy's hunting cabin in the Silver Mountains.

He slung the duffel over his shoulder and headed down

the hall toward Sydney's room. The plush carpet muffled his footsteps. Her door was closed. First he tapped softly. Then, when he got no response, a bit harder.

No answer. Her door remained closed.

He tried the handle. It wouldn't turn. Locked?

Alarmed, he backed away and, giving himself a good start, used his shoulder as a battering ram. The wood gave. He crashed inside.

The room was empty, save for her cello and suitcase. Her second-story window was open. He ran to it, just in time to see a white cargo van pulling away. Below her window, a wide concrete ledge led to the roof over the kitchen, which gently sloped over the storage room.

Damn it! Heart hammering, he spun and ran for the stairs. Taking the steps two at a time, he hurtled toward the front door.

The gates! They were closed and required special equipment to open.

Instead of barreling down the long drive, he reversed direction and headed toward the security room. The gates were controlled remotely from there. Unless Sydney's abductor had a bypass password, they wouldn't open without approval.

If he got there in time, he could stop the van.

Skidding around the corner, he ran into the room in time to see Carlos turning from the console. The screen from the front-gate camera showed only the closed gate. There was no sign of the van.

"What the hell is this?" He stabbed his finger at the screen. "What happened to the camera? Did it show the white van?"

"White van?" Carlos looked up in alarm. "No, it froze up. The security guy went to check on it. He asked me to monitor the rest."

"What about the gate?" Chase barked. "Tell me you didn't open the gate?"

Wide-eyed, Carlos nodded. "I just did, but that was only Jim."

"Jim?"

"He had to run an errand."

Chase couldn't believe his ears. "An errand?" He swore. "Sydney's been abducted."

"Abducted?" Carlos jumped to his feet. "When?"

"Just now. By Jim's white van." He took off running. But by the time he reached the garage, grabbed a set of keys to a powerful little roadster, and roared down the driveway, there was no sign of the van.

First he drove toward the highway. Despite the way the winding curves gave him glimpses of the road ahead, he saw no sign of the van. The wild countryside flashed past, and finally the sign for the highway came into view.

At the entrance ramp to the highway, he pulled a U-turn. Four lanes of traffic zoomed by. If they'd made it onto that, he'd never catch them.

Just in case, he continued on in the other direction, toward town. As he'd expected, the van had disappeared. Along with Sydney and Jim.

When he got back to the lodge, the chopper had arrived. William waited with Carlos and the pilot.

"The duke wants to know what's going on." Carlos looked wild-eyed. "I didn't know what to tell him, so I told him you'd phone him back."

"What about Jim? Has anyone been able to make contact?"

"We tried Jim's cell phone," William told him. "But one of the maids found it in his room. He left it."

"So he's untraceable." Chase ran his hand through his hair. "Where's the security guard who was on duty? I want to review the tapes. Now."

"He's back in the security room."

Before he'd finished speaking, Chase was already headed there. The security guard was waiting.

"What the hell happened?"

"Someone disabled the front-gate cameras."

In no mood for generalities, Chase restrained himself from grabbing the man's shirt. "Disabled how?"

The guard scratched his neck, grimacing. "They've been set to play rather than record. You see it all the time in movies. Someone inserted a tape to run continuously."

"Let's see the others."

But a review of the tapes revealed nothing.

Chase wanted to punch something—anything.

"Maintain control." William handed him a cell phone. "It's the duke. He says we're all supposed to be en route to Silverton."

Biting back a groan, Chase spoke into the phone. "Savage here."

"What on earth is happening down there? Your men couldn't give me a straight answer."

"They've got Sydney."

"Who's got Sydney?" The duke's icy calm grated on Chase's nerves. "Slow down. What are you talking about?"

Trying to speak as concisely as possible, Chase relayed the afternoon's events.

To his shock, the duke didn't believe any of it. "I think you're all jumping to the wrong conclusion. I doubt she's been kidnapped. She must have gotten wind of the investigation and simply taken off."

"No. Jim was the inside guy."

"Jim's been a loyal employee. Like you, he started as a bodyguard."

"I'm aware of that. But someone got to him."

"Has he—or anyone—called and made demands?"

Chase swallowed. "No, that's what worries me. They've been trying all along to kill her."

"I'll alert Interpol. Leave this up to them, they are trained to handle these things."

Chase's heart pumped so hard and so loudly he feared the duke could hear it over the phone lines. While intellectually he understood what Carrington meant, he knew in his heart he couldn't leave finding Sydney up to the pros."

He had too much at stake. She was his everything.

Carrington wasn't finished. "I still need you here. Once Interpol is on the case, I want you to head back to Silvershire."

Even though his boss couldn't see him, Chase shook his head. "I can't leave now. I've got to find Sydney."

"Send William and Carlos. Your assistant quit yesterday. She couldn't handle the pressure. You've got to get back to the office and take control of things. Otherwise, I'm afraid it'll be a public relations disaster."

Once, hearing something like those words would have made Chase ecstatic. Now, all he could think of was Sydney. "I'm sorry, but William will have to head up the office in my absence. He's fully trained and capable."

"But Chase—" Carrington started to protest. Chase cut him off by flipping the cell phone closed.

William waited expectantly and Chase gave him the order to head back to Silverton in his place. Then he motioned to Carlos.

"I need your help. We've got to figure out a way to rescue Sydney, and quickly. Before they decide to kill her."

Carlos grinned, a flash of white teeth. "Just like in the old days, huh, boss?

Wearily, Chase gave a nod. "Except this time the target is much more important."

"Do you want me to involve the local police?"

"Not yet. We'll let Interpol handle all that. Hunt down the usual sources and see what you can learn from them. We've got to discover where they've taken her."

And pray she was still alive when they found out.

Chapter 14

When she woke, squinting in bright fluorescent light, her heart sank as she realized two things. First, she'd been taken captive and second, they hadn't bothered to blindfold or tie her. If they weren't worried about her seeing what they looked like, it could only mean one thing.

They meant to kill her—and her precious baby.

Sitting up slowly, she swallowed against nausea and swung her legs over the side of the—couch? Yes, she'd been placed on a worn and filthy faded orange couch, the like of which even the most needy charity would turn down.

Head pounding, she stood. Her tongue stuck to the roof of her mouth. Trying to swallow, she gagged. Water. She needed water. Unsteadily she staggered to the door—steel?—and tried the handle. It was locked from outside. Wherever she was, she was a prisoner.

The room swirled. Blinking, taking deep breaths, she tried to focus.

Stay calm. Stay cool.

She had to take stock of her surroundings.

The room, which had concrete walls and no windows, resembled a ten-by-ten basement storage room. *Basement* being the key word. Was she being held in someone's home? Not with concrete walls and a steel door. This seemed more likely to be some kind of underground bunker, like a safe house for high-ranking officials. But where?

Her suitcase hadn't come with her—no surprise there. Her purse lay on the cement floor. She unzipped the top, surprised to find the contents intact.

A moment later, she heard the sound of a key fitting into a lock and a deadbolt sliding back. As the door handle turned, she slowly backed away.

Jim entered, face expressionless. Closing the metal door behind him, he used the key to lock it. When he'd finished, he pocketed the key. "Feeling better now?"

She nodded, trying not to stare at the plastic water bottle he held. Seeing where her attention was fixed, he handed it to her.

Though her mouth was dry, she hesitated.

"It's not drugged." He indicated the steel door. "I've no need to drug you now."

Knowing she had no choice but to believe him, she drank greedily, not stopping until she'd drained the bottle. At least her mouth no longer felt full of cotton.

He continued to watch her without speaking.

She stared back, keeping her gaze on him while she placed the empty bottle on the concrete floor.

"Why, Jim? Chase trusted you. Why'd you do this?"

He grimaced, smoothing his hand over the top of his gray crew cut. "Money, why else? I'm not getting any younger."

"You sold out your government so you could retire?"

His eyes narrowed. "No. You're Naessan. Agreeing to kidnap you has nothing to do with my government."

"Does the duke know you've done this?"

"Of course not." Scorn rang in his voice. "He's an honest man."

And you're not. But she held her tongue, asking instead, "Was it you all along trying to kill me?"

"No. There is more than one faction involved. I was hired to get you out of the line of fire. I came late into the game. Consider yourself lucky," he told her.

"Lucky?"

"Yes. I was told originally one group hired someone to kill you. But he couldn't seem to do the job. He was behind the shootings at the hotel, blowing up your rental car, the car that tried to run your limo off the cliff and the smoke bombs."

"Told by who?"

He didn't answer, merely smiling.

"The jet crashing, too? Did this nameless someone cause that?" She couldn't keep the sarcasm from her voice.

"Unfortunately for him, no. No one knew you'd be on that jet, though if you'd died in the crash it certainly would have simplified things for him. I've been told he even tried to get to you after the crash, before you could be rescued, but the royal chopper beat him to it."

"On that island? How'd he know about that?" She swallowed, refusing to look away. "For that matter, how did he always know exactly where I was, if there wasn't a man on the inside? No matter where I went, he always found me."

He laughed, reminding her with a sharp pang that this was Jim. Jim, who'd always been the quietest member of Chase's team, the consummate grandfather, a family man.

Damn.

Casting a meaningful look at her purse, he held out his hand. "Let me see your purse and I'll show you."

For a moment she stared at him. Finally, she handed it over.

Once he had the black Fendi in his hands, he set it down next to him and pulled a switchblade from his pocket.

Sydney winced out of reflex, making him grin.

"This blade isn't for you. I'm using it to do this." Turning her purse over, he used the sharp knifepoint to pick at the bottom seam. Prying apart a small opening, he used the tips of his fingers and pulled out a tiny, silver disc and held it up. "See?"

She went closer, trying to see. "It's a—"

"Remote tracking device." His grin spread. "This wonderful device is how we knew where you were every second of every day."

A bug. She suppressed the urge to rub her eyes. She felt like an actor in a James Bond movie. "How was that put in my purse? And when? I never let it out of my sight."

"When you perform with the symphony you do. An operative broke into your locker when you were playing in Silverton."

Right about the time she'd started dating Reginald.

"Why? Was it because I was dating the prince?"

He shrugged. "I don't think so. Remember I said there were different factions involved? The first group, the one that wanted to kill you, threatened your father. They tried to use you against him."

"My father?" Dazed, she rubbed her temples. "I don't have a father."

"Really?" Lifting a brow, he wagged a finger at her. "Prince Kerwin would be disappointed to hear that. He saved your life."

"Prince Kerwin?" This was getting stranger and stranger. "He's the mysterious person you keep mentioning? You work for him?"

"Yes. When the first group tried to have you killed, he took care of their hired assassin."

"Took care of how?" She hoped the effects of the chloroform would begin to wear off soon. "What happened to the assassin?"

He shook his head. "In order to gain control of the situation, he eliminated your would-be killer. Right after that maid got shot instead of you."

Eliminated. She swayed, forcing herself to stay focused on his face. She didn't want to know how, or by whom. "And then you were hired by Prince Kerwin? To do what, kidnap me?"

"I was recruited to do exactly that."

"Why?" She crossed her arms. The man who'd sired her had never wanted anything to do with her before. Other than setting up her trust fund, he'd never even attempted to make contact. Why now, and in such a way?

"He hired me to bring you here, get you out of the clutches of the Silvershire people. He didn't want you under their influence until he had time to make an offer."

"Politics?" Her head swimming from more than the chloroform, she tried to make sense of his words. "Now you've really got me confused. You're telling me I was brought here for political reasons?"

He shrugged. "I'm only the messenger."

"But this makes no sense. Politically, I'm worthless. I have no status, no rank, no pull. I'm not worth anything to anyone."

"Ah, but you are more valuable than you realize. Your father is Naessan royalty. And, as an added bonus, you carry the only blood heir to Silvershire's throne. If the people can be convinced that your child must be made next in line for the throne... An explosive combination."

"Illegitimate," she pointed out. Whether she spoke of herself or of her baby, she wasn't sure. Right now, hand cradling her slightly rounded belly, they were one and the same. "The duke will rule in place of Reginald. Royalty never puts a bastard on the throne, you know that."

"Perhaps not in the past. But your father feels that can be changed. Recognized officially or not, you are Prince Kerwin of Naessa's daughter." He waved a hand. "And as far as the baby you carry, whether you and Prince Reginald married or not is irrelevant. Your child is his only known issue. Your child is heir to Silvershire."

Openmouthed, she stared. Jim's eyes burned. He actually believed this nonsense. Fervently. And if he did, others might, as well.

Oh, for the love of... This was ridiculous!

For her baby's sake, she had to figure out a way to make this work to her advantage. She bit her lip. She needed to keep her mouth shut and quit giving them reasons to kill her.

Deep breath. Shoulders back. "Where are we?"

"On Chawder Island."

"Where the jet crashed?" Again he'd succeeded in shocking her. "How is that possible?"

"One of your father's corporations owns this island. After you were rescued, Prince Kerwin opened up this reinforced, underground bunker he had built years ago."

"Bunker? How is that possible? This island isn't that large. You shouldn't be able to dig very far before hitting water."

"Volcanic rock. Surely you noticed that when you were here before? This little mountain used to be a volcano. Your father explored here and found caves. That led to this bunker."

As though he suddenly remembered whose money lined his pockets, his smile disappeared. "Your father will be here soon. He wishes to make his offer in person."

"And you? What do you get out of this?"

"Besides money?" He took a step closer, still smiling. "I will have the honor of knowing I indirectly saved the future king of Silvershire."

"But the money's more important, right?" At his nod, she took a deep breath, then changed tactics. "How much is he paying you?"

He chuckled. "More than my salary after working ten years for the PR department."

"I'll pay you more."

Shaking his head, he sighed. "Sydney, look. I like you. While I know you have a trust fund, I read the papers. I know you only get two hundred and fifty thousand a year, plus what you earn playing for the symphony. The amount Prince Kerwin offered me is more than you could afford."

Maybe, if she only dipped into her savings. But Chase had offered her seven hundred and fifty thousand. If she could convince him to send it to her...

"Don't bet on that."

He raised one graying brow. "Your father is paying me half a million pounds. Tell me you can beat that."

"I think I might. What if I can give you seven hundred and fifty?"

"Interesting." He frowned. "I don't know. If Prince Kerwin were to find out, I'd be dead. Your father is not a forgiving man."

Steady. "He'll never know. All you'll have to do is say I've escaped."

Jim dragged his hand across his mouth. "I'll have to think about it."

She made an effort to shrug, as though her heart wasn't racing. "Don't think too long. I'll need to make a phone call to get the money here. I want to get away before Prince Kerwin arrives."

"Why?" His gaze bright with interest, Jim stared at her.

"Because my father has never cared about me. Ever. Once he's here, I honestly think he'll kill me himself, so no one can ever threaten to use me against him again."

Without another word, Jim let himself out. Sydney glanced at the filthy couch and looked for somewhere else to sit. She settled on the concrete floor, back to the wall, facing the door. If Jim took her offer, everything would depend on Chase.

Barely half an hour had elapsed before Jim returned.

"I'm taking the seven-fifty," he announced. "Now who do you have to call?"

She kept her face expressionless. "Chase. He has the money. It was given to him by the duke to buy me off."

"Chase?" Jim's face reflected his disbelief. "I'd rather not deal with him."

"You won't have to. I'll call him."

"That's not what I mean." Panic glinted in his eyes. "You don't know Chase."

"He'll pay it." She spoke with more confidence than she felt. She *thought* he'd pay to save her, but the money actually belonged to the Crown. And, ever since Reginald, she no longer trusted her judgment where men were concerned.

"Oh, I know he'll pay. That's not what I mean. After I get paid, I'd planned on taking the money and then disappearing, maybe to a Caribbean island someplace. But not if Chase is involved. No one messes with people he cares about. He'll hunt me down."

A lump stuck in her throat. "That's assuming he cares about me."

"He does." Jim sounded certain. "You forget I was around the two of you. I've seen the way he looks at you."

Sydney tried to look positive, too. Ironic that the fate of her and her baby now rested on the head of royal PR. What a field day the papers would have with that!

"I'll make him promise to leave you alone." She needed to hear his voice. "Are you going to let me call him?"

"No. I'm making the call. That way there's no funny business. But—" his smile seemed overly bright "—he's probably going to insist you talk with him, to prove you're alive. I am going to ask him to give his word to leave me alone. Chase never goes back on his word."

He stared at her a moment longer. "You can't mention Prince Kerwin or the deal's off. Understood?"

"Yes." She had no choice. Nor did she much care. All she wanted was to get herself and her baby out of here alive.

Studying her, he seemed about to ask her something else. But instead, he drew a cell phone out of his pocket. "Then let's give him a call."

* * *

When his cell phone rang, Chase almost missed it. He'd just turned on the shower and was preparing to step into it.

Picking up the phone, his heartbeat skipped. The caller ID showed unknown caller. It had to be Jim with a new cell phone.

"Speak to me, Jim. What have you done with Sydney?"

"She's here. Safe. She tells me you have quite a bit of money on you."

The ransom demand. Every nerve stilled. "Money?"

"The seven hundred and fifty thousand." Jim spoke quietly, as if he was embarrassed.

"Jim, why are you doing this? You've worked with me a long time, going back to when we were both royal bodyguards."

The line went silent. Finally, Jim cleared his throat. "I have Sydney. Do you have the cash or not?"

"It's a bank check—certified. As good as cash." He took a deep breath. "What about Sydney? Is she alive? Unharmed?"

"She's fine."

"Put her on the line."

"No can do. Not yet. Not until you commit to pay."

"I'll pay. If she's all right." Grimly, he contemplated what he'd do to his former employee if he so much as harmed one hair on Sydney's head.

"Give me your word."

"If she's returned to me unharmed, I'll pay. You have my word."

"I also want your word that you won't come after me later, once you have her."

Chase clenched his jaw. He wanted to rip the man apart

with his bare hands. "You have my word," he ground out. "I won't come after you."

"Ever?"

Chase swore. "Ever."

"Good enough. I know you keep your promises." Jim sounded cheerful. "I'll put her on the line."

"Chase?" When Chase heard Sydney's shaky voice, he felt some of the crushing weight lift from his chest. At least in this, Jim hadn't lied. She was still alive. Thank God.

"Sydney, are you all right? You're not hurt, are you?"

"No." He could hear her licking her lips, as though trying to get moisture into her mouth. "I'm not hurt."

"Where are you?"

"Chawder Island, he said. The place where we were—"

"I know." He bit back an oath. "Sydney, listen to me. We've got to—"

"Got to do what?" Jim was back on the line. "Chase, you'd better listen. For the first time in a long time, you're not calling the shots. Here's what I want you to do…"

After Jim concluded the call, he went to the door with the phone still in hand. "Looks like you're going to have to stay locked up a bit longer." He sounded apologetic, as though none of this was his doing. "I don't know how long it'll take him to get here."

"Have you heard from Prince Kerwin?"

"Not yet. We have a little time. He's been busy. I've seen him on the telly. He had to attend some kind of a summit in Tice. Dignitaries from all over the place are there." He smiled at her. Sydney couldn't believe she'd once seen his smile as kind.

"When that's finished, I imagine he'll head out here."

Still smiling, he left, closing the steel door behind him. A moment later, she heard the sound of the dead bolt sliding into place.

Time crawled by. How much time, she couldn't say, since she had no watch. She paced, she raged, she tried to think.

She walked the confines of her cell until her legs hurt. Then, sitting on the edge of her mattress, she examined her perfectly manicured fingernails and sighed. One by one she began methodically picking at the cuticle.

Jim brought her food and she ate it, judging the time of day by what he brought. Since the first meal he brought her was an undercooked piece of chicken and beans, she judged that was her supper. She slept a little, though the cold concrete floor was so uncomfortable, she finally made herself move to the couch.

For breakfast, Jim brought a tasteless porridge, for lunch, runny soup.

When she heard the sound of the dead bolt moving, she guessed it was dinnertime again. But Jim entered the room without a tray, wild-eyed, his shirt half buttoned, as though he'd dressed in a hurry.

"We've got a problem." Clearly agitated, he couldn't stand still. "Prince Kerwin's chopper has radioed they should be landing soon. They'll be here within half an hour."

Sydney closed her eyes. When she opened them, she swallowed. "What about Chase?"

"I don't know. He said he'd be here. But he thinks we've got plenty of time."

Her heart stopped. *Where was Chase?* "What are we going to do?"

He shrugged. "You're going to have to meet with your

father. If Chase shows up afterwards, we can still make it look like you've escaped. This might even work out better."

As the door closed behind Jim, Sydney felt chilled. For the very first time in her life, she was about to meet the man who'd sired her. Once, hearing this news would have been the answer to a little girl's lonely prayers. But now, Prince Kerwin's desire to meet with her had come far too late and was for all the wrong reasons.

He'd never even visited the home she'd shared with her mother, preferring to meet Frances Conner somewhere else to avoid having to see his by-blow.

Did he truly think she'd greet him with open arms? That little girl had grown up long ago.

Yet, when the door of her cell swung open and a tall, silver-haired man dressed in a Gucci suit strode in, her heart still caught in her throat.

Prince Kerwin.

Though she'd seen his face on television and in newspapers, none of that had prepared her for the sheer force of his commanding presence. She tried to breathe normally, act nonchalant, yet found herself wishing for a mirror to ensure she'd pass muster. Dumb. The man she refused to call Father looked, with his broad shoulders and arrogant profile, every inch the royal prince. Silver hair graced his temples, and the cut of his expensive suit flattered his trim body. One brilliant, square-cut diamond flashed from his right pinky.

Oddly enough, he brought Reginald to mind.

A conqueror viewing the vanquished, he entered the room alone, surprising her. She'd expected him to arrive surrounded by bodyguards. No doubt his men waited just outside her cell door. After all, how much damage could an unarmed pregnant woman inflict?

Behind him, framed in the doorway, Jim flashed her a nervous smile before pulling on the heavy steel door. It swung closed behind him with a clang, leaving Sydney and her sire alone.

From across the room, they stared at each other.

"Hello, Sydney." His deep voice sounded warm.

Unable to help herself, she studied his face. She saw her own chin and nose when she looked at him. She'd also gotten her blue eyes from him, but little else. He was tall and lean, while she made up in curves what she lacked in height. He looked royal, while she...was as ordinary as could be. Her best feature was her flame-red hair.

She started to speak and found she couldn't. Her throat felt tight, closed. Odd how meeting him still made her want to cry. Even now, with all he'd done and all he'd refused to do.

Finally, she cleared her throat. "Prince Kerwin."

"I've wanted for years to meet my daughter."

Startled, her gaze flew to his. "You've wanted?" She couldn't keep the bitterness out of her voice. "For years I've longed for a father, but you never once came or called. I even worked up the nerve to ask mother why you didn't want me." She blinked, refusing to cry in front of him.

"And your mother? What did she say?"

Her mother had merely laughed, her cold gaze raking over Sydney in a way that left no doubt she was lacking.

"Sydney?"

"She didn't really answer." She shifted her weight from one foot to the other. "What does it matter? You've never had anything to do with me in the past."

He looked surprised and—unexpectedly—hurt. "Your mother said you both wanted it that way. I paid for everything, and stayed out of the picture. She'd only let me visit the house when you were away at school. Otherwise, we met at a flat I kept in town."

Sydney could only stare, her ears roaring. Was this another trick? Or truth? Had her mother stooped so low as to deny her child her own father? To what end?

So as not to take attention away from herself.

Her mother hadn't wanted to share the prince with anyone, not even their little girl.

Not knowing what to believe, Sydney slowly shook her head. "My mother—Frances—told you that?"

A frown creased his brow. He took a step closer. "Of course. Otherwise I would have made an effort to get to know you. You *are* my daughter, after all. She told me you wanted a quiet life, that I would disturb you."

Either her mother had sunk to new depths of selfish narcissism, or Prince Kerwin was a bold-faced liar. She was betting the actual truth was a combination of both things. "She said you didn't want me."

They stared at each other from identical blue eyes. Finally, he dragged his hand through his perfectly groomed hair. "I should find it no surprise to learn your mother lied to me all these years."

Sydney shrugged. She hadn't spoken to Frances in eighteen months.

The tall, silver-haired man watched her. She couldn't tell if that was sorrow darkening his eyes, or if he was playing her the same way her mother had supposedly played him.

When she didn't answer, he sighed.

He came closer, bringing with him a whiff of expensive cologne. "Haven't you dreamt of having it all? Living at the palace, being part of the court? The luxury, the prestige, the respect—all you've ever wanted, can be yours at the snap of my fingers."

Without thinking, she blurted the truth. "All I ever wanted was your love."

After a moment of silence, while he studied her as if she were a specimen under a microscope, he laughed. And laughed longer, a rich, masculine sound that brought sudden tears springing to her eyes. His laughter mocked her, ridiculed her the same way her mother always had.

Who was she to think such a man could ever love her?

She wanted to shrink back inside herself, to rebuild her protective shell, but her pride wouldn't let her.

"Come now." He grinned at her. "You're as good an actress as your mother. I promise I will make this worth your while."

Actress? If only he knew. Once she would have traded all her toys for a smile from this man.

She drew herself up and looked him straight in the eye. "Do not ever insult me by comparing me with my mother."

Sobering, he nodded. Something must have shown in her face, telling him he'd gone too far. "It's not too late. We can change things." His warm smile invited her to come closer.

Now, she knew he wanted only to use her. He didn't really care about establishing a relationship or getting to know her.

It shouldn't have hurt, but it did. More than she'd expected.

She wanted to tell him to go straight to hell.

But she couldn't. Provoking him might only make him decide to finish what the assassins had started. She had to stall for time until Chase could get there and she could escape. She no longer had only herself to think of. She had her unborn child to protect.

Chapter 15

"With all due respect, Prince Kerwin, let's dispense with the lies. I'm aware that you couldn't care less about me." She hoped she wouldn't gag on the next words. "Your offer interests me. What do you want from me in exchange?"

He smiled approvingly. "I knew you were your moth—"

She shot him a glare of warning.

"All right, then. How much do you know? I'm sure Jim explained everything to you." He reminded her of Reginald at his most arrogant.

"Not everything. I know you were going to have me killed." Carefully, she watched for his reaction.

"Not I." He looked offended. "I saved your life. My colleagues would have preferred you were permanently out of the way. I had their hired gun removed."

"Why?" Though Jim had already told her, she wanted to hear her sire answer in his own words.

"You can be more useful to me alive than dead. I have great plans for you."

She crossed her arms, hugging herself. "Plans? Could you be more specific?"

Obviously, Prince Kerwin wasn't used to being questioned. He looked down the length of his aristocratic nose at her, brows raised. "Honestly, didn't your mother teach you anything? My plans are not your concern."

"Ah, but they are," she told him, her voice as silky-smooth as his had been earlier. "If you want me to stand firmly on your side, tell me what you're planning."

Again he glared at her in ringing silence. Motionless, Sydney waited him out.

Finally, he sighed again. "Now that Silvershire is without an heir, I think the people will accept your child. Once you ally yourself—and your precious child—with me, we will choose you a husband." His laughter had a sharp edge. "I'm involved in negotiations with two neighboring countries, Besel and Leandra. Both the kings have sons of marriageable age. Once you marry one of them, your child will speak for the combined countries."

"They'd marry me, knowing I carry another man's baby?"

He laughed, the sound sharp. "Don't you understand? Your unborn child is the key. Joined with you, your husband's country will gain a great deal of power. Naessa will no longer stand alone against Silvershire."

"And what of Silvershire?" she asked softly, cradling her slightly rounded belly.

His eyes gleamed. "Silvershire will no longer be the only powerful nation. Naessa will also have that status, under my guidance and leadership."

"Shouldn't that come from within the country first? We are a small nation, without a large army or—"

"Of course." He cut her off. "I plan to expand Naessa. My father doesn't have much faith in my ability to lead. This will prove him wrong."

King Charles had to be eighty, at least. "So you act without the throne's authority in this?"

He narrowed his eyes. "They will back me, once it becomes obvious I can win. That's where you come in. You and your wonderful, doubly royal baby. Heir to the crown of Silvershire. What better way to sway the people to my side?"

She could only stare. For so long she'd dreamed of meeting this man and now…he made her skin crawl.

"When you talk about expanding Naessa, are you thinking of starting a war with Silvershire?"

He didn't even blink. "If that's what it takes. Silvershire has grown complacent. I'm working with various allies, in secret of course, to gather an army. With you on my side carrying the heir to their crown, bloodshed might not be necessary."

Like any good politician, he'd put the ball squarely back in her court. "You're saying if I don't agree with you, people will die?"

"Perhaps."

Another horrible thought occurred to her. "Speaking of dying, did you kill Reginald?"

For the first time, she managed to startle him. "No. Quite honestly, I was planning to buy him off. If he'd lived, he would have made a perfect puppet. With his excesses and low moral fiber, he would have done anything for money."

How could he, with his plots and secret plans, talk about someone else's low moral fiber?

Something of her thoughts must have shown in her face. He flashed an arrogant smile that told her he didn't care.

"Think about my offer. Join forces with me. Proclaim to the world that you and the next heir to Silvershire will be aligned with Naessa, plus the country of whichever prince you marry."

"And if I don't?"

"If you don't?" He gestured at the concrete walls. "I could have you killed now, but I won't."

"You'd let me go?" She couldn't believe it. "Just like that, you'd let me go free?"

His expression went cold, remote. "That's not what I said, Sydney. You know too much to let you live. I will keep you here, a prisoner, until the baby is born. As far as the world will know, you will have died in childbirth. In truth, I'll order my men to kill you."

So much for fatherly love. Compressing her lips into a tight line, Sydney stood motionless, expressionless, and watched the man she would never call Father take his leave.

Take his offer or die. Not much of a choice. Unless…for the first time in her life, Sydney knew she'd have to think and act just like her enemies. That was her only hope—to pretend to go along with their plans, and hope she could warn Chase in time.

Even if Prince Kerwin paid Jim the money he wanted, no doubt he had a small army camped outside. Trying to help her escape, Chase could get killed. Now she not only had to worry about the safety of her unborn child, but also the man she loved.

Chase bailed out over the ocean at night, at thirty-five hundred feet. The plane—one of the new, superquiet, superlight aircraft built specifically for the Silvershire air force—sped silently away.

Because he was jumping from so low an altitude, he immediately pulled his ripcord, feeling the swift, sharp pull upward as his parachute billowed into the pitch-black sky. His knapsack contained night-vision goggles and, of course, the certified bank check for seven hundred and fifty thousand pounds.

Drifting toward the beach, he came in on the opposite side of the island from where the jet had crashed, away from the shadow of the mountain where he and Sydney had nearly made love for the first time and where, according to Jim's instructions, he was to bring the money.

No longer bribe money, the check had become blood money. He planned on turning over none of it. Not one red cent. Instead, he meant to free Sydney and bring troops swooping down on the island.

He only hoped he wasn't too late.

Chase had come an awfully long way, taken a huge risk, and enlisted the help of Silvershire's military forces, all on his gut instinct. Things were bigger than they seemed. Whoever had paid Jim would come eventually, and he wanted to catch the bigger fish as well as the small.

Most importantly, he wanted to find Sydney.

The landing was soft and good, and the lack of a breeze kept the parachute from carrying him too far down the beach. Dragging his parachute into the underbrush, he slipped on the night-vision goggles. He moved silently and kept to the forest as he made his way to the mountain.

A sound made him freeze. Damn—that could only be the sound of a low-flying chopper approaching.

It flew over him, heading toward the mountain.

In the morning he was supposed to meet with Jim at the base of the mountain to exchange the money.

Who was in the chopper? Jim and Sydney? Or was it the one behind Jim's defection, the one in charge?

He supposed he'd find out in the morning.

Before then, he'd do a bit of recon work and see what else he could discover.

For a good while the only sounds he heard were the normal, night sounds of the forest. Small animals moved about in search of food, but he was the only human.

So far so good. He kept his steady path toward the small mountain. A few minutes later, he heard the faint hum of man-made machinery. Jeeps and generators, several men. Jim's associates?

Circling around the pond, he kept going. He remained in the shadows as he drew closer. A dog barked and he froze, only cautiously moving forward when it was quiet again.

There was some sort of camp at the base of the mountain. Careful to make no sound, he peered through the foliage to take a head count.

There were only a few men, less than he'd expected. He counted three, before a fourth emerged from a tent, whistling as he walked. All soldiers in camouflage. All armed to the teeth. They were camped around a door that had been cut into the side of the mountain.

A door? He'd climbed this mountain when he and Sydney had been trapped here before, done his share of exploring, but hadn't noticed the door. How had he missed it and where did it lead? Underground bunkers? Then he saw the elaborate screen they used to cover everything and understood why the place had gone undetected. Once the screen was in place, covered as it was with leaves and dirt and rocks, no one would ever find the door.

What kind of covert operation had captured Sydney?

A second later, he had his answer. A royal one. The helicopter he'd heard earlier sat on a well-lit landing pad built at the edge of the beach. The sides were painted with the royal crest of Naessa. Two large German shepherds were chained to stakes near the helicopter. He recognized the dogs from television. They were Prince Kerwin's pets and traveled everywhere with him.

Prince Kerwin. That explained the soldiers and the underground bunkers. Naessa might be small, but it was a wealthy country.

So why the phone call from Jim demanding money? And how was Sydney involved? Her birth father was Prince Kerwin. This brought more questions he couldn't answer.

He couldn't help but wonder if he'd blundered into some kind of trap. Since he had no choice, he supposed it didn't really matter.

For now. Once the military got here, there'd be answers, he guaranteed it.

Now, before anything else, he'd need to focus on the most important question of all. Where was Sydney being held and how was he going to get to her?

After he got her out, he was home free. One press of the button he wore on his belt, and the transmitter would send a prearranged signal. Silvershire Special Forces would swoop down on the island and secure it. But until he found Sydney, he worked alone.

He hunkered down to wait and plan.

Flanked by two burly bodyguards, Sydney followed Prince Kerwin down the long hall. At each corner, the incline became more and more steep.

"I had this underground bunker designed incorporating several natural caves. This path will gradually emerge on the surface," the prince said, expansive now that he thought he had another fan. "Masterpiece of a hiding place, don't you think?"

Was it ever. "I can't believe we didn't find any signs of this place when we were trapped here."

"Ah yes, you and that man." They turned another corner. "Your fiancé? What became of him?"

As she struggled to find an answer, the lights went out, plunging them into darkness.

Though she was as surprised as the rest of them, Sydney knew an opportunity when she saw one. Spinning past her bodyguards, she elbowed one in the gut. The other one grabbed her arm, so she kicked him, her toe connecting with his soft parts. Grunting in pain, he let her go.

She ran like hell in the pitch-black hallway, up, always up, heading toward the exit. Slamming into walls, careening off corners, bruised and battered but always protecting her abdomen, she kept ahead of the furious prince and his guard.

Then, rounding another turn in the darkness, she realized she could see her hands. Ahead of her she saw light. Outside! She was that close!

As she barreled into a holding room that led to the main hallway, the way looked miraculously clear.

A few more feet and she'd have her freedom.

A shape loomed up in front of her. Big, bulky. A man. Crap! She attempted to dodge. He grabbed her arms.

No. With an inarticulate sound of rage, she fought him.

"Sydney, stop." Chase's voice. She froze, long enough to focus on his face. Chase. Here. She didn't have time to wonder how or why. It was enough that he was.

"Run," she managed, pushing away an unbelievable swell of joy. "No time to explain. They'll be up here any minute."

Two men lay on the ground, face down.

"I took them out. Come on."

They sprinted, running side by side, crashing full speed into the forest. Without stopping they rushed, jumping over the occasional fallen log, pushing aside the undergrowth, and hoping like hell the dogs weren't released.

When they reached the deepest part of the woods, a good distance from the camp, they rested. Doubled over, Sydney tried to listen for sounds of pursuit. She heard nothing.

Chase bent over next to her. "Until they send the dogs after us, we're okay. I disabled the four guys outside."

Trying to catch her breath, Sydney gasped for air. "Dead?"

"No. Unconscious."

"Good." She frowned. "Chase, I haven't seen Jim."

He shook his head. "We'll deal with him later. Silvershire troops will be here soon. I've sent them a signal. We've got to keep going."

"Where?"

The sound of dogs barking carried through the trees.

"Damn!" Chase jumped to his feet. "The only place dogs can't track us is water. Come on, we're going to have to go back to the pond. Remember I told you about the underwater route to the hidden caves I found?"

She nodded.

"Let's go."

Though exhaustion had her stumbling, Sydney pushed herself up.

As they drew nearer the pond, the sound of barking and baying grew louder. Chase wondered how many dogs they were using in the search. No matter. Water would stop the dogs from going any further. Unless their pursuers knew about the hidden cave, they'd be safe until reinforcements arrived. Until then, they needed to hide.

More than anything, Chase wanted to keep Sydney safe.

Finally, they reached the pond and waded in together to their knees. After a quick look at Sydney, Chase held out his hand. She took it without hesitation, allowing him to pull her chest-high into the murky water.

"Once we're under, open your eyes and follow me. I did this when we were here before. There's a rock wall that leads to the caves on the right. We'll follow that and, just when you think you can't hold your breath any longer, we'll surface in an underground cave. It's like a huge air bubble. There's a ledge and a couple of other flat places to climb, which we'll need to do to get out of the water. We're going to hide in the cave for a little while. Are you ready?"

She swallowed and nodded.

He pressed a quick kiss to her lips and then, releasing her, he waited while she dove in. A second later, he followed.

The rock wall was exactly as he remembered and, lungs bursting, he felt his way quickly along the smooth surface. Sydney was right with him. Then, when the rock abruptly ended, he grabbed her arm and pushed them both up the craggy face of the ledge.

As he'd done the first time he'd tried this, he wondered if he was going to make it. Then, miraculously, they popped out of the water, gasping for air.

He held on to the rock face with one hand, Sydney with the other. "Are you all right?"

Still trying to pull oxygen into her lungs, she nodded. "I think so."

Hauling himself up on the ledge, he reached for her.

Shaking her head, she pulled herself up. They rested a moment, before climbing the rest of the way.

As they reached the small cave, she was shivering. Chase pulled her close, holding her.

God, she felt good wrapped in his arms once more. Where she belonged.

He nuzzled her wet hair. She raised her face to his, a question in her eyes. "What are we going to do?"

"Wait here until help arrives."

Sydney seemed to accept this answer, relaxing slightly. Somehow, despite all she'd been through, she still managed to look sleekly pampered. And, he admitted to himself, sexy as hell.

"When'd you get here?"

He smiled. "Last night. Right about the same time Prince Kerwin did. Now tell me what's going on."

She filled him in. Once she'd finished, Chase gave a low whistle. "Talk about convoluted. And the sad part about it is he was right about Reginald. I know how you felt about him, but Reginald would have sold out his country for a good time."

"How I felt about him?" Twisting her hands in her lap, she sighed. "I realize now I never really knew Reginald. I heard the stories, of course. But he was different with me. Right up until he ended it, he acted as if I'd changed him, made a difference."

He kissed her, hard. "You probably did, for a while."

"Maybe. But I know now I never really knew him. Nor he me."

Chase had to know. "What about the baby, Sydney?"

"He and I never discussed the baby, after the first time. Once I told him I was pregnant, as far as he was concerned

I didn't exist. He wouldn't see me. He ignored my e-mails and refused to take my calls. He pretended not to know me."

Again, Chase found himself wondering at Reginald's monumental stupidity. To have had the love of a woman like Sydney, and then to discard it....

His own thoughts struck him like a sledgehammer.

Love. He pushed the thought away for later.

"So, what do you think?" He gestured around them. "Even though they can't be reached by land, the tops of these caves are above ground. See all the light? There must be some small holes somewhere."

Taking in their surroundings, she smiled. "Pretty neat. I've never been caving."

"As caves go, it's not much. But it's hidden, safe and dry. We can hang out here until we know the island has been secured."

She pressed against her stomach. "How long?"

"As long as it takes."

"Without food or water?"

"The pond water is safe to drink. I've tried it. Worst comes to worst, we can go a day or so without food."

She nodded, though she looked so uncertain he couldn't resist kissing the side of her neck, making her shiver.

"I'm worried about my baby."

He drew back and turned her chin to face him. "Did anyone hurt you?"

"No, it's not that. I have to make sure I'm getting enough nutrients. I don't have my vitamins or—"

He covered her mouth with his. This time, he deepened the kiss and she sagged against him. When he lifted his mouth, she sighed. "I can't help worrying, Chase."

"We'll be fine," he told her, aching for more than a kiss.

He never wanted to be parted from her again, though now wasn't the time to tell her that.

"Yes, I'm sure we will be." Pushing herself out of his arms she stood and wrapped her own arms around herself. She sounded strong as she met his gaze, her own determined.

"Anything's better than being a prisoner in that underground concrete bunker of theirs."

To distract himself, he fished a plastic bag from his pocket. "Waterproof," he said, breaking the seal. "This is the transmitting device I told you about. I've activated the signal, so it's only a matter of time."

Shaking her head, Sydney laughed. "Shades of James Bond, eh?"

"Maybe." He grinned back.

"Silvershire has a hell of a PR department. What's up with that?"

"We're prepared for anything." He placed the small metal box on a nearby rock ledge. "Not only do we protect the royal reputations, but we are all trained to protect their lives, as well. Some of us are former bodyguards, like William, Carlos and Jim." He clenched his jaw, wondering how the man he'd known for years had come to betray him.

"Chase?" Sydney came back to Chase's side. "We need to talk."

Before, in any of his previous relationships, those four words had inspired dread. But this was Sydney, and Chase merely nodded and pulled her into his lap.

"Come here."

Breathless, she put up a mock struggle. "I said talk, not cuddle." But still, she let him pull her close, settling nicely in his lap. Heaving a sigh, she leaned her head on his shoulder.

"I've missed you," he told her. Holding Sydney, he realized he never wanted to let her go.

They spent the remainder of that night wrapped in each other's arms. At first, he checked his watch every hour. Then, as Sydney dozed, he finally fell asleep.

When he woke, he saw it was seven in the morning.

Gently easing Sydney out of his arms, he stood and stretched, working out the kinks in his body. When he looked at her again, he saw she was awake, and watching him.

They shared some water and some of his military rations.

Fidgety, he tried to pace. The small confines made this difficult. He did it anyway.

She exercised. Sit-ups, push-ups, jumping jacks. He thought about joining her, but settled back to watch instead.

Finally, he couldn't take the silence. "They should be here by now. I'm going to go check."

"Out there? Do you think it's safe?"

He touched her arm. "We won't know until I find out. We can't stay here forever."

She nodded. "I'm going with you then."

"No. Let me—"

"Hey." She pressed her nose against his, making a mock growling sound. "Don't mess with a hungry pregnant woman. I'm going for the food."

"No. The baby's better off away from bullets. You wait here."

Grumbling, but because she knew he was right, she moved back over to the large rock they'd used as a seat, and sat.

The mournful look on her face made him smile.

"Be careful," she said.

"I'll be back as soon as I know it's safe." He pressed a

kiss on her mouth. Then he went to the ledge and slid into the dark water.

He surfaced in the center of the pond to a sun-dappled forest.

No gunshots. Did that mean it was over or that it hadn't yet started?

Chapter 16

Moving through the forest toward the Naessan camp, Chase listened carefully. If he heard Prince Kerwin's dogs, he'd know things hadn't gone as planned.

When he reached the trail that led to the bunker, he saw Silvershire troops guarding the door.

He'd asked Carrington for a few paratroopers. The Silvershire Royal Air Force had delivered.

Emerging from the woods, he kept his hands up, in plain sight. They held him at gunpoint and summoned their commander, who recognized Chase and ordered him released.

"Is all secure here?"

The lieutenant nodded. "But we've been unable to locate Sydney Conner. Prince Kerwin has been taken into custody. Due to the delicate situation with Naessa, we've notified Duke Carrington himself. He is on his way here. ETA is approximately one hour."

"Great." Chase swallowed. "What about Jim Keesler? Older man, gray hair. He worked for me in the PR department. Have you seen him?"

The other man's expression turned grim. "I'm sorry, sir. He didn't make it. There was some initial resistance. We returned fire. There were three casualties, all theirs. He was one. We didn't know he was there."

"He'd switched sides." Sighing heavily, Chase wished he'd had a chance to talk to the other man once more. He still didn't understand what had happened to motivate a good man to turn bad, to sell out his friends and country for money.

"Would you like to view the body?"

"No." Chase turned to head back the way he'd come.

"Where are you going, sir?" The young officer appeared confused. "You should wait to speak with the duke."

"To fetch Miss Conner. I had to hide her until you guys showed up." Chase lifted his hand in a quick wave. "I'll be back before the duke arrives."

Sydney couldn't sit still. She paced, she roamed, she talked to herself in Chase's absence. And she prayed. If she lost him…

Blinking, she swallowed to try and dispel the hot ache at the back of her throat. Chase would be fine. Any moment now, he'd emerge from the depths of the pond.

A splash, and he erupted from the water, gasping for air. Delighted, she ran to the edge and helped him pull himself up. Then, before he could catch his breath, she kissed him on the mouth. Running her fingers over his face, his arms, his hair, she couldn't seem to stop touching him.

"Hey." He grabbed her hands. "It's all right."

"You're safe." Knowing her heart was in her eyes, she met his gaze and then kissed him again.

When they drew apart, he shook his head. "Yes, I'm safe." Smiling tenderly, he touched his mouth to the tip of her nose. "And if you don't stop that, we'll never get out of here."

"It's safe?"

He nodded. "After I catch my breath, we'll go. My boss—the duke—is on his way here."

"Prince Kerwin?"

"Your father has been arrested."

She searched his face. "What about Jim?"

His smile faded. "Jim's dead. He didn't make it." Eyes dark, he held out his hand. "Come on. Let's get out of this place."

A half hour later, Sydney watched nervously as a chopper landed on the beach. A handsome man wearing a black Prada suit headed toward them. He moved with a loose-limbed, elegant sort of grace.

Sydney recognized him from television. She stiffened. "The Duke of Carrington," she whispered, wondering if he still thought she'd killed Reginald.

Putting his arm around her shoulders, Chase drew her close. He kissed her cheek. "No more worries."

"Easier said than done," she muttered, studying the man as he approached.

The duke's coffee-colored eyes were sharp as he took in the way Chase stood protectively close to Sydney.

Flashing Sydney a quick smile, he clapped Chase on the back. "When you took off, I thought you'd lost your mind. But loving my Amelia has shown me what love can make you do. She pointed out how important you are to the public relations department and that I shouldn't be too harsh on you. I've decided to take her advice."

Listening, Sydney didn't know what to say. Shortly after telling Sydney they were over, Reginald had announced his engagement to the very same Princess Amelia. Now, after a whirlwind courtship, Carrington had married her.

"Now that Reginald's dead…" Her eyes widened. "I apologize. I didn't mean to say that out loud."

"No apology necessary." The duke didn't seem offended, and Sydney let out the breath she'd been holding. "You're absolutely correct. The press has been having a field day."

Chase winced. "This was why you wanted me back in Silverton, wasn't it?"

Carrington nodded. "But you had something more important to do. I'm glad to know I can still count on you."

Filling him in on Prince Kerwin's plot, Chase kept his arm around Sydney. She tried not to keep looking for a glimpse of her sire, but couldn't seem to help herself.

"It was an added bonus that looking for Sydney uncovered the plot against Silvershire." The duke fixed Sydney with an intense look from his warm brown eyes. "I'm sorry about your father."

She started to reply automatically, "He wasn't my—" Closing her mouth, she dipped her chin in a nod. "Me too," she said instead.

The duke held out his hand. "Russell Carrington."

Stepping forward, she took it. "Pleased to meet you."

"I'm glad to finally meet you, Princess Sydney. I've heard you play and must say I thoroughly enjoyed it."

She looked at Chase. With a small shake of his head, he told her not to argue about the title.

"I've been in touch with your country. King Charles has denied any knowledge. Naessa's official line is that Prince Kerwin acted alone."

"He mentioned a few other countries." She named them.

"Thank you." He signaled to the lieutenant, who snapped to attention. "Check that out immediately."

"Yes, sir."

Carrington turned his attention back to Chase. "I have more good news for you. You two can let go of this pretend engagement of yours. Miss Conner is no longer a suspect."

Pretend engagement. Hearing the words, Sydney wondered when she'd started to forget the engagement wasn't real. The shell-shocked look on Chase's face told her he was thinking the same thing.

"Evidence has surfaced proving Sydney wasn't behind the blackmail threats or the murder. We're looking at other suspects now, chiefly a terrorist group which might be linked to Sheik Kadir Al-Nuri."

Seeming to refocus, Chase groaned. "He's coming in a month for the Founders' Day gala, isn't he?"

"Yes. And we must follow standard diplomatic procedure and assign him an aide during his visit. I'm thinking Cassandra Klein."

"Why Cassandra? Kadir's a worse playboy than Reginald was."

Carrington shrugged. "She speaks Arabic."

"Any other suspects?"

"Nikolas Donovan has requested a meeting with me."

Clearly shocked, Chase narrowed his eyes. "Why?"

"He says he wants to discuss the future of Silvershire."

"Sounds like a threat."

"Could be. Amelia doesn't think so, and I trust her judgment. But rumors are starting to circulate that Reginald's death has made Silvershire vulnerable to our enemies." The duke waved his hand toward the bunker. "Which is what must have inspired Prince Kerwin to do what he did."

"Will he stand trial?"

"I don't know. Naessa has requested custody."

"Excuse me." Sydney cleared her throat loudly. "I know you two have forgotten I exist, but this is really important to me. I'd like to make sure I heard you correctly. You said that I'm no longer a suspect in Reginald's murder, yes?" Holding her head up proudly, she eyed the duke.

He grinned. "Well done, princess. I like the way you face me, nobility to nobility." He winked at Chase. "You know, maybe you should consider making this engagement real. Sydney has a hell of a lot more class than most of the true-blue royals I know."

"I—" Chase looked trapped. He pushed a strand of his long blond hair away from his face and blew out his breath in a puff.

Sydney wanted to curl up and die.

Carrington's smile faded. "I understand. You two need to talk about what's happened, right? I'll quit meddling." With a sigh, he shook his head. "Being in love so deeply makes me look for such happiness for everyone else. Again, I apologize."

Expression now a stony mask, Chase wore his impersonal, private face. "Sydney and I have a lot to talk about. I've got some explaining to do, I think."

Her heart shattered. Just like that, she knew. Now that his assignment was clearly over, Chase clearly regretted everything.

Just like Reginald had.

Except Reginald had been a mere infatuation. She knew that now. She also knew that what she felt for Chase was the real thing.

And he, like the prince before him, like her mother and the man who'd never been her father, was going to reject her love.

She didn't think she could bear it again.

One thing she did know for certain, she wouldn't run after him as she had Reginald. Wouldn't beg him to stay. She had no reason to, apart from her love. After all, she didn't carry his child.

Her precious unborn child.

She and her baby would have each other. She'd be fine. Happy, even. Eventually.

Directing her attention to the duke, she forced a nonchalant smile. "Now that I'm no longer a suspect or in danger, I assume I'm free to go back to Naessa?"

"Correct."

"How soon?" She refused even to glance at Chase again.

Chase answered, still in PR mode. "We'll need to have a press conference and clear things up. Plus—"

"No." Interrupting him, Sydney kept her gaze on the duke, who looked puzzled. "No press conference for me. You people do what you need to do on your end to handle it. Just get me home as quickly as possible."

"Sydney—"

She made herself look at him, doing her best to hide any emotion. The wind lifted his hair to caress his square jawline and his hazel eyes looked puzzled.

He was so damn beautiful that looking at him now hurt.

"That's all right, Chase. I understand." Proud of her steady voice, she tried for a smile. It felt more like a grimace. "You're good at your job, especially the body-guard part of it. Thanks for keeping me safe."

"We still need to talk," he said. "To figure out…"

"To figure out what?"

The duke interrupted. "Can you two do this at another time? Chase, you've got to get back to work. We've got reporters here, as well as the makings of an international crisis."

The not-so-subtle reminder should serve to refocus Chase on what was important to him. He'd almost lost his job for her once. She knew he wouldn't do so again. He'd told her he lived only for his job. She was no longer his concern.

After all, she was safe now.

Turning to Carrington, she looked him up and down, as though she really was a princess, outranking him. "You're a duke, therefore you can accomplish whatever you want, no matter how much it inconveniences others. Send me home."

Glancing from her set face to Chase's, the duke looked thoughtful. "I suppose I can send you in the chopper."

"Good. Notify me when it's ready." Back straight, she walked away, making herself a solemn vow. Chase would never know he'd broken her heart, even if it killed her.

Screw his job. Sydney wouldn't even look at him. Chase started to go after her, but the duke's grip on his shoulder stopped him.

"You need to come with me. We've got a press conference to hold."

About to snarl at his boss, Chase took a deep breath.

"Chase?" Carrington watched him closely. "You've got to start working on what to say to the reporters. Spin's your specialty, and God knows we can use that now. It's not every day a crown prince from another country gets charged with a crime."

Spin? Chase shook his head. "Are the reporters here on the island?"

"Yes." Mouth quirking in a smile, the duke watched him. "They're down in the bunker, waiting. I allowed two—*The Quiz* and the *Daily Press*—to come along."

Chase's heart sank. "I'm sorry, but you'll have to go it alone. I'll understand if you no longer wish to employ me."

Still watching him closely, the duke inclined his head. "I want to make certain you understand what is important here."

"My job?" Chase let his tone show his disbelief. "I'm sorry, but—"

"No, your woman." The smile became an all-out grin.

"I want our engagement to become real." Chase dragged a hand through his hair.

"Have you asked her?"

"Well, no. But—"

"Do you love her?"

Chase swallowed. "I can't live without her."

"I see. But do you love her?"

"Yes," Chase snarled. Then, softening his tone, he started forward. "I've got to go after her. I'm sorry about the press."

"I can handle them." Carrington waved him away. "Go after her, man. I'll finish up here without you."

Chase searched the camp, and the beach. She wasn't there. One of the soldiers had seen her walk into the woods, toward the pond. But when Chase got there, he couldn't find her.

He came out of the woods on the other side of the island,

near the old shelter he'd constructed from pieces of the broken aircraft.

Back to him, Sydney stood facing the water, her hair gleaming in the sun like a newly minted penny.

She took his breath away.

As he started toward her, he rehearsed what he wanted to say for the tenth time. After all, the Wizard of PR still had a trick or two up his sleeve.

She turned to face him, sapphire eyes searching his face, and all his carefully rehearsed words flew from his head.

"Sydney." He reached for her, crushing her to him

Pushing him away, she stepped back. "What are you doing here? Oh, I nearly forgot. You said you have some explaining to do. So let's hear it."

"I wanted to explain about our engagement."

She shook her head. "No need. I understand it's not real."

Though her tone was indifferent and she tried to keep her face expressionless, he caught a glimpse of pain in her eyes.

Did she truly think he didn't love her? How was that possible?

His breath caught in his throat. "Sydney, you know how I feel."

She folded her arms across her chest. "Do I?"

"Have I not shown you?"

When she still looked doubtful, he began to speak. Not the words he'd so carefully prepared and rehearsed, but straight from his heart. "Do you remember the first time we kissed, right here?"

She gave a hesitant nod.

"I'll never forget it. You pressed a kiss against my throat, and I was lost. The first time I held you in my arms? I thought I'd drown in the storm of your eyes, I—"

She held up her hand. "Stop. You don't have to do this. I totally understand. You'll go on with your job, your life, and I'll go on with mine." She touched her stomach without hesitation. "In case you've forgotten, I'm expecting another man's baby."

He shook his head. "My baby. Ours."

Her eyes filled with tears. "What are you saying?"

"I want us to be a family. I want to raise your baby with you, as my own, and to be the only father that child will ever know." Blinking back tears of his own, he cleared his throat. "I want our engagement to be real."

Her lush mouth curved in the beginnings of a smile. "But Chase, you've never asked me."

He dropped to one knee, right there in front of their old shelter, with the ocean crashing on the rocks behind him, and the cloudless May sky as his witness.

As he opened his mouth to speak, a reporter stepped from the shadows of the trees, camera snapping.

Paul Seacrist from *The Quiz* gave them the thumbs-up sign. "Got it," he said. "Would you care to make a comment?"

Growling a warning, Chase shook his head. "Go away."

Sydney laughed. "No comment."

"Please." Chase's voice was somewhere between a snarl and a plea.

The reporter looked from him to her. Something he saw in Chase's face softened his eager expression and he nodded. "Let me give you two a little privacy."

He backed off, until he stood a comfortable distance down the beach.

"How about that?" Brows raised, Sydney looked at Chase. "Now, you were saying?"

Carefully, reverently, he took her hand. "Sydney Conner, I love you. You are all that matters to me. Will you do me the honor of truly becoming my wife?"

She smiled. "Of course, I'll marry you, Chase. How could you ever doubt it? You're my heart, my life, my everything."

With a joyous whoop, he took her in his arms. They shared a long, lingering kiss to seal the bargain. Neither paid any heed to the photographer's frantic snapping.

The following day, the picture made the front page of *The Quiz*.

* * * * *

THE SHEIKH AND I

BY
LINDA WINSTEAD JONES

Linda Winstead Jones has written more than fifty romance books in several sub-genres. Historical, fairy tale, paranormal and, of course, romantic suspense. She's won the Colorado Romance Writers Award of Excellence twice, is a three-time RITA® Award finalist, and (writing as Linda Fallon) winner of the 2004 RITA® Award for paranormal romance.

Linda lives in North Alabama with her husband of thirty-four years. She can be reached via www.eHarlequin.com or her own website, www.lindawinsteadjones.com.

For The Children.
May all your dreams come true.

Chapter 1

Kadir stood on the balcony of his villa on the sea, and watched the waves come in as the morning sun glinted on the gentle surf. From this vantage point he could usually see his yacht anchored in the near distance, but it had been gone for several days now. His crew was sailing the ship to the coast of Silvershire. Having his own familiar space available during his weeks there would make the long stay more tolerable, he was certain.

A private jet waited at a nearby airstrip, ready to carry Kadir and his retinue of bodyguards and aides to Silvershire. There he would not only attend the Founder's Day Gala to which he'd been invited; he would also meet with Lord Carrington, the apparent king-in-waiting. The old king was very ill, and his only son, Prince Reginald, had died under mysterious circumstances some months back. There were, of course, many suppositions about who had killed the obnoxious prince, and why, but Kadir paid little attention to rumor.

In truth, Kadir didn't care who ruled Silvershire. He desired an alliance with the ruler of that country—whomever he might be—in order to strengthen Kahani. Every affiliation he formed or strengthened, every handshake, every smile, every friendship brought Kahani another step into the modern world. Kadir wanted, more than anything, to see the country he loved move into the twenty-first century with dignity and strength.

There were those who wanted Kahani to turn back the clock a thousand years. Most citizens wanted nothing more than peace and prosperity. A home. Food for their loved ones. Safety for their family. But for some, that was not enough. For some, life was one battle after another, and they did not want that peace. A tightness grew in Kadir's chest. Dissidence in Kahani was not new. Zahid Bin-Asfour had been a thorn in his side for a very long time. Fifteen years and four months.

Every alliance cemented Kahani's place in the new world, but there was another reason Kadir desired a meeting with Lord Carrington. Reliable intelligence indicated that Zahid and Prince Reginald had met not long before the prince's death. Three days before, to be exact. Kadir didn't know why Zahid and the late prince had met. If Carrington had intelligence himself he did not…a sharing of information might be most useful to both parties, and both countries.

Kadir watched a familiar figure approach from the east, the sun at the old man's back. Mukhtar ran a local market and delivered fresh fruits and vegetables several times a week. He carried a canvas bag that bulged with lemons, grapes and almonds—Kadir's favorites—and whatever vegetables had looked best that morning. The bodyguards who surrounded the villa at all times were accustomed to the friendly vendor. As Mukhtar drew closer, Kadir could see that he did not wear his usual smile. He was not only in an uncustomary bad mood, but had apparently forgotten that Kadir was leaving the country today and would not return for several weeks, therefore having no need for this morning's delivery. Something must've distracted the usually pleasant man.

"Good morning," Kadir called as the man approached the balcony. Mukhtar's feet dug holes into the sand, and he kept his head bowed.

Before he reached the balcony, Mukhtar stopped. He did not raise his head.

"Is everything all right?" Kadir rushed down the steps to join the old man on the sand. "You're looking rather pale. If you need a doctor…"

Mukhtar lifted his head. There were tears in his eyes. "I'm very sorry," he croaked. "I didn't have any choice, you must understand. They have my children. My daughters, and my son. My new grandson." He shivered visibly. "I must do as they say. Forgive me."

The canvas bag Mukhtar carried bulged in such a way that Kadir knew— too late—that it did not contain the usual fruits and vegetables. Mukhtar's distressed face and the cleverly disguised handcuffs that Kadir had not seen until it was too late told him what was in that bag.

Kadir wondered, as he took a step closer to the old man, if the explosive apparatus would be triggered by a timer, a remote device or the frightened vendor himself. "Let me help you. The king's guard can rescue your family. Whoever has done this, you can be sure that he has no honor. A man who would kidnap innocents to force you to this will not release his captives, no matter what you do."

Mukhtar took a step back. "He told me you would say that. He also said I should remind you that you could not save *her*."

Kadir took a deep breath. *Zahid.* In the past few years, Bin-Asfour had spent most of his time in neighboring countries. Was he back in Kahani? Was he watching? What had precipitated this newest and boldest attempt on Kadir's life? Whatever the reason, now was not the time to allow his old enemy to taunt him into making a foolish decision. "That is the past. All that matters is now. All that matters is saving your family. I can have an explosives expert here in moments. We'll disarm the bomb, free you and set about rescuing your family. You can help me end the tyranny of a madman who wants to drag us all into the past. You can be a hero."

Mukhtar lifted his chin, and Kadir could see that his decision had been made. "Don't come any closer." He took a small step back, and then another. "I did not know what to do, Excellency. Forgive me. I am a foolish old man."

"No, you're…"

Kadir got no further before the man turned and ran. Not toward him, as was surely Zahid's intention, but away—toward the sea. The guards saw what was happening and moved forward, guns drawn, to place themselves between Kadir and the source of danger.

"Don't shoot!" Kadir called. There was no need. At the moment, Mukhtar was a threat only to himself. When he reached the edge of the water Mukhtar turned, and in that instant his eyes met Kadir's. The old man no longer cried. Instead he was stalwart and determined.

One hand moved toward the bag that was handcuffed to the vendor.

"No," Kadir whispered.

A powerful explosion rocked the peaceful morning, and those guards who were closest to the bomber were thrown backward and to the ground. None were close enough to be injured—though Sayyid appeared to be stunned by the jolting fall. The sound of the blast rang in Kadir's ears, and a cloud of sand danced where the old man had once stood. Sayyid and the others who had run to stop Mukhtar from his foolishness shook off their surprise and slowly regained their footing in the sand.

Kadir turned his back to the violence and climbed the steps to the balcony. Household servants and political aides who had been preparing for the upcoming trip ran onto the balcony and were met with horror.

Kadir did not look back at the beach, as he had no desire to see what was left of a decent man. He caught his personal secretary's eyes and issued a command. "Get Sharif Al-Asad on the telephone." Sharif was a highly placed officer with the Ministry of Defense. He and Kadir had once worked together, but years ago their careers had taken very diverse paths. Still, they had managed to remain friends. Their methods of operation were different, but their ultimate goals were much the same.

Hakim nodded curtly, snapping, "Yes, Excellency," before returning to the house to do as he was told.

The others remained on the balcony, watching the scene on the beach in horror and surprise. There should be no surprise at unexpected violence, but horror…yes. An old man blowing himself up in a vain attempt to save his family was the height of horror.

Kadir had sacrificed much in the name of what was best for Kahani. He was thirty-six years old and had no wife, no children. There had been a steady succession of women in his life, all of them fun for a while but in the end…uninspiring. He could easily arrange a marriage with a suitable woman he had never met, but that would mean calling upon the ways of the past. Ways he was determined to change.

His parents were gone, and his brothers had lives and families of their own. And of late, Kadir was not always certain of what he most wanted. One thing was certain: He wanted Zahid Bin-Asfour destroyed. He would not rest easy until that was done.

Hakim had Sharif on the line within minutes, and Kadir shared all the information he could, as he set the rescue of Mukhtar's family into motion. There had been a time when he would have been one of the men storming the terrorist camp in order to rescue the innocent, but these days his role in defeating terrorism took a different slant.

When Kahani was properly and securely aligned with a number of powerful nations who would come to their aid when the need arose, Zahid and those who followed him would be reduced to nothingness. These days, Kadir did his best to defeat his enemies in a different way—with a smile, a handshake and the sincere promise of alliance.

Zahid Bin-Asfour could not fight the entire world, and Kadir intended to bring that world down on his head.

"He's a *what?*" Lexie plopped down onto the couch.

Cassandra glanced at her sister. Of all the possible mornings for an unannounced visit, this had to be the worst. "You heard me the first time."

"A sheik," Lexie said with a grin. "A genuine, sweep-me-away-on-your-white-horse sheik. Very cool, Cass. What's the catch? Is he old? Married? Ugly?"

Lexie was a sweet woman, but diplomacy was nothing more than a vague concept to the eldest of the four Klein sisters. Fortunately, Silvershire foreign relations were safe from Alexis Margaret Klein Harvey Smythe Phillips, whose only agenda at the present time was finding husband number four.

Cassandra Rose Klein's ambitions had taken a different vein. She wanted to make a difference in the world. She wouldn't call herself power-hungry, but she was ambitious. It wasn't that she didn't want to love somebody, but there was more to the future than a man…or as in her sister's case, a series of men.

"He's single," Cassandra said. She grabbed the file she'd been studying over her morning coffee and tossed it onto the couch. "And *not* old."

Lexie snatched up the folder and opened it. A recent photo of Cassandra's latest assignment filled most of the first page. "Ooohhh. Not ugly at *all*." She read aloud, "'His Excellency Sheik Kadir Bin Arif Yusef Al-Nuri, Director of European and American Affairs for the Kahani Ministry of Foreign Affairs.'" Her nose wrinkled. "Do you have to memorize all that?"

"Yes."

"What will you call him? Kadir? Yusef? Arif? Honeybunch? What?"

"I'll address him as Excellency, unless he invites me to call him Sheik Kadir."

Lexie leafed through the rest of the file, not at all interested in what was truly important. She didn't care what Al-Nuri had done for his country, or what he wanted to do in the future. Lexie didn't care about politics, reform, or alliances. She only noticed Al-Nuri's physical attributes. If she had even a clue what his bank account looked like…

"How did you get so lucky?" Lexie asked as she closed the file. "I understand when it comes to politics, blackmail works wonders. Or are you sleeping with your boss?"

Cassandra laughed. "My boss is a very small, very sour woman who's probably old enough to be my grandmother."

"Weren't all the diplomatic aides fighting over who'd get him? Taking charge of the sheik for the next couple of weeks is not exactly going to be a chore."

Cassandra took a deep, calming breath. "I was given this assignment because I'm fluent in Arabic and I'm familiar with Kahani customs. Don't let your imagination run amok. My relationship with Al-Nuri will be strictly business."

"Everything is strictly business with you, Cass," Lexie teased. "Doesn't that get boring after a while?"

"I didn't enter foreign service so I could meet men."

"You can't tell me you don't find the sheik the least bit attractive."

Cassandra remained cool. "It doesn't matter if he's attractive or not."

"Of course it matters," Lexie said with an aggravated sigh. "You're twenty-five years old, and I can't remember the last time you were the slightest bit serious about the opposite sex. What are you waiting for?"

Love. Cassandra bit her lip and didn't answer aloud. Lexie had been involved in one destructive relationship after another since the day she'd turned seventeen. She knew no caution where love was concerned.

Cassandra, the youngest of the Klein sisters, knew nothing *but* caution. She also knew hope, though it rarely showed. How many times had her mother told her about the first time she'd seen the man she'd immediately known she was destined to spend a lifetime with? A glance across a crowded café. A fluttering of the heart and an inexplicable feeling of familiarity followed, then came an out-and-out flip of the stomach. Two months after that meeting they were married. A year later, Lexie had been born. Growing up, that story of love at first sight had been the fairy tale for Cassandra.

She'd been waiting from the age of fourteen for the fluttering and flipping of her insides, but she had begun to think it would never come. There had been no glance across a crowded room. No butterflies in the stomach. No swelling of love at the sight of a face, no breath held in anticipation at the sound of a voice.

Lexie rose and reached into her handbag. She came up with a jangling key chain. "Here." She tossed the keys and Cassandra caught them. "In case you want to take the hunky sheik to my beach house. I won't be back for a month."

"Where are you going?"

"I'm going to Greece, with Stanley."

Cassandra bit her lip. She didn't like Stanley Porter, Lexie's latest love interest, but Lexie wouldn't listen to her little sister's concerns. "Be careful."

"You're the one who needs to be careful. That sheik of yours is a ladies' man."

"How can you tell from one photograph—"

"The eyes," Lexie interrupted. "Your sheik has bedroom eyes, Cass. One proper glance from eyes like those, and a woman doesn't stand a chance."

For this afternoon's initial meeting Cassandra had chosen her most austere gray suit, and her long pale hair was pulled back in a neat French braid. Her heels were low and comfortable. This was a big assignment, the most important of her career, and she was ready to take it on. "His Excellency does have a bit of a reputation as a playboy. Nothing I can't handle." She dangled the keys to the beach house Lexie had gotten in her second divorce. "I won't need these."

Lexie didn't take the keys as she passed on her way to the front door of Cassandra's small but neat flat, chosen because it was affordable and less than ten minutes from the building where the Silvershire Ministry of Foreign Affairs was located. "Keep them anyway, just in case. Maybe you'll get lucky. I keep condoms in the master bathroom cabinet, under the sink."

For a moment, Cassandra considered tossing the keys at her sister's back, but that wasn't her style.

When she collected the file on Al-Nuri from the coffee table, she glanced at the photograph that had so impressed Lexie. His Excellency had a nicely trimmed mustache and beard on a ruggedly handsome face. Wavy dark hair barely touched broad shoulders, and his olive complexion was warm. But it was the eyes that drew and held her attention. Bedroom eyes, Lexie called them. *Is this literally what a man's eyes look like in the bedroom?* A shiver walked down Cassandra's spine, and the hairs on the back of her neck stood and danced.

She had no idea what a man looked like in that situation, and at the current rate of her nonexistent love life, she'd never find out.

* * *

Cassandra paced in the shade of a hangar. Al-Nuri's plane was scheduled to land at this small, private airport in less than fifteen minutes.

This new wrinkle was alarming, but she felt up to the task. If she wanted to rise in the ranks, she could not allow any twist or turn to alarm or distress her. If she became the aide who was able to handle any situation—even this one—she would soon be indispensable.

More than anything, Cassandra wanted to be indispensable.

His Excellency, Sheik Kadir, had requested a meeting with Lord Carrington, to take place as soon as possible. For a variety of reasons, Lord Carrington was not yet ready to meet with the sheik. Just as she had been about to leave for the airport, Cassandra had been asked by her superior, Ms. Nola Dunn, to keep the man entertained—no, *distracted* was a better word—until such a time came that the meeting was desirable for both parties.

Cassandra didn't know precisely why Lord Carrington didn't want to meet with his visitor from Kahani just yet, but she did know that something important was going on in the palace. Something to which a woman of her station would not be privy. There was an electricity among those in the know, an unnatural energy that kept them all on edge. Even Ms. Dunn had been edgy.

It didn't matter. One day she would be privy to everything. One day.

Cassandra knew this assignment could make or break her career in foreign service. For years, she'd studied other cultures and languages in hopes that one day she would be Silvershire's representative around the world, in places where the small country she called home had never held a position of importance. For now she was a low-level diplomatic aide, but one day—one day she would see the world.

She had done her best to make herself valuable in her present station, hoping to be noticed and promoted. During the latest computer upgrade, she'd stayed late almost every day, making sure everyone's station was in proper working order, if they asked her to help. They often did, since she was quite good with computers, and always available to assist. When Ms. Dunn's latest disaster of a secretary had made a mess of her files, Cassandra had volunteered to work on the weekends until order was restored. She was very good at restoring order.

Keeping up with news from around the world was quite important, and was a big part of her job. She had bulging files on all the countries that would be represented at the upcoming Founder's Day Gala, and she'd shared what she'd gathered with the others in the office. Still, none of the assignments she'd taken on to this point were as important as this one.

She recognized the sheik's jet as it landed and taxied toward the hangar. The flag of Kahani was proudly painted on the side of the jet. The time of the sheik's arrival had been a carefully guarded secret, so there was no fanfare, and no curious onlookers clamored for a peek of the entourage. There was just her, and a driver who waited in the parking lot on the other side of the hangar. Cassandra straightened her spine and took a deep breath of air. Not only did she have to assist the foreign minister from Kahani with a fine balance of respect for his customs as well as respect for her own, now she had to stall him in his quest for a meeting with the duke. Too bad Lexie had already left the country.

She was an expert at keeping men of all types diverted. Cassandra had never been good at diversion. She was much better suited to directness…often to the point of bluntness. Why be subtle when directly spoken words were so much more, well, direct?

If Lexie was a soft feather of seduction and distraction, Cassandra was a mallet.

The jet came to an easy halt on the runway. After a short pause, the door opened and a stair was lowered. For a moment no one descended. Cassandra's nerves were none the better for the delay. She'd just as soon get this difficult assignment under way.

A tall, thin man in a severe dark suit was first down the stairs. He studied the area as he descended, one hand held ready over his right hip, where a weapon no doubt was housed in a holster of some type. At a crisp word from the tall man, two others descended the stairway—more quickly and not quite as openly aware. Cassandra stepped toward the jet, and immediately had the attention of all three men. She could see that they instantly assessed her as nonthreatening, but they were prepared for anything. No one answered her smile.

"Good afternoon," she said, speaking in perfectly accented Arabic. "I'm Cassandra Klein, and I will be His Excellency's guide during his stay in Silvershire." She received no response from the men, none of whom was the sheik she had been sent here to meet. Was it possible that he had canceled his appearance and one of these men was his replacement? No, these men were muscle. Bodyguards, no doubt. Kahani wasn't the hotbed of terrorism some of the neighboring countries had become, but neither was it an entirely safe place. Leaders who worked to bring about change were often endangered, and she imagined Al-Nuri was no exception to that rule.

She heard a soft, deep voice from just inside the jet, and a moment later a man she recognized as Sheik Kadir appeared at the top of the stairs. Another guard was positioned behind him, and she caught a glimpse of two others—not muscle, from what little she saw of them. They were administrative assistants, no doubt. From the top of the stairs, the sheik looked down at her and smiled. Cassandra's stomach did an unexpected flip. Her heart fluttered. Oh, dear, the man's photos did not do him justice, not at all. Her smile remained in place, a wooden mask as she gathered her wits about her. Her stomach only flipped because she'd eaten that salad dressing at lunch. It had tasted good enough, but obviously it had gone bad. She steeled her heart against another flutter as the man she had been sent here to meet descended the stairs with the grace of an athlete and the smile of a movie star. Like the others, he was dressed in an expensive suit that fit him perfectly. Unlike the others, he continued to smile.

"What a pleasure to be greeted by such beauty."

Cassandra hated it when someone, *anyone,* commented on her physical appearance, when whether or not she was pretty had nothing to do with diplomatic service. But of course, she could say nothing to reprimand the sheik.

Oh, my, those eyes. Bedroom eyes, Lexie had called them, and so close…yes, that description made sense. In a moment of utter insanity her innards began to react again, and an unexpected and unwanted thought flitted through her mind.

He's the one.

No, Cassandra insisted to herself as she pushed her surprising reaction aside. Aside and down with a vengeance, until it was buried deep. The dance of her stomach, the knot in her chest, it was surely nothing more than the ill effects of bad salad dressing. She couldn't allow it to be anything else.

Chapter 2

Kadir gave a curt bow to the woman who was waiting at the foot of the jet's stairway. He'd received a communication days ago giving him the woman's name, so her gender was no surprise. He had not, however, expected that she would be so beautiful. Though she dressed in a conservative suit, and her shoes were of the sensible sort, and her pale blond hair was twisted back in a severe style that only accentuated her fine cheekbones and large gray eyes, she exuded an unexpected sensuality he could not ignore. The day had not been a pleasant one thus far, so it was surprisingly enjoyable to get lost in her beauty for a moment.

"Excellency," she said, her voice professional and curt. "Welcome. It's my pleasure to be given the opportunity to assist you during your stay in Silvershire. A car is waiting." She indicated the direction of the car with a wave of her delicate hand. "Whatever you require during your stay with us, you need only to ask."

What he required as a man was very different from what he needed as a diplomat. He'd had little time or opportunity to care for the man in himself these past few years. Unfortunately, that fact had not changed.

"I understand an estate near the palace has been prepared for me and my staff."

"Yes." Ms. Klein led the way to the waiting limousine while Sayyid and Fahd collected the luggage from the jet. "The Redmond Estate. Mr. Redmond and his new wife are vacationing in Paris and will not return for several months, and they graciously offered their home. I understand your guard detail has already been informed of the existing security system."

"Yes. They believe it will be satisfactory."

Since his yacht was anchored near a small shore town a relatively short distance from the palace, he would be able to slip away on occasion. Living in someone else's home was often awkward. He preferred his own quarters, even if they were small rooms on a modest but familiar seagoing vessel.

"It's very kind of the Redmonds to offer their home. Hotels are so impersonal and…" Dangerous, though he did not tell her as much. He did not normally concern himself overmuch with safety issues, but this morning's incident made it clear that Zahid was determined to remove Kadir from the picture. "Shall we say, they do not have the warmth of a real home. I am most appreciative."

The limousine was large enough to accommodate his entire party. Four bodyguards, his personal secretary, a junior aide from the Ministry of Foreign Affairs and himself. And Ms. Klein, of course. Tension from this morning's unfortunate episode remained, clear in each of his associates. Kadir did his best not to appear tense with his escort, who would surely take it as a sign of unease with the current situation. As a precaution, his bodyguards searched the car inside and out—and underneath—and they also searched the driver. He saw no need to explain to Ms. Klein that just this morning an attempt had been made on his life.

Once they were settled in the vehicle, and it moved away from the small airport, Kadir turned to his assigned aide and smiled. It was a diplomat's smile—wide and guarded and touched with hope. "I am looking forward to meeting with the duke. We have much to discuss."

To her credit, Ms. Klein did not blush. But he read the answer in her eyes, as they all but shut down. That gray, which had been soft as a dove's wing moments ago, grew ever so slightly harder. Given her profession, she really should be more difficult to read. She was young, however, and had time to develop a more stony expression.

What a shame that would be. He liked the expressiveness of her eyes, even when she was about to disappoint him.

"Lord Carrington's schedule is quite full at the moment, I regret to say. I'm sure he's anxious to meet with you, and will do so as soon as is possible. Until then, I hope you'll be interested in seeing more of Silvershire. It is a beautiful country, and I have a number of activities planned for the coming weeks."

Kadir had no interest in seeing more of Silvershire—or anywhere else. He would have his meeting with Carrington; it was the reason for this trip. He was not annoyed by Ms. Klein's answer, however. He would play whatever game she had planned for him.

He had a feeling games with his appointed aide would be quite interesting.

The estate where Sheik Kadir would be housed was an old and dignified home that actually resembled a small castle. It sported stone walls and well-tended gardens, rooms furnished in flawless antiques, servants around every corner and even a small, unused tower. It was very much like stepping back in time three hundred years.

The owner of the estate, Prentiss Redmond, was not titled. His money was new. Well, relatively new. His father had made a fortune in steel and oil refineries. Prentiss seemed better suited to spending money than to making it, and his new wife, who was fifteen years younger than he, would likely be glad to help him spend every dime. Redmond very much wanted to be *in* with the royals, and that was the reason he'd offered his home for the use of their guests.

The sheik's bodyguards immediately took over the estate security. They had received information about the household staff and cleared them all weeks ago. None of the servants could be considered threatening. Most of them looked as if they might've actually been here three hundred years ago.

Cassandra stifled a smile as Oscar, the ancient butler, led Al-Nuri up the wide, winding staircase. The old man moved very slowly, and with great dignity. The sheik did not seem at all perturbed to be moving at a snail's pace—and that was a definite point in his favor. While you'd think patience was a requirement of all diplomats, she had met many who had none.

She did her best to once again dismiss the physical reaction she'd had to the sheik when he'd stepped off the plane. Salad dressing, nerves, a virus coming on—it could be any of those things, and she much preferred any of them, even the virus, to the possibility of a strong physical attraction to Al-Nuri. Even though she had, at times, bemoaned the lack of love in her life, when it did come it couldn't possibly be with a man who lived in a country where women might as well be trapped in the nineteenth century—no, the *first* century! She was a thoroughly modern woman, with plans for a career. An important career.

Besides, when she experienced that feeling of love her mother had so often told her about, it really should be with a fellow citizen of Silvershire. A quiet and intelligent man—she had never cared for show-offs or comedians—who would support her in her career. And he really should be blond, so their children would all be blond. Logically she knew that setting hair color as a criteria was nonsensical, but she was grasping at straws to convince herself that the man who climbed the stairs ahead of her would not do. The sheik was more than ten years older than she. That was surely much too great an age difference for true compatibility. She mentally listed all the reasons she couldn't have any sort of physical attraction to the sheik, and it almost worked.

Then at the top of the stairs he turned and smiled at her. It was a truer smile than the one he had flashed at her earlier, and she saw what was surely a hint of the real man in that smile. He was amused by Oscar—by the pace, the uniform, the dialogue as the old butler shared the history of the mansion as they endlessly climbed the stairs. She liked that, that he could be amused. Amused, and kind enough not to hurry the older man along or reprimand him for his slowness or a tale that often rambled.

Cassandra had always prided herself on being all-business. She was the mallet, after all. The sledgehammer. The ice queen, Lexie had called her more than once. It had seemed like an insult at the time, but she could use that quality to her advantage now.

If she found that her resolve was not strong enough, she could always ask to be removed from the assignment. But how would that look on her employment record? "Resigned for reasons of uncontrollable physical attraction to a totally unsuitable man" would ruin her career.

With effort, she returned Al-Nuri's smile. "Excellency, I'm sure you'd like an opportunity to settle into your new accommodations before we begin our tour of the country. Tomorrow morning we'll visit the Maitland Museum of Fine Arts an hour before it's opened to the public. The museum opened just last year, and is quite impressive. You'll have the rest of the day today to get settled in your quarters. If there's anything you need…" She was ready to make her escape—at least for now.

"I do have many questions about the current political state of Silvershire."

Of course he had questions about the prince's death, the king's medical condition, the possibility that the duke would soon take the throne. She was prepared to answer all of his questions—within reason, of course.

"After you've settled into the estate, we'll have a chance to discuss anything you find of interest."

Oscar was continuing toward the suite of rooms that would be Al-Nuri's during his stay in Silvershire. The elderly butler was unaware that he'd lost his audience. He was mumbling about something that had taken place in this very hallway, a hundred and twenty-four years ago.

Cassandra locked eyes with the sheik, and she knew very well what he found of interest. Just because she was inexperienced, that didn't mean she was blind. She steeled her spine—again. If he intended to make this assignment difficult for her, so be it. He would find she wasn't eager for his attentions, as most women he met probably were. This was business, and their relationship would remain professional.

"Tonight," the sheik said as he turned to follow a doddering Oscar. "I'm sure dinner here in the estate can be arranged. Eight o'clock."

Cassandra was tempted to decline the invitation, but this was her job. And no man, not even this one, would make her run.

Kadir received an important phone call from Sharif late in the afternoon of his arrival in Silvershire. Intelligence indicating the location of Mukhtar's family had been obtained, thanks to a neighbor who had witnessed the kidnapping and had given a detailed description of the driver and the vehicle used. With that information, Sharif had tracked the kidnappers and Mukhtar's family to a quiet neighborhood just a few miles away from the market. The planning of the rescue operation was under way. There was no indication of whether or not Zahid was in the same location—but it was certainly possible. In the past they had been close to Bin-Asfour many times, but he always escaped, leaving his followers to suffer for his ambitions and his tendency to do violence.

Kadir very much wanted Mukhtar's family to be rescued, but in truth this wouldn't be over until Zahid was caught—or killed. No matter how many success-ful battles were waged, no matter how many soldiers Zahid lost—he always managed to survive. His army could be decimated, and within days he would have a new army. Bin-Asfour was known for his silver tongue, for his ability to convert otherwise sane men to his insane cause.

Kadir would love to be the one to pull the trigger and see Zahid dead, but he'd left that part of his life behind when he'd decided to be a diplomat. He could not battle for his country's future in both ways—only one. Violence required less thought, and was in many ways much easier than diplomacy. A soldier did as he was told and the results, good or bad, were immediate. In his current position he had to be cautious about every word, every decision. Yes, in many ways being a soldier was easier…but he was no longer a soldier, and very little in his life was easy.

Sharif wanted to see Bin-Asfour dead as much as Kadir did, but for his own reasons. There had been a time when they'd discussed those reasons…but no more. The time for talk was long past.

He could've ordered dinner for two to be served in the elegant formal dining room of his home-for-the-moment. Ms. Klein no doubt expected that, and would come prepared to maintain her all-business attitude toward him. She was his contact here in Silvershire, his advocate—though she did not yet see herself in that way. She was his key to gaining access to Lord Carring-ton, and he would do whatever was necessary to woo her to his way of thinking. In order to do that, he must first charm her.

He suspected where Ms. Klein was concerned, a gun would likely be much easier than diplomatic charm.

In order to keep her off guard, he arranged dinner for four to be served at a small table in a cozy drawing room. He invited his clerk and his aide to join him and Ms. Klein for dinner, and as with all else they complied. Sayyid and Haroun would keep watch, while Fahd and Jibril slept. They would take over at midnight, and until he left Silvershire they would maintain that schedule— two men midnight to noon, the other two noon to midnight. He was growing so accustomed to the constant presence of bodyguards, he sometimes forgot they were with him. After all, they could usually blend into the background—a necessary precaution, a part of the job.

In the past few years, Zahid had not been a direct threat. He and his followers moved from country to country, searching for and occasionally finding support for their cause. They performed acts of terrorism outside of Kahani, and at the same time they built their fortune through the sale of drugs. Kadir didn't know why Zahid had tried to have him killed at the present time, but neither could he deny the new danger. No matter how much he would like to, he could not entirely forget why he had such a close guard at hand.

It was pleasant to see the expression on Ms. Klein's face when she was escorted into the sitting room precisely at eight o'clock. She was still dressed in her severe suit, and had added no makeup or jewels to make the ensemble more appropriate for evening. It was surely her way of telling him that their relationship was purely business and would remain so. She was dedicated, in that way only the very young can be. What would it take to make sure that she was dedicated to him and his mission of meeting with the king-in-waiting?

"Thank you so much for taking the time from your busy schedule to dine with us this evening." Kadir watched as her eyes took in the small table set for four and the silent presence of his aides. She then turned her eyes to him. Was she surprised to find him dressed casually and comfortably? His pants were freshly pressed, but the shirt he had chosen was unbuttoned at the collar, and he wore no tie. He had not even trimmed his mustache and goatee, so a bristly shadow roughened a portion of face. He needed a haircut, as usual, but he was not by any means disheveled. Just casual, as if the meeting were of no real importance.

"We do have much to discuss," Ms. Klein said, almost suspiciously. "I can tell you all about the schedule for this coming week, and if you have any questions about the events surrounding the Founder's Day Gala, I'll be happy to answer them."

"Lovely." He eased her chair away from the table and waited for her to sit. After a split second of indecision she did so, and he made sure she was in place before he sat across the table from her. Hakim and Tarif took the remaining chairs, while Sayyid and Haroun maintained their posts at the two doors that opened off the small sitting room.

Kadir listened attentively as Ms. Klein told him all about her plans for the week. Museums, gardens, tours of homes much like this one. Nothing of substance, and nothing he had not seen before. He did not tell her so, of course, but smiled and expressed interest in each and every event. As the simple meal progressed, she became more and more relaxed. She

was never entirely relaxed—he suspected that was
not in her nature—but at least she was no longer suspicious of his motives.

After dessert, Hakim excused himself, stating that he
had work to do before retiring for the night. Tarif was
not far behind him. Kadir asked Ms. Klein about the state
of Silvershire's public education system, and she gladly
began a well-practiced and seemingly attentive diatribe.

Kahani's public education system was in bad need
of an overhaul, and the subject was of great interest to
him. But it wasn't long before Kadir's attention's
wandered. His Silvershire aide had such attractive gray
eyes, and such a wonderfully lush mouth, it was impossible to concentrate on test scores and curriculum when
she was looking at him. He was not a man who could
be easily distracted, but that's what Cassandra Klein did.
She distracted him to the extreme.

What man would not be distracted? The suit she wore
did not entirely disguise the fact that she had a nicely
rounded female shape. He had hoped that at some time
during the evening she would remove her suit jacket, but
she had not. Of course not. She was determined to be
professional and proper, which was a true waste. Her
eyes were lively, and her mouth was made for better
things than talking business. The lips were soft and full,
and made for kissing. He wanted to see her laugh, at
least once.

As nice as his wandering thoughts were, he didn't
have time for such nonsense. Like the woman sitting
before him, he needed to concentrate on the reasons for
this visit.

"You have made such wonderful plans for my time
here, and I certainly don't want to miss a single event.

I do wonder if there would be an opportunity to tour Barton College while I'm here?"

The question took her by surprise. Her eyes widened slightly, and she held her breath for a moment. "Certainly," she answered. There was a short hesitation before she added, "You do realize that Barton is a women's college."

"Of course." Ms. Klein would find that she was not the only one who came to this meeting well prepared. "If my memory is correct, Barton College was founded in 1873, and has been a school of privilege until the past seventeen years, when generous scholarships funded by the government have allowed those who otherwise would not be able to afford such a fine education to attend."

Ms. Klein looked slightly suspicious at his knowledge. "I attended Barton myself. My mother teaches there."

"Wonderful! I can expect a most thorough tour, in that case."

She cocked her head slightly. "May I ask why you wish to tour Barton?"

"Education is the answer to so many of the world's problems, don't you agree?" He didn't give her an opportunity to answer, but he read the yes in her eyes. "I am interested in forming just such a facility in Kahani. How can I work to bring my country into the new millennium without offering an adequate education for one half of our population? The educational needs of women in Kahani have been neglected for so long, it seems only right that we rectify that disservice in as practical and effective a way as possible."

She shook off her surprise quickly. "I will make the arrangements. The summer session is much smaller than fall and spring, but we can tour the facilities and meet with the dean, if you'd like."

"I would like that very much. Will I have the opportunity to meet your mother?"

Again, the question took her by surprise. He liked surprising her; her reactions were so genuine, they cracked her tough facade and revealed the woman beneath. "Perhaps."

She glanced at her watch, and appeared to be surprised at the lateness of the hour. "I really should go, Excellency." She stood quickly. "Thank you so much for dinner. I will collect you at quarter of nine in the morning, so we can begin our tour of the museum before it opens to the public."

Kadir cared nothing for museums, but did not say so. "I look forward to seeing you again." He bowed gently. "May I…"

She turned to face him as she collected her handbag from the small table by the door. Sayyid was posted just outside that door, but was out of sight.

"May you?" she prompted.

"May I call you Cassandra? It's such a lovely name, and we will be spending many hours together in the weeks to come. I would, of course, like it very much if you'd call me Kadir. 'Excellency' has never suited me. I keep looking over my shoulder for the stuffy old man who answers to that dignified title." He tried a smile, even though the woman who was poised to flee didn't look as if she were about to say yes to his proposal. But then again, she did want to please him, to keep him happy. It was her job, and she was a woman who took her job very seriously.

"I don't think that would be a good idea," she said softly, and before he could ask her why, she was gone.

* * *

Every Tuesday night, Cassandra wrote her mother a letter. It had become a habit, and she could not sleep on Tuesday nights until her letter was written. She always posted the letter from the office on Wednesday morning, and it was delivered on Thursday afternoon. Sometimes the letters were brief, if she was busy or if the week had been uneventful, but on other nights the letters were pages long.

These days e-mail made keeping in touch easy, and Cassandra did use that form of communication regularly. But her mother had told her how she loved receiving an old-fashioned handwritten letter now and then, and this tradition had been born. Now it was a ritual, one she didn't dare miss.

> *Dear Mum,*
> *Lexie is off to Greece with Stanley. I suppose you already know that, but since Lexie is not the best of communicators I thought I'd pass the news along She'll be gone a month.*

Dressed in loose-fitting yellow pajamas, a cup of cooling tea at her elbow, Cassandra tapped the end of her pen against the pad of blue paper. The paper was unlined, and was decorated with a smattering of pink and lavender flowers along the left margin. The pad sat on her desk, and she perched on the edge of her chair. Should she mention the sheik or not? Her first instinct was *not,* but there would be no hiding the man if they took a tour of Barton College. Cassandra straightened her spine. And why on earth would she hide His Excellency, Sheik Kadir? She often wrote about her work, and the sheik was all about work. Nothing else.

I began a new and very exciting assignment today. A representative of the Kahani Foreign Ministry is visiting the country for the next three weeks, and I am to be his guide and aide for the duration. All those nights of studying Arabic have finally paid off. This is a plum assignment, and I'm happy to have it. You could say it's the chance I've been waiting for. Ms. Dunn, who is always so hard to please, said I had the qualifications necessary to fulfill this assignment.

The sheik is very well-known. The short version is His Excellency Sheik Kadir Al-Nuri. Perhaps you saw his picture in the newspaper. There was an article in the Silvershire Times about his impending visit, and I believe it ran three or four days ago.

Again she tapped the end of her pen against the paper. She could leave it at that but her mother was practically psychic, in that way only mothers can be. She seemed to know things she should not, and this short letter might illicit a "what aren't you telling me?" response. It was so unfair.

We will likely be taking a tour of the college. That was Al-Nuri's suggestion, not mine. I never would've thought he'd be interested. He has ideas of founding a women's college much like Barton in his own country, which is quite ambitious if you remember how archaic some of their customs are.

He wants to make changes, and I suppose I must
admire him for that. In any case, the sheik and I
will probably be there sometime in the next three
weeks. I'm not sure when. I'll have to tinker with
the schedule. Perhaps we'll see you while we're
there.

Cassandra wasn't about to tell her mother that Al-Nuri
had actually asked if he could meet her during the tour
of Barton. That request sounded so personal, and it would
certainly raise questions she didn't want to answer. She
started to sign off, but thought better of it. Perhaps she
should end the letter on a more personal note.

I think I ate some bad salad dressing at lunch
today, but tonight all is well.
Love,
Cassandra

She sealed the letter in an envelope that matched the
notepaper, and placed it beside her purse so she
wouldn't forget it in the morning. That done, she
dumped out the half-empty teacup, brushed her teeth,
turned out the lights and crawled into the waiting bed.

Her mother had always called her Cassandra, but
almost everyone else was determined to shorten her name
to Cassie or Cass. After a while, it sounded petulant to
insist that they call her by her full name, so she simply
accepted whatever they wished to call her. Her sisters
called her Cass, and always had. Even her dad called her
Cass, and she really didn't mind. Coming from her family
the name sounded fitting enough. When people she'd just
met immediately shortened her name, it annoyed her.

Al-Nuri had asked if he could call her Cassandra. Not Cass, not Cassie…Cassandra. The way he said her name, the way the word rolled so sensually off his tongue as if he could taste it… Heaven above, the man could be trouble. If she allowed him to be, that is. And she would not.

She pulled the covers to her chin, then closed her eyes and insisted that sleep come quickly and deeply. Right before she drifted off, she whispered the fervent hope that she not dream of bedroom eyes and slightly accented *Cassandras*.

Chapter 3

The museum was only mildly interesting. The building itself was large and modern, not at all in keeping with the rest of the city. There was lots of glass and sharp lines that did not mesh well with the older, more quaint sections of the city. Large rooms that connected like a twisted maze were filled with paintings and drawings, intricate carvings and displays of ancient weaponry that had some significance to Silvershire history.

As much as Kadir admired fine art, no painting or sculpture could hold a candle to his personal tour guide, the lovely Ms. Klein. Once again she had dressed in a plain and conservative suit, and her pale hair was pulled back severely. Today, however, he occasionally caught her in a blush, and there was a light in her eyes she could not disguise, no matter how she tried. Like it or not, she was affected by his presence.

As he was affected by hers.

She was a wealth of information, telling him something about each artist and each artifact. Soon her words began to run together, and he simply watched and enjoyed her. Every display in the museum dulled beside her beauty, and he did not feel guilty to enjoy watching her instead of the artworks he was meant to appreciate.

Photographers were awaiting their departure from the museum, alerted to his presence by a museum employee, no doubt. Kadir was accustomed to camera flash bulbs and unflattering photographs plastered in newspapers around the world. In truth, no part of his life was his own—and so he smiled for the cameras as he strode along the paved path, and waved when his name was called. Ms. Klein held back, allowing him and his guards to be the focus of the photographs. Too bad, since a picture of her would be much more pleasant than one of his own.

Fahd and Jibril were tense. Yesterday's assassination attempt, which they had managed to keep out of the press, had them on edge. Rightfully so. This trip to Silvershire had been well publicized in the past few weeks, so Zahid surely knew where Kadir was. Would Bin-Asfour be bold enough to make an attempt here, in another country, or would he wait for Kadir to return to his home before trying again?

As they reached the parking lot—Fahd and Jibril alert, Hakim and Tarif lagging behind, and Ms. Klein doing her best to hide—a photographer made his way past the barricade and moved in for a closer shot. He lifted his camera and took a series of photographs before Jibril rushed to the photographer and forced the man back to his proper place.

Jibril was a large man, so it was unexpected that the

smallish photographer would put up a fight. He did, however, and Fahd did his best to hurry Kadir to the waiting limousine, which was bulletproof and could move very, very fast when necessary. As Kadir increased his step in order to accommodate his bodyguard, the unmistakable sound of a gunshot reverberated through the humid air.

Kadir spun away from Fahd and away from the limousine, instinctively grabbing Ms. Klein's arm. He pulled her to him, protected her as best he could with his body and threw them both toward the opened car door and safety. Behind them onlookers and photographers shouted and fell to the ground, and Jibril shouted orders in crisp Arabic. Ms. Klein screamed as they vaulted through the air and into the back seat of the limousine, where he landed on top of her. Fahd slammed the door shut, but as no more gunshots reverberated, Kadir deduced that the immediate danger was over.

Two attempts on his life in two days, and all he could think about was the softness of the woman beneath him.

Her cheeks reddened, and her lush lips parted slightly. One of her slender legs was caught between his, in an awkward and yet somehow apt position, and she'd instinctively wrapped her arms around him. Though they were no longer vaulting through the air, she did not loosen her hold. Her heart beat so hard and fast he could feel it, pounding against his own.

"Are you unharmed?" he asked, his voice low.

"Yes." The single word trembled. "You?"

"I'm fine." They had moments—mere seconds, perhaps—before they were joined by the rest of the party.

And still, Kadir did not move. The body beneath his fit very nicely, and no suit, no matter how severe, could disguise the softness he felt. Cassandra Klein was very much a woman, and he did not want to move. Not yet.

"Perhaps you should…get off of me," she suggested, not as forcefully as she could have.

"Perhaps I should." And still he didn't.

She was so close, and so tempting. It would be very easy to lay his lips over hers. There wasn't time for a true, deep kiss, but even a quick brushing of his lips against hers would be delicious. It was entirely inappropriate to kiss one's diplomatic aide. Even to think about taking such an action was improper. And yet he did think….

Outside the car, his bodyguards shouted to one another in Arabic, and bystanders yelled in excited English. The commotion seemed rather distant and was easily dismissed from his mind. Kadir watched the intriguing parting of lush lips just inches from his own, saw the flash of passion in dove-gray eyes and thought of more pleasant days. And more pleasant days to come, perhaps?

"Now may I call you Cassandra?"

She opened her mouth to say no. He could see and feel the no coming, just as clearly as he had seen her desire. In her eyes, on those lips…the no was right there. And then she hesitated.

"Perhaps when we are alone you can call me by my given name," she said. "There's nothing wrong with that, I suppose. Of course, we shouldn't be alone," she added in a quicker voice. "Between your bodyguards and assistants and the press and the staff at the estate and—"

As if to prove her point, the car door opened swiftly. "The shooter escaped, Excellency." Jibril very neatly ignored the compromising position in which he found his employer. "Fahd tried to give chase, but when it became clear the would-be assassin was gone, he returned."

Kadir sat up slowly, and Ms. Klein—Cassandra— followed. She tried to straighten her mussed hair, but flying through the air and landing in the back seat of the car beneath him had undone the severity, and he suspected it could not be easily repaired. Her skirt had ridden up her leg, and the hem sat nicely high on her thigh, a pleasant diversion she quickly remedied.

Hakim and Tarif gratefully scrambled into the safety of the limousine, both visibly shaken. Neither of them had ever been in the military, and at the moment it showed. They were scared, and would not easily shake off the morning's excitement.

"The duke has top-notch security personnel at hand, and they will begin investigating the shooting immediately," Cassandra said in a purely business voice, as if she had not just been beneath him, as if she had not been inches from a kiss.

"That is not necessary," Kadir said calmly.

"What do you mean it's not necessary?" she asked, her voice almost sharp. "Someone took a shot at you, and you might've been killed. That is unacceptable."

"No investigation is necessary, as I know full well who ordered that shot."

Again she tried to straighten her hair. Again she failed.

"Zahid Bin-Asfour," he continued. "I doubt he fired the weapon himself, but he surely ordered it done."

"Terrorists will not be allowed a presence in Silvershire," Cassandra said, as if her words alone could stop them.

Kadir leaned back against the seat as the car sped away from the museum. "That sounds very logical, but there is no logic in terrorism. Zahid took an old and precious ideal of tribe and unity and love of ancient culture, he took the concept of brotherhood and twisted it into a thing of hate and bloodshed. In the name of taking the people he claims to love back to a simpler yet harsher time, he is willing to kill anyone who disagrees with him. He wraps his own twisted need for power in words of heritage and dignity, and then he destroys both in violence and hate. Zahid Bin-Asfour is a criminal. A murderer and a drug dealer. There is no logic in his reasoning, Ms. Klein."

"I'm sure you're right, b-but…" She stammered, and blushed again. He was quite sure this woman never stammered.

Kadir leaned closer to Cassandra and whispered, "Ah, you are worried about me?"

"No!" she answered quickly. Then she retracted her denial. "I mean, of course as your escort your safety is my responsibility. I'll order a new guard to add to your own, and adjust the schedule," she said. "From now on no one will know of our planned activities in advance."

"No additional guards," Kadir said in a soft voice that left no room for argument.

"But…"

"No more."

Cassandra took a deep breath and said nothing, but he expected she'd argue for an increased guard again. And soon. He would refuse again. While he was not foolish enough to ignore security concerns, he would not hide behind an army—not Kahani's, and certainly not Silvershire's.

He should promise her, and himself, that he would not behave so inappropriately again, that he would not think of kissing her—and more. He should vow to keep their relationship professional and distant, as was right and proper.

But he didn't.

* * *

Her heart continued to pound because someone had shot at her. At least, that's what Cassandra tried to tell herself, even though the shooting had taken place hours ago.

Al-Nuri and his entourage were back at the estate they called home for the time being, and she was waiting for Ms. Dunn to finish with an important phone call so she could have a word. Sheik Kadir didn't want extra security, but he was going to get it anyway. If anything happened to him while he was in her care… If anything happened to him *at all*…

Cassandra was called into Ms. Dunn's office, after waiting almost half an hour. She was so wound up, she began talking as she walked through the door and toward the older woman's desk. "His Excellency Sheik Kadir is most anxious for a meeting with Lord Carrington. I understand that the timing is not best for Lord Carrington, but surely something can be arranged in a timely manner."

Ms. Dunn leaned back in her large leather chair—all ninety pounds or so of her dominating the room in an eerie but unmistakable way. "Take a deep breath and relax, Cassie. The meeting Sheik Kadir desires will take place in due time, most likely."

Ms. Dunn indicated that she could sit, but sitting was impossible when her heart was pounding this way and she could feel the blood rushing through her veins. Cassandra stood at the end of the wide walnut desk. "What do you mean, most likely?"

Assistant director for the Ministry of Foreign Affairs, a woman who had been in foreign service for more than forty years, Nola Dunn was an imposing figure. Cassandra had never spoken sharply to her before. It had probably been years since anyone had dared to say much more than "Yes, ma'am."

Ms. Dunn did not seem annoyed by Cassandra's brazenness. "When I gave you this assignment, I informed you that Prince Reginald met with Zahid Bin-Asfour shortly before his death."

"Yes, ma'am, I recall that very well." It was for that very reason that the terrorist was suspected in the prince's murder.

"And you are also aware that Bin-Asfour and the government of Kahani are all but at war, and have been for a very long time."

"Yes, ma'am."

Ms. Dunn placed thin arms on her desk and leaned forward. "What if Bin-Asfour isn't responsible for the assassination of Prince Reginald? What if he and Reginald were working together, and the government of Kahani is behind the murder?"

"But…"

"Until we know with certainty that Kahani is in no way involved in the prince's assassination, there can be no meeting between the Duke and your sheik. It has the potential to be a public relations nightmare. At the same time, we can't treat Al-Nuri as if he or his country is suspect in the matter, not when all we have is a theory. Keep him happy. Promise him the meeting he desires will take place when the time is right. And keep him far, far away from the palace. Is that clear?"

Cassandra knew, without a doubt, that Al-Nuri was in no way involved in Prince Reginald's murder. Even if his government had a hand in the assassination, *he* would not be involved. He was too good. Too kind and well-meaning. That was an argument she could not put forth at this time. Not without proof.

So she asked, "Why would Prince Reginald align himself with a terrorist?"

Ms. Dunn waved a bony hand. "It's just a supposition, and an unlikely one at that. But until we know more, it's best that Al-Nuri be kept a safe distance from the palace. And Lord Carrington."

"Yes, ma'am."

Ms. Dunn studied Cassandra up and down, her eyes cautious. "You were the target of a shooting today."

"Al-Nuri was the target," Cassandra corrected. There was quite a bit of difference, in her mind.

"Still, you were there. I'm sure it was a harrowing experience."

"It was…" She thought about the confusion that had followed the gunshot; the way Al-Nuri had grabbed her with strong arms; the slamming of the car door that had separated them from the melee; the weight of his body on hers, and the way he had looked at her with those bedroom eyes. "It was distressing, that's true, but the entire episode was soon over and no one was harmed."

Ms. Dunn's eyes actually twinkled. "I have great hopes for you, Cassie. You're a tough girl, and you're very smart. One day you could very well find yourself in this chair. For now I'm glad to have you on my team."

Cassandra wanted to tell her superior that she preferred "Cassandra" to "Cassie," and "woman" to "girl," but she'd likely pushed her limits enough for one day.

Ms. Dunn neatly changed the subject. "The king had surgery earlier today. The tumor was removed, and the physician says the procedure was a success."

It was privileged news, though likely not for long. "So he'll recover?"

Ms. Dunn shrugged, but it was not a casual, uncaring gesture. "It's too soon to tell. He remains in a coma."

Cassandra wondered if there was a hidden message in Ms. Dunn's bit of gossip. The future of the country was more important than the wishes of one man. In such uncertain times, any detail might be crucial—including keeping Al-Nuri and Lord Carrington separated until they knew more. She turned to leave the room, wondering how she'd keep Al-Nuri occupied for the duration of his stay. He was determined to have his meeting, and she couldn't arrange it for him. Not yet, at least.

Ms. Dunn had told Cassandra she could one day be in that chair. It was everything she had ever hoped for. For the first time she reached deep and asked herself: Was that really what she wanted? Did she want to be like Nola Dunn? Powerful, intelligent, very much in the inner circle.

And also very much alone.

"Cassie," Ms. Dunn called.

At the doorway, Cassandra turned. Oddly enough, the usually sour old woman was smiling. It was quite disconcerting.

"Mind yourself. Al-Nuri is a handsome devil and can be a womanizer, from what I hear. I wouldn't have given you this assignment if I didn't think you could handle him."

"I appreciate the confidence, ma'am."

Ms. Dunn waved a hand in dismissal. "Just be careful."

Cassandra nodded, quite sure the warning had nothing to do with bullets and assassination attempts.

* * *

Late Thursday morning, Kadir received a short but informative phone call from Sharif. Mukhtar's family had been rescued, and in the process a number of Zahid's recruits had been killed. Two of the soldiers with Sharif had been wounded, but there had been no loss of life on that side of the fight. The terrorists were well settled into the series of old buildings, making it clear that Zahid was trying to reestablish himself in Kahani. No wonder he'd attempted to kill Kadir. No one would fight Bin-Asfour and his ambitions harder—except perhaps Sharif.

Kadir had been hoping that perhaps Zahid would be there when the raid took place, or that one of his men would give up information on his whereabouts. Neither of those hopes came true.

On Thursday afternoon, the lovely Cassandra Klein took him on a tour of well-tended private gardens at an estate north of the capital city of Silverton. They were pretty but unexciting, and Kadir could not get the important matters that ruled his life out of his head. Zahid Bin-Asfour. The meeting with Lord Carrington. Mukhtar's violent end. The shooting at the museum, just yesterday morning. It was difficult to become excited about a rare flower when such events crowded his mind.

Fahd and Jibril had placed themselves on opposite ends of the neat garden Kadir and Cassandra explored, ready to defend their charge if necessary, but also lulled by the quiet and serenity of the well-manicured grounds.

Kadir stopped in the middle of the neat pathway and turned to face Cassandra. Now this was a sight that could clear all unpleasantness from his mind. He saw no imperfections on her face, no flaw on her carefully and conservatively clad body. There was a spark of passion in her eyes, as he had noted often in the past two days. Was there a man in her life who awakened that passion?

"Do you have a man in your life?"

She was so startled by his question, she actually twitched. "My personal life is really none of your business, Excellency."

"I'm simply curious," he responded. "A husband, a suitor, an affianced one…"

"No," she answered curtly, blushing slightly. "I'm a single woman. My career is very important to me, and that leaves little time for…for…"

"Romance?" Kadir supplied.

"Whatever. Now, that's all I intend to say on the subject of my personal life."

That suited Kadir, since the fact that she was unattached was all he needed to know. He gladly changed the subject. "Do you like this sort of garden, Cassandra?"

She was startled by his use of her name, but a quick look around assured her that they were—for all intents and purposes—alone. "What do you mean? It's just a garden. A very nice garden, of course. Aren't all gardens of the same sort?"

He smiled, and again she blushed. "No, all gardens are not of the same sort. Not at all. Personally, I prefer a garden where the plants are allowed to grow wild, where to make your way along the path you must push around and beyond untamed growth. I prefer large blooms that are red and bright yellow and deep purple, bright colors that remind us that life is beautiful." He studied the pastel flowers along the methodical path. "It takes a sturdy plant to survive that sort of gardening. These pale blooms would not survive in such a garden. They would be choked out by the brighter blooms that dare to reach for the sun. Their thin roots would be overtaken by thick, healthy roots that reach for nutrients and claim the soil with a vengeance." He glanced down to find Cassandra studying him with wide, curious eyes. "A wild life is not suitable for something too delicate."

It occurred to him, as he finished, that he wasn't talking about gardens anymore. In the past his life had been wild and untamed. On some days it was still bright, but he'd become so entrenched in his job, so dedicated to his mission, that the colors had dulled somewhat. Dulled, but not entirely faded.

The danger to his life was very real, and while he could and did take all proper precautions, there was no way to make his life entirely safe. Cassandra Klein was a pale and delicate flower that would not survive in such terrain.

And, of course, she would never be called upon to try.

He wanted, very much, to kiss her. The desire to do so was improper, imprudent. It was definitely foolish. And yet, he did want a kiss. Maybe if he laid his lips over hers and took a proper kiss, he would taste the wildflower in her soul. Perhaps she was not as delicate as she appeared to be.

"I'm sorry you're not enjoying the outing," Cassandra said, her voice all business once again. "I can see that these gardens are not of interest to you. Tomorrow we'll…"

"Barton College tomorrow," he said with a smile, not bothering to tell her that certain gardens were very much of interest.

"But…"

"You said we would vary our schedule so no one would know where to find us. I wish to see Barton College tomorrow."

Her shoulders squared. "All right. If that's what you wish."

He leaned slightly toward her. "And I will meet your mother?"

Cassandra sighed and glanced away. "I suppose you will."

"Good. We'll leave early, and I'll drive."

"But…"

"I'll drive," he said again.

Kadir took Cassandra's arm and led her down the well-manicured garden path, the scent of summer blooms filling the air, wondering as he walked toward Jibril how he would manage to separate himself from the dedicated security staff that was determined to protect him twenty-four hours a day. He was tired of the order of his own life. Tired of the dullness that had taken hold.

He longed to be a wildflower himself again, just for a while.

Chapter 4

Cassandra closed her eyes and tried to keep her stomach from completely leaving her body. Once again the sheik was messing with her insides, only this time it was his driving skills that had her feeling light-headed. She had never traveled this familiar road so *fast*.

She opened one eye and glanced at Al-Nuri. The man smiled widely, enjoying this insane trip. With the wind in his shoulder-length hair, sunglasses hiding those sinful bedroom eyes and wearing clothing much more casual than he normally wore, he looked like a different man.

He turned his head to her and the grin grew even wider. Oh, no, he truly was insane.

"Watch the road!" she commanded.

He did as she instructed, and she closed her eyes again.

Al-Nuri had very sleekly ditched his bodyguards this morning, leaving poor Tarif with a tale to tell—a tale of a long day of important phone calls that could not be interrupted, a tale of boring diplomatic work that required a full day alone in the estate office the sheik called his own for this trip. That done, Al-Nuri had slipped into Prentiss Redmond's garage and appropriated a small black convertible—with Oscar's assistance, of course.

At this rate they'd arrive at Barton College in half the time it usually took Cassandra to make the trip.

This road was a fairly good one, but it was in need of repair here and there, and it twisted and turned along a few stretches. Al-Nuri didn't even slow down for the sharpest of curves, and the slightest bump took them airborne.

Heaven above, he was going to kill her. She was going to die a virgin, without knowing the love she'd waited for *or* the meaningless sex Lexie recommended. At this rate she'd never know the joy of being an almost-psychic mother, like her own mum. She was going to die in a perfectly acceptable but definitely dreary navy blue suit, with her hair tangled and hopelessly mussed by the wind that had undone her French braid long ago.

The car whipped around, jerking the very breath out of her, and came to a sudden stop. Cassandra very cautiously opened her eyes. Al-Nuri had pulled the car to the side of the road. Just ahead was a sign that read Barton 8 kms.

She glared at him. "You were speeding."

He was so obviously enjoying himself, she couldn't remain angry. "I know," he said. "It was marvelous."

She didn't want to smile, but how could she help herself? Sheik Kadir, His Excellency, looked like a ten-year-old boy who had just discovered the joys of the roller coaster. There was such delight on his very masculine face. "Why did we stop?"

To her surprise, he leaned across the console, cupped her head in his large hand and pulled her mouth to his. Slowly, and yet with urgency. That hand was firm but gentle, and she had time to pull away when she realized what he was about to do. She didn't.

He kissed her. Deeply, completely and with the same joy with which he had driven this borrowed sports car, he kissed her. She kissed him back, even though it was entirely inappropriate and unexpected and wrong. This time her stomach did more than flutter. It clenched, leapt and danced. So did her heart. The tip of his tongue just barely teased her bottom lip, and she felt something powerful climb into her throat. A moan. A demand.

Something she had to drive down and ignore.

Cassandra drew away, confused by her intense reaction. She should be stronger than this. She knew better. *He* knew better! "Excellency, I have known you three days."

"I know." One masculine hand brushed away a wild strand of blond hair that teased her cheek. "Three days is a long time to wait for a kiss, but…"

"No, it has not been a *long time,*" she said sternly. "The point is, I barely know you!"

He was not chastened, that she could tell. "You sound disapproving, and yet you did not kiss in that way. Should I believe my ears, or my mouth?"

"Believe whatever you want. Just don't do that again."

He pulled back into the driver's seat and studied her. She could not see his eyes behind those dark glasses to judge his reaction. "If I misread your interest, then I apologize."

"Apology accepted, Excellency," she said.

He sighed. "I thought you might call me Kadir when we are alone."

"You thought wrong." *About a lot of things.*

Al-Nuri drove the rest of the way more sedately, and he kept his eyes on the road. The wide smile that had been so oddly enchanting was gone now, and that was for the best. She knew he was a playboy of sorts. Did he always seduce his female aides for his own pleasure and entertainment? Did he keep notches in his headboard? Were there broken hearts spread all around the world?

Fluttering stomach or no, she would not be made a fool by a man whose only interest was a bedmate for his three-week stay. Two and a half weeks left, she noted, as she mentally counted down the days.

Barton College was an old and prestigious campus, and the grounds were well kept. They were not as annoyingly tidy as the manicured garden he had visited yesterday, but still the grounds were neat. There were old trees and precisely trimmed hedges on soft green hills, and the buildings that made up the campus were constructed of sturdy gray stone that looked cold even beneath the early-afternoon sun, which shone down brightly.

Kadir had met the dean—a stern and intelligent middle-aged woman—and he'd spoken with several students. A few of the students had giggled in an annoying and inexplicable manner, but they were very young and silly, so he'd dismissed their inappropriate behavior.

He had more important things on his mind.

He'd been planning to move to his yacht this weekend, at least for a few days. It was clear that Lord Carrington had no intention of agreeing anytime soon to the meeting Kadir had requested, and Kadir had no desire to play tourist for the next two weeks, before the gala he had come here to attend was held. The yacht was anchored near the north shore town of Leonia, in the quiet Leonia Bay, and a few days of peace in a place he could truly call his own would be welcomed.

But moving onto the yacht so far away from Silverton would surely mean leaving his assigned aide behind, and he was not ready to walk away from Cassandra Klein. She intrigued him in a way no woman ever had.

Cassandra had been unusually silent during the tour of the college. Not just silent, but subdued. Withdrawn. It was the kiss that had done it, he knew. Even though she had enjoyed the kiss and had participated fully, it continued to disturb her. It was easy enough for Kadir to decipher the true reason for her mood.

They walked along a shaded path that led to a small park that overlooked the Lodan River. He found an empty bench and sat, leaving room for Cassandra beside him. She chose instead to stand behind the wooden bench, rigid and unforgiving.

He patted the seat beside him with patient fingers.

"No, thank you," she answered softly.

"I won't bite," he said. "Or kiss." He waited a moment, and she didn't move. "Please," he added in a lowered voice.

Eventually Cassandra rounded the bench and sat beside him—if you could call perching at the far opposite end of the bench "beside." She'd been forced to take her hair down, since the brisk ride in Redmond's convertible had mussed her hair so that there was nothing to be done but let it down and brush it out. He had not realized her hair was so long. It was always tightly restrained, which he could now see was a true crime.

"I don't normally kiss diplomatic aides," he began.

She scoffed.

"Actually, I have never kissed a diplomatic aide before today. It's unprofessional and potentially messy."

"Exactly," she said, obviously relieved. Apparently she had mistaken his comment to mean that he agreed with her. He did not.

"But you, Cassandra, you are different."

Her head snapped around, and soft, pale hair danced. "I am *not* different," she argued. "And you can't expect me to believe…" Her sentence trailed off, but he understood her meaning. How odd, that he could look at her face and know what she was thinking. It had been years since he'd felt so deeply connected to any person. And a woman he wanted to sleep with? Never.

"It has been a very long time since I wanted anything for myself," he said. "Years. So many years, I can't even say how many." Well, he could, but he wouldn't. There would be time for that later, perhaps. "I have been caught up in my purpose, my career, my mission, until there is nothing else in my world. You make me want something else. From the moment I saw you—"

"Stop," she commanded. "Excellency, this is…"

"Kadir."

She turned her head to glare at him. "*Excellency,* I am not the kind of woman you obviously think I am."

"I think you are beautiful and intelligent and kind. Am I wrong?"

Her lips pursed slightly. "I'm not the kind of woman who can give a man…something else." She blushed. "Anything else. My career is very important to me, Excellency. I won't do anything to tarnish it."

Sleeping with him would definitely tarnish her reputation. And his. If they were caught, that is. He was not blind to the fact that they had no future. Her life was here in Silvershire. His was in Kahani, and as Kahani's representative around the world. They were too dissimilar to even think of anything beyond the span of his visit in her country, but did that mean they had to deny what they both so obviously felt?

"Your career is more important than the excitement and the beauty of life?" he asked. "More important than joy?" More important than love? He would not put that question to her, since he had not known her long enough to speak the word *love*. He would not promise—or even hint at—anything he could not offer.

"My career is the most important thing in my life," she explained, and her eyes begged him not to make the coming days difficult for her. "In truth, it's the only important thing in my life. Don't misunderstand, I love my sisters and my parents, and I have friends. But I've dedicated myself to my career to the exclusion of everything else. Yesterday you asked about my personal life, and I made it very clear that I don't have one. I don't have time for anything beyond my career. One day, perhaps, but not now." She appeared flustered, and more uncertain than she wished to be. "I can't allow you to come in here and ruin everything I've worked for."

Kadir sighed. There was nothing he could say to make Cassandra understand that his interest in her wasn't entirely casual. They had no future—that was true enough—but still…she was special. Different. There was no way he could sit here and make her understand that he couldn't replace her with another woman and be just as happy if that woman welcomed his attentions.

He wanted her. No one else would do. And judging

by the expression on her face, he was not going to have
her. He could try to change her mind, if the opportunity
arose, but he could not—would not—push her into a
temporary relationship that she obviously didn't want.

A pair of students walked by. One carried a sloppily
folded newspaper. They both tittered.

Kadir was suddenly easily annoyed. "What is wrong
with these idiotic, snickering students?"

Cassandra purposely saved the visit to the art de-
partment for last. The least amount of time Al-Nuri and
Piper Klein spent together, the better off they'd all be.
Hello, goodbye, we're back on the road again.

Oh, she did not look forward to the return trip.

"Cassandra!" Piper rushed forward, leaving behind
her desk piled high with books and papers. "I was just
about to go out and hunt you down. I heard hours ago
that you were on campus."

With a smile Cassandra said, "I was saving the best
for last, of course."

Piper turned calculating and approving eyes on Al-
Nuri. "You must be the sheik." She offered her hand.
"Piper Klein. Pleased to meet you."

Cassandra took a deep, calming breath. "Mum,
you're to address him as Excellency. That's what's
proper."

Al-Nuri turned on his most brilliant smile as he took
Piper's hand. "Don't be proper on my account. I have
told your daughter many times that I care little for what
is proper." He continued to hold her hand. "Call me
Kadir, please."

Oh, no, no, please don't, Cassandra thought.

"Kadir," Piper said. "What a lovely name."

So much for almost-psychic Mum.

Piper Klein was fifty-six years old, still trim and still pretty. She had lively blue eyes and a sense of adventure, and usually had paint or clay—or both—under her fingernails. Cassandra had gotten her gray eyes from her Dad, but everything else in the gene pool came straight from her mother. She had missed the sense of adventure, however, which was just as well. That sense of adventure hadn't done Lexie any good at all.

For a few long minutes, Piper regaled Al-Nuri with tales of her years at Barton College. Cassandra listened closely. If her mother ventured into "When Cassandra was a baby…" territory, this visit was *over*. But their conversation remained all about the college, and about Al-Nuri's plans to fund one much like it in Kahani.

He was a man like all others in many ways—the kiss had proven that point—but in many ways he was unique. He did want to change the world for the better. He wanted to make a difference in a country where a college like this one would affect countless lives.

She wouldn't kiss him again, but that didn't mean she couldn't admire him, as a man and as a politician.

Cassandra knew she would probably never forget that kiss, and though she would never let Al-Nuri or anyone else know…she wanted another one. Strictly as an experiment, of course. Would another kiss be as wonderfully alarming? Would it make her heart do strange things? She might be a virgin, but she *had* kissed men before.

None had ever kissed her the way Al-Nuri did, sinfully and with a delicious completeness. None of those previous kisses had made her want more than she could have. Surely her reaction to his kiss was an aberration, and another would prove that he was no different from any other man.

The dean arrived with a folder of papers that contained some details about finances and curriculum for Al-Nuri, and the sheik wandered in her direction. Piper took that moment to scurry over to her daughter.

"Oh, my goodness," she whispered. "He's amazing. Handsome, rich, powerful and *nice*." Piper waved a dismissive hand. "I'm sure he has qualities that are less than wonderful—all men do—but what I have seen so far is absolutely perfect." She smiled widely. "You were right to wait for a man like this one to come along."

Cassandra's expression didn't change. "I have no idea what you're talking about."

Almost-psychic Mum's answer was a gentle slap on the arm. "Don't be embarrassed. Bad salad dressing, indeed. Even if you hadn't told me, I still would've figured it out on my own."

"I didn't tell you anything," Cassandra argued, her voice low.

"You told me everything I need to know in your letter, though I did have to see beyond your little code. He's marvelous, he's smart, I ate bad salad dressing."

"I think it was rancid."

Piper snorted. "Besides, I saw the picture. Did you think I wouldn't?"

Cassandra cocked her head to one side and blinked, confused. What on earth was her mum talking about? "What picture?"

"Isn't it a little late for playing innocent, Cassandra? Really, a man doesn't go to such measures unless he feels *something*. It's very gallant and romantic, and…"

Piper narrowed her eyes as she studied her youngest daughter's puzzled eyes. "Oh, dear, you really haven't seen it, have you?"

It was the expression on her mother's face that caused Cassandra's wave of sick dread. "Haven't seen what?"

Piper rushed to her desk, and Cassandra followed closely. A quick glance back showed her that Al-Nuri was keeping the dean entertained for the moment. At the messy desk, Piper moved a stack of books aside and grabbed a newspaper.

One quick glance, and Cassandra knew what newspaper it was. "Mother! You read that trash?" The *Silvershire Inquisitor* was nothing more than a tawdry gossip tabloid. The *Quiz,* as it was called by most, was certainly not fit for Barton College's esteemed art professor.

Piper folded the paper so the top half of the front page was revealed. The logo of an eye—all-seeing, apparently—dominated. But just beneath that eye was a photograph that grabbed Cassandra's attention and held on.

It was her. And Al-Nuri. Well, it was their legs, more specifically. Entangled and extended from the back seat of the limo, moments after he'd grabbed her and thrown her toward safety.

Al-Nuri's legs were covered by his dark trousers. Since her skirt was riding high on her thighs, her legs were very much bare. And rather…spread, so that he was, for that second in time, between them. Beneath the photo, in bold type, words screamed, Sensational Sheik Saves Sexy Secretary!

"I am not a secretary!" Cassandra protested.

"Don't take it personally, dear. I'm sure the word choice was strictly for the alliteration."

Beneath the photo, on the bottom fold of the front page, there were two less sensational photos. One head shot of her, and one of Al-Nuri. No wonder the students had been giggling all day.

A quick glance at the article did nothing to ease her dread. Apparently the *sensational sheik* had thrown himself in front of a bullet in order to save her. There had been one bullet, and it had been intended for *him,* not her. Why did they have to make him out to be a hero? Later in the article, there was a not-so-subtle hint that perhaps Al-Nuri and the diplomatic aide he risked his life for were "involved." "Stay tuned for more juicy details," the author of the article promised.

All her care about sacrificing for her career, and this is where it got her. If people believed she and the sheik were improperly involved, it was just as bad—well, almost as bad—as if they really were....

Stealing kisses. Sharing personal confessions. Starting to like one another in a very undiplomatic way.

"What's this?"

That deep voice at her shoulder startled her, and she tried to crumple the paper in her hands. Al-Nuri reached out and took the *Quiz* from her, unfolding it slowly until the horrible photo was fully revealed.

"I'm going to sue," she said in a calm voice.

"Why? It's a very good photograph."

"It is not!"

He cocked his head to one side, as if he could see more that way.

"You were there, Excellency," Cassandra said. "There's no need to study the photo so closely."

"I did not see the incident from this angle," Al-Nuri said as he continued to peruse the photograph.

She tried to take it from him, but he was taller and stronger—and he managed to hold the newspaper out of her reach. Maybe it was foolish, but looking at that photo reminded her of how she'd felt at that moment. Not when he'd tossed her into the car, but just after, when his weight had been on her body and his lips had been so close....

"Please give me that paper, Excellency."

"I'm not finished."

"Yes, you are."

"I have not read the article."

Her heart leaped in pure dread. "Since half of it is untrue, there's no need, Excellency."

He looked down at her and smiled. The man had such a wicked grin. "Call me Kadir, and it is yours."

She hesitated, and he turned his attention to the article. The article in which he was a hero who'd saved her life, and they were lovers.

"Please give me the newspaper, *Kadir.*"

He stopped reading and looked her squarely in the eye. "Again."

"Kadir," she said, her voice softer.

It was enough to satisfy him, and he handed her the paper.

Kadir. It was a nice name, and it suited him much better than Excellency or Al-Nuri. She had suspected all along that simply calling him by his given name would make him feel too close. Too real. Too much like *hers.*

She'd been right.

Chapter 5

For the return trip, Al-Nuri had put the top up on the convertible. It looked as if they might run into a rain shower down the road, so it was a reasonable precaution. He also drove much more slowly, which was a relief.

Still, Cassandra missed his wicked, joyful smile. It was an unexpected response that she could not afford to indulge in. She never, ever, indulged in anything just for herself, or missed anything so inconsequential as a grin, or even considered placing her career second on her list of priorities. That had made perfect sense to her…until today. Suddenly she wasn't so sure her well-laid plans for the future were actually well-laid.

And wasn't that an unfortunate choice of words?

A few minutes more than half an hour from the college, the rain began. It didn't storm, but fat drops fell on and around the car. Al-Nuri turned on the windshield wipers and dropped his speed, since visibility on the winding road was not what it had once been. The radio was off, and they both remained silent. There was just the sound of rain and the wipers, swishing away at the intense quiet.

Cassandra turned her attention to the *Silvershire Inquisitor,* reading the front-page article about the museum shooting once again. The article was no less alarming than it had been the first time she'd read it.

"The story distresses you," Al-Nuri said in a lowered voice that sounded loud and ominous in the confines of the vehicle.

"Yes," she confessed as she turned to page two. "It should distress you, as well. We both have reputations to think of."

"You said the paper is not well-respected. Will anyone of importance give credence to the story?"

Cassandra sighed. "Probably not," she conceded. "But we will have to be very careful. There can't be any hint of impropriety between us."

Without warning, Al-Nuri pulled the car to the side of the road, put it in Park and then turned the key— silencing the engine and the wipers. For a long moment there was no sound other than the rain all around them. Raindrops fell on the canvas roof and the windshield, pattering softly. After a moment, Cassandra realized that she was holding her breath.

"Are you distressed because some unimportant person might believe you behaved inappropriately, or are you distressed because they might believe you're involved with an Arab from Kahani?"

Cassandra's head snapped up and around. "My annoyance with the *Quiz* has nothing to do with where you come from or who you are. I've worked very hard to get where I am within the Ministry of Foreign Affairs, and to have people think I use my position as an opportunity to—to hook up with men is insulting."

He seemed a bit relieved, but she couldn't be sure. "They will be watching us closely now, yes?"

"Yes. We can expect photographers to be waiting outside the estate, and if we want to go anywhere without them, we'll have to sneak out, as we did this morning. That won't be as easy as it was a few hours ago. The *Quiz* hadn't hit the stands when we left the estate."

Al-Nuri draped one arm across the steering wheel, in a casual—and yet not quite casual—pose. "Should I ask for another aide from your department for the duration of my visit?"

For a moment, Cassandra considered answering "Yes," but it didn't take long for her to reconsider. "No. I'm afraid that would only fuel the flames of the rumor. We must continue to work together as professionally as possible." Let the press take their pictures. Let them try to find something—anything—inappropriate.

"No one is watching us now," Al-Nuri said.

"No."

"This might be the last time we are truly alone."

She didn't like that idea, not at all. "I suppose so."

Al-Nuri didn't make a move, as he had on the breakneck trip to Barton College, but the way he looked at her…it was enough to make any woman's heart beat faster.

"Asking for one more kiss would surely be inappropriate," he said. "You've made it clear that you don't wish to become involved with me in any way other than professionally. I like you very much. I wish we had met under different circumstances, so I could pursue you with a clear conscience. But wishes are for children who still believe in dreams, not for grown men who are confronted each and every day with the harshness of reality. There are those who want me dead. I live surrounded by bodyguards because to ignore the danger would be foolish. And yet today I left that danger, that reality, behind, and I'm not sorry. I'm not ready for the day to end, Cassandra. I imagine you think I do this sort of thing all the time, but in that supposition you would be wrong. I admire you. I'm drawn to you. In a little more than two weeks I'll be gone, and your life will go on as it did before I arrived. You've made it clear that you don't wish anything to come of what we feel."

Cassandra thought of arguing that she felt *nothing,* but it would be a lie—and he'd know it.

"So, I wish for one more kiss," he said. "Here, where we are truly alone and no one will see. One last kiss, before reality returns. If the idea does not appeal to you on any level, say as much. Reject the idea and I will continue on, and will not mention it again. But if you feel, as I do, that such a kiss is necessary…"

Cassandra leaned slightly toward him. She'd liked it better when he'd just taken the kiss. Now he was making her choose, he was making her *think.* And she didn't want to think about this anymore.

One more kiss would prove to her that her reaction to the first one had been a fluke. One more kiss would remind her that Al-Nuri was no different than any other man. "Just kiss me, Kadir," she said. One more kiss to set her mind straight, and then she could dismiss the inappropriate feelings that grew stronger every time she looked at this man.

Al-Nuri—Kadir—placed his lips on hers, and as

before he cradled the back of her head in one large, warm hand. The kiss grew deeper quickly, and this time she tasted desperation as well as desire. She leaned closer, he held her tighter and her lips parted more widely. This was the last kiss—this was all they could have—and so she didn't want it to be over quickly. It had to last a while longer. His tongue danced gently with hers, and her arm snaked around his shoulder so she could hold on tight.

Sensations—passion, need, tenderness—all swelled inside her. It was as if her body pounded with what it wanted...what it needed. Like Kadir, she wished, for one impossible moment, that they had met under different circumstances.

But like him, she knew that was a foolish wish.

Had she really thought this kiss would remind her that he was just like any other man? He was not...and the kiss was truly extraordinary.

Cassandra drew away, breaking the kiss because she knew if she didn't, she'd soon be unable to stop. She was not a woman accustomed to losing control. Kadir dropped his head to her shoulder, and after a moment he laid his lips on the side of her neck. Briefly, warmly, tenderly and with emotion. He drew away slowly and looked her in the eye.

She hadn't eaten bad salad dressing for days, and yet...and yet...

Three photographers were waiting outside the Redmond Estate gates when Kadir and Cassandra returned, but as it was just after dark, the photographers couldn't tell who was in the vehicle. The sight of those photographers who had not been there that morning annoyed Kadir; it proved that Cassandra had been right, and in the coming weeks they must be very careful in the ways in which they presented themselves to the public.

Once they were inside the estate, Cassandra said a quick and obviously distracted farewell, and made her way to her own vehicle. She was anxious to escape. From the photographers and the article that disturbed her, and from him. He felt as if he were losing her as she drove away, though in truth she had never been his to lose.

Sayyid had discovered Kadir's escape late in the afternoon, but thanks to Tarif's and Oscar's explanations, the security guard was not overly concerned by the absence of his employer. Irked, yes, but not worried. No matter how annoyed he might be, Sayyid could say very little.

Kadir closed himself in his office and tried to attend to the business he had neglected all day. If he could arrange a meeting with Lord Carrington quickly, perhaps he should make an excuse for leaving before the gala took place. That meeting was his primary purpose for being in Silvershire, in any case, and his departure would certainly make Cassandra's life easier.

If he could do that for her, perhaps he should. She was not like the women who occasionally came in and out of his life, and there would be no opportunity for more to develop between them. It was best that he take care of the business that had brought him to Silvershire, and then leave, as quickly and quietly as possible.

Tomorrow morning he would call the Silvershire Ministry of Foreign Affairs and demand the meeting with Lord Carrington. Even on a Saturday morning, someone would be available to take his call.

It was getting late, and he was thinking of retiring for the evening, when Hakim knocked briefly, then opened the door and walked into the office with a brisk step. "You have a visitor, Excellency."

For a moment, Kadir wondered…Cassandra? But he knew it wouldn't be her, no matter how he wished it to be so.

"A Mr. Nikolas Donovan," Hakim finished.

"It's rather late. Can he wait until morning?"

Hakim's eyes were very tired. "I don't believe so, Excellency. He apparently waited for the photographers at the gate to leave, as he did not wish his visit to be recorded. Tomorrow morning the photographers may very well return."

The fact that Donovan didn't wish to be photographed entering the estate was intriguing. "Show him in."

Kadir knew, of course, who Nikolas Donovan was here to represent. He was well-informed of all the political factions in Silvershire, including the Union for Democracy.

Donovan had been searched for weapons, and still Sayyid insisted on being in the room during the meeting. As Kadir trusted the bodyguard with all his secrets—well, all of his *political* secrets—he didn't mind. The guard's presence did seem to distract Donovan at first, but Sayyid did his best to blend into the woodwork.

When introductions and cordial greetings had been made, Donovan took a seat on the opposite side of Kadir's desk.

"I'll get right to the point," Donovan said briskly. "You're well-respected in the diplomatic community, and I'm here to ask for your support for my cause."

"You want me to publicly support the Union for Democracy?" Kadir asked.

"Yes, Excellency," Donovan answered. "I believe we can be of some use to one another, if we align."

Aligning with the Union for Democracy would be in direct opposition to Kadir's planned affiliation with Lord Carrington. Though he personally admired what Donovan was trying to do, he could not condone that organization and still ask for an alliance with the monarchy of Silvershire. Besides, there were well-substantiated rumors that some factions within the Union for Democracy had begun to advocate violence as a way to meet their goals. Kadir was quite sure that Donovan was not among those who would turn to violence, but it was a chance he could not take.

"I'm afraid I must decline," Kadir answered without any softening of expression that might give away his personal feelings on the matter.

"Believe me, I understand that your position here is precarious. It's for that reason that I waited until the photographers left before calling. I don't want to put you in a difficult position. All I ask is that you consider my proposition."

Kadir shook his head. "I am here as a representative of my government in order to form an alliance with Lord Carrington, and as soon as I meet with him I'll return home."

"Good luck with that," Donovan said sharply. "Carrington has just left the country, and I don't believe he plans to return until a day or two before the Founder's Day Gala."

A small knot formed in Kadir's stomach. "Are you certain?"

"I met with him last night. He and his wife, Princess Amelia, were getting ready to leave for a visit to Gastonia."

Last night. Kadir sighed. Would nothing of his duties in this country proceed as they should?

"What do you think of Lord Carrington, Mr. Donovan? Will he make a good king?"

Donovan's jaw went tight and hard. "He's a decent man, a much better man than Prince Reginald."

Kadir smiled. "That isn't saying much, from what I hear of the departed prince."

"With the king in a coma, Carrington refuses to even discuss altering our antiquated system of government. The people should be able to decide who leads their country. I know that Kahani is also a monarchy, but you've been advocating change for years. What you and I want is not so very different."

"I'm not trying to overthrow a government."

"Neither am I," Donovan argued. "I want my country to advance into a new and more modern world, which is what you want for your country. Together we could advocate for that change in a much more powerful way than we can alone."

It was almost tempting, and there was something very likable about Donovan. He was intense, in that way visionaries often are. And yet—Kadir had no choice in the matter.

"Again, I must decline."

Donovan was disappointed, but not angry. It was a point in his favor that he didn't fly into a rage when he didn't get what he'd come here for. Of course, he was well aware that Sayyid watched his back, so perhaps he didn't dare lose his temper.

Business done, Donovan leaned back in his chair

and offered a gentle smile. "I saw your picture in the *Quiz* this morning."

Kadir lifted his eyebrows slightly. "Did you? I wouldn't think you'd waste your time reading such a disreputable newspaper."

"I never miss it. Between the stories of alien visitations and the adventures of dog boy, there's the occasional bit of truth that catches my eye."

Dog boy? Alien visitations?

Donovan's smile widened. "No one will admit they read the *Quiz,* but somehow everyone knows what's in it. It's one of our guilty pleasures, I suppose. Do you have guilty pleasures, Excellency?"

Not nearly enough. "If I did," Kadir said with a smile, "I would not admit as much to you."

"Of course not." Donovan stood, offering his hand across the desk.

Kadir rose and took that hand, shaking it firmly. "Good luck, Mr. Donovan."

"And to you, Excellency," Donovan answered. "If you change your mind, please contact me at your convenience. I'm easy enough to find. I believe you and I would work together well, given the chance."

Sayyid escorted Donovan from the room. When his visitor was gone, Kadir sat in his desk chair and leaned back, relaxing for a moment. Lord Carrington had left the country, so there would be no meeting in the near future. Why hadn't Cassandra told him Carrington was in Gastonia? Was it possible that she didn't know? Or was she keeping secrets from him?

In any case, it seemed there was no reason for him to remain here at the Redmond Estate. Tomorrow morning he would go to Leonia and take up residence on his yacht. Given the atmosphere following their trip to Barton College, Cassandra would probably be very happy to see him go.

Cassandra was just about to crawl into bed when the phone rang. The jangling noise startled her. Who would call so late? Was something wrong? Maybe it was Kadir, calling to say good-night.

She lifted the receiver from her bedside phone. "Hello?" she answered, her voice just slightly suspicious.

"I was hoping you wouldn't be asleep yet."

Cassandra breathed a sigh of relief at the sound of her mother's voice. "No, not yet. I'm headed in that direction, though."

After a short pause Piper asked, in a very soft voice, "Is he there?"

Cassandra didn't have to ask who *he* was. "No! Of course not! I told you, Mum, you have the wrong idea about what's going on here. Rather, what's *not* going on. My relationship with the sheik is entirely professional." At least, it was *now,* and would remain so for the duration of his visit. There would be no more kissing, no more conversations about dreams and wishes.

Piper sighed. "Too bad. I was rather hoping to have a sheik as a son-in-law one day. We could vacation in Kahani, which I hear is lovely. Would your sons be sheiks, too? I'm afraid I really don't know how that works. And Kadir really is a very nice man. I like him. And oh, my, he's so handsome. Are you sure he's not there?"

Cassandra couldn't help but laugh. "I'm sure."

"Too bad. It's long past time for you to take the plunge, Cassandra. You're smart not to fall for every line that's thrown your way, you're smart to wait for something more than out-of-control hormones." Again she sighed. "But really, darling, sometimes you're too smart. There comes a time when a woman has to follow her heart and forget what her head tells her. Love is a rare and precious thing, and if you allow love to pass you by without making a grab for it, it might never come again."

"What makes you think love has anything to do with this?" Cassandra tried to sound lighthearted, but she wasn't sure she succeeded.

"Because I know you," Piper answered confidently.

Cassandra reclined on the bed with the phone to her ear. "You're such a nosy mother," she said without anger. "All right. Since you're determined to pry where you should not, answer one question for me."

"Fire away."

Cassandra waited a moment before proceeding, and her mother remained silent. And then a dam burst and Cassandra began to talk rapidly. "How does a woman know if it's her heart speaking or her hormones? 'Out-of-control' hormones, you said. You know how I hate being out of control." A knot of uncertainty and unease formed very near to Cassandra's heart. "Is a man, any man, worth throwing away years of work and dedication and planning? How can a woman know if a man who speaks to her heart, or her hormones, cares for her in anything other than a physical way? And if you know a relationship can't possibly last, is it worth the pain of a potential heartbreak? Lexie was deliriously happy with each of her husbands and boyfriends, at least for a while. Would she have been better off turning her back on the good times to avoid the bad, or are the good times worth the pain that follows?"

Piper didn't answer immediately, and then she said slowly, "That's more than one question."

Frustrated, Cassandra said, "Well, pick one."

"All right." Piper took a deep breath. "Yes. The answer is yes."

"Which—"

"I have to go," Piper interrupted. "Your father's calling. I promised him a sandwich before bedtime."

"But—"

"Good night, darling. I love you."

The line went dead, and Cassandra was left holding a receiver. She stared at the receiver for a moment, as if that stare might bring her mother back. She needed real concrete answers to her questions, not a simple, single and nonspecific word. Soon there was a soft click, and the sound of a dial tone took the place of her mother's voice.

Cassandra replaced the phone on her cradle and fell back to the bed with a gentle bounce. *Yes.* Which question had her mother been answering with that one-word response? It didn't really matter, did it? A yes to any one of the questions pointed her in the same direction.

But Cassandra wasn't like her mother, or her elder sisters, where men were concerned. She didn't have their sense of adventure, their sense of confidence, their love of all things romantic. She was more cautious than the other female Kleins.

She was also the only one sleeping alone tonight.

Chapter 6

When Cassandra stopped her car at the Redmond Estate gates the next morning, three photographers started snapping away. She maintained her composure, and even turned her head toward the cameras for a moment to offer a professional and cool smile. She could not let them see that she was affected by their silly photographs and articles. She remained calm, even when one of the photographers winked and grinned in a suggestive way. Why did she get the feeling he was the one who'd snapped the picture of her bare legs?

Today the suit she wore was her most severe. The blouse was high-necked and the skirt hem fell well below her knee. The color was a limpid gray-green. Ms. Dunn adored this particular suit, and complimented Cassandra every time she wore it.

When the gates opened, she managed a small and

dismissive wave for the photographers—even the smarmy one.

Cassandra was greeted at the door by a flustered Oscar, and walked into a foyer that was crowded with suitcases and one very large trunk.

"What's going on?"

"They're leaving," Oscar said, obviously fretting. "I'm afraid I must've done something to offend them. Oh, it's all my fault. That one very large man, Jib…Jib…"

"Jibril," Cassandra said.

"Yes, I don't think he likes me. I offended him somehow, though I don't know what I might've done. They're angry because I helped the sheik escape for a while yesterday. I never should've done that." Oscar wrung wrinkled hands. "The sheik is the boss, I understand that, but if the others are angry with me, then he can't very well remain here. He's angry, too. Oh, he's in such a foul mood this morning, and it must be my fault. I failed at my job, and that's why they're all leaving."

"Don't be silly." Cassandra patted the old man's arm as she walked by. "I'm sure they're not going anywhere." The luggage said otherwise, but surely there was an explanation. "I have a tour of Silverton-upon-Kairn planned for today, and tomorrow…"

Kadir walked into the foyer, immediately claiming her full attention. Her heart fluttered…and she convinced herself it was because he had startled her with his brisk entrance.

"I'm afraid we won't be here tomorrow," he said crisply. Judging by the expression on his face, Oscar had been correct in his assessment of Kadir's mood. "As I have been informed that Lord Carrington is out of the country and will not return until shortly before the gala, there's no need for me to stay here."

Kadir walked toward one of the larger suitcases and Cassandra followed, her sensible heels clacking on the tile floor. "I'm sorry, Excellency. I had no idea Lord Carrington was leaving the country."

He turned and looked down at her, raising his eyebrows slightly at her formal use of the term Excellency. Still, others were listening. Well, Oscar was listening, and she had no desire to become the subject of estate staff gossip.

"There's no need to fly home," she said sensibly. "I have many activities planned for the coming two weeks. There's much more to Silvershire than a single meeting with Lord Carrington."

"I'm not going home," Kadir said. "My yacht is anchored in Leonia Bay, and I'm going to stay there for several days. I'm sorry to ruin your plans, but…" He glanced up, and Cassandra followed his gaze. Oscar had left the room, and they were truly alone—at least for the moment. "I'm not good at pretending, Cassandra," Kadir said in a lowered voice. "I don't believe I can see you each and every day and pretend that I don't want more than you're willing to give. This is for the best."

Since no one was watching, and there were no photographers nearby, she boldly looked him in the eye. "You're running away."

"Yes."

Cassandra shook her head in frustration. "Don't you understand that running will only make matters worse? People will assume that we either had a lover's spat, or that we're trying to pretend nothing happened."

His expression turned fierce. "I am trying to pretend that nothing happened!"

"Yes, but we can't *look* as if we're pretending."

"Cassandra…"

"Kadir."

When she said his name his expression softened. "You're testing me," he accused in a lowered voice.

"No, of course not." She was, however, very much testing herself. "Leonia is a lovely village. There are several nice restaurants in the area, and the view is lovely. It's a popular spot for a holiday."

"You've been there."

"My sister has a cottage just outside town. She's on vacation and has offered me the use of her home while she's away, so I have a place to stay while you live on your yacht. I'll continue to serve as your aide, of course, and we'll tour the area if you'd like. We can even go fishing. The photographers who are currently waiting outside the estate might follow, but within three days they will all be gone, because we won't give them anything interesting to photograph and nothing else ever happens in Leonia."

"Your plan is to bore them into leaving us alone."

"Precisely." It seemed like a logical enough plan, even worded so plainly.

Kadir looked her up and down, taking in the shoes, the conservative suit, the tightly restrained hair. "You will pack clothing more suitable for fishing than this dismal outfit?"

Dismal was a little harsh as a word choice to describe her suit, but… "Yes, of course."

Kadir studied her for a long moment, and she felt as if he were testing her somehow. He wanted distance from her. Distance would ruin her career. If he dumped her here while he went to his yacht for the duration of this visit, she'd be viewed as a failure. This was her most important assignment ever, and the man she'd been charged to assist couldn't run away from her.

"Go home and pack a bag," Kadir finally said. "We leave in one hour."

She almost did as he instructed, but a shimmer of warning stopped her. It looked as if the sheik and his entourage were ready to leave now. She couldn't take the chance that he'd leave her behind and she'd be forced to follow him to Leonia. She shouldn't be put in a position where she had to chase Kadir across the countryside.

"My sister and I wear the same size," Cassandra said. And there was a very nice little shop in town where she could buy those things she did not wish to borrow. Underwear, toothbrush, makeup—all the essentials. "I can leave whenever you're ready." She gave Kadir a professional smile.

Maybe he wanted to be rid of her, but she couldn't make herself easy to shake off. Besides, he'd soon realize that she was indispensable—as a political aide, of course.

Leonia Bay was indeed beautiful. Kadir had always loved being near the ocean, and he looked forward to settling in on his yacht.

But not right away, apparently. Cassandra offered a quick tour of the village, and he could not turn her down. Sayyid and Haroun accompanied them, while the others took a skiff weighted down with luggage to the yacht.

Only one of the photographers followed on the long trip from Silverton to Leonia, his older-model car keeping pace on the winding road. The others apparently thought they'd have a better chance of taking a marketable photo in the capital city. Cassandra was obviously concerned about the lone photographer. She didn't say so, of course, but her eyes flitted to the car often, and Kadir could see the worry in her eyes.

A woman like her should never have to worry. She should be pampered and protected and given all that she desired.

Haroun drove the conspicuous limousine through the picturesque town, and Sayyid kept a sharp eye on those they drove past. Tourists, retired couples, children…there was no obvious danger here. After making a quick stop at a small shop, they simply rode around for a while. Cassandra pointed out several interesting shops, a bakery that made wonderful cookies and fresh bread, the restaurants she preferred and a small museum that was very much unlike the Maitland Museum of Fine Arts in Silverton. This one was nautical in nature, and was not much bigger than the foyer of the Redmond Estate. Cassandra's dialogue was lively and professional and somewhat distant, considering that he still remembered what she'd tasted like just yesterday.

Kadir didn't understand Cassandra Klein, and he was a man who usually understood women quite well. She kissed like a woman who was interested in more than politics and propriety, and then she acted as if they had never kissed at all. She dressed conservatively, even gloomily, and yet now and then there was an intriguing gleam in her gray eyes that was anything but conservative or gloomy.

It had been a very long time since he'd met a woman who could take his mind entirely off his mission—and that was not a good thing. It would have been better if he'd left the Redmond Estate before her arrival this morning, as he had planned. Now that she was here, how was he going to get rid of her?

And he did need to get rid of her somehow. He could not possibly spend the next two weeks pretending that he didn't want her.

They ate lunch at a small, outdoor café that looked over the bay, drawing stares—since they were not dressed as the other tourists were, and Sayyid and Haroun were obviously bodyguards, not friends or guests. The photographer who had followed them from Silverton took a number of photographs, but the scene they presented was boring, as Cassandra had planned. To any eye, the lunch was purely professional.

The photographer soon turned his attention to different subjects—the sea, a pretty girl, three siblings who looked remarkably alike, but for their size. There was much beauty, many scenes of interest to an artist or a photographer in this small village. As the man with the camera wandered away from the café, Cassandra relaxed visibly.

She was very beautiful when she relaxed, and Kadir wished for his own camera to capture the expression on her face. Would he remember this moment clearly enough?

Cassandra was intent on keeping him busy throughout the day. Fishing was next on her list of things to do. She assured Kadir that her sister had all the proper equipment at her cottage. As they left the café she watched for the photographer to follow. He didn't. A pretty girl in a skimpy bathing suit had grabbed his attention, at least for the moment.

The cottage Cassandra spoke of was rather isolated,

located just beyond the edge of town and very near an outcropping of rocks that met the ocean waves. It was plain but neat, consisting of a main room, a kitchen, two bedrooms and two baths. All the rooms were large, which made the entire cottage feel airy and comfortable.

After checking the cottage thoroughly, Sayyid and Haroun positioned themselves at the entrances—Haroun on the front porch, Sayyid at the back door. Cassandra put on a pot of coffee, then disappeared into one of the bedrooms. After watching the closed door for a long moment, Kadir went to the wide window that looked out over the sea. The waves soothed him, as they often did, and he tried to take his mind off of Cassandra.

He knew how to be rid of her once and for all, but could he do it? Did he dare? It was not in his nature to be cruel, especially when he cared more than he should for the subject of that cruelty. And yet he had to do something. He had to take the matter in hand.

Cassandra exited the bedroom a few short minutes later, and he couldn't help but smile. She wore blue jeans that had been rolled up to just beneath her knees, tennis shoes with no socks and a pink T-shirt that advertised a local café—the very one where they'd eaten lunch. Her hair had been pulled back into a long, loose ponytail, and she looked years younger. She looked carefree and relaxed.

It was quite a transformation.

"I think these will fit you," she said, offering him a stack of clothes on outstretched arms. What she presented was worn blue jeans, much like hers, as well as a T-shirt. His was beige instead of pink. A pair of canvas shoes, stuffed with white socks, sat on top of the stack. He might've sent one of the bodyguards to the yacht to collect proper clothing for the afternoon's activities, but Cassandra had insisted it was not necessary. "They belong to Lexie's boyfriend, or one of her ex-husbands. I'm not sure which one, but they're more suitable for fishing than what you're wearing."

The suit he wore was dark and conservative and expensive, and definitely not intended for sea spray and live bait.

Cassandra glanced toward the front door. "Will your bodyguards want to fish with us? I can find old clothing for them, as well…."

"That won't be necessary," Kadir said as he headed for the bathroom so he could change his clothes. In order for his plan to get rid of Cassandra to work, he needed his bodyguards at a distance.

Cassandra hadn't been fishing in many years, but she still remembered how, for the most part. Kadir was very comfortable with a rod and reel, decked out in someone else's jeans and a snug-fitting T-shirt. When the wind caught his hair and blew it away from his face, and he looked so intent on his chore, he was quite fetching.

If a man could be fetching, that is, and if she could afford to notice. Which she couldn't.

Lexie's cottage was wonderfully secluded, so she didn't worry about curious eyes watching or listening. Well, other than Kadir's bodyguards, that is, and they weren't close enough to hear anything that was said. They remained alert, but the serenity of this place soothed even them, and she could almost forget that there were those who wanted Kadir dead, and these bodyguards were not a luxury but a necessity.

"Do you come here often?" Kadir asked, his eyes on the ocean.

"No."

"Why not?"

So, he wanted to add conversation to their fishing. It would be tricky, to be friendly with him without allowing things to proceed beyond friendly. "Lexie and I don't always get along. She and I are...very different." And that was putting it mildly.

"I have a villa on the ocean. Even in the worst of times, the water soothes me. I'm not sure why." Kadir sounded almost wistful, which surprised her. "I would rather be on my yacht than anywhere else in the world." He turned his head and looked at her, with those dark, bedroom eyes. "The living quarters are small, but very nice. You'd like them." For a long moment he was very thoughtful, and then he reeled in his line and turned to Sayyid. One step, and the bodyguard was all but rushing to meet him. The two men spoke in low tones, and it appeared that they were arguing with one another. And then, much to Cassandra's surprise, both bodyguards left.

Sayyid cast more than one glance back, but he and Haroun eventually got into the limo and drove back toward town.

"Where are they going?" Cassandra asked.

"Back to the yacht."

"But..."

"The photographer who followed us was left behind in town, snapping pictures of pretty girls and soothing scenery. No one knew in advance that I was coming here today. By tomorrow, word will be out, and anyone who knows the yacht is anchored here will arrive, and the possibility of danger will be real once again. But for today, just for today, no one knows where I am." His eyes on the ocean once again, he appeared to breathe deeper. He actually seemed to relax.

"How will you get back to the yacht?" Cassandra asked.

He shrugged his shoulders. "I'll call a taxi, or maybe I'll walk. A skiff will be left for me at the pier where we unloaded the luggage. That's no more than a mile from here, if I remember correctly. A pleasant enough walk."

They didn't catch anything at all, but the atmosphere was much more relaxed with the bodyguards gone. Kadir truly did look to be lost in the beauty of the ocean. In his position, did he have many truly free moments like this one? Probably not.

She wanted peaceful moments for Kadir, not because he was her first really big assignment, not because he was trying to change the state of his country for the better, not because his position was very much what she envisioned for herself, one day. She wanted him to have peaceful moments because she liked him. Not for the position he held, not for his dedication to making Kahani a better place. She liked *him*. His smile, his bedroom eyes, the way he kissed.

Time didn't stand still as they stood on the rocks and fished, but it did pass more slowly. Cassandra's heart rate slowed, and she breathed deeper than usual, taking in the sea air. The waves had a soothing rhythm that seemed to take on the cadence of her heart as she stood on the rocks and relaxed. It was very nice, and very *real,* and whether she would admit it or not, she liked simply being with Kadir, for a while.

But, of course, nothing good lasted forever. Eventually Kadir reeled in his line and walked toward her, fishing rod held casually in his hand. "We should head back to the yacht," he said. "It'll soon be time for dinner. You will join me, won't you?"

Cassandra reeled in her own line. "Dinner? Thanks for the invitation, but…" She'd planned on grabbing a can of soup from Lexie's cabinet. "I should get settled in here. You go ahead." He smiled at her, and suddenly eating a can of soup in Lexie's kitchen seemed very lonely.

"Sayyid left here with orders to have a catered supper waiting for the two of us. He was to go to one of the restaurants you pointed out today, the one you said was your favorite. You didn't mention which dish you preferred, so I asked that he have all of them made available."

Her heart skipped a beat. "All of them?"

They walked to the cottage, slowly and casually. This village, the cottage, the sea Kadir liked so much, they all had a way of doing that to a person—making them slow down and take deep breaths and relax. Cassandra almost never relaxed, but this was very nice. She hadn't known that she needed this holiday from her structured life, but apparently she did.

With the fishing gear stowed back in Lexie's storage shed, where they'd found it, Cassandra and Kadir began the walk toward the pier. For a few minutes, all was well. Kadir asked questions about Leonia and Lexie, and there was no talk of Lord Carrington or assassination attempts or alliances. Now and then he seemed to be about to say something, and then he changed his mind and turned the subject to something unimportant. The weather, fishing, food. All too soon she saw the pier ahead. A small skiff waited, as Kadir had said it would.

On the pier he turned to her, stopping so suddenly she almost ran into him. She stopped short, but not until she'd come so close she could smell the sea spray that had washed over him while they'd stood on the outcropping and fished the afternoon away. When she started to back away, he reached out one arm that encircled her and pulled her close. A strong hand settled at the small of her back, holding her firmly but gently in place.

"No eyes will be watching us tonight, Cassandra. Tomorrow that will change, but for tonight…"

"Don't," she said softly.

"I want you," Kadir said, ignoring her plea to stop before he went too far. "Sex between two adults who are obviously attracted to one another is nothing to be ashamed of. I know why you insist on hiding what you feel, but for tonight—just for tonight—why can't we take what we want? No one but the two of us ever needs to know."

A part of her was tempted, more tempted than she'd ever been or ever thought to be. She was drawn to Kadir, but was she willing to ruin her career for a flutter? Was any man worth throwing away years of planning and work and dedication?

As she was wondering, he leaned down and kissed her. No one was around to see, so she had no excuse to draw away. Besides, she wanted the kiss. She wanted the connection.

She wanted Kadir.

His mouth moved over hers, and she slipped her body closer to his. His arms held her close. She slipped her arms around his waist and held on as the kiss deepened. Her response was much more than a flutter, and she considered very seriously taking him up on his offer. There was more here than the desire for a sexual connection. She cared about this man she'd met less than a week ago. She cared very much.

It was Kadir who ended the kiss, taking his mouth from hers. "Say yes, and you won't be sorry," he whispered. "I won't allow you to be sorry."

The full weight of what she'd actually been considering hit her, and her knees wobbled. He meant something to her, in an unexpected way. But what did she mean to him? Did she mean anything at all? "I can't. You're asking me to throw away my job for a…a what? What is this, Kadir? A fling? A one-night stand? A diversion because you can't yet meet with Lord Carrington?"

"What does it matter?" he asked, more than slightly testy. "Do we have to give what's happening between us a name of some sort for you to file away in a neat box? Do all your relationships belong in a certain category, and until you know where I belong you're going to deny me, and yourself?"

She didn't want to tell him that *all her relationships* were…him.

"I'm not asking you to run away with me," he said sharply. "I'm just asking for one night. Just because we're working together, that doesn't mean we can't also enjoy a casual sexual relationship. It's been a difficult week. Sex will help us to relax."

It was easy to step away after he said that. She was drawn to him; he liked her. But she wasn't about to endanger her career for *one night*. She wasn't about to throw it all away for *casual*. "I think you should have dinner alone," she said sharply as she backed away from him.

"And tomorrow?" he asked, his voice remaining sharp. "Will you once again don a drab suit that does not suit you and pretend that nothing happened?"

"Nothing did happen," she insisted.

"Pity," Kadir said. He jumped into the waiting skiff and quickly untied the lines that lashed it to the dock. Before starting the engine, he turned those dark eyes to her. "Call the Ministry of Foreign Affairs and tell them I require another aide for the duration of my visit. One who is more…hospitable." He glanced to the west, where the sun had already disappeared behind the horizon. "It's almost dark. Wait here. I'll send Sayyid back with the keys to the limousine. He will drive you home."

Speechless, Cassandra watched him steer the skiff toward the waiting yacht. For a few moments she didn't move at all. His last words had been cruel, and she had not thought him capable of cruelty. Had he only been charming when he'd thought she'd sleep with him? The kissing, the fishing, the smiles… Had they been a part of his attempted seduction?

And what would Ms. Dunn say when she called and requested that someone else be assigned to His Excellency during the remainder of his time in Silvershire?

The skiff disappeared as it rounded the yacht. Maybe there was a ladder or something on the other side of the large vessel. He'd tie up the skiff, climb the ladder—anger took the place of her confusion and hurt, and Cassandra's attitude took a sharp turn—and choke on his romantic dinner for two.

As she allowed anger—which was much easier for her to manage than the initial hurt—to take over, she realized that she was much better off discovering this crude side of Kadir's nature now, rather than later. His charm had disguised the seedier side of his nature, and he'd almost had her fooled. Almost. She'd been so close to making a mistake she'd have regretted for the rest of her life.

No way was she going to stand here and wait for Sayyid or anyone else to collect her and drive her back to Lexie's cottage. She was perfectly capable of walking there, even if she ended up arriving after the night turned pitch black. Cassandra left the pier and stalked to the road that would lead her back to the cottage, glad for the opportunity to walk off some of her anger.

How dare he? It had all been a game to him, one seduction in a line of many, and she'd almost taken him seriously. Tears threatened, but she pushed them away. Al-Nuri didn't deserve her tears. He was a macho, spoiled, demanding *pig*. If there was ever a time for her to be the ice maiden Lexie had called her in the past...

She hadn't taken two steps down the road before a thundering explosion startled her breathless, and she spun toward the ocean as a fireball claimed Kadir's yacht. Another explosion followed, sending flames into the air and ragged pieces of the once fine vessel into the sea.

She was stunned for a moment, and then the truth hit her between the eyes like a sharp-bladed knife. Kadir was on that yacht.

Unable to control her own legs, Cassandra dropped to her knees and started to scream.

Chapter 7

Cassandra didn't have her cell phone with her, but as it turned out she didn't need one. By the time she stopped screaming, she heard the approaching sirens. Of course, everyone in town had seen the explosion. Local authorities would take charge, they would search for survivors in the sea and begin an investigation.

She'd seen the explosion, and she didn't think there would be any survivors for the authorities to find. Bodies, yes, but survivors…no.

She gave a brief and almost hysterical statement to the officer who assisted her from the road. Leonia had a local police force, but it was small and the officers were unaccustomed to dealing with anything of this magnitude. As she watched the authorities scramble to handle the situation, she had one clear thought. A call to Ms. Dunn would get proper investigators on the scene quickly. Whoever had done this must be made to pay.

But no amount of justice would bring Kadir, or the other people who'd been on that yacht, back. It was so unfair, so *wrong*.

The same officer who took her statement, such as it was, drove Cassandra back to the cottage. He asked her if she needed help, if she needed a doctor or someone to sit with her for a while, but she declined. She wanted to be alone. She wanted to cry some more and scream again, and she couldn't do that with this stranger, or any other, watching her.

Inside the cottage, Cassandra called Ms. Dunn and passed on the news about the explosion and Kadir's death in an insanely calm voice. Tears stung her eyes, but she didn't allow her boss to hear those tears in her voice. Still, apparently the astute Ms. Dunn heard *something*.

"Cassie, are you all right?" the older woman asked when the short report was completed.

"I'm…" The word *fine* stuck in her throat. She could've been on that yacht when it had exploded, but she hadn't been. She was safe because she'd allowed Kadir's less-than-romantic invitation to sway her decision, because she was the ice maiden Lexie accused her of being, because when love had presented itself to her, it hadn't come in the neat, pretty package she'd expected, so she'd thrown it away. Her knees wobbled, and she was forced to sit on the floor, phone still in hand.

"I prefer to be called Cassandra," she said in a too-soft voice.

"Of course," Ms. Dunn replied gently.

Her anger flared, pushing away the confusion. "Sheik Kadir was a very nice man, you know. Smart, funny, dedicated to his country the way we are dedicated to ours. He didn't deserve to die this way. Whoever Lord Carrington sends to investigate the explosion—the *assassination*—make sure they're the best. I want those responsible caught and I want them to be punished."

"Of course. I would have it no other way, Cassandra." There was a short, expectant pause before the woman added, "I'm going to send Timothy Little to Leonia tomorrow to collect you." Once again, Ms. Dunn's voice was all business, if not quite as sharp as usual.

Cassandra had no desire to see the overly eager diplomatic aide Ms. Dunn offered to send, or anyone else from the office. She wanted—needed—to be alone. "No, thank you. I'm going to stay here for a few days." There was no way she could return home now, and she certainly couldn't go back to the ministry tomorrow or the next day as if nothing had happened. Her brain wasn't working correctly, and her heart was broken in so many ways she didn't know how it could ever be fixed. How could any man do this to her in just a few days? How could Kadir matter to her so much that his death and the knowledge that she would never see him again devastated her, when in truth she barely knew him?

"Yes, certainly, if that's what you want, Cassandra," Ms. Dunn agreed. "Call me when you get the chance. I'd like to know that you're doing well."

"Of course."

When the call was done, Cassandra remained on the floor. Her legs were weak still, so she leaned against the couch and hugged herself with trembling arms. She did her best to ignore the tears that dripped down her cheeks. She needed to call her mother before the news of Kadir's death began to spread, but…not now. Not yet. She needed to be better composed before she spoke to her mum. For now, she was content to sit on the floor and allow the emotions she'd tried to deny wash over her.

Instead of throwing herself wholeheartedly into what she'd felt for Kadir from the moment she'd seen him, she'd allowed her reservations to keep her at a distance. Even when he'd kissed her, when she'd kissed him, her misgivings had come between them and she'd held so much of herself back. Why couldn't she be more like Lexie? More bold where men were concerned. More daring. Why did she find it impossible to take even the smallest chance?

If she'd invited Kadir to come into the cottage to share a can of soup, he'd still be alive. He might've stayed and kissed her some more. Perhaps on this very couch. He would've held her closely, if she'd allowed it. Would she have? She didn't know, and she'd never have the chance to find out. If she hadn't been so damned concerned about her career, she would have a warm memory or two of the man who caused her stomach to flutter.

If she'd given in to her feelings, she wouldn't feel as if she'd thrown away the only man she'd ever loved.

If, if, if. Cassandra lay down on the floor and covered her face with her hands, as if she could hide in that childish way. Shaking, dry-eyed, terrified—she could not imagine that she'd ever have the energy or the drive to get up off the floor.

This was what she'd been trying to avoid in being cautious, and look where it had gotten her. She'd kept Kadir at a distance, she'd maintained her professional attitude—for the most part. She'd done her best to keep him and his flutters at a distance...and still her heart was broken.

* * *

Amala ran on the beach, laughing and skipping, as little girls did. Kadir tried to catch her, but he couldn't quite keep up. His big sister was older than him by three years, and even hampered by a skirt that brushed the sand, she ran faster than he did. Her legs were much longer and even stronger than his own, and she pulled away from him, slowly and then with a speed that stole his breath away.

Suddenly Kadir knew something bad was about to happen. Dark clouds moved in, and the waves grew tall and threatening. Amala pulled farther away from him. He tried to run faster, but instead it seemed his legs wouldn't move at all.

A wave washed over the sand, grabbed a screaming Amala…and then she vanished, lost to the sea.

When Amala was gone, the wave came for Kadir. He stood there, unable to move or to say a word, while it rose up above him, broke down and swallowed him like a monster made of saltwater. The water was in his eyes, in his mouth, and it tried to drag him down.

He reached out in desperation, but the monster was too much for a small boy to fight and he could no longer breathe….

With a gasp, Kadir reached out. His hand found a ledge of sharp rock. Another wave—just a wave, not a monster—tried to grab him, but he held on tightly to the rock. He blinked the stinging, salty water out of his eyes, and gasped for air. He hurt everywhere. He could barely breathe. And if he wasn't careful, the next wave might pull him down and down, and there would be no coming back up.

The sky was dark, with nothing but a half-moon to

light the waves and the jagged rock. There was a moment, not much more than a second or two, when Kadir believed he was trapped in a dream. But then he remembered.

He'd been about to climb the ladder that would take him on board his yacht when his conscience had forced him to change his mind. True, his treatment of Cassandra would send her away, as planned…but faced with the reality of his success, he didn't want her to believe that he didn't care for her at all. He didn't want her to think he was a shallow playboy who cared only for women who would come to his bed when called.

So he'd turned the skiff around and headed for the pier. He'd watched, in the dying light of day, as Cassandra stalked away from the pier, not waiting for Sayyid as he had instructed her to do. She was angry, rightfully so. All he had to do for his heartless plan to succeed was allow her to continue to be angry….

And then the first explosion had come without warning. Kadir had been blown into the water. The blast stole his breath, and tossed him from the boat as if he weighed nothing. Before he fell into the waves, something—a sharp piece of flying debris—cut into his arm. The skiff was tossed and broken, and he sank. The other explosion had come as he'd been fighting to find the surface, and then…darkness.

He wasn't sure how he'd survived. Somehow he'd fought his way to the surface for air, but he didn't remember doing so. Somehow he'd floated or swum or drifted to this piece of rocky shore—but he had no recollection of making his way here. Perhaps those memories would return to him in time, but then again, they might not.

He had the fleeting and nonsensical feeling that his sister, Amala, who'd been dead for fifteen years, had somehow guided him to the surface. For a moment he was quite sure that the spirit of his sister had saved him from the monster of the sea.

It was with great effort that Kadir pulled himself onto the rock, using his left arm for leverage since his right was unusually weak. He lay back, exhausted and unable to move, while his mind began to clear somewhat.

After a few moments, he asked himself the question. Who was responsible for the explosion? Who had known he would be on the yacht tonight? Who would've been able to get word to Zahid that tonight was the proper time and place for assassination? His bodyguards, Hakim and Tarif. The lone photographer, whose name he did not know. The small and trusted staff on the yacht.

And Cassandra.

He didn't want to believe she could be involved, but she had refused his invitation to join him for the evening—not that he had bothered to make the invitation suitable for a woman like her—and that refusal had kept her safe from the blast.

In truth, anyone might be behind the explosion. Zahid's followers had kidnapped Mukhtar's family in order to force the old man to do as they wished. They were not above doing the same again, which meant he could trust no one.

No one.

Without the sun to warm the rock and his body, the night very quickly turned cool. A breeze on his wet clothing made Kadir shudder. His life had not been entirely safe for the past fifteen years, but he had always had people around him he could trust completely. Zahid had not always been an immediate threat, and there had been moments of peace, and people he could rely upon without fail.

But somehow, amidst his determination to bring about change and stop Zahid and his followers, Kadir had managed to separate himself from almost everyone, even those who had earned his trust. He was no longer close to his brothers; in truth, he barely knew them anymore. Their wives and children were strangers. Women came and went, none ever getting too close to his heart. For fifteen years he had kept a shield between him and everyone else in his life.

Why did it seem, at this moment, that he was more alone than he had ever been? Why did it seem that he could trust no one but the dead? His parents. Amala. Everyone who had been on the yacht when it exploded.

He grew so cold he was compelled to move off the rock and toward the road, though he had no destination in mind. Where does a man go when he can truly trust no one? He walked slowly, up the jagged rock and across a collection of loose pebbles, before finding himself on the narrow road. And there, directly before him, was Cassandra's cottage.

Her sister's cottage, to be more precise. Illumination from inside warmed one window with yellowish light. Other windows were dark. Was she there, sitting in that one lighted room? Or was she in the darkened room, not alone but with a man? A lover. Zahid, perhaps. Had she been putting on an act for him all this time? Was Cassandra Klein one of Zahid Bin-Asfour's converts? Maybe she was simply his mistress....

Light-headed and more confused than he had ever

been, Kadir closed his eyes tightly. No, he could trust Cassandra. She had nothing to gain by aligning herself with Zahid. And…she would not. She was a modern woman, a woman who valued her career and her independence. Cassandra was everything Zahid despised.

Cassandra was everything Amala would've liked to have been, but Amala had not been given the same opportunities. If she had, would she be alive today?

Kadir walked toward the lighted window. He must be cautious; he must always be cautious. But when the day arrived when he could truly trust no one in the world…he would just as soon be dead.

Sleep was impossible. Maybe she would never sleep again.

Cassandra sat on Lexie's small couch, a light blanket wrapped around her shoulders to ward off the chill that had nothing to do with the temperature of the air. Two lamps burned in this main room. The rest of the cottage was dark.

She'd telephoned her parents, before it got too late, to assure them that she was fine. If she didn't call and they heard she was here, they'd jump in the car and drive overnight and be here by morning. She wasn't ready for company—not even theirs—so she'd told them Ms. Dunn had offered to send someone to collect her and drive her back to Silverton. She didn't bother to note that she'd declined the offer.

A soft knock at the back door caught her so by surprise, she twitched sharply. At this time of night it could only be bad news. Maybe Lexie had returned because she and Stanley had had a fight and the vacation was over. Maybe the police had found Kadir's body.

That thought caused a bone-deep shiver. Maybe Ms. Dunn had ignored Cassandra's insistence that she was going to stay here for a few days, and Tim Little was here to collect her.

But why hadn't she heard a car?

Cassandra stood and dropped the blanket from her shoulders. Once again, the soft knock—a scraping, almost—came from the direction of the back door.

Someone had killed Kadir. Did that same someone want her dead, too? Lexie kept a small, old revolver in the drawer of her desk. They had argued over that weapon on Cassandra's last visit. Lexie said she needed some sort of protection in the remote house, even though nothing much ever happened in Leonia. Cassandra had argued that Lexie was more likely to accidentally shoot herself with that six-shooter.

But now Cassandra rushed to the desk, opened the drawer and withdrew the weapon. She didn't know much about guns. Was it even loaded? Was the safety on? She looked for a safety as she walked into the kitchen, but didn't see one anywhere on the gun. Maybe all she had to do was point and shoot.

That was the big question. Could she point this weapon at a human being and shoot to kill? The uncertainty didn't last long. If the person who'd killed Kadir was on the other end of the gun, she'd have no trouble pulling the trigger.

Again, the knock—which was not quite a knock, but was once again more of a scraping—sounded. Maybe what she heard on the other side of the door was an animal. If it was any of the people she'd first thought of, she would've heard a car. If it was a person planning to do her harm, they likely wouldn't knock at all. It would be easy enough for an intruder to break the glass, reach inside and unlock the door. Yes, maybe what she heard was an animal who'd wandered onto the back porch.

She kept the six-shooter in her hand, just in case.

At the back door, Cassandra stood to one side and lifted the curtain that covered the four small window-panes. Even though the light in the kitchen was off, she saw nothing beyond the window but darkness. Maybe it had been an animal, after all—a wandering dog, per-haps—and the creature had already moved on. She'd almost relaxed when a hand shot out of the darkness and pressed against a pane of glass she'd unveiled. Her heart jumped, she raised the gun and then a soft voice said, "Cassandra?"

She knew that voice. Hands trembling, she unlocked the door and opened it wide. Kadir stood there, leaning beside the door as if that was the only way he could continue to stand. He was wet, his eyes were strangely unfocused and his clothes were torn and bloody.

But he wasn't dead.

She reached out and took his wrist in her hand, drawing him gently into the kitchen.

Once he was inside the kitchen, she closed the door and placed the six-shooter on the counter. When she reached for the light switch, Kadir stopped her with a whispered, "Don't. Someone might be watching." Those words of caution reminded her to lock the door again, before leading Kadir into the main room and the light of two lamps, so she could study him more closely. Here the windows were tightly covered, so they didn't need to worry about prying eyes.

She supported him with an arm around his waist, as he walked slowly toward the couch where moments earlier she'd been grieving for him. His right arm was bleeding, she noted, and he shivered to the bone.

When they reached the couch, he all but fell onto it. Cassandra put her panic aside and assessed what had to be done immediately, then she reached for the phone.

Kadir moved quickly, much more quickly than she'd thought him capable of, and clamped his hand tightly around her wrist. "Don't call anyone."

Obviously he wasn't thinking clearly. He'd had quite a shock, and might be delirious. "You need a doctor. When that's taken care of I'll call Ms. Dunn, and she'll contact the proper authorities in Kahani. Would you prefer to make that call yourself? Someone needs to get started with those calls right away. Everyone thinks you're dead, Kadir. We need to let them know—"

"No," he said sharply. "No doctor. No phone calls." His eyes met hers, and she saw in his gaze that while he was still not himself, he was thinking clearly. He was not delusional. "If everyone thinks I'm dead, this is a good thing. For now, at least. I don't know who I can trust, Cassandra. Only you. Tonight I trust only you."

She returned the phone to its place on the end table and covered Kadir with the blanket. "Your arm is bleeding."

"Is it?" He glanced at the torn and bloody sleeve and the damaged flesh beneath as if he had not yet realized he was wounded. "So it is. You'll have to bandage it for me."

"I'm not a doctor."

"No, but your medical care will suffice. It has to, for now. If word gets out that I'm alive, we will both be in danger." He reached out his left hand to caress her face. "I have always known that my life could be cut short by those who oppose me. But you—you should not be put in harm's way because you're with me. If you cannot keep my secret, if you must call someone and tell them I'm alive, then I'll leave right now. By staying with you I could bring those who would kill a dozen people or more in order to get to me, those who murdered everyone on that yacht because they thought I was there, to your door. I won't do that."

Cassandra leaned down and gave Kadir a quick kiss. She touched him, her fingers brushing against his damp shirt and then his too-cool hand. Her mind and her heart were still reeling with the knowledge that he was alive. That he was here. That he trusted her.

"I won't call anyone." She'd doctor him as best she could, telling him again and again that she was relieved beyond belief to see him alive. She wanted to kiss him again, once his arm was bandaged and she dressed him in warm, dry clothes. And after that?

Cassandra had no idea where they were headed or what would happen next. She did know that they had no choice but to deal with "after that" tomorrow.

Chapter 8

Kadir woke with a start, gasping as if reaching desperately for air.

Unlike the last time he came to consciousness with such ferocity, he found himself warm and dry, lying in a soft bed, safe and secure—and not alone. He assessed the situation quickly. His arm had been cleaned and bandaged. He remembered Cassandra leaning over him and tending the wound with great care. She slept beside him now, her warm curves close to his body. Her slumber was deep, but one of her small feet was draped over one of his legs, as if she had arranged herself to awaken if he dared to leave the bed or even roll away from her.

Morning was coming, after a night so long he could not fathom that twenty-four hours ago he had been sleeping at the Redmond Estate. A touch of light turned the sky beyond the bedroom window gray, as a new day approached.

But morning had not yet arrived, and for the first time in a very long time Kadir relaxed completely. There were no bodyguards at the ready, no precautions to be taken, no danger waiting outside the bedroom door. Everyone but Cassandra thought he'd been on the yacht when it exploded. Zahid and whoever had betrayed Kadir thought he was dead.

At the moment Kadir liked being dead. He liked it very much. As he reached for Cassandra, wanting only to stroke his fingers against her warm skin, sleep crept upon him, gently and completely.

The jangling of the phone woke Cassandra, and she came awake with a start. The ringing woke Kadir, too. He sat up and looked at her, not yet fully alert. Cassandra took a deep breath and reached for the bedside phone, answering with a sleepy "Hello."

Cassandra relaxed as her greeting was returned. It was Ms. Dunn calling, asking if she'd changed her mind about being collected by Timothy Little and being brought back to Silverton. There was work to be done at the Ministry of Foreign Affairs, Ms. Dunn imparted sharply. Particularly so at this time as the Founder's Day Gala was just two weeks away. Two weeks from yesterday, to be precise.

Ms. Dunn was of the opinion that hard work was the proper cure for any ailment—including the shock of watching a yacht filled with innocents being blown out of the water.

It was the older woman's way of checking in with Cassandra and assuring herself that all was well in the cottage in Leonia. She would never come right out and ask, but

Cassandra had worked with Ms. Dunn long enough to know what the intentions of the call really were.

Cassandra assured her boss that she still wanted to take a few days off, and that she'd return to Silverton by the end of the week. She didn't know if that was true or not—she had no idea when she'd return to Silverton—but it would do for now.

With Ms. Dunn properly and completely dismissed, Cassandra turned her attention to Kadir. "How do you feel this morning?"

"Better," he said. "Much better."

He looked much better. In fact, he looked large and handsome and healthy and well-rested. There was some stubble around his usually well-trimmed beard and mustache, and his black hair was mussed. She imagined this was what he always looked like in the morning— stubbly and warm, with his longish hair slightly wild and very curly, and his eyes, his bedroom eyes, dark and sleepy and filled with a promise she did not entirely understand.

Last night she had helped him dress in a pair of cotton pajama bottoms that likely belonged to Stanley. They had not seen much wear, and fit well enough. But his chest was bare, and it was the finely sculpted, slightly hairy chest of a real man. She should move away…but she didn't.

"How's the arm?" Her eyes dropped to the bandage on his right biceps, and Kadir's gaze traveled there, as well.

"Fine. You're a good doctor." He actually managed a small smile, one she returned.

She tried to sound as if she were completely unaffected to be sharing a bed with this man. "The cut wasn't as bad as it looked at first, but we'll have to keep an eye on it and make sure it doesn't get infected."

Now that they were awake, she really should scramble out of the bed and put some distance between her and the man she'd slept with last night. It wasn't entirely necessary that she be here. She could've retired to the other bedroom last night—but Kadir had still been mostly out of it when she'd put him to bed, and she'd been half-afraid that if she left him here alone, in the morning he'd be gone as if his appearance at the kitchen door last night had been nothing more than a dream, or the magical answer to a heartfelt wish.

But this morning he remained very real.

Kadir scooted closer to her, and she did not back away from the blatant advance. He wrapped one arm around her, and she took a deep breath that filled her lungs with his scent as she swayed very slightly in his direction. One of her hands settled against his bare midsection. Yes, he was warmer than he had been last night, fresh out of the sea and stunned by the explosion. He felt more solid, more real, more *safe*. Her hand remained there, pressed lightly to his muscled abdomen. It was a nice, comforting reminder that he was real and alive and *here*.

"I thought you were dead," she whispered. "I saw the yacht explode, and in my mind you were already on it and…" The rest caught in her throat. "What happened? Were you thrown clear?" She didn't see how that was possible, but Kadir was here, so obviously something had happened.

"I wasn't on the yacht when it exploded," he said, his mouth settling near her throat, there where shoulder curved into neck. A quiet quiver passed through her body in response to that contact. "I had a change of heart and was returning to you."

In order to try again to seduce her? In order to tell her again that she was not suitable as an aide? At the moment, she didn't care what had made him turn around and come back to her. Turning back had saved his life, and she could only be glad.

"I didn't want you to think that I didn't care about you," he said softly. "Even though I knew it was best if you remained angry with me, even though I purposely pushed you away, I didn't want to leave things between us unpleasant. I do care for you, Cassandra."

Was he saying that because they were in bed together, dressed in nothing more than skimpy nightclothes that could be easily discarded? Or was he sincere? At this moment she didn't care why he said he cared for her. The words sounded true to her jaded ears, and so she accepted what he said. It was enough, for now.

In trying so hard to be independent and carefree of heart, she'd thrown away a chance at knowing true passion. She wouldn't throw it away again.

She shifted her head and nuzzled Kadir. She tasted his neck, his jaw, and finally brought his mouth to hers and kissed him deeply. Her entire body shuddered, and she instinctively pressed herself more securely against him. This time there was nothing and no one to stop her. No second thoughts, no worry about her heart. It was impossible to guard the heart completely without shutting it down. Turning it off and denying moments like this, in order to remain free of heartbreak, also robbed her of a chance at knowing passion.

She didn't care if Kadir broke her heart, eventually. All she cared about was now. This moment, this touch, this celebration of the fact that he was alive.

And so was she.

The kiss was not desperate, but it was far from sweet. A depth she had never suspected was possible arose and grew in the meeting of two mouths. The kiss fused Kadir to her in a way that went beyond the physical, beyond the mere meeting of lips and teasing of tongues.

Kadir's hand held her head, fingers speared through her hair. His beard was rough, and at times she felt it scraping across her chin or her cheek, but she didn't care. Their lips barely touched, and then fused together. The kiss was light for a moment, and then it deepened. Her heart beat hard, her blood raced, and as for the flutter…it grew swiftly to something well beyond a mere flutter. She had never wanted anything so much….

"Cassandra," Kadir whispered, pulling his mouth from hers for only a moment.

If he asked her if she was sure about what was about to happen, she might falter, so she didn't allow him to say more. She spread her fingers through his curls and pulled his mouth to hers, tight and firm. She slipped her tongue deep into his mouth and wrapped one leg over his hip. He was right there, with nothing but a few scraps of fabric between them. Was she sure? *Yes,* more sure than she had ever been.

He slipped his fingers just barely into the waistband of the pajamas she'd borrowed from Lexie's chest of drawers. Fingers brushed against skin no man had ever touched before, and she quivered. She quivered intensely, and a sound crept up her throat and escaped as something near a moan. It was a sound she had never made before.

Kadir's hand slipped lower, and she found herself arching slightly to bring him closer. Closer and closer…

When the phone rang, she jumped, but she did not roll over. She kissed Kadir more deeply, then drew her well-kissed lips away and whispered against his mouth, "They'll call back."

He made a sound much like her little moan, and answered, "Or else they will come here to the cottage to check on you. We don't want that." The phone had rung three times. Four. Five. Another kiss. Six. With a groan, Cassandra rolled over and snatched at the receiver.

"Hello!"

She scooted slightly farther away from Kadir. "Oh, hi, Mum."

"Is everything all right?" The voice on the phone held all the concern of a woman for her daughter. More than anyone, Piper Klein understood how much Cassandra had come to care for Kadir. What timing. Almost-psychic Mum strikes again.

"Yes. I…you woke me up." Cassandra sat up, not quite at ease to remain entangled with Kadir while she spoke to her mother.

"I'm sorry. You're usually up so early, I just assumed you'd be awake by now. I know you had a late night, and…oh, honey, I'm so sorry. We can come up there to stay with you for a few days, or we can meet you in Silverton."

She'd made the same offer last night, and Cassandra had declined. She did so again. "No, thank you. That's not necessary. Ms. Dunn is urging me to get back to work as soon as possible. I think she believes staying busy will help. I might head back this afternoon and take her advice." She hated lying to her mother, but what choice did she have? "I'm fine, Mum, truly I am."

The bed creaked and undulated as Kadir rolled away and off the other side. He headed for the bathroom, closing the door behind him.

Cassandra turned her back on the bathroom door.

She wanted, so much, to tell her mother that Kadir was alive. But she couldn't do that. Not only would it mean breaking her word to Kadir, it could very well put Piper Klein into a dangerous situation. In a lowered voice she said, "You were right when you said I've been too cautious. I should've thrown myself at Sheik Kadir the moment he walked off the plane and those flips and flutters appeared and surprised me. I should've told him the first night that I knew when I first saw him that he was the one for me."

"You've always been prudent."

"I've always been afraid," Cassandra replied. She heard the shower begin to run. She could speak more loudly now, since Kadir was occupied and the shower would mask her words even more than the closed door, but she didn't. Her voice remained soft. "I've always been afraid of being hurt the way Lexie has been, so many times. She was always so desperately heart-broken when an affair or a marriage ended, and seeing her that way scared me. I only want what you and Daddy have."

"One day you'll have it." The promise sounded less than authentic, like a mother telling a small child that one day her Prince Charming will arrive on a white horse and after that there would be happily ever after.

"Maybe," Cassandra answered. "But I won't get it by being afraid all the time and not even allowing myself to try. I suppose I could take a few lessons from Lexie."

"Let's not take this to extremes!"

Cassandra laughed lightly at her mother's hint of panic. "I'm still me, Mum. I'm just…" Different. Bolder. Less afraid. "God, I feel like I'm a hundred years older than I was this time yesterday."

Piper Klein sighed into the phone. "That's it. I'm coming to Leonia today."

"Don't do that. I might not even be here this afternoon. I really might decide to take Ms. Dunn up on her offer of burying myself in work." She told her mother again that she was fine, and then she hung up the phone and fell back onto the bed, wishing Kadir was still here with her.

The shower continued to run on the other side of the bathroom door. Kadir was in there, naked. She knew he wanted her. He had always wanted her. She'd been the one who'd put on the brakes, time and time again. She'd been the one to insist that their relationship remain professional.

She walked toward the bathroom door, unbuttoning the pajama top as she went. These pajamas had been a Christmas gift from Mum, but apparently they were too conservative for Lexie, because until last night they'd never been worn. They still had that crisp fold of newness, and until last night the tag had still been on the pants. No, Lexie slept in sexy lingerie—or nothing at all. She knew how to seduce a man. Cassandra did not. Her mouth was dry with nervousness, and she was a woman who never allowed herself a moment of nervousness.

She opened the bathroom door without knocking. Kadir's slightly distorted figure beyond the steamy shower glass was intriguing and arousing. He was tall and lean, but not too lean. He had nicely honed muscles and a pleasantly masculine shape, and what she'd felt in the bed had only been a hint of the possibilities that lay ahead. She allowed the unbuttoned pajama top to slip off and hit the floor.

Before she could take a step toward the shower and the naked man within it, a deep voice stopped her with a single word.

"Don't."

Puzzled, she stood in the middle of the bathroom, half-dressed. "Don't what?"

"Don't step into this shower with me," Kadir said. His voice was just loud enough for her to be sure she heard every word clearly. "Don't have sex with me simply because you're relieved I'm not dead."

"Kadir, I'm not…"

"And don't lie. Not to me and not to yourself. It's easy to get caught up in what I want when you're kissing me, when your body is warm against mine, but stepping away gave me time to think. You have resisted me until now. What's changed?"

She recognized that whatever might've happened if her mother hadn't called likely wasn't going to happen now. "Maybe you think too much," she argued.

What might've been a rough, humorless laugh that didn't last long rumbled from the shower. "I wish I didn't have to think at all, but I have no choice. There is one man in the world I can trust, and I've not yet decided how I might get in touch with him without alerting others to my survival." In a lower voice he added, "There is one woman in the world I can trust. If I sleep with her in her moment of weakness, if I take advantage of her obvious relief that I find myself still among the living, will she come to regret what should never be cause for regret?"

"I won't…"

"You don't know, not today. Not this morning, when it seems there's no one else in the world but the two of us." She heard his remorse, and it made her sad. "We're not alone in the world, Cassandra, and before much longer it's going to come crashing in on us with a vengeance. When that happens, will you still feel as you do now?"

"I could promise you I won't have regrets, but you're not going to believe me, are you?"

"Not today," he said softly.

"All right." Cassandra picked up the pajama top from the floor and carried it into the bedroom, closing the bathroom door behind her. She didn't cry. Tears were for death and destruction and heartbreak, not simple failures. That's what this was, after all. A failure. She was a failure at seduction.

She slipped on the pajama top and buttoned it as she left the bedroom. A large breakfast was called for, and she didn't remember what Lexie had in her kitchen. Surely the makings for pancakes or muffins were in the cupboard.

No, she didn't cry, and she didn't get a little angry. Her mind whirled with possibilities and plans and scenarios. Maybe she was a failure as a seductress, but she hadn't had any practice in the past so she had to start from scratch. Since she had no doubts that Kadir wanted her, she didn't think the task would be too terribly difficult.

And even though she had failed, thus far, she wasn't about to give up. What she'd wanted had changed, but her personality had not. She was still a sledgehammer, and she still went after everything she wanted with fierce determination.

A heavenly scent assaulted Kadir as he left the bedroom behind. Sweet and cinnamony, the smells of something baking filled the house. He'd been afraid that Cassandra would take offense at his refusal of her proposition, but that was a chance he had to take. A woman didn't change her mind overnight. Well, sometimes she did, but it was never a well-thought-out change of intentions. It was nice that she was relieved to find him alive, but he didn't want Cassandra to sleep with him this morning, and lament doing so by the time night fell once again.

But since he heard cheerful humming drifting from the kitchen, along with the heavenly smell, she had apparently survived his refusal quite well.

She still wore her pajamas, he saw as he stepped into the kitchen. He himself had found some clothes in the spare bedroom closet, which came very close to fitting him, as the fishing clothes had done yesterday. Worn blue jeans, a green cotton button-up shirt and worn deck shoes would do until he could buy something new.

With what, he did not know. He was wealthy man, but he had no cash on him and he was believed to be dead.

"Do you like muffins?" Cassandra asked as she peeked into the oven. "Hmmm. Almost done. Another three or four minutes, I'd guess." She stood and turned, and when she saw his face her smile faded and he actually saw her twitch. "Good heavens, what have you done?"

Kadir laid a hand on his smooth cheek. "I shaved." He did not tell her that the idea of shaving had originally come from glimpsing the redness of her cheeks and chin after they'd kissed. He did not want to hurt her, not even in that small way. "I would like those who believe me to be dead to continue in that belief. After we eat those muffins, I would like for you to cut my hair. With the physical changes and other certain precautions, no one will recognize me."

Once her shock faded, she smiled in obvious approval. "I like it. You look younger without the beard, and—" she cocked her head slightly and studied him well "—different. The clothes make a big difference, too. Once we cut your hair, only someone who knows you very well will recognize you."

He didn't bother to tell Cassandra that it was likely someone who knew him very well who had been the one to betray him.

She walked toward him, still seeming not at all disturbed by what he had counted on as being a bone of contention. Most women did not take rejection so well. Maybe she'd recognized that he was right in calling an end to what had almost happened in her bed. That was always possible. Not likely, but possible. Cassandra Klein was a sensible woman, after all.

Upon reaching him, she lifted her hand and touched his cheek. "Nice." And then she went up on her toes and laid her mouth over his.

She kissed him. Her arms did not go around him; his did not go around her. Still, his body responded. His very world tilted.

And then she dropped away, with a smile on her face. "No need to look at me that way, Kadir. I had to know what it was like to kiss you without the beard, now didn't I?"

It sounded like a woman's convoluted reasoning, but he didn't dare to argue with her.

As if nothing had happened, she said, "The muffins are ready. I hope you're hungry. A woman can't just make two or three muffins, so we might as well eat hearty."

If the kiss was Cassandra's idea of revenge, if it was her way of tossing his well-meant refusal back in his face and making him taste regret all over again—then she was winning this particular battle.

So Kadir did the only thing he could think of. As he

sat down at the small breakfast table with coffee and milk and a plate of muffins, he said, "Last night you had a gun." He reached for a warm muffin. "I want it."

Chapter 9

Kadir handled Lexie's six-shooter in a way that assured Cassandra he was more familiar with weapons than she. He'd found the proper tools for cleaning the gun in a kit that was stored in the back of the hallway closet. Extra ammunition was stashed there, too, and he had gladly retrieved it. He'd very precisely and smoothly inspected and cleaned the six-shooter and loaded it. He was now examining the weapon once again.

As if he felt her gaze, Kadir lifted his head and looked squarely at her. She still wasn't accustomed to the smooth cheeks and chin, but she liked the look. Losing the beard changed his appearance drastically. Once his hair was cut, no one would recognize him.

Well, he'd likely need dark sunglasses to make the disguise complete. She'd recognize those eyes anywhere.

"You're staring," he said, only slightly accusing.

"Sorry. I've never before seen a diplomat who was so comfortable and capable with guns."

He shrugged and finished putting the weapon together. "I wasn't always a diplomat."

To be sure. Kadir was unlike any other ambassador she'd ever met, and since she had decided he was the one man in the world for her, should she ask for more details? On the one hand, he might feel such questions were too personal, not proper for a diplomat and his aide. He remained leery of her this morning, suspicious of her motives. If she pushed too hard, he was very likely to go off and handle this alone. She wanted to help; she needed to be involved.

But on the other hand, she wanted to know Kadir as deeply and completely as possible, and she didn't know how much time they had for such luxuries.

"You were a soldier?"

"Yes," he answered briefly.

"What made you decide to become an ambassador?"

The gun was reassembled, cleaned and readied to Kadir's satisfaction. He placed it on the table before him, and studied her with eyes that sometimes seemed to see too much. "If you really want to know, I'll tell you while you cut my hair."

They went into the hallway bathroom, which was slightly larger than the one off the master bedroom, and Kadir sat on the edge of the tub. Cassandra ordered him to remove his shirt, and he did. When that was done, she tossed a towel over his shoulders and began to cut. Cautiously, carefully, she cut his curling hair.

Just as she was about to prompt him to begin, he spoke.

"I had a sister," he said. "Her name was Amala, and she was three years older than I."

Kadir spoke of his sister in the past tense. That, and the tone of Kadir's voice, told Cassandra that Amala was dead. She thought of how hard it would be to lose one of her sisters. There was no need to tell him she was sorry, that she felt his pain. He knew.

"At the age of twenty Amala fell in love, but my father refused to give his permission for the marriage she desired. He arranged a marriage with a more suitable man, a wealthier, more powerful, more influential man. Amala didn't care for this man who was chosen by our father, but she had no choice but to do as was directed. That was the custom."

It was a barbaric custom, but she didn't point that out. Again, Kadir knew.

"Amala was a good daughter, so she married the man our father chose, and for a while she seemed content enough. Not happy. I don't believe I ever saw happiness in her after she was wed, but neither did I believe her to be unhappy. If I had known…" He took a deep breath and exhaled slowly. "But I did not, and it does no good to wish to step into the past and correct our mistakes. We can only move forward."

"That's true," Cassandra said gently.

"He killed her."

The news came without warning, and Cassandra flinched.

"Her husband caught her communicating with the man she had once desired to take as her husband, and he murdered her. He wrapped his hands around her neck and choked the life out of her, and crammed the letter she'd been writing down her throat. When that was done, he claimed that the taking of life was his due as husband to an unfaithful wife. As if to write a letter to an old friend was infidelity. As if Amala belonged to him, and it was his right to extinguish her life."

"I'm so sorry." Cassandra stopped cutting and laid her hands on Kadir's shoulders. Yes, he knew, but still she wanted to say the words to comfort him. He laid a hand over hers, briefly, and then dropped that hand as if it were not a good idea to touch her in even such a simple way. "That must have been very difficult for your family."

"Yes, it was. We wanted justice, but there was no justice for Amala. The taking of her life by a wronged husband was considered appropriate in the eyes of the law."

"What happened to him?"

For a moment Kadir was silent, and Cassandra cut a longish strand of hair. Her fingers brushed his scalp, ruffling newly cut curls and offering a bit of silent comfort.

"Nothing," he said softly as her fingers raked across the back of his head. "My father became ill and never recovered. He died a year later. My mother, whose joy died with her only daughter, passed away less than six months later. But Zahid went on as if nothing had changed. For him, I suppose nothing *had* changed."

"Zahid Bin-Asfour, the man who's trying to kill you?"

"Yes. There have been so many times when I've wished that I'd followed my first instinct and put a bullet in his brain when I heard the news. He left Kahani a few months after he murdered my sister, even though he had broken no law. I almost followed him. It would not have been easy, but I could have tracked Zahid down and killed him in such a way that no one would ever have known I did it. I was twenty-one years old, a soldier who believed that such vengeance was not only possible but just."

"But you didn't."

"No." For a moment he was silent, and Cassandra suspected he was finished, at least for now. And then he continued. "I wanted Zahid dead, but more than that I wanted the country I call home to be a place where such things don't happen. To transform the very customs of a people takes a long time. It takes handshakes and compromise and perseverance. Big changes don't occur with the pulling of a trigger…but there are days when I wish I had made that choice, instead of the one that brought me to this place in time." He squirmed a little, obviously uncomfortable. "It is no longer acceptable in Kahani for a man to take his wife's life as if she were a possession of no importance to be done away with on a whim."

"And you did that," she said in a lowered voice. "You brought about that change."

"Not alone, but I was there." Kadir became silent again, and this time he was truly done.

Cassandra decided not to push for more. She had questions, but he'd told enough of the story for now. She continued to cut his hair, snipping the strands shorter and shorter, watching as the short black strands curled gently.

"Someone in town might've seen something," Kadir said as she was taking a few last snips. "I'll go to town and listen to what the locals are saying."

"*We'll* go to town," Cassandra corrected. "Tomorrow would be better than today. About half the shops are closed on Sunday, and today the town will be crawling with investigators, anyway. Besides, you need to rest today. You're recovering very well, but your arm was cut deeply and you nearly drowned."

"I'll go alone. I don't wish to involve you in this," Kadir argued.

"I'm already involved," she said angrily. "In case you have forgotten, both of us might've been on that yacht when it exploded. If I had accepted your dinner invitation, we'd both be fish bait right now. Someone tried to kill me, and that means I'm definitely involved."

He turned his head and looked up at her. Wow, what a change a shave and a haircut made. Kadir looked not only younger, but was actually approaching pretty. "I've always known that my dedication to bringing change to Kahani might cost me my life. It's a sacrifice I'm willing to make. I am not, however, willing to sacrifice your life."

Cassandra didn't so much as pause before answering. "That's very nice, but I'm not staying here while you go to town on a fishing expedition of a different sort. I don't come to Leonia often, but I know people in town and they know me. If you want all the gossip, you have to be part of the in crowd. Or at least a sister to someone who's a part of the in crowd."

"But…"

"Besides, I know where the keys to Lexie's motorcycle are kept."

His eyes lit up. "Motorcycle?"

"Motorcycle."

"That is not a motorcycle!" Kadir insisted. "It's a motor *scooter!* And it's *pink!*"

"So?" Cassandra responded with a decided lack of outrage.

"How are we supposed to remain inconspicuous on a pink motor scooter?"

"Don't be a baby."

"A baby?"

Cassandra's smile wiped away almost every trace

of Kadir's outrage at the knowledge that his only mode of transport lacked power and was obviously made for a woman.

He'd taken her advice and rested most of the day yesterday. Sleep had claimed him often during the day. He hadn't realized how exhausted his body was, but Cassandra had known. She had recognized his weakness when he had not, because she knew him so well. How oddly disconcerting.

During the day she'd tended him often as he'd rested, feeding him, changing the bandage on his arm, touching him in casual ways that felt anything but *casual*.

Kadir was still determined to keep his distance from Cassandra. Last night he had attempted to sleep in the guest room, but when he'd awakened in the night he'd found Cassandra's body close to his. They both wore nightclothes, and the touching involved during the night was incidental and casual, but still…to sleep with her and not have her in all ways was a kind of torture.

She was still stunned and relieved that he'd survived the explosion that had been intended to take his life— and hers. He didn't want her to sleep with him because she suffered from a type of posttraumatic stress. That was the only explanation he could come to, since she'd denied him vigorously on Friday night and again on Saturday night, and then openly offered herself to him Sunday morning.

One day she would thank him for being so circumspect. Today was not that day.

"I suppose we could walk…." Cassandra began.

"No." Walking to town and back would be a waste of precious time. One commodity he did not have to spare was time.

They had a plan, of sorts. His role was to be that of a boyfriend who'd come from Silverton in the dead of night to comfort Cassandra after her close call. Kadir was to remain as quiet as possible while she pumped the locals for information. Even though he looked very different—wearing another man's clothes, with his hair cut short and his facial hair gone—his voice remained the same. Cassandra would ask the questions; he would listen. There should be no danger in today's excursion. Everyone thought he was dead.

She had taken one of his ancestor's names which was a part of his full name—Yusef—and shortened it to Joe. That's what she would call him, if introductions were called for. Joe, he of the pink motor scooter.

When they returned to the cottage this afternoon, she would make a call to the Kahani Ministry of Foreign Affairs and try to get a message to Sharif.

Sharif, who had loved Amala and probably still did. Sharif, who would gladly die before throwing in his lot with Zahid Bin-Asfour.

It would have to be an innocuous message, since they could trust no one else with the secret that Kadir lived. Not yet. They could only hope that Sharif would return the call.

Kadir scoffed at the ridiculous scooter, and took the helmet Cassandra offered. At least it wasn't pink, but instead was black. Hers, however…

Cassandra didn't immediately put the helmet on her head. She had something to say. At moments like this she was endearingly transparent, as if she had never known a moment of deception. Coming from a world where deception was a part of everyday life, this trait was one of the things he most admired about her.

"There's something I think I should tell you, even though I'm not supposed to tell you, or anyone else. It might have nothing to do with this, but I can't be sure." She wrinkled her nose, ever so slightly. "I just feel like you should know everything before we get started."

"I will keep anything you tell me in strictest confidence."

"I know, but…I've never shared proprietary information with anyone before." She looked at him with those amazingly intelligent and changeable gray eyes. "It feels a little like betrayal, but if I don't tell I might be betraying *you* and I can't do that."

"Anything you tell me stays here, in this shed." Morning sun slanted through the open doors, touching Cassandra's ponytail and making her glow with an unreal beauty. "I would never betray you in any way."

She hesitated, but not for long. "You believe that Zahid Bin-Asfour is behind the attempts on your life."

"I have no doubt," Kadir said.

Cassandra nodded, as if she understood. "It isn't widely known, but Prince Reginald met with Bin-Asfour just a few days before he was murdered. Investigators are trying to find out more about the meeting, in case it might have something to do with the prince's death, but no one's sure why they met."

"Drugs," Kadir said. "Zahid made a delivery, and he remained in the prince's company for several hours. Our own security council learned of the meeting weeks ago. Zahid makes much of his money through the sale of narcotics. Usually he does not participate in those dealings himself, but when royalty is involved…" He shrugged. "Illegal drugs were delivered to your prince in exchange for money or promises. I suspect there was more to the meeting than a simple sale, but it's likely we will never know."

Cassandra didn't chastise him for not sharing this information with her sooner. Instead she nodded, satisfied that he was armed with all the information she had to share.

"One more thing," she said, tucking the pink helmet under one arm and looking him squarely in the eye, in that fearless way she had. "Can I have a kiss for luck?"

He should say no and keep some distance between them, but this was one request he could not deny her.

As Cassandra had suspected, the village was buzzing with news of the explosion. Many people spoke of seeing the sheik on Saturday, never suspecting that before the end of the day he'd be blown to bits.

They were all anxious to talk to her, since she'd been with Kadir on his tour of Leonia. No one questioned her presentation of Kadir as "Joe," her silent boyfriend from Silverton. He didn't look like a sheik, in ratty hand-me-downs from Stanley—or one of Lexie's ex-husbands who'd left a few things behind. With the haircut and shave, and the dark glasses hiding his eyes—it was possible *she* wouldn't have recognized him if she hadn't witnessed the transformation for herself.

For the time being, she didn't even think about what she wanted from Kadir on a personal level. This was business, and she had always been able to throw herself into the task at hand at the expense of all else. She did that now. They didn't learn much, but apparently everyone in Leonia had been outside their homes and shops at the time of the explosion and had seen it firsthand.

It was late afternoon when the photographer from the

Quiz found Cassandra and Kadir sitting at an outdoor café, sipping coffee and comparing notes. Sadly, they had learned nothing that would help them discover who had been behind the explosion. A number of investigators from Silverton were still in town, questioning everyone who'd claimed to witness the explosion. They'd had all day yesterday to interrogate the citizenry, but since just about everyone in town claimed to have seen the explosion, the complete investigation would take days—perhaps even weeks. So far Cassandra had been able to avoid the investigators, but she knew they'd catch up with her sooner or later. She'd tell them the same story she'd told the local officer. That was the truth as she'd known it at the time, so it wasn't exactly a lie.

The photographer who had followed them to Leonia on Saturday very boldly walked up, introduced himself as Simon York and asked if he could join them. Then he sat before they had a chance to respond. Ignoring the insignificant Joe, he offered a hand across the table. Cassandra ignored the hand.

"What do you want?" she asked coolly.

"Now, don't be that way, Cassie. I know you're probably upset about that little picture in the *Quiz* last week, but I was just doing my job."

Since York had been ignoring Kadir, the photographer was surprised when a large hand shot out and grasped the wrist of the offered hand.

"She's Ms. Klein to you," Kadir said in a lowered voice.

"Sorry," York said. When Kadir released his hold, the photographer rubbed his wrist and frowned at Cassandra. "I didn't take you for the type who'd go for a thug."

"Joe's very protective," she said. "If you behave

yourself you won't have any problem with him. Now, why are you here?"

The photographer leaned onto the table, listing slightly away from Kadir. "I was taking shots of the sunset Saturday," he whispered. "I got a few perspectives that included the yacht. A man crept into the far right side of my view, but I wasn't worried about that. I figured if the photo was a good one I'd just crop him out. He stood there and watched until the yacht exploded, and then he turned away." York paused for effect. "He was smiling."

"You got a shot of his face?" Kadir asked.

"Yes." York clearly did not want to include "Joe" in the conversation, so Cassandra gave a little wave of her fingers, and Kadir leaned back in his chair to observe.

"Have you told the investigators?" Cassandra asked.

"No." York sounded horrified. "If I do they'll confiscate all the film. I can't have that, now, can I? It isn't as if knowing that man was watching will bring the sheik back, right? My developing lab is back in Silverton. I didn't want to wait, but I'm afraid if I go home I'll miss something here. There's no telling what might happen next! I left the film at the local photographer's shop. The old man there said he'd have them ready in—" York checked his watch "—a little less than one hour."

"Why are you telling me this?"

York smiled. "I just take pictures at the moment, that's true, and I love my camera. But I'm quite a writer, too. If I have the photographs and an exclusive interview with the woman who watched Al-Nuri ride out to his death, a woman who had been connected to him romantically in a previous story in the *Quiz,* I'll be set. My name will be made overnight." His grin widened. "I'll be a *star,* Ms. Klein."

The idea of giving this man anything repulsed her, but… "I want to see the photos as soon as they're available."

"Of course." York cut a suspicious glance to Kadir. "Does he have to come along?"

"Yes," Cassandra said, calling up a tone that left no room for argument.

York ordered his own cup of coffee, and he carried the conversation. He had spoken to the same people Cassandra and Kadir had interviewed. No one else had mentioned the man York had caught in his photograph. Still, once they had the picture in hand, someone would surely recognize him. This was a small village, and even though tourists came and went, they had to stay somewhere, and they had to eat. Someone in Leonia would remember him.

Simon York could already taste what it would be like to be a star.

A few minutes before the photos were supposed to be ready, the three of them left the café. Kadir remained protectively between Cassandra and York. He wanted the photos, but he didn't like or trust York. The distrust and dislike was clear on his transformed face.

York pointed. "There, just beyond the candy shop at the end of the next block."

A puff of black smoke danced from the area York indicated. It was curious, but not alarming. Then another puff followed, blacker and larger than the last one.

It was Kadir who began to run first, his long legs quickly picking up speed. He glanced back and shouted, "Fire!"

Chapter 10

By the time Kadir reached the photo shop, black smoke was drifting from the building in thick clouds, and people had begun to step out of the surrounding shops to see what was happening. On the sidewalk just outside the shop he removed the sunglasses and tossed them aside, took a deep breath to fill his lungs with air and then opened the front door.

Behind him, someone shouted that it wasn't safe to go into the building. With the door open, black smoke billowed out, wafting around and behind Kadir, alarming those who had gathered to watch. Again, someone shouted that they'd called the fire department and it really wasn't safe to go in there.

Kadir didn't retreat. The fire was growing quickly. If anyone remained in this shop, the fire department would likely arrive too late to be of any assistance.

Flames shot ominously from the back room. Kadir stared into the flames for a moment. If the photographs were in that section of the building, it was too late to save them. He glanced at the front counter, which was surrounded by smoke but not yet afire. If the photos were there, waiting for York to pick them up, he didn't see them…and there was no time to search.

An elderly gentleman lay facedown on the floor. It looked as if he'd been trying to reach the door when he'd fallen. Kadir kneeled down beside the fallen white-haired man and placed a finger at a fragile-looking throat. He found a pulse, weak and uncertain, but steady enough. Again, Kadir glimpsed into the fiery back room, wishing he had come here sooner, wishing he could get a glimpse of the man in the photograph, the man who had watched his yacht and all the people on it destroyed.

But the time for those wishes was gone; the film, the photographs, the negatives—if they were in that back room, they had all been destroyed. Kadir lifted the unconscious man off the floor, and as he did so he felt something warm and wet on his shoulder, where the man's head lolled. Blood, no doubt. Apparently this man had not been overcome by smoke, but rather had been bashed over the head so he could not escape.

By the man in the photograph? Almost certainly.

The rescue took mere moments. On the sidewalk the neighboring shopkeepers and customers gathered around. Seven people watched, and they all breathed in relief at the sight of the old man. Cassandra and the photographer hung back, watching expectantly.

"Thank you, sir," a plump woman wearing a chocolate-stained apron said as Kadir gently laid the injured man on the sidewalk, well away from the smoky entrance to the fiery shop. She touched gentle fingers to the bloody patch of gray hair. "Poor dear, did he fall trying to get away from the fire?"

"I believe so, yes," Kadir said, lying easily as he retrieved the sunglasses he'd tossed to the sidewalk before entering the shop. Cassandra had said they were a necessary part of his disguise, so he slipped them on.

All eyes were on him, and in the distance sirens wailed. The last thing he needed was to spend the rest of the day being interviewed and thanked. The investigators would expect a last name, and proof that "Joe" was who he claimed to be. It crossed his mind that he could run back into the shop for a few moments to search for the photos, but since the old man had been hit on the head—not accidentally injured trying to escape—it was certain the photos had been destroyed, or taken. "I wish I could stay but I must go. Please see to the old fellow until proper assistance arrives."

"Yes, of course, but…" As Kadir made his way toward Cassandra, the plump woman asked, "Who are you? William will surely want to know who saved him."

"My name is Joe," Kadir answered.

"Joe *who?*" a customer asked, raising her voice as Kadir increased his step.

"Just Joe," he called. He took Cassandra's arm and walked quickly away from the scene. "The pictures have been destroyed or stolen," he said in a lowered voice. He turned his gaze to the photographer. "Can you describe the man you saw?"

Distraught over losing his precious photos and chance at stardom, York sighed in disgust. "I suppose. But what difference does it make now?"

Kadir's patience was near an end. He could drag the annoying photographer into the nearest alleyway and force him to tell all he knew. He could, but he would not. "If you can lead me to the man who watched the explosion and then walked away with a smile on his face, I will give you an exclusive story that will indeed make you a celebrity. Everyone in Silvershire, and well beyond, will know your name."

"Why should I believe a thug like you?" York asked sullenly.

"If I were a thug, I could very easily beat the information out of you," Kadir said calmly. "You are small, and without an excess of toned muscles in your upper body. It would not be difficult."

For the first time, York looked at Kadir with analytical eyes. "Where are you from? Not Silverton, I'd guess."

Kadir glanced at the little fellow. "An exclusive, in exchange for everything you know about the man you saw."

"Sure, *Joe.* Why not? What have I got to lose at this point?"

They made two more turns, and found themselves on a narrow, deserted street. There York stopped. He leaned against a quaint stone building and began to give a description. Kadir listened carefully. Most of the information was useless. The man was of average height, appeared to be Arabic, dressed in an expensive black suit and was clean-shaven.

"That's it," York said with hands offered palms up. It was an expression of total surrender. "Now, what about my exclusive?"

"After I find him," Kadir said as he took Cassandra's arm.

"What?" York followed them down the sidewalk. "That wasn't part of the deal."

"How do I know you told the truth?" Kadir asked. "You do not strike me as being the most scrupulous of men. When I know what you told me was true, then you'll get your story."

"Who are you, anyway?" the small man persisted. "You're no *boyfriend,* I know that much. You're not from Silverton, either, I'd wager, and English is not your first language. A spy, maybe? That in itself will make for interesting reading. Sexy Secretary Spotted in Company of Stupid Spy, or something along those…"

Kadir moved fast, spinning, catching York by the throat and pressing him against the nearest stone wall.

"Sorry about the stupid thing," York croaked. "I'm just…" He struggled to take a breath. "Come on, give me something, man. I lost all my pictures. You can't blame me for being in a bad mood."

Kadir leaned in close. "If you ever again write a word about Ms. Klein without first obtaining her permission, you will regret it." He lowered his voice. "And she's not a secretary."

He released the small man, and this time when Kadir and Cassandra walked away, York did not follow. When they were several steps down the unevenly paved street, Kadir took Cassandra's arm. She listed in closer, and he was undeniably relieved and glad to have her body so close to his.

But now was not the time for such a simple pleasure. "I believe the man York saw worked for me."

Kadir wasn't sure that the man York had seen was one of his employees, but he suspected it might be true.

After all, how many well-dressed Arabs had been in Leonia on Saturday evening? No one had known they were coming here, and only the one photographer had followed. Still, he did not want to discuss the matter until he had more information. Cassandra tried to do her own calculations. Average height—that ruled out Jibril and Haroun, who were both very tall. Clean-shaven—not Sayyid or Hakim. Who did that leave? Tarif, Fahd and the crew she had never met.

Would anyone from the yacht's crew dress in a suit?

She also had to consider that the man York had seen might've shaved that very afternoon, and perhaps his idea of average height was not the same as her own. In truth, they had eliminated no one.

Cassandra called the Kahani Ministry of Defense and left a message for Sharif Al-Asad—who was not available. The message had to be simple, and could not even hint that Kadir was alive. Cassandra left the message that she was a friend of Sheik Kadir's and would very much like to speak with Sharif to relay her deepest sympathies on the loss of his friend.

She left the phone number to Lexie's cottage with a surly man, hoping that Sharif would return her call. She wasn't at all convinced that the message would be passed along.

Dinner was soup without conversation. Kadir was lost in thought, occasionally frowning and always distant. He was understandably distraught at the possibility that the assassin was one of his own, and just as distraught that he could not identify the culprit. Tomorrow they would go to town once again, and this time the questions would be different. More specific.

But for tonight they needed to rest and wait for a phone call that might or might not come.

Kadir settled on the couch to watch the evening news. His assassination was still a major story, even though two days had passed since the explosion. Better tidings were also shared, once the announcer had passed on the fact that there were no leads as to who might be responsible for the sheik's assassination. Princess Amelia was expecting a baby. Lord Carrington and his wife had been trying to keep that bit of intelligence a secret for a while longer, but someone in the know had leaked the story.

Someone in the know was always willing to leak this story or that. Simon York would be devastated that he'd missed yet another scoop.

Cassandra sat next to Kadir, and when the news turned to insignificant weather and local interest, she leaned into him. "There's nothing to do now but wait," she said.

"That's true," Kadir said in a lowered voice.

"You might as well relax tonight." Her fingers traced the bandage beneath the fabric of his shirt. "I should probably change your bandage."

"It's fine," Kadir said absently. "The cut is healing nicely."

She sighed and laid her head on his shoulder. It was very nice, just to sit this way—close and connected and warm. But it wasn't enough, and Cassandra had decided that Lexie's way could not be her way.

"I've been trying to seduce you for almost two days, now, and my efforts have been wasted," she said bluntly.

"Cassandra, don't—"

"Let me finish, please."

She took his silence as agreement.

"It's not surprising that I'm a failure as a seductress,"

she admitted. "Hints and flirting and girlish smiles are not my style at all. I prefer to be direct in all matters, and perhaps I should be direct in this one, as well."

She slipped one possessive arm around Kadir's mid-section. "I've never held a man like this. I've never kissed a man the way I've kissed you, I've never cuddled and kissed and felt as if my heart was about to burst out of my chest. Until the night you were injured, I'd never slept with a man, not in any sense of the word." She took a deep breath and made the big confession. "I'm a virgin."

Kadir sighed. "All the more reason—"

"You said I could finish what I have to say without interruption."

Another sigh. "Proceed."

This was better than hints and not-so-subtle brushes of her hands on Kadir's body. This was not a game; it was her life. "For as long as I can remember, I've been waiting for something special. A feeling. A bond." She might as well say it. "Love."

She felt Kadir's body stiffen, but she didn't release her hold on him, and he didn't push her away.

"My mother always told me that the first time she saw my father she knew he was the one for her. Her heart fluttered, and her stomach flipped over and she *knew* in an instant. I've waited for that feeling since the age of fourteen, Kadir, and when I saw you walk off the plane…"

"Don't," he whispered.

"I felt it for you," she continued. "Maybe what I feel is purely physical and in time it will pass, fading away or simply disappearing. Maybe it's more than physical, but in the end what I feel and what I want won't matter. I don't know. Maybe I'm not supposed to know. Maybe I'm just supposed to accept what I feel and trust that what comes is meant to come. All I know is I want you, and you have become annoyingly determined to fight me at every turn."

Kadir placed a hand in her hair. "You fought against any attraction for me from the moment I first saw you. When you changed your mind so suddenly, what was I supposed to believe? More than anything, I don't want to hurt you. I don't want you to regret a moment of our time together."

"I've been fighting my feelings for you since that first moment because you didn't arrive in the way in which I'd always imagined." It was an embarrassing admission. "The arrival of love should be neat and tidy, or so I thought. I should meet a suitable man—*the* suitable man—at a social function or on the beach, at the market or in the museum as we both studied the same painting." It all sounded silly now. Who could plan their life to the last detail? What was life without a few surprises? "It shouldn't arrive in a way which forces me to choose between my career and the love I've always wanted. Love should be neat, I decided, not messy and complicated. So I pushed the flutter aside and dedicated myself to my work, and tried very hard not to like you too much.

"And then I watched the yacht explode, and I knew that to set aside something so special and extraordinary was a mistake." She rose up slowly and laid her mouth on Kadir's neck. He tasted so good, and she wanted this and more. "Enough explanation. I want you to make love to me. If that doesn't happen, if I turn my back on something so exquisite, it will be like passing by a beautiful flower and not taking the time to smell it, or closing my eyes when a breathtaking sunset appears because I know it won't last. If you really and truly don't want me,

I'll understand. But I think you do." She laid her hand over the erection that strained his jeans. "I think you do."

Kadir's arms encircled her, and she knew that tonight he wouldn't deny her. "I can make you no promises beyond tonight, Cassandra. We don't know what tomorrow will bring."

"I'm not looking at tomorrow. Just tonight. I waited for you, Kadir, I waited a long time. I don't want to wait anymore."

He threaded his fingers in her hair, held her head gently and kissed her. Deeply and completely, he kissed her. One hand slipped beneath her T-shirt and then simply laid there against her skin as if he were trying to absorb her. Could he feel her heart pounding? Could he feel the rush of blood that made her light-headed and shaky?

She had used the L-word, but Kadir had not. Maybe he didn't love her at all, but wanted her in a purely physical way. Maybe he was afraid of love. It didn't matter. She didn't want to pass up this beautiful moment in the name of keeping her life neat and tidy.

Life wasn't supposed to be neat and tidy, and it took this crisis to teach her that fact.

With a suddenness that startled her, Kadir drew away, ending the kiss. "I wasn't thinking." He moved a strand of hair away from her face, and let his fingertips trail against her cheek. "I don't have any form of birth control with me, and I suspect you don't, either. Leaving you carrying my child is a chance I won't take."

Kadir didn't mention that there was a madman out to kill him. He didn't mention that nine months from now he might be dead, or fighting his battles on the other side of the world. He didn't have to.

Cassandra reached into the back pocket of her borrowed jeans and pulled out a condom that crinkled in its package. "My sister has a box of these under the bathroom sink. Will they do?"

Kadir sighed, in what seemed to be relief, and took the condom from her. "Yes, they will do."

Kadir slipped the condom into his own back pocket, for now. What Cassandra thought was love would soon prove to be purely physical, as she suspected it might. Still, he did not want her to regret revealing her deepest sentiments to him.

Even when they went their separate ways, when she returned to her job and he returned to his—if he survived he didn't want her to regret this.

Kadir unfastened and unzipped Cassandra's jeans. Every move he made was slow, deliberate. His fingers raked across the sensitive, pale skin of her belly, and she trembled. She was so soft. So delicate. More than anything, he did not want to hurt her. He lowered his head and kissed the sensitive flesh, letting his lips linger there for a moment. Kadir didn't take much time to revel in those things in life which were fine, those things which made life worth living. The love of a beautiful woman, even if it was not meant to last, was certainly one of those things.

Cassandra's thighs parted slightly, in a purely instinctive move, and her eyes drifted to a sensual half-closed state. The gray of her eyes was soft now, as soft as the wings of a dove and filled with what she believed to be love. With every stroke of his fingers, with every brush of his lips, the desire in those expressive eyes grew to a new height.

Kadir pulled Cassandra's shirt over her head and tossed it aside, and while she was in that vulnerable state, half-undressed and flushed with desire, he drew her body against his and kissed her deeply. Her mouth met his with hunger and anticipation and desperation. She knew as well as he did that this relationship was temporary. Even in the best of circumstances, they came from two very different worlds. She was a modern woman; modern women were not welcomed in his country, not even now.

No, this was a passing alliance, one that could not last, but it was also deeply meaningful. Cassandra meant more to him than a short-lived liaison, but he couldn't tell her that. Unlike her, he had to guard his innermost thoughts. He could not afford to be so brutally honest, as she had been.

In a matter of minutes, he could take her here on the couch, quickly and fiercely joining and making love to her. Her body trembled, her heart pounded and she was ready in all ways. Kadir had been ready for this woman since the moment he'd seen her, but now…now he wanted her with an unexpected intensity. He had never wanted any other woman quite this way.

But Cassandra had shared everything with him, and he knew this was her first time. Her first time should not be fierce *or* quick. It should be memorable, and those memories should make her smile and shiver for a long time to come.

Her bra was easy to remove with a flick of his fingers and a gentle plucking, which removed the lacy fabric from her breasts. When the undergarment had been tossed aside, he lowered his mouth to take a nipple deep, and Cassandra arched her back and gasped. The sensation was a new one for her. New and powerful and delightful. Her fingers settled in Kadir's newly short-ened curls, and she pulled him closer. He drew her deeper into his mouth, then pulled back and traced the hard nipple with the tip of his tongue. She sighed and shuddered, and he slipped his fingers into her opened jeans.

Pushing her jeans down over her hips, he slipped his fingers between her legs. There she was hot, wet and quivering. He touched her, teased her, aroused her with his mouth on her neck and breasts and his fingers stroking until she was rocking beneath him in a gentle and instinctive sway, trying to draw him closer, deeper.

She whispered his name, her body shook and Kadir rose up to take her mouth with his. His tongue speared into her mouth while his fingertip just barely entered her eager body. Her gasp of surprise at the new sensations caused her entire body to jerk. He kissed her, and one finger brushed against a sensitive nipple while another moved inside her.

Cassandra climaxed with a cry and a lurch, her body undulating against his as the orgasm made her entire body quiver. He held her, and reveled in the release as if it were his own. Even as the tremors faded and she relaxed, she continued to kiss him. The kiss turned gentle. She was satisfied, for the moment.

The way she touched his body told him she would not be satisfied for long. One hand settled over his erection and moved languidly.

"Oh, my," she said when she was capable of speech. "That was definitely worth waiting for." She smiled at him.

Kadir's heart lurched at the sight of that passionate

grin. He dismissed the reaction to one of pure, unsatisfied lust and that wandering hand.

"To bed?" Cassandra said in a soft voice that spoke volumes.

"Yes," Kadir said, drawing away from her and caressing the perfect, half-dressed body she presented to him. Had he ever seen anything more beautiful? Had he ever wanted anything so much?

He promised himself at that moment that even when morning came, Cassandra would not be sorry she'd waited for him.

Chapter 11

There was a new and almost palpable energy in the atmosphere, as if a storm was coming. The very air Cassandra took into her lungs felt different, as if it had been charged with electricity. She'd wondered earlier if she might be shy if the evening progressed as she'd planned, but she was not. There was such joy in making love, there was no time for shyness.

She and Kadir undressed one another as they made their way to the bedroom and the bed, and like the kissing, each and every move seemed very right and natural. Buttons, zippers, the occasional awkward move to rid oneself of an unnecessary article of clothing—it was all as natural as taking a deep breath of the electrified air.

Heaven help her, at the moment she needed Kadir the same way she needed air and the beat of her heart. He was that important, that necessary.

Together they slipped beneath the covers, and Kadir's naked body rested against and then pressed against hers. Legs entwined, and arms encircled. They were so close, so near to coming together in all ways.

He wrapped his arms around her and kissed her, gently and then deeply, as if they were just beginning again. Oh, the feel of his bare body against hers was heavenly. That sensation of skin to skin was a delight in itself, as sensual and exquisite as any touch could ever be.

They kissed and touched, and reveled in the friction of one body against another. Kadir's erection pressed into her hip, but he didn't seem to be in any rush. Time moved very slowly, so that every kiss, every caress, was elongated. Savored. Cassandra's body reached for something new and untasted, but like Kadir she didn't rush. She allowed him to lead her, to guide her in this new, sensual experience.

Kadir touched her with his fingertips, as if learning each of her body's curves and swells. Shoulder, neck, breast, the soft skin above her belly button, the crook of her elbow. He watched the sight of his hand against her skin, by the light of the moon that shone through the bedroom window, as if he felt the same wonder she had discovered.

She watched his face, when she could, wondering at the beauty and mystery of this night, wondering if she truly knew the man behind that handsome face. She did more than look, of course, enjoying an exploration of her own. She traced Kadir's newly shaved jaw, which was sharp and masculine, and then she pressed one hand against the well-muscled chest and feathered her fingers through his short, black curls while pulling his mouth to hers for another, deeper kiss.

After much kissing and touching, she felt bold enough to wrap her fingers around his erection, to stroke and explore and arouse. Kadir's response was to growl low in his throat and roll her onto her back. He swiftly put on the condom and spread her thighs with his knee, and she awaited the joining she wanted so badly. But Kadir didn't immediately give her what she wanted. Instead he touched her, he traced her with his fingers and slipped one finger inside her again.

He was making sure she was ready in all ways. He was thinking of her, even now.

"It's time, Kadir." She wrapped her legs around his hips as he guided himself to her and slowly, very slowly, pushed inside her waiting body. She held her breath, savoring and wondering and, yes, worrying a little. Kadir wasn't accustomed to inexperienced women, she knew that. Would he be disappointed in her? She wanted him to experience the joy that overwhelmed her. There should be no disappointment in this night.

When he was fully and completely inside her, every worry danced out of Cassandra's mind. Her body had already begun to tremble in anticipation. Ripples of pleasurable sensation flickered through her.

Kadir began to move slowly, tenderly, and she moved with him, her hips rising and falling, her heartbeat racing. Her body had not only adjusted to accept his, it welcomed him. They fit together perfectly, in a way that surely no other two people ever had, or ever would. He had been made for her, and she had been made for him.

She quit thinking while he made love to her. Her instincts took over completely, and she found herself holding on, rising higher in order to take him deeper, and they found that rhythm that took them beyond all questioning, all worrying. There was just this, and for now that was fine. It was very fine.

Cassandra gasped and held on to him as the sensations grew, and then she shattered, crying out as the orgasm washed through her body with a force she had not expected. Kadir came with her, his body stiffening and lurching as he drove deeper than before.

Everything slowed, and eventually she was able to breathe again. Her body was exhausted, in a new and entirely wonderful way.

What she felt at this moment, it was so powerful it must be love. What else could fill her heart this way? What else could make her feel as if the entire world had changed just for the two of them? She wanted to tell Kadir that she loved him, but since she had already mentioned the L-word once tonight, and he had not, she decided to leave it alone. For now. If love was meant to come, she suspected there would be no stopping it.

Kadir rolled away from her and headed for the bathroom to dispose of the condom. If he was going to be around for a while, she might want to see about some other form of birth control, something that wouldn't come between them or require that momentary delay. It was unlikely he would be around long enough for her to address that concern. She dismissed the worry from her mind because she didn't want anything, not even thoughts of the future, to spoil what they had tonight.

Very soon, Kadir slipped back into bed, large and warm and naked, and he pulled her body against his. He was silent for a moment, and then he whispered, "Are you all right?"

He was worried about her because this was her first time, because she had been a virgin.

"I'm fine," she said, and then she laughed lightly. "No, I'm more than fine. I've never felt so absolutely wonderful in my entire life."

"Good." Kadir sounded relieved.

They found a comfortable position where arms and legs linked and bodies fit together, and very soon Cassandra fell into a slumber so deep it was unlike any other she had ever known. All was right with the world; her world, at least. It was the dreamless sleep of a well-loved woman.

Kadir remained awake long after Cassandra's breathing fell into the deep, even breathing of sleep.

Cassandra was a beautiful, sensual woman, and he had wanted her beneath him for what seemed like a very long time. Still, he had attempted to be prudent where she was concerned, knowing their future was not only uncertain, it was nonexistent.

Her talk of flowers unsmelled and sunsets unseen had undone him and all his prudence, but that wasn't the only reason he'd so gladly taken her as the lover she'd asked to become.

Betrayal from within had always been a possibility, and still he was greatly disquieted by the possibility that the person responsible for the explosion that had taken many lives had been a comrade, if not a friend. A part of him wanted to believe that York had seen one of Zahid's soldiers, a terrorist who had somehow managed to follow Kadir and his party to Leonia and plant the explosive.

But that was not logical. Logic insisted that the assassin had come to Leonia *with* Kadir, and that he'd had an opportunity to plant a bomb because he was welcomed on the yacht.

Tonight he had allowed himself to dismiss logic and

hide inside Cassandra, for a while, to lose his fears and his anger in her in a way that was undeniably magnificent. She thought what she felt was love, but she'd soon enough discover that was not the case. What she felt was physical. Women often confused the needs of the body with the needs of the heart. Kadir did not.

But this was nice. He liked to feel her lying beside him, to watch her smile and moan and touch with the amazement that can only come with something new and beautiful. Cassandra and all she offered, however temporary, might very well save his sanity while he searched for the truth.

The truth would not be easy to find, but if Zahid had been involved in Prince Reginald's murder, then the proof was likely here, in this country. Uncovering the facts of Zahid's involvement would help them all. Cassandra would be a hero for solving the mystery of the royal assassination. Simon York would get his damned exclusive.

And Kadir would be able to turn the entire world against Zahid Bin-Asfour and his followers. Fostering a primitive culture was one thing; assassination was another entirely.

He would be in this country for a while longer. Days, perhaps weeks. In that time, he would gladly keep Cassandra as his lover. He admired and liked her, he was intensely attracted to her, he enjoyed her company. But before he left, she had to understand that this was no more than any other short-lived affair. They could comfort one another, they could find pleasure and companionship in this bed. But when it was over, it would be well and truly *over.*

She did not belong in his world, and he had no place in hers.

* * *

Kadir had half expected a visit from the police sometime Monday night. He'd given his name as Joe, after pulling the injured man at the photo shop from the fire, and several people had seen him leave the scene with Cassandra. It wouldn't exactly be difficult to make the connection, since they'd been all over town that morning and he'd been introduced a dozen times as her boyfriend.

But no one came looking for Kadir, or Joe. No one arrived to question Cassandra, either. She didn't understand the why of that, not until she received an early-morning call from Ms. Dunn.

The older woman almost always appeared to be tough and uncaring, but she did care, in her own brisk way. Her frequent calls were intended to make sure Cassandra was all right, and during Tuesday morning's call—a call which awakened Cassandra from a sound sleep—Ms. Dunn asked pointedly if the investigators had dropped by the cottage to ask questions. Cassandra assured her boss that since the evening of the explosion, no one had questioned her about what she'd seen.

"Good. I told the investigators that were dispatched to give you a few days to recover from the shock," Ms. Dunn said, apparently relieved. "The local police have your statement, and that's sufficient for now."

"Thank you." Cassandra glanced over at Kadir. He was awake, but still drowsy. He didn't look as if he'd slept well. "I could use a few more days to myself, and it isn't as if I can tell the investigators anything I haven't already told the local officers."

"Precisely," Ms. Dunn responded. "You can certainly have a few days. I would like to have you back in the office by the weekend," she added. "Next Monday at the very latest. The week before the gala is always hectic, and I'll need you here." Once again, the tone was sharp.

"Of course," Cassandra answered, having no real idea when she might return to the ministry.

When the call was done she closed her eyes. It was early, the sun was barely up, but she didn't expect sleep to return. She was well rested, but also languid. Maybe they could stay in bed and make love all day. It was a nice idea.

Kadir pulled her close, as if his thoughts mirrored hers. He nuzzled her neck and cupped one breast in a warm, large hand. Long fingers rocked and danced over her skin. That easy, familiar touch made Cassandra feel as if she were literally melting.

"Good morning," he said, his voice deep and slightly gruff.

"Good morning." Cassandra smiled. He was seducing her all over again—not that she actually needed to be seduced. His hands already seemed to know her body well, and she responded to him without taking the time to think about the whys and the shoulds, the why nots and the should nots. She just enjoyed. In fact, she reveled.

She raked her fingers along his back, his side, his hip. Caressing him this way was much easier than she'd thought it would be. There had been such a steady wall between her and the opposite sex until she'd met Kadir. She knew very well how to keep men at a distance; she'd been doing that for years. Now she was learning how to draw one in, and in spite of her inexperience she didn't think she was doing too badly.

If she thought too much about what she was doing, she might find reasons to stop. So she didn't think. She touched, and kissed and whispered.

She more than half expected Kadir to roll her onto her back and push inside her. After all, there were condoms on the bedside table, not so very far away. But he didn't reach for one. Instead, he sighed and rolled away from her, leaving the bed altogether.

"Much as I would like to spend the day in bed," he said, "we have work ahead of us today."

"I'm rather tired of working," she confessed.

Naked, aroused…beautiful…Kadir stopped at the bathroom door, turned slowly and grinned at her. And her heart did all sorts of unexpected tricks in response.

"It would be too easy to spend the day in bed with you," he confessed. "Much too easy." The grin faded. "It would, in fact, be very easy to remain dead. To become Joe and have nothing in the world to do but love you."

Love in the physical sense, Cassandra knew without being reminded.

"It would be too easy, Cassandra, to hide here with you. But that's not who I am, so this morning I will take a cold shower and go to town without you. You should stay here and rest. Sleep a while longer. Think only of pleasant things. Let me deal with the unpleasantness of the world, just for today, while you rest here."

Kadir went into the bathroom and closed the door behind him, and a moment later Cassandra heard the water begin to run. And a few minutes after that, she slipped from the bed and joined him. They didn't have time to waste, she knew that. He wanted her; she needed him.

Today she would not allow Kadir to shower alone, any more than she'd allow him to take on the unpleasantness of the world without her.

* * *

For someone who'd been a virgin yesterday, Cassandra was quite insistent about what she wanted. Insistent, and persistent and unfailingly determined.

He had given her what she'd wanted when she'd joined him in the shower. How could he not? Afterward she had insisted on coming with him to the village once again. This time he had argued more strenuously—for all the good it had done him. If Sharif called, he would leave a message or call back, she'd argued. If the police stopped by to question her—or him—wouldn't it be best that she not be there? If they were going to keep their stories straight, then they really should stay together.

None of those arguments had swayed Kadir, but Cassandra knew how to get what she wanted from him. She'd asked the question…

What if the man who blew up your yacht and started a fire in the photo shop comes here and I'm alone? What will I do, Kadir?

It made no sense for the man who'd attempted to assassinate him—the man who had killed many innocents on the yacht in order to get to Kadir—to go after Cassandra. But there was also no guarantee that he would not.

Kadir parked the pink motor scooter not too far from the ruined photo shop—and just a short walk from Simon York's room at the small, nearly ancient Leonia Inn. The inn was four stories tall, narrow and near crumbling, but it was the cheapest hotel in town. Kadir was hoping to get to the inn without seeing anyone who might recognize him, but the plump woman he had seen outside the photo shop yesterday saw him and rushed from the candy shop to intercept him. He tried to ignore her, but she waved and shouted his false name.

"Joe!" Pudgy fingers wiggled on her outstretched arm. Her run was an effort, and there was much jiggling as a result. "Joooooe!"

On the sidewalk, he and Cassandra stopped and turned to face the woman. He never should've given her a name yesterday when she'd asked, not even a bogus one.

The woman slowed down considerably when she realized that Kadir and Cassandra were not going to run from her. "Thank goodness I saw you," she said in a loud, gasping whisper. "You really should know…" She stopped to catch her breath.

"Know what?" Kadir asked as the plump woman came to a stop before him. Today she wore a name tag on her chocolate-stained apron. *Mary.*

"It was very clear to me, and to the others, that you didn't wish to speak to the police. I don't know why." Mary sounded slightly disapproving. "But you did a good thing, Joe, and we decided it wasn't right that a good deed should bring you trouble. So, Henry told the officer who questioned us that he saw the smoke and pulled William out of the shop before the flames got out of hand. William was unconscious, so he can't very well dispute the fact."

"Who is Henry?" Kadir asked, amused and relieved.

"Henry is the red-haired fellow who was in my shop yesterday when all the ado took place. He's a regular customer," she added with a touch of pride. "He can't get enough of my toffee."

"There were several witnesses," Cassandra said.

"Yes, but none were tourists. We all agreed that it would be best if Joe didn't have to…well, we're grateful that William was saved, and no good deed should bring a man unwanted attention. We all agreed."

"I take it William has regained consciousness?" Kadir asked, leaning slightly forward in anticipation. "Did he see anyone? Does he remember how the fire started or…" How much did Mary and the others know? "Does he remember anything at all?"

"Not a thing," Mary said in a no-nonsense voice. "He smelled smoke, turned and then he apparently fell and hit his head on the counter."

If that was what William remembered, then that's what everyone would believe. Everyone but Kadir, at least. "I'm very glad that your friend is well." He took Mary's hand, bowed slightly and then kissed her knuckles. "Thank you, and many thanks to your friends, as well. I very much appreciate your discretion." When he rose up again and looked at the candy maker's face, she was blushing. Her cheeks were an outrageous shade of red.

"It was nothing, really," she said, breathless once again. "I just thought you should know."

"The fire was contained to the photo shop?" Cassandra asked.

"Yes, luckily. None of the adjacent buildings were damaged, since no one shares a common wall with William's shop. I have complained many times about keeping kids out of those narrow alleyways, and keeping them clean is always a chore, but today I'm grateful the alley between my shop and William's is there."

"I'm very glad to hear that no one else suffered damage," Kadir said.

The candy maker waggled a finger at him. "You should stop by and try my toffee when you have the chance. Skinny girls like your girlfriend here don't eat much candy, I understand that, but a strapping young man like yourself doesn't have to worry about a few extra calories."

No one had called Kadir a young man in a very long time, but he supposed *young* was relative. "I will most definitely stop by and purchase some of your fine toffee."

Again Mary blushed.

They said goodbye, and once again Kadir and Cassandra headed for Simon York's inn.

Just before they reached the doorway that would take them into a dimly lit and sparsely furnished lobby, Cassandra laughed.

Kadir held the door open for her. "What is so funny?"

She took his hand as they stepped inside the inn. "If you expect to pass yourself off as a Joe, you're going to have to work on the accent, and for goodness' sake, stop being so charming."

"Charming?"

She squeezed his hand and her grin widened. "No one named Joe kisses a woman's hand quite the way you do."

Chapter 12

It was obvious to Cassandra that Kadir didn't care for Simon York. She didn't, either, for that matter. He'd hounded them, after all, and was responsible for that embarrassing photo that had gone into the *Quiz*. But it was possible the annoying photographer had knowledge they didn't, so for now the three of them were working together.

At the moment Kadir was speaking, and York furiously scribbled notes in a small tablet. The man wanted his exclusive—one way or another—and he listened to Kadir's words as if there might be gold hidden among them.

"Did you know," Kadir said solemnly, "that Zahid Bin-Asfour and Prince Reginald met not long before the prince's assassination? Three days before, to be precise."

"Yes, of course I knew that," York said. It was an obvious lie. The sparkle in his beady eyes and the way he hurriedly scratched the information on his paper told Cassandra that much.

"Bin-Asfour delivered illegal drugs to the prince," Kadir continued, "but we don't know what, if anything, he received in exchange. Do you?"

"I can find out," York promised. "The *Quiz* has people everywhere, and I do mean everywhere. If anyone knows what went on between the prince and Bin-Asfour, we can find it."

Cassandra felt a decided shimmer of unease. If anyone in the ministry ever found out she'd been a party to handing this kind of information to an employee of the *Silvershire Inquisitor,* she'd be out on her ear in a heartbeat. Ms. Dunn had never been known as a forgiving woman.

"Very good," Kadir said. "I expect you will get the investigation started immediately. Until then, it would be best if we keep the information about the meeting under wraps."

York's head snapped up. "Under wraps? Are you kidding me? This is hot stuff. I can't keep it to myself!"

Instead of arguing, Kadir smiled. "Hot stuff? I thought you said you already knew about the meeting." He shrugged, very casual and uncaring. "That is up to you, of course. I imagine once this bit of information becomes public knowledge, everyone will be scrambling to find the rest of the story. I thought it might be best if you waited until you had everything, but if you want to divulge what we have thus far…"

"No, no," York said, very grudgingly agreeing. "This had better pan out, mate. The princess is preggers, and I could be in Gastonia snapping photographs."

"You and every other photographer in this part of the

world," Kadir argued. "I thought you wanted to be different. Special. A star among celebrities."

"Yeah, yeah," York mumbled.

Cassandra was still stuck on "The princess is preggers." It would make a typical *Quiz* headline.

"Now—" Kadir leaned back in his chair and stared at York "—what can you tell me that I do not yet know?"

Kadir dominated the small rented room Simon York called home, not only with his size but with his energy and his force of will. No matter where he went, no matter how crowded or sparsely populated a room might be, how could every eye not turn to him? How could any person he spoke to not give his every word their full attention?

No one would ever mistake him for a Joe for very long, no matter how diligently he worked to lose his accent and his charm.

Cassandra wished fervently that he *was* a Joe. That they could date for a few months, and spend weekends here at the seashore or down in Barton. He'd ask for her father's blessing, in a few months—maybe a year—and then they'd be married. At night they would each talk about their day, before falling into bed to make love. They could live in Silverton, where she'd continue to work until the babies came. Maybe even after the babies came. Wouldn't he be wonderful with babies?

But he wasn't a Joe and never would be. Dammit.

Before the meeting was over, York promised to do some discreet digging into the meeting between the prince and Zahid Bin-Asfour. This new research would require a trip to Silverton, as he did not feel secure in sharing too much information over the telephone. The three of them planned to meet here, in this room,

Thursday evening. By that time York was sure to have something of importance to share.

At least they could hope that would be the case.

Cassandra was certain Kadir would immediately head back to the cottage, once the interview with York was done. But he didn't. Instead he walked around town, his movements slow but his eyes sharp. He studied tourists and shopkeepers with equal intensity. Once she even caught him staring at a man and his children with what might be called melancholy. Perhaps it was only her imagination, but she was sure she saw some emotion on his face. It took her immediately and completely back to that insane moment when she'd decided he would be a wonderful father...and wasn't that an unusual bit of fancy for her to indulge in?

He even stopped at Mary's shop and bought some toffee, with cash he borrowed from her, as he was presently without funds. The woman was thrilled to see him, and was equally pleased to sell him a small container of her special candy.

Kadir remained lost in thought as they walked back toward the scooter. For the most part, he'd been silent as they'd walked about town, but now he mumbled to himself. He even cursed.

"What are you talking about?" she asked as he reached for his helmet.

"I don't have any idea if he's still here, so why do I waste my time looking into every café and alleyway?"

"Who exactly are you looking for?" Kadir knew the men in his entourage very well. Surely he suspected one—or more—over the others.

He shook his head. "I don't know. I still don't want to believe that any of the men who worked for me would do such a thing. If indeed I was betrayed from within my own household, surely the traitor has left."

"But you're not *sure*."

Instead of answering, Kadir leaned over and gave her a quick kiss. "Maybe he's waiting for my remains to be discovered. Zahid is not a trusting man. He might very well insist upon concrete proof of my death."

"But you don't know that."

"No," Kadir said.

"Who do you think might've…"

He shook his head and mounted the scooter. She climbed on behind him and held on.

"I refuse to speculate on the possibilities," Kadir said. "Logic aside, I very much hope I'm wrong in my suppositions, and the man who tried to kill me is a stranger who left Leonia soon after the explosion took place."

Cassandra raked her hands against Kadir's midsection, in an instinctive offer of comfort. She didn't know what to say. Heaven above, she always knew what to say, in any situation, no matter how awkward. It was her job to know what to say!

But this was Kadir, and she loved him. She wanted to protect him from what he saw as the only logical explanation. While she searched for words, he lifted her hand and kissed the knuckles. Then he put the scooter into motion, and the time for speaking words of comfort or support was gone.

The afternoon was a long one. The phone only rang once, and it was a call from Piper Klein, who wanted to know if her daughter was well. It was touching to think that those who knew Cassandra well believed she'd be devastated by the death of a man she barely knew. But then again, women seemed to understand one another in a way men did not.

Sharif did not call. Would another message from Cassandra so soon be too much? Would someone question why she was trying so desperately to contact Sharif? Kadir decided it was too soon for another message. It would only draw attention to her, and he didn't want that.

She sat next to him on the couch, close. Very close. Her thigh brushed his, and that simple touch was enough to make him hard.

"What do we do now?" she asked, as if she had been reading his mind.

"We wait."

She fidgeted, very slightly. He had a feeling she did not *wait* well. "Maybe we should go back to town and directly ask people if they've seen the man who was photographed. We do have a vague description, thanks to York, and we can visit the shops nearest the pier and…"

"No," Kadir answered sharply. If he asked the villagers about identifying a man who was supposed to be dead and they verified that he had indeed been seen, would they all be in danger? Would Mary the candy maker and William from the photo shop and the employees at the market close to the pier all be targets for a man who would surely prefer to remain among the dead?

If Kadir was right in his presumption, of course, and if the traitor was still in Leonia. Neither of those was certain. "We will wait for York to return and see what sort of information he can give us."

"That's two days, Kadir. What are we going to do for the next two days?"

That was one question he could easily answer. He

kissed her, and she yielded quickly beneath his touch. One of her delicate hands rose up and touched his hair, and her lips parted.

He'd never known a woman like Cassandra Klein. In his country women were not allowed the kinds of freedom what would produce a wonder like her, but it was more than that. In his duties as ambassador he had been around the world. He had spent time with women from all cultures. He had even slept with more than his share.

But Cassandra was special. No one else had ever been able to draw him in so closely, so intimately. Not intimately of the body, but of the spirit. It was as if she were inside him, all the time. It was as if he had known her forever, as if they had shared more than a few precious days.

When the time came, leaving her would be difficult. Fortunately, now was not the time for thinking about leaving.

She slipped her fingers into the waistband of his jeans, teasing him with her incredible softness and the bold warmth in her touch, and he forgot everything but the physical. He wanted to be inside her. He wanted to feel her quiver and hear her make those sounds low in her throat. He wanted to hear her cry out his name as she reached orgasm.

Kadir tried not to think about the importance of her being a virgin before last night, but he could not entirely push that knowledge away. She had waited for him. For *him,* and no one else. He didn't want her to regret a moment of their time together, even when it was over and they were living their lives thousands of miles apart.

They undid buttons and zippers while they kissed,

neither rushing nor dawdling, but moving slowly and without hesitation toward what they both wanted. Cassandra was wonderfully responsive to his touch. Kadir saw her response in the way she moved, in the flush that rose to her skin, in the swell of her breasts and the change in the way she breathed. And he saw it in her eyes, gray and soft and so full of spirit that the gaze alone touched him in a way nothing, and no one, ever had.

Before he removed her jeans, she reached into the back pocket and withdrew a condom. She had come to him prepared, and he was glad. Tonight he didn't want to stop. He didn't want to call even the shortest halt to the progression of their lovemaking.

Cassandra insisted that he be as naked as she, and soon he was. She touched him boldly, with delicate fingers that drove him beyond all rational thought. He wanted her around him, and nothing else mattered. Nothing.

Soon she reclined on the couch and drew him to her, her long legs wrapped around his hips, her eyes closed and a small smile teasing the corners of her mouth. Kadir just barely began to enter her, and then he stopped.

"Look at me," he whispered.

Cassandra did as he asked and opened her eyes. Dove-gray eyes so soft and desirous and loving, they touched his heart. Kadir was determined that his heart not be involved in this. Even if it was, even if he could not stop what he knew was impossible…he could never tell her. He could never tell anyone.

Their eyes were locked as they came together. Cassandra's body quivered. He adored that quiver, the sigh, the way she lifted her hips to meet his, in a rhythm that came so naturally to her. In her arms, in her body, he forgot everything and everyone else. There was nothing in the world but pleasure and beauty. There was nothing in the world but Cassandra and the way she came to him.

She climaxed quickly, almost as soon as he was fully, deeply inside her. Kadir did not wait, but joined her in a moment of pure, powerful release that wiped all the ugliness and uncertainty of the world away, for a short while.

As soon as she caught her breath, Cassandra laughed lightly. Kadir lifted his head and looked down at her. Light from the lamp at the end of the couch shone down on her exquisite face.

"What's funny?"

"Me," Cassandra said. "Us," she whispered in a lowered voice. "I didn't know sex could be so furious and wonderful and unstoppable. Like a freight train." She laughed again. "The bed's not so far away, and yet it seemed as if it was, when going there meant moving my body even a fraction away from yours."

Kadir lowered his mouth and kissed her throat, so slender and pale and soft. "I want you in every room of this house," he whispered.

"It's a small cottage," she responded, her fingers teasing his hair. "And we already have the master bedroom, the master bath and the main room covered. That just leaves three rooms."

He lifted his head and looked down at her. In this light, with that expression on her face, she was the most beautiful creature he had ever seen. A woman like this could very easily steal a man's heart away.

Her fingertips touched his cheek. "Kadir, I…"

He saw the expression in her eyes, he felt the weight of what she was about to say in the very air around them.

So he kissed her to stop the words from leaving her mouth. He wanted Cassandra to the depths of his soul, but he could not allow love to come between them.

Wearing Lexie's pajamas, Cassandra sat at the desk in the main room, where just a couple of days ago she'd found a six-shooter. Kadir had that weapon now. It was never far from his hand.

A tradition was a tradition, no matter where she happened to find herself. It was Tuesday night, after all. Lexie's only stationery was plain white and lined, but it would do.

Dear Mum,
Lexie's place is beautiful, and very relaxing. I
didn't realize how much I needed a holiday until
I was forced to take one. The sound of the waves
is unexpectedly soothing, and there are moments
when the sight of the sea takes my breath away.
No wonder Lexie loves it here.

There was no need to let her mother know that Kadir was alive, not yet, and if Piper Klein knew there had been fires set and assassins spotted, she'd be here in a matter of hours. Mothers were like that, almost-psychic or not. It was definitely best that her parents remain in Burton.

I'm feeling much better than I was just yesterday.

And how.

You were right. You and Lexie and Daisy and
Paula, you were all right. Bet you never expected
to hear me say that. But it's true. When you told

*me to enjoy my life instead of planning it so care-
fully, when you told me that not everything can be
planned to the last detail like an itinerary for a
visiting dignitary, when you said I needed to enjoy
my life, you were all right. Some things can't be
taught, they have to be lived, and love is one of
those things. Loss, too. The sheik and I became
good friends in his short time here, as you suspected. Nothing anyone could've told me would
have prepared me for the sight of Kadir's yacht exploding before my very eyes and the devastating
emptiness that followed.*

Even though she'd learned just a few hours later
that Kadir hadn't been killed, that moment would haunt
her forever.

*I'm much better, now, truly I am. Ms. Dunn wants
me back in the office by the weekend. There's always
so much to do in preparing for the Founder's Day
Gala. Will you and Dad be making the trip to Silverton this year? I can get you tickets to the gala,
but Dad has to wear a tuxedo. Tell him I said the
tux he wore when you were dating won't do. The
ruffles are disturbing, and it hasn't fit him well in
years.*

The gala was an exclusive event, but as an employee
of the foreign service, she could always manage to
wrangle a couple of extra tickets, if need be. As far as her
father was concerned, nothing ever went out of style, and
if an outfit was a little tight, well, as long as it covered everything that needed to be covered, he felt it was just fine.

He had not always fared well living in a house full
of fashion-conscious women.

When I write next Tuesday's letter, I'll be back in my apartment and life will be back to normal.

She didn't know if she'd be home by next Tuesday or not, but expected she might be. Once Kadir had his answers, he'd be gone. As for normal, well, she didn't think any part of her life would ever be the normal she had come to expect. Still, she'd learn to manage. She wasn't the type to fall apart when things didn't proceed as she wished. She was, after all, a realist.

Would losing Kadir when he walked away from her be any less painful than watching the yacht explode? Of course it would. She wanted to know he was alive and well, that he breathed and smiled and maybe even went fishing. Somewhere in the world.

But it would be painful.

See you soon, I hope.
Love,
Cassandra

Eventually her mother would learn that Kadir had survived the assassination attempt, and there would be plenty of explaining to do. But those explanations were not necessary tonight.

Letter written, Cassandra turned off the main room lights and crawled into bed with Kadir. He seemed to be asleep, but she didn't think he was. She placed her body close to his, and draped one arm across his torso. She would miss this holding as much as the sex, when he was gone.

Was that why Lexie always found another man so

quickly after her romances failed? She knew what it was like to be held and cherished and loved, and that had to make the loneliness sharper, more painful.

Cassandra wasn't sure how she'd adjust to sleeping alone, once Kadir was gone. She was smarter than her eldest sister, though, and she knew he could not be easily replaced. Kadir could never be replaced.

The timing of Kadir's quick, deep kiss on the couch, earlier in the evening when she'd still been trembling from making love, had reminded her that he didn't want her to tell him that she loved him. It was a complication he didn't know how to handle, and she understood that very well. So she wouldn't tell him again. He knew, and that was enough. It would have to be. She would take what she could get from this short-lived relationship and store it all away in a glorious memory that would never fade.

Memories were a poor substitute for the real thing, but if it was all she could have then she'd make it be enough. Her body trembled, and she pushed away the acute pain that threatened to rise to the surface. She hadn't known, all those years she'd waited for her true love to arrive, that she wouldn't be able to keep him forever.

Chapter 13

Cassandra was willing to drive the pink scooter into Leonia Wednesday morning to post her letter. It would be a short enough and safe enough trip, she imagined. Kadir didn't plan to do any more investigating, not until after York returned—hopefully with some new information—so there was no reason for him to go with her. She was very aware that with every appearance in town, Kadir took the chance that someone might recognize him. Try as he might, he wasn't a very good Joe.

Still, he refused to allow her to go to town alone. Since just yesterday she'd argued that they should not be separated, she didn't fight him on the matter for very long.

There was no reason to tarry in the village today. She mailed her letter, Kadir bought a larger supply of toffee, which he said was quite good, and then they headed back to the cottage.

It did not escape her attention that while they were in Leonia, Kadir once again kept a sharp and curious eye on the people around them. It was as if he suspected every man woman and child in town of being a potential assassin, and she couldn't blame him for that. He carried Lexie's six-shooter, but it was well concealed. If she hadn't known where he carried the weapon, she wouldn't even realize it was there.

It was also apparent to her, as they ran their errands, that in spite of her concerns the townspeople were fooled by their cover story. They truly believed that Kadir was her boyfriend from Silverton, come to comfort her. *Boyfriend* was such an inadequate word to describe their relationship, but when they held hands and he leaned in to whisper in her ear, she imagined that's just how it appeared to onlookers.

She looked forward to a quiet day at the cottage. A quiet day and a half, to be precise, since York wouldn't return until late tomorrow. She and Kadir could make love in every room of the cottage, and then they would start all over again. They could fish in the afternoon, and maybe Kadir would make love to her on the rocks—though she did wonder if the rocks were too hard and sharp for that activity. Only one way to find out, she supposed. She'd cook for him, and make him laugh, and ask questions about the life she would never get to share, and do her best to make him forget all his troubles—for a while.

She had a day and a half to make enough memories to last a lifetime.

Cassandra and Kadir entered the cottage through the kitchen door. She glanced around the cozy room, wondering where and how, exactly, Kadir planned to make love to her here....

Before the door was closed, Kadir grabbed her hand and yanked her down and behind him, at the same time dropping the tin of candy and smoothly drawing the six-shooter. Cassandra grabbed on to the denim of his jeans in order to steady herself, and peeked around his leg to see what had startled him. A man stood in the door between the kitchen and the hallway, his own gun drawn and steady.

The gunman had olive skin, like Kadir, and long black hair that was mostly pulled back in a ponytail. A few strands escaped and framed a harsh, thin face. His beard was untended, and that, along with the narrowed eyes, gave him a wild and decidedly dangerous appearance.

Kadir almost immediately relaxed. "You startled me," he said as he returned the weapon to its proper place.

The armed man who had broken into the cottage while they'd been in Leonia lowered his own weapon—which was a much more modern gun than Lexie's six-shooter—and cocked his head to one side. "Kadir?" The man's voice was truly puzzled, but after a moment's study he grinned. The smile changed his face entirely, and he wasn't quite so scary. "You're alive."

Kadir assisted Cassandra to her feet as the armed man strode into the kitchen. When she was standing, brushing off imagined crumbs from Lexie's kitchen floor, the bearded man stepped past scattered pieces of toffee and threw his arms around Kadir, laughing—not quite maniacally.

When the laughter and the relieved hug ended, Kadir placed his arm around Cassandra's shoulder. "This is Sharif Al-Asad, assistant to the Kahani Minister of Defense and my oldest friend. Sharif, this is Ms. Cassandra Klein, the aide I was assigned upon my arrival in Silvershire."

Cassandra offered her hand, and Sharif shook it briefly. "A very pretty aide, if I may say so." His eyes were appraising, and she imagined Al-Asad realized that she and Kadir were involved. Eyes like that didn't miss much. Sharif didn't have bedroom eyes, like Kadir, but those eyes were sharp as a hawk's, and unfailingly apprising.

"You didn't return my call," she said, only slightly accusing.

"When my oldest and dearest friend is assassinated, you expect me to sit in an office and reply to telephone messages?"

She looked Sharif Al-Asad up and down. His beard and his hair needed tending, but his clothes were expensive and fit him well. He handled his pistol with the ease that came with years of experience. He was, she knew instinctively, indeed a dangerous man. "I suppose not."

This was the man Kadir trusted. The only man, he said. As the three of them walked into the main room to share the happenings of the past few days, a chill walked up and down Cassandra's spine.

Kadir might trust this odd man with his life, but she did not.

Sharif's smile faded as he watched Cassandra walk into the kitchen. When his old friend had asked if she could make him a cup of hot tea, Kadir had realized that he wished to speak alone.

"We can leave now," Sharif said, standing nimbly. "We'll walk out the front door while she's in the kitchen, and I'll have you to a safe place within two hours. When you're secured, I'll return to Leonia to personally conduct the investigation."

Kadir did not stand. He reached up and laid a stilling hand on Sharif's forearm. "I'm safe here, for now."

A touch of sharp anger crossed Sharif's face. "You have known that woman for a *week,* and you're willing to place your life in her hands? I have never known you to be a fool, Kadir, but that is a decidedly foolish decision. Zahid might've bought her, or blackmailed her, or threatened her. She could poison you at any time, or shoot you while you sleep, or…"

"She would do none of those things."

"You have no way of knowing that with any certainty."

But he did know, in a way that would be difficult to explain. "She thinks she loves me," Kadir said with a sigh.

Sharif's features softened a little. "It could be a game…."

"This is no game."

"You've been blinded," Sharif said as he reluctantly sat once again.

"I didn't say that I love her." Even if he thought he might, one day, love was impossible in these circumstances and it was a useless exercise to even consider such a thing. "I do like her, very much."

"That's clear enough," Sharif grumbled.

Kadir actually smiled. "I like her well enough to protect her while I can, and I certainly like her well enough to walk away when I'm finished here." There was no need to point out that as long as Zahid lived, no one Kadir dared to care for would be safe.

While Cassandra was busy in the kitchen, Kadir told Sharif of his suspicions. Sharif was surprised, but not shocked. Nothing had the power to shock him anymore; he had seen too much. Still, he was as disturbed as

Kadir that someone who'd been within the tight circle might've been behind the explosion. A phone call this afternoon would get an investigation into everyone who was thought killed on the yacht into motion.

"We have discovered why Zahid came here to meet with Prince Reginald," Sharif said once plans for the new investigation were complete.

Kadir awaited the rest, an eye on the doorway Cassandra would walk through, his ear partially tuned to the sound of her work in the kitchen.

"Zahid offered an alliance," Sharif continued, contempt clear in his voice. "An allegiance between Silvershire and Bin-Asfour in exchange for all the recreational drugs the prince desired."

"And the prince's response to this ridiculous offer?"

Sharif shrugged his shoulders. "That we do not know. If the offer was rejected, then Zahid would have felt it was within his rights to kill the prince. I have a man on the inside, and in a few days…"

"You have someone within Zahid's camp?"

Sharif nodded. "My informant has been disillusioned, but realizes if he tries to walk away from the organization he and his family will be killed." Again, that shrug. "If he's caught sharing information he should not he will surely be killed, but that's a risk he's willing to take."

Before Cassandra was finished preparing the requested tea, Sharif left the cottage by way of the front door. He was not one to sit still and wait, and if there was even the smallest possibility that the culprit remained in Leonia, he wanted to be on the watch. Sharif did not leave the cottage without a soft warning for Kadir to take care, and a suspicious glance toward the kitchen.

Cassandra returned to the main room with a tray

bearing three cups of steaming tea, along with sugar and cream. She searched the room quickly, looking for their guest, and Kadir informed her that Sharif had departed.

With a sigh that spoke of relief, she placed the tray on the coffee table and sat beside him—close, as she so often chose to do. The expression on her face said it all. "I don't trust him."

"Why not? He wants Zahid dead as badly as I do. Maybe more. He's the one man in the world Bin-Asfour can't buy or blackmail." He thought again of Sharif's assertion that Cassandra herself might've been bought, and he dismissed it just as quickly. She could've killed him a hundred times in the past four days.

No, the danger Cassandra presented had nothing to do with Bin-Asfour.

She wrinkled her nose as she considered his assertions. "Your friend strikes me as a man who knows no boundaries. He'd do anything to get what he wants, including sacrificing you. You say he wants Bin-Asfour as much as you do, and I believe you. Let me ask you this. Would Sharif give his own life to take down Bin-Asfour?"

"Without doubt," Kadir answered.

"What makes you think he values your life more than his own? Maybe Sharif would be willing to sacrifice you in order to gain Zahid's trust, if it meant getting his hands on the man."

"Perhaps," Kadir answered softly, and more thoughtfully than he'd intended. With each passing year, Sharif seemed more desperate, more hungry, as if he had begun to realize that the man who'd murdered Amala might never have to pay for his crime.

"He doesn't like me at all," Cassandra said as she leaned snugly against his side.

No, his lover and his friend did not like each other. Sharif saw the potential for danger in Cassandra, and she saw the potential in him. Kadir supposed that no one or nothing in his life was entirely safe, but that was no way to live. He didn't want to spend the rest of his days looking over his shoulder and expecting the worst even of those he cared about.

Better to take a chance now and then than to completely close himself off from the few real joys of life. "Life is never entirely without risk."

Cassandra scoffed at that, but maybe she agreed because she did stop arguing.

That was fortunate, as they had better ways to spend the afternoon than in argument.

The next day and a half were everything Cassandra had hoped for, and more. She and Kadir made love and they fished and they laughed. They laughed a lot. They had late-night conversations about their childhoods and their siblings, their hopes and their fears, telling the sorts of secrets lovers share. They held hands and kissed often.

The only unwelcomed interruption came in the form of Kadir's scary, hairy friend, Sharif, who dropped by on occasion, usually appearing in such a way as to startle Cassandra. It didn't take long for her to realize that he did that on purpose. When Sharif was present, he and Kadir whispered to one another, sharing secrets they did not want Cassandra to know.

Fortunately Sharif never stayed at the cottage for any length of time. He came and went as he pleased, but he never remained in their company for very long.

On the Thursday evening scooter ride to Leonia, Cassandra held on to Kadir with all her might. Their time together was almost over. She knew it; she felt it to her bones as the wind whipped past them, and the smell of the sea filled each breath she took.

She'd expected to be in on the meeting with Simon York. Whatever he had discovered—if he had discovered anything at all—might actually have something to do with solving Prince Reginald's murder. She'd likely be forgiven anything—even lying about Kadir's death— if she could play a part in solving that mystery. Ms. Dunn would still disapprove, but she would offer forgiveness much more quickly.

But Kadir didn't lead Cassandra to the front door of the Leonia Inn. Instead he took her hand and they walked a narrow alleyway that led them to a deserted courtyard. There, Sharif waited. Kadir's friend was no more glad to see her than she was to see him.

Kadir spoke to them both in a tone of voice that left no room for argument. This was the voice of a high-level diplomat, a man who was accustomed to having his every order obeyed without question. "Sharif, I want you to escort Ms. Klein back to Silverton. Stay with her until I tell you otherwise."

Sharif's response was curt. "No."

Kadir's response was in Arabic, and spoken so quickly and so softly Cassandra didn't have a chance to understand what was said. She only heard one word she could decipher. *Amala.*

Panic welled up inside her. She didn't want to be sent away...she wasn't ready to say goodbye.... But when Kadir took her by the shoulders and looked into her eyes, she saw goodbye.

"Listen to Sharif, and stay safe."

Cassandra was incensed on so many levels, she didn't

know where to start. "I don't need an escort, a body-guard or a babysitter."

"I do not agree."

"I'm not a child, Kadir, and I don't appreciate being treated like one." So many emotions danced within her, she didn't know what to feel, what to say. "If anyone needs Sharif's assistance, it's you."

"I need no assistance."

"You're planning something, I can see it. What are you up to?"

He kissed her on the forehead lightly, as a friend might. "You'll know soon enough, and I don't want you anywhere near me when it happens."

"That does not sound good, Kadir. Not at all."

He smiled at her, but the smile died when Sharif began to argue with him once again. Again, Sharif spoke in Arabic, but this time his voice was loud enough and slow enough for her to translate easily.

Sharif didn't want to leave Kadir any more than she did.

Her heart beat too hard. This could be it. This could be the last time she saw Kadir. Whether he lived or died, whether Bin-Asfour succeeded in killing him or not. She'd lived safe all her life, and she was tired of living safe. Life is not without risk—everyone she'd ever loved had told her that.

"I love you," she said, speaking quickly so Kadir didn't have time to stop her. "I waited all my life for you, and now you're just going to walk away from me as if none of it matters?"

Sharif quickly took himself out of the circle, moving several steps away and pretending to search the alleyway for interlopers or eavesdroppers.

"You only think you love me," Kadir argued in a

lowered voice. "That happens, sometimes, when sex is involved. Women don't seem to be able to separate the heart from the physical act of love, when in truth the two usually have little in common."

The pain cut to the quick. Was there nothing but sex between them, after all? "Do you love me, just a little?" she asked.

Kadir brushed a strand of hair away from her face, sighed and said, "No, I don't love you at all. I like you. I wish you well. I will carry the memory of these past days with me until the day I die, whether that happens tomorrow or fifty years from now." He looked her squarely in the eye. "But I don't love you, Cassandra. Please understand."

Tears stung her eyes, but she refused to shed them. She would not be an overly emotional, needy girl. And if she had to cry, she'd save it for a time when she was alone. But she did feel she could argue with Kadir.

"You could be a gentleman and…and…*lie*." She'd convinced herself that he did love her, but maybe this was nothing more than she'd suspected all along. He'd needed a woman to warm his bed, and she was convenient. It wasn't as if she hadn't known that was possible the entire time they'd been together.

And still, it hurt. Everything hurt.

"Goodbye, Cassandra." Kadir kissed her hand, much as he had the candy maker's, and then he turned his back on her, leaving her in the company of a man she did not like at all.

The way Sharif took her arm and all but dragged her away indicated that he felt the same way about her.

The heaviness of heart was unexpected, as was the undeniable sadness that welled up inside Kadir on a wave as unstoppable as those in Leonia Bay. It would be easy enough to dismiss his distress as the effect of what he was about to do, but he could not lie to himself any longer. He could lie to Cassandra, and had, quite well. But he should not lie to himself.

If everyone he loved was not a target for Zahid, if he thought he could protect her, if he believed that they had even half a chance at a happiness that would last more than a few days, then things would be different. Things *could* be different. But all that was nothing more than a few fanciful wishes, and he was a grown man who had put aside such indulgences long ago.

At the Leonia Inn, Kadir ran up the steps to the third floor, deciding to forego the rickety elevator in favor of the upward jog that helped him to release some of his unexpected emotion—or should. The run didn't seem to help much, as he'd thought it might. Lately nothing was as it should be.

York answered Kadir's knock anxiously, glancing around for Cassandra as Kadir entered the room.

"Did you discover anything of interest?"

"Not a lot," York confessed. "Apparently Zahid Bin-Asfour and Prince Reginald met several times during the six months before his murder. From what I've been able to discover, it was nothing more than two men of like interests sharing drugs and women. An elite party, you might say."

There was more, but if York had not discovered the rest on his own, Kadir would not tell him.

"Now," York said, "about my exclusive."

York would get his exclusive, even though he had provided scanty information that would not prove to be useful. "Is there time to get a story in tomorrow's edition of the *Silvershire Inquisitor?*" Kadir asked.

"If it's hot enough, yes."

Hot enough. An apt enough description.

Kadir stood and gave the little man a well-practiced bow. "Sheik Kadir Bin Arif Yusef Al-Nuri, Director of European and American Affairs for the Kahani Ministry of Foreign Affairs, very much alive and at your service."

Chapter 14

On Friday morning, Cassandra took great care to prepare herself for a long day. Makeup disguised the fact that she'd not slept well, and while nothing could be done for the redness of her eyes—crying much of the night would do that to a girl—all things considered she didn't look too bad.

Her suit was expensive—one of her best—and it was perfectly cut. The dusky blue was a good color for her. Maybe her face did look too pale against the darkness of the suit, but she doubted anyone at the ministry would notice or care.

She could lose herself in work. There was much to do, as Ms. Dunn had pointed out more than once in their telephone conversations in the past week. It wasn't as if she'd ever actually believed that anything lasting could come of her affair with Kadir.

Sharif insisted on driving her to work. Since they'd left Lexie's cottage in his rental car after collecting the few belongings she'd had there, he hadn't said more than half a dozen words. But he had been attentive, rather like an ugly but dedicated guard dog. He did not take no for an answer, and he never led her to believe that she was, in any way, in charge of this operation. He refused to so much as discuss Kadir with her.

In front of the ministry, he searched the parking lot with sharp eyes. As she opened the door and stepped out he said, "Act surprised."

Cassandra leaned into the opened passenger door. "What?"

"You know nothing," Sharif said sharply. "You are shocked at the unexpected news, just as everyone else is sure to be."

"I have no idea what you're talking about."

"It's what he wants. Remember that."

Confused and annoyed, Cassandra slammed the passenger door. As she walked into the ministry building, she shook her head. Sharif knew English, she knew Arabic and yet half the time she had no idea what he was talking about.

As she walked into the office, all heads turned in her direction. She'd expected curious stares, but this scrutiny was more intense than she'd imagined. How on earth would she handle all the questions that were sure to be thrown her way?

Before she'd taken three steps into the office, Ms. Dunn bellowed her name.

Cassandra stepped quickly toward the director's bellow. What now? All week Ms. Dunn had been kindly and concerned about the situation, but there was no kindness in the voice that filled the ministry and had some employees staring at Cassandra as she passed, and others cowering at their desks as if nothing unusual was going on.

Cassandra walked into Ms. Dunn's office with her head held high. "You wish to see me?"

Ms. Dunn's answer was a hard-eyed glare, as she tossed the newest edition of the *Silvershire Inquisitor* onto her desk, front page screaming, Sheik Kadir Lives!

Cassandra's knees actually wobbled, and suddenly Sharif's parking lot warning made sense. Act surprised? There was no acting involved, at the moment. Why hadn't Kadir told her what he planned to do? Why had he left her in the dark?

She all but collapsed into the chair that was reserved for those employees Ms. Dunn interrogated, and she reached for the paper. When she spoke, she said, very softly, "Oh, dear."

"You didn't know," Ms. Dunn responded in a significantly lowered voice.

Cassandra lifted her head, and all she could do was offer a meek shake. She opened the paper fully. Kadir had actually pushed the news about the princess's pregnancy to the bottom half of the page. There was a photo of Kadir with his hair cut and his beard shaved, and he held a copy of the Leonia newspaper, which was dated several days after his reported death.

She scanned the article York had written. Kadir said he'd been wounded—and that was true enough—and that he'd found a remote home where he'd taken the time to heal. Also mostly true.

And then he said that he planned to return to the Redmond Estate on Saturday morning, where he'd wait until a new security detail could be dispatched from Kahani. He ended by stating that he still wished to meet with Lord Carrington as soon as the man returned to the country.

"Stupid," she whispered.

"What did you say?" Ms. Dunn asked.

Cassandra lifted her head and looked Ms. Dunn in the eye. "I said, *stupid,*" she repeated angrily. "There have been two attempts on his life since he arrived in Silvershire, and he's just told everyone where he'll be this weekend, and he's also informed the assassins that he has no security detail." She felt a heat of real anger rise to her cheeks. "That's incredibly foolish."

"Yes, well, I'll make sure there's local security at the estate until his own bodyguards arrive."

Would it be enough? Cassandra suspected not. Kadir was setting himself up as bait, hoping to catch the man who had betrayed him.

Ms. Dunn was much more relaxed, now that she believed Cassandra had not lied to her. "Would you like to resume your duties as aide to Al-Nuri?"

Cassandra almost said yes, but caught herself in time. Kadir had made his wishes clear. He didn't love her, and he didn't want her involved in this new, foolish scheme. She'd be better off staying far, far away from the Redmond Estate. And him.

And as far as Ms. Dunn or anyone else knew, Kadir had allowed her to believe he was dead for the entire week. No self-respecting woman would pick up where she left off as if nothing had happened. "I think not," she said coolly. "His English is almost perfect, so no knowledge of Arabic is necessary. Anyone from this office will be sufficient to assist him."

"Good. I'll send Timothy to the Redmond Estate in the morning, early enough to greet the sheik."

"Timothy is a fine choice. I'm sure he and Sheik Kadir will get along quite well."

In fact, Kadir and Timothy Little had nothing at all in common. They'd likely get on one another's nerves from the moment they met. That was not her problem—not anymore.

Cassandra stood, her knees much steadier than they'd been when she'd first sat down. Instead of surprise or worry, what she now felt was anger.

"Would you like to take this copy of the *Quiz?*" Ms. Dunn asked, pushing the newspaper toward her.

"No, thank you," Cassandra answered coldly. "I have no desire to read the article again."

Ms. Dunn would assume Cassandra's animosity was the result of Sheik Kadir not contacting her about his survival instead of telling his tale to a reporter. Cassandra didn't care what Ms. Dunn assumed, at the moment. The anger was very real.

As she left Ms. Dunn's office, the receptionist flagged Cassandra down. "Your mother's on the line for you."

Cassandra sighed. Talking to almost-psychic Mum would only make her feel worse. All that foolish talk about love and taking risks had made her vulnerable. Her mother would ask questions she couldn't answer—not yet.

This is exactly what she'd been trying to avoid in setting love aside. She hurt, and she'd been forced to lie to her boss and now she was supposed to lie to her mother, as well?

"Tell her I'm busy and I'll call her back," Cassandra said as she headed for her desk, hoping to lose herself in work, as Ms. Dunn had suggested.

And why not? Her work was all she had.

* * *

The Redmond Estate seemed too large and too cold, after his time at the cottage in Leonia. It had nothing to do with the size of the rooms or the view beyond the windows, Kadir knew. The estate was cold because Cassandra was not here.

But that was for the best, since *here* was not safe.

Kadir swept into the estate early Saturday morning, calling upon every ounce of arrogance he possessed. He sent the staff away, ordering them on a forced vacation. Kadir told the estate employees that he wanted time alone on the heels of his ordeal, but in truth he wanted them all out of harm's way. Most of them were elderly and would only be a hindrance if Zahid fell for his trap. Oscar took the rejection especially hard, wondering what he'd done wrong.

There were official representatives from Silvershire who were determined to act as bodyguards, as well as a small man with a tinny voice who had been dispatched from the Ministry of Foreign Affairs to take Cassandra's place. The small man, appropriately named Little, was easily intimidated and even more easily dismissed. The security guards were tougher to be rid of, but Kadir did manage to toss them out of the house and off the grounds, insisting that if they did not accede to his wishes it might cause an incident between their two countries. Eventually they, too, departed, though he imagined they'd keep a close watch on the estate.

By Saturday evening he was alone in the large house. Alarms had been set—not that he expected any security system would stop Zahid Bin-Asfour. The photographers had wandered off shortly after dark. Slipping into the estate would not be all that difficult, even with the security system on. Turning the system off would make it much too clear that Kadir expected company.

Kadir kept a number of weapons close by, including Cassandra's sister's six-shooter. It was by far the least sophisticated of his weaponry, but he felt a fondness for it, just the same.

The hours dragged by. He had been alone in the past. At times he had treasured those few times when he was truly and completely alone. But tonight he simply felt desolate. He had grown accustomed to the voices of others in his circle. Most of all, he had grown accustomed to Cassandra.

Sitting in a darkened room of the deserted estate—the office he had claimed as his own on the second floor—Kadir allowed his mind to wander.

Maybe if he caught Zahid, maybe if he killed the man who had threatened his life on many occasions—maybe then he could indulge in a private life. At the moment, he could not imagine a private life that did not have Cassandra Klein in it.

What would she think of Kahani? Would she find peace in the villa by the sea, as he did? Would she join him in his quest for change? To marry a woman from Silvershire and ask that his countrymen and coworkers accept her would not be easy, and yet…love was universal, and in Cassandra there dwelled all that a woman could be if she were offered the right opportunities. She was the living, breathing embodiment of what he wished to bring to his country.

Kadir sat in the dark for hours and waited for an attack of some kind of come. A bomb, a bullet, a knife in the back. The estate had been under surveillance, so another explosion was unlikely, as there had been no opportunity for a bomb to be planted. No, since the first two attempts had failed, he expected this one would be conducted face-to-face. With any luck, he'd see the attack coming and get off a few shots first.

Without luck—he was as good as dead.

Cassandra's anger toward Kadir had bled over to his friend Sharif, who'd known all along what was going to happen. Their conversation about the situation had been short and without satisfaction, since Sharif was no more happy about the plan than she was.

For once, they actually agreed about something. That agreement was not at all comforting.

Sharif didn't want to be here, she knew that, but he refused to leave—even when she ordered him to do so. He'd followed her to the market this morning, sullen but ever present. Since returning to her flat, he'd split his time between pacing the halls talking to himself and pacing in the kitchen, drinking the incredibly strong coffee he'd made in her machine. No wonder he didn't sleep!

After a long Saturday of shopping, cleaning, doing laundry and worrying, Cassandra ate a salad in her kitchen for dinner before settling onto the couch to watch television. Well, the television was on. She didn't pay much attention to what was on the screen. Sharif was in the kitchen, pacing, drinking coffee *and* talking to himself. Now and then she picked up a word she could decipher. *Stupid. Dangerous. Nonsense.* Apparently some of his thoughts mirrored her own.

When her mother called—not for the first time today—and started to leave an almost panicked message on the answering machine, Cassandra picked up. She'd put this conversation off for two days, and she supposed it was time to get it done, as best she could.

At first, Cassandra allowed her mother to rant. Piper Klein was worried, after all, and rightfully so. It was a mother's privilege. Cassandra didn't say much. In the end she told her mother she was fine, and that she really didn't want to talk about Sheik Kadir and what had happened. Not yet. She couldn't lie to her mother the way she had to Ms. Dunn and everyone else at the ministry, not even by allowing assumptions that were untrue. It was for that reason that she'd avoided talking to her mum for so long. So she told her mother that she simply could not discuss what had happened—not yet—and then she ended the call with relief.

She only gave a moment's thought as to how she'd handle the face-to-face meeting with her mother next week, when her parents came to Silverton for the Founder's Day Gala.

Cassandra plopped back onto the couch, relieved that the conversation she'd dreaded was over. She didn't bother to turn up the volume on the television. The images cast oddly broken light around the room, but she didn't really care what the people on the TV had to say.

She'd passed many nights just like this, alone in her apartment. But she had never felt quite this alone—not even on her worst days. It was all Kadir's fault, because he'd introduced her to the reality of not being alone. Was it worth it? Was the pain she was suffering right now worth the joy she'd experienced for a few short days?

At the moment she couldn't answer with a hearty yes…but she couldn't answer no, either.

She thought she heard a soft shuffle from the hallway that led to her bedroom. Or was it just misdirected sound from the television? Sharif continued to mumble in the kitchen. Maybe that was what she'd heard. And then she heard the shuffle again.

Just what she needed. Mice! Mrs. Thatcher, who lived alone in the flat next door, had had a rodent problem last year, but Cassandra had never seen any mice in her place. She knew, of course, that didn't mean they weren't there.

Sharif continued to talk to himself, even as Cassandra made her way to the kitchen pantry to grab a broom. While it would be nice to pretend she hadn't heard that soft noise, she'd never get to sleep tonight unless she found out for herself. A broom seemed a proper enough weapon. Her reluctant bodyguard watched her depart from the kitchen with the broom in hand. If he'd been any other man, she might've asked him to handle her mouse problem, but he wasn't any other man—and she wasn't a girl who ran to anyone to fix her problems.

Cassandra stepped into the hallway and reached for the light switch. Before she could flip the switch, a hand flew out of the dark and grasped her wrist tightly. She started to scream, but not much sound escaped before the intruder—not a mouse after all—clapped a hand over her mouth. The broom dropped to the floor as he edged her toward the light of the main room, where the television continued to play.

Sharif stood in the kitchen doorway, eyes hard, mouth grim, gun in hand and trained…on her. Heaven above, she had never trusted that man….

And then she felt the press of cold steel against her temple, and a voice she had heard before said, "Drop it, Al-Asad, or she dies here and now."

Slowly, reluctantly, Sharif allowed his weapon to drop.

"Toss it to the floor," the intruder commanded, and Sharif complied.

Her reluctant bodyguard took one decidedly unthreatening step forward. "Let her go. You and I can…"

He didn't get a chance to say more. The press of steel at Cassandra's temple lessened, she saw the tip of a suppressor as the weapon changed direction and then the man who held her fired. The weapon made a coughing sound, which was louder than she'd expected, but not loud enough to alarm the neighbors. Sharif dropped to the floor, and Cassandra watched as blood bloomed on his trousers, just above the knee.

The man who held her relaxed considerably once Sharif was down, and he allowed her to turn just enough to see his face. She should not be surprised, not after listening to Kadir's suppositions about who might've betrayed him. The first thing she said was, "You shaved."

Hakim, Kadir's timid personal secretary, turned his weapon on her once again.

The phone near his hand rang, and Kadir answered. Sharif was supposed to call every three hours with a report on Cassandra, and he was fifteen minutes late. Sharif was never late.

Kadir said hello, fully expecting another tirade from Sharif on how he should be here, instead of guarding a woman who meant nothing to him or to Kahani.

The voice that responded to Kadir's greeting was not that of Sharif.

"I have them both," Hakim said, his voice distinctly recognizable.

Kadir did not have to ask who both were. There were

only two people in the world he cared about. "Let me speak to them."

"No."

"How do I know you have them?"

Hakim sighed. "Don't be tiresome, Excellency. Apparently Al-Asad did not take your concerns about Ms. Klein seriously. Security was dismal. I entered her apartment through a window. It was very easy to slip the insufficient lock. Once I was in the apartment, she came after me with a *broom*." He had the nerve to laugh lightly. "Taking Al-Asad was no problem at all, once I had Ms. Klein in my hands."

"I wish to speak with them."

"No, there is no time. If you ask again, I will shoot one of them."

Kadir's heart leapt in his chest. "Have they been harmed?"

"Not yet," Hakim answered. "If you cooperate, they might both very well survive this night."

Anything, Kadir almost shouted into the phone. *Anything at all.* Instead he answered calmly. "What do you want in exchange for their lives?"

"Yours," Hakim answered without emotion.

Hakim had been Kadir's personal secretary for years. Had he always been aligned with Zahid? Had he been blackmailed into assisting Bin-Asfour in his quest? "Why?" Kadir asked calmly. "If Zahid has threatened you or your family, if he's forcing you to do things you don't want to do, I can help. Sharif and I can help you, Hakim, if you'll allow us to do so."

"It's not that simple, Excellency. Bin-Asfour has offered me a lot of money to deliver proof of your death. I won't have to work, not ever again, once this chore is done. I'll have a villa of my own, and workers to serve me and my days of answering to your call, to *anyone's* call, will be over."

Kadir placed a tired hand on his forehead. All this for money. Dozens dead, Sharif and Cassandra threatened, all for wealth. "If you believe Bin-Asfour will part with that kind of money, you're mistaken. He'll kill you without a second thought before he'll part with even a fraction of his fortune."

"I don't believe you," Hakim said gently. "Zahid wants you dead so badly he'll gladly pay anything."

"When did he make you this offer?" After all, there had been many times in the past when Hakim could've put a bullet in his employer's brain. Not without being caught, however.

"A few months ago. Planning an execution that didn't leave me in the hands of your security detail was trickier than I thought it would be."

"So you came up with a plan to kill them all."

"Yes," Hakim said, without so much as a touch of remorse. "Now, quit stalling and let's get to tonight's business. You know where I am. If you're not here in fifteen minutes, the first shot will be fired. If you don't come alone and unarmed, two shots will be fired. One into Al-Asad's brain, the other into Ms. Klein's."

Kadir didn't bother to say another word. He hung up the phone. Before heading for the garage, he yanked up the receiver once again and dialed Cassandra's apartment. Maybe Hakim had been bluffing, and Cassandra and Sharif were fine. He could be ambushed making his way to Cassandra's rescue, when she wasn't in any danger. But Cassandra's phone rang twice, and then Hakim's voice answered with a proper

"Klein residence," which would not alarm an unsuspecting caller.

Kadir didn't answer, and very soon Hakim laughed again. "You now have thirteen minutes, Excellency."

Hakim's last words had painted a frightening picture in his brain, and Kadir could barely think. He did, however, think to grab the six-shooter before he ran from the room.

Sharif wasn't dead, but he'd been badly wounded.

Her next-door neighbor, Mrs. Thatcher, knocked loudly on the door shortly after Cassandra's short scream, and with Hakim's gun at her head, Cassandra explained through the closed door that she'd seen a mouse and been alarmed. The woman was satisfied, and she headed to her flat to call the building manager to make a complaint. She was not going through *that* ordeal again, she vowed.

Cassandra assisted Hakim with Sharif's body. The man with the gun allowed her to bind the wound with a strip of a sheet she'd just laundered, and she worked quickly, since Hakim did not seem to be blessed with patience. That done, they eased the wounded man into a kitchen chair, and Cassandra tried to make sure Sharif was comfortable before Hakim began to duct tape him to the straight back and the legs of the chair.

And then Hakim did the same thing to her, at gunpoint, of course. While he strapped her ankles to the chair, Cassandra pushed her panic down and asked, "You work for Zahid Bin-Asfour, don't you?"

"Don't be nosy, Ms. Klein. No good can come of it."

"Did you murder Prince Reginald?"

His head snapped up. The question took him very much by surprise. "No. Why do you ask?"

"It's suspected that followers of Bin-Asfour murdered the prince. I just wondered…" She shrugged her shoulders, as best she could.

When she was taped to the chair to his satisfaction, Hakim placed his face close to hers. "Why would Bin-Asfour have Prince Reginald killed when the prince had just agreed to align himself with the organization after he took the throne? It would be quite a blow to the Kahani government for Bin-Asfour to be officially recognized and embraced by the throne of Silvershire. Zahid was quite upset when he heard of the prince's death."

"So, do you think someone from the Kahani government murdered the prince?"

The formerly humble secretary shook his head. Of course, she imagined his humility had always been an act. "What difference does it make? You should be worried about your own life, not that of a prince who's already dead."

"I just want to know, that's all. When I get out of here, I might get a promotion if I can shed some light on the murder." In truth, she was merely stalling for time, but if she did get out of here alive, and if she could give new information to those who were investigating the prince's murder…maybe she'd be forgiven for not telling a few secrets along the way.

Hakim left Cassandra and Sharif alone in the kitchen, not that they were in any position to do anything. He was wounded, unarmed and constrained. She was not in much better shape.

"No one from the Kahani government had any part to play in Prince Reginald's death, I swear it," Sharif said in a lowered, less-than-steady voice.

"As if you'd tell me if you knew any differently," Cassandra responded.

Sharif locked his eyes to hers. "There's no reason for me to lie to you about anything. Hakim's going to kill us, you know," he said calmly.

Cassandra's heart leapt. "Maybe not…"

"Even if Kadir comes to save us, which is no doubt the plan, Hakim will still kill us. I just hope Kadir is smart enough to stay away, but I suspect he is not." There was a decided edge to Sharif's voice.

"He'll know it's a trap…" she began.

"And he won't care." Sharif sighed in evident disgust. "Do you wonder why I'm here with you when I should be with Kadir? Do you wonder why I have been guarding you when I should be watching my old friend's back? Do you wonder why I did not attempt to shoot Hakim while he held you?"

"Yes," Cassandra whispered.

Again Sharif looked her squarely in the eye. "Since we're going to die, I might as well tell you. Maybe you should know, since it's come to this. Kadir told me, back in Leonia, that he cared for you the way I once cared for Amala, and that if anything happened to you, he would never forgive me. I care little for his forgiveness, but Amala loved her little brother, and if he loves you then I have no choice but to do as he asks, for her sake as well as his."

"But he…" *He doesn't love me,* Cassandra started to say. The words froze in her mouth. No, Kadir did love her; he just hid that love for his own reasons. "Thank you for telling me," she said.

"You should know, before you die." Sharif sounded like a man who accepted death easily. Maybe he didn't have anything to lose. Maybe he was ready for death. He'd lost his love a long time ago. He shook his head dismally. "I should have taken the shot when I had the chance, but I was afraid Hakim would move and I'd hit you. Kadir would never forgive me if that happened."

Sharif began to work against the bonds at his back, but minutes passed and he didn't seem to be making progress.

Hakim reentered the kitchen, saw Sharif struggling to free himself and raised his gun. He fired one shot, and Sharif went still.

Cassandra gasped, and then she screamed. Hakim turned the weapon on her. His hands were oddly steady, his eyes decidedly cold.

"Be quiet, or you're next. His Excellency is on the way, and it looks as if I no longer need either one of you."

Chapter 15

Kadir parked a short way down the street from Cassandra's apartment building, pulling the black sports car he'd driven to Barton, what seemed like a lifetime ago, to the curb. The security personnel who had been assigned to watch him had tried to follow as he'd sped from the estate, but the sports car was too fast for them and he'd managed to lose them quickly.

He had a few minutes left before Hakim's deadline was over. Now was not the time to panic and rush forward. Now was the time to stop and think. Was Hakim working alone? That was likely, since money was involved and Hakim would probably not want to share, but Kadir could not be sure. He left the car and walked toward Cassandra's building. If he went to her front door he'd be dead within seconds—and so would Cassandra and Sharif, if indeed they still lived.

Kadir stepped into the shadows of an alleyway and dialed Cassandra's number on his cell phone. After two rings Hakim answered, once again using his most professional voice to say, "Klein residence."

"I'm outside the building," Kadir said in a voice that held no emotion. "Give Ms. Klein or Sharif the telephone. When you walk outside and I can see you while I still hear your hostages' voices and know they are well, then you'll get what you want."

Hakim scoffed. "No. You come to me, or there's no deal."

"Then there's no deal." Kadir sincerely hoped Hakim could not hear the panic in his voice. "If I walk in that front door, we're all dead, and I know that well. You're not going to leave witnesses to the assassination if you have an opportunity to avoid it."

"You've just condemned your friends to death," Hakim said solemnly.

"Have I?" Anger crept into Kadir's voice. "Zahid isn't paying you a dime to kill Ms. Klein and Al-Asad. I know you're willing to murder others in order to get to me. Sayyid and Fahd and Haroun and all the other men you knew and worked with, you killed them all to get to me. But if you waste your time murdering Ms. Klein and Al-Asad while I walk away, how does it benefit you? It doesn't. I'm on the north corner, as you exit the building."

"Say hello," Hakim instructed, his mouth far from the receiver.

Cassandra answered. "Don't come up here, Kadir!" she said in a loud voice. "Sharif is…"

The connection ended abruptly—by Hakim's hand, no doubt. Sharif was *what?* Dead? Hurt? A part of the plan, as Cassandra had once suspected?

Kadir dialed the number once again, but the phone rang until the answering machine message came on the line. He headed with a quick step toward the entrance to Cassandra's building. No matter what he'd said in trying to draw Hakim away from his hostages, he would not, could not, leave Cassandra and Sharif in the hands of an armed man who meant them harm.

Before Kadir reached the entrance, Hakim walked out of the building. He was not alone. Cassandra was held before the traitor, and though Kadir could not see the gun, he knew it was there, between Hakim and Cassandra.

It was late at night, and the street was deserted and dark. A lone streetlamp shone down on the three of them, providing the only bit of significant light. Kadir and Hakim each stepped closer to one another, cautiously, slowly. Kadir kept the six-shooter down, slightly behind him and in shadow.

"I'm here," he said tersely. "Let her go."

"No," Hakim responded.

Kadir stuck the six-shooter into the waistband of his pants, there at his spine, and lifted his hands high. "I only want to see the others go free. You can have me. I'm tired of fighting at every turn, I'm tired of watching Zahid win all the time. What do I have to live for, anyway? Zahid took my life from me a long time ago, when he compelled me to sacrifice everything in the name of what he'd done. At this point death will be a relief."

Hakim smiled. "Good."

With a shift of his hand, Hakim allowed Kadir to see the weapon with which he threatened Cassandra.

"Let her go," Kadir said once more.

"No." Hakim's focus was now almost entirely on Kadir, who still had his arms raised. The gun was pointed at him, and Hakim's grip on Cassandra was not as earnest as it had once been. Kadir looked Cassandra in the eye and nodded once, and somehow she knew what he silently asked of her. She yanked once and stumbled away from Hakim. Kadir dropped to the ground as Hakim fired the first shot. He rolled away and drew the six-shooter he'd concealed at his spine.

Hakim was surprised; he'd expected no resistance at this point. From the ground Kadir fired twice. Hakim fired again, but again his bullet went wide.

Kadir fired again and Hakim fell. The gun he'd held went skittering across the sidewalk.

Kadir ran to Cassandra, who floundered as she regained her footing.

"Are you all right?"

She nodded, and he steadied her with one hand.

"Sharif?"

"He's hurt badly. Hakim shot him." Cassandra lifted her head and looked Kadir in the eye. Maybe now she realized why he couldn't afford to love her. By knowing him, by being important to him, she had become Hakim's target. She could've been killed.

The security guards Kadir had managed to lose temporarily pulled their car to the curb and jumped out simultaneously, their trained eyes taking in the situation. At the same time, residents of the apartment building stepped outside to see what was going on.

Kadir turned his attentions to the security guards. "This is the man who planted a bomb on my yacht. I'm quite sure he also hired someone to take a shot at me as I left the Maitland Museum, no doubt to impel me to make the trip to Leonia sooner than I'd planned. A member of the Kahani Ministry of Defense is in Ms.

Klein's apartment, and he's been wounded. I would appreciate it you could call for assistance."

The two men jumped to do all that needed to be done, and Kadir led Cassandra back into the apartment building, weaving past curious neighbors and avoiding all questions. He wanted to take Cassandra's arm, he wanted to steady her. But he didn't. They could not appear to be close, not even now.

Sharif was bound to a sturdy wooden chair in Cassandra's kitchen. He'd been shot twice, once in the thigh, once in the shoulder. The injury to his thigh had been bound, but the shoulder wound was raw and continued to bleed. His head hung forward, limply.

Kadir began to cut the tape that held Sharif to the chair. "The wound in his shoulder doesn't appear to be too bad."

A growl rose from the man seated in the chair. "That's because it's not in *your* shoulder."

Kadir smiled. Sharif was going to be fine. Grouchy, until his shoulder and leg healed, but, still, alive and well.

When Sharif was free, Kadir steadied the wounded man and turned his attention to Cassandra. "I'm sorry you were pulled into this," he said. "This is not your war, and if Zahid's soldiers had any nobility at all..." He tamped down the anger. "But they do not. I'm sorry," he said again.

Sharif lifted his head and looked at Cassandra. Kadir could not help but notice the glance that passed between them, but he could not even begin to decipher it.

"We survived," Sharif said. "For a while there, I was certain we would not."

"I know what you mean," Cassandra said, her voice shaking slightly. "For now, let's worry about getting you to a doctor. Help is on the way."

Sharif grunted. "I hate doctors."

Kadir wished he could feel a moment's ease, knowing the man who'd tried to kill him, a man who had murdered many innocents on board the yacht, was dead. But unfortunately Zahid Bin-Asfour never lacked for soldiers, and he knew another would soon arrive to replace Hakim. Someone else could be paid, blackmailed or seduced into doing all that Zahid desired.

Kadir supported Sharif to the best of his ability, trying to be strong and yet easy with the wounded man. He was afraid to so much as move Sharif to the sofa in the other room, even though he would surely be more comfortable there. It would be wise to leave even the smallest of movements to the medical personnel that were on the way.

Sharif had signed on to this risk long ago. He knew the possible cost of fighting Zahid Bin-Asfour and his followers, and he'd gladly accepted that risk. But Cassandra was innocent in this. She should not be in Zahid's sights, not tonight, not ever.

It was possible that only Hakim knew how Kadir felt about Cassandra. It was possible that Zahid was blessedly ignorant of the fact that Kadir had been foolish enough to think, for even a few days, that he could have a personal life.

Kadir continued to kneel beside Sharif, but he lifted his head and stared at Cassandra. "Perhaps you should wait in the other room," he said briskly.

"What?" She sounded confused, and scared and... surprised.

"Go to your bedroom, lock your door and when people start to ask questions don't tell anyone that you ever knew me as anything more than a representative of my country. You were caught in the middle, you were at the wrong place at the wrong time. That's all."

"But…"

"When I get Sharif to the hospital, I'll make a few calls of my own. As far as anyone is concerned, you barely know me. You didn't realize that I'd survived the explosion until you read it in the newspaper, and it will suit you well if you never see me again."

"Kadir…"

"Go, Ms. Klein."

She stiffened, took a step back and then spun on her heel and walked away. He watched her until she was out of sight. She slammed her bedroom door heartily.

From the bloody seat where Sharif awaited assistance drifted an uncertain, whispered, "I really did think we were going to die…."

Cassandra did exactly as Ms. Dunn asked. She threw herself into preparations for the gala and made sure everyone was aware of the special needs of those dignitaries visiting from other countries. Food, religion, personal eccentricities. There was a detailed file for each and every foreign guest of note.

Her despondency over losing Kadir had been lifted, on that night when she'd been kidnapped and Sharif had been shot. Odd that such terrible events could make her feel better.

Kadir did care about her. He did love her. And even if she never saw him again, knowing that made it all worthwhile. The tears she still shed, the pain she still felt, the deep emptiness she didn't know how to discard…it was all worthwhile. She knew love.

Kadir had only called her once, to tell her that Sharif was well. He'd be out of commission for a while, and was apparently extremely grumpy, but he'd live, and even regain full use of his wounded arm and leg, with therapy. After that—nothing. She'd heard that Kadir would get his meeting with Lord Carrington on Wednesday evening. Would he even bother to remain in Silverton for the gala? He had a new Kahani security detail in place and had settled back into the Redmond Estate, but once his meeting with Lord Carrington was done, there was no reason for Kadir to stay in Silvershire at all.

The news Cassandra had obtained from Hakim, before his death, had answered some of the questions surrounding Prince Reginald's death. Zahid Bin-Asfour had not been involved, and neither had the government of Kahani. There was no longer any fear of potentially embarrassing press to keep Lord Carrington from meeting with Kadir. Who knows? Maybe they'd even form that alliance Kadir wanted so very badly.

It was very difficult to remain angry with a man who so obviously wanted to do good for his country.

Cassandra kept herself busy during the day, but when evening came, her mind wandered to Kadir. Some nights she actually expected him to come to the door and confess his love for her. But of course he didn't come.

On Tuesday night, Cassandra donned her plain blue pajamas and sat down to write her mother a letter.

Dear Mum,
This is a busy week at work, as you know. There's still so much to be done, I'm surprised Ms. Dunn doesn't just chain us to our desks and make us stay until the gala is done.

She hadn't told her mother about the kidnapping, about seeing a man shot, or about learning that Kadir did, indeed, love her. The events of Saturday night had been kept under wraps, and only a handful of people knew what had actually happened. It would be best, however, if she kept her parents away from Mrs. Thatcher this coming weekend....

I do love Kadir. Not that it matters, much. He's going back to Kahani this week. Maybe tomorrow, after his meeting with Lord Carrington, maybe Sunday, after the gala. The sheik and I are too different in too many ways. We could never make it work, and I'm smart enough to understand that. I love him, and he broke my heart. Even though it still hurts, I'm not sorry. I'll never be sorry. Don't worry about me. I truly am fine.
See you Saturday. I hope Dad got a new tuxedo!
Love,
Cassandra

She sealed up the letter, prepared it to post in the morning, as usual, and walked through her familiar flat, turning off lights and preparing for bed.

When someone knocked on the door, she wasn't surprised. She should've been, given the late hour, but she wasn't. She looked through the peephole, and again, she was not surprised.

Cassandra opened the door. "So, are you here as Excellency or as Kadir?"

He took her in his arms, and that was answer enough. Kadir came into her flat, kicked the door shut behind him and then took the time to lock it.

"Are there guards in the hallway?" she asked. "Spies lurking outside my window?"

"No. No one knows I'm here. I slipped away from my new bodyguards." Kadir laid his lips on her throat and sighed, in what felt and tasted like relief. "It's the only way."

Cassandra put her arms around Kadir and held on. This was secret, she understood that. No one could know…and it wasn't going to last much longer.

"Kadir…"

He placed a finger beneath her chin and tipped her face up so she was looking him in the eye. "No talking," he whispered. "No questions, no tears, no whispered wishes that we know won't ever come true. If you can't agree to that, then I'll leave now."

"You're here just for the sex, then?"

"Yes," he whispered.

She kissed him, knowing that once again he was lying to her, glad for this one last night, trying once again to make memories that would last a lifetime. There was desperation in his kiss, and in hers, but the desperation was quickly replaced by the passion they'd always shared.

Cassandra wanted to take her mouth from Kadir's and tell him that she loved him. But she didn't—and she didn't have to. He already knew.

And she knew, just as well, that he loved her. He would never tell her so, but she knew it to the depths of her soul. Sharif's words, when he'd thought they were going to die, only confirmed what her heart knew without question.

They kissed and took one step and then another toward the bedroom, fingers unbuttoning and unzipping as they went, hands exploring and arousing. Since her clothing consisted of pajamas and panties and nothing else, getting her undressed was easy work for Kadir.

Kadir, on the other hand, was fully dressed. He also carried Lexie's six-shooter, which had been tucked away in a shoulder holster he wore beneath his jacket. As they reached the bed, he removed the six-shooter and laid it on the bedside table. By this point, she was already completely undressed, and several of his buttons and half a zipper had been undone. She lay back on the bed and watched as Kadir finished undressing himself. He had come prepared, and placed a couple of wrapped condoms on the table, there near the six-shooter.

He didn't rush, but neither did he dawdle. And he kept his eyes, his beautiful bedroom eyes that spoke of love even when he denied it, on her the entire time.

When he crawled onto the bed, she wrapped her arms around his bare body and pulled him closer. The sensation of his skin against hers was heavenly, and she closed her eyes and drank him in. He kissed her throat, and then her mouth and then moved back to her throat again. Such soft, talented lips he had. She wallowed in the kiss, and in her body's response.

One hand skimmed her body from breasts to thigh, and then back to breasts again. Fingers raked—gently, barely touching here and there and then rubbing much harder in other places. There was no rush, though her body seemed to spiral toward their joining. It spiraled slowly. Inexorably, but without even a hint of haste. Making love, even for the last time, should never be rushed. It should be savored, and that's what they did. They savored.

Kadir kissed the crook of her elbow, and let his lips

linger there for a moment. The sensation was wonderful, and she smiled as his tongue flickered in and out. He teased her with his fingers, but never too boldly. Each movement was languid, unhurried. Maybe he was making memories, too.

When it seemed she couldn't take any more, Cassandra rolled Kadir onto his back and explored his body as he had explored hers. She kissed his throat and his mouth, raked her hands over the length of his body, searched for those unexpected places where a kiss or a proper stroke made him moan or quiver. Beneath the ear, just beneath his navel, the inside of his thigh.

She raked her fingertips up and down his erection, and then straddled him to lower her head and taste him, very briefly and with a flick of her tongue. It was that flick of the tongue that made him reach for the bedside table and the condoms there.

Kadir made love to her as slowly as he had aroused her. They didn't rush, because they knew when this night was over it would be truly *over.* After he walked out of her apartment—in a few minutes or a few hours— she'd probably never see him again.

So she felt the beginning waves of orgasm with a touch of sadness. Too soon. It was all too soon. She couldn't tell Kadir that she loved him...not if she wanted him to stay a while longer...but as her body cracked and quivered beneath his, she grabbed on to him and cried out his name, and when he came with her, his own completion coming as her body still trembled around his, she said, "I'm not sorry, Kadir. I'll never be sorry."

It was near dawn when Kadir rose from Cassandra's bed, leaving her sleeping deeply and with evident contentment. He dressed without making a sound, but when it came time to return the six-shooter to the holster, he hesitated. The small weapon was not his. It had been borrowed, and it had served its purpose.

Cassandra didn't wake. He could simply walk away. It would be easier than saying goodbye, even if she tried to make the parting easy for him.

He sat on the side of the bed, dressed and ready to go—and yet *not* ready to go. He drew down the covers and placed one hand on Cassandra's bare back. She had a beautiful back, perfectly shaped and feminine and strong. Had he ever told her that he loved the sight of her bare back? As well as the curve of her hips, and her smile, and her feet with the pink toenails, and the grace of her long fingers and…everything. Everything about her was beautiful, and well-loved.

Kadir leaned down and kissed Cassandra's spine. She squirmed, sighed and then smiled in response.

"Goodbye," he whispered.

Still more asleep than awake, she said, "Already? No…don't…it can't be time…."

When she tried to turn over, he pressed his mouth to her shoulder and very gently kept her in place. He couldn't walk out without saying goodbye, but neither did he wish to wallow in the pain.

"You are amazing," he whispered. "There is no woman on the earth quite like you, Cassandra Klein."

She was fully awake now. He felt it, in the tension of her shoulder and the change in her breath.

"Will you be at the gala on Saturday?" she asked. No wonder she didn't turn to face him. Even though she tried to hide it, he heard the tears in her voice. She was not a woman to weep easily, and it hurt him to know he had caused her even a single tear.

"No. After my meeting with Lord Carrington, I'll return to Kahani immediately. After all that's happened, it's for the best."

"Too bad," she said, trying to sound nonchalant and failing badly. "I never got to see you in your traditional Kahani dress."

"Trust me," he said, kissing her shoulder again. "You've missed nothing."

They tried to make light in this last moment together, but could not, and eventually Cassandra turned to him— red eyes and all. She barely lifted up.

"I'll miss you," she said sincerely.

He kissed her quickly, then moved away while he still could. When he reached the door he whispered, lowly so she would not hear, "I'm not sorry, either."

Even though at the moment, he hurt like hell.

Chapter 16

Thursday morning found Sharif Al-Asad a cross, short-tempered patient. All the nurses were afraid of him. He was scheduled to be released the following afternoon, and no one on the staff would be sorry to see him go.

Cassandra arranged the cut flowers she'd brought to cheer up his room, even though he'd already declared that he hated flowers and did not want them in his sight. She'd decided that Sharif was not nearly as irritable as he pretended to be. Maybe he was, but it suited her to believe that he was putting on a show.

When Sharif realized that she wasn't going to toss the flowers or take them with her when she left, he sighed in pure disgust and leaned back against a pile of soft pillows.

"Did you see Kadir last night before he left?" Cassandra asked.

"Yes." Sharif did not elaborate.

Did he think she was going to cry on his wounded shoulder? That wasn't her style, and loving and losing wasn't going to change that. Besides, if she did want to cry on someone's shoulder, it wouldn't be Sharif's. He was seriously lacking in the empathy department. "I hear his meeting with Lord Carrington went very well."

"So I heard," Sharif said suspiciously.

Cassandra quit fiddling with the flowers and smiled down at Sharif, giving him her full attention. He had refused to allow the nurses to shave his face or cut his hair, so he still looked very much like a wild man. The wildness was mostly in his eyes, however, not in his untended hair and scruffy beard. She sat on the side of the bed, startling him with her easy familiarity.

"Since things went so well with Lord Carrington, I expect Kadir will come back to Silvershire, now and then," she said in a lowered voice, so no one passing in the hall would hear her.

Sharif's face hardened. "Don't fool yourself into believing—"

"I'm not fooling myself," she interrupted. "I don't expect Kadir to come riding in on a white horse to sweep me away. I have my life, and he has his, and they don't exactly suit one another well. I've known that all along. There's no fairy-tale ending waiting for us." Still, she had hope—an unexpected, perhaps foolish, girlish hope—that she would see Kadir again. If all she could have was a night here and there…she'd take it. Gladly.

"Why are you here?" Sharif asked, his voice brusque and gruff.

She straightened his covers with a nervous gesture. "To bring you flowers, of course. Besides, I wanted to see you before you go, to make sure you're on the mend and…"

"And what?" he snapped when she faltered.

Cassandra looked Sharif in the eye. "I'll be blunt. No one loves Kadir the way you and I do. I just…" She'd practiced what she wanted to say all last night and this morning, and now the words wouldn't come as she'd planned. Best to be plainspoken.

"Watch his back, please. Keep him safe, if you can." She sighed and once again fiddled nervously with the top edge of the sheet. "I'd like to think that one day soon the two of you will see Zahid dead, or in prison, and I'd like to think when that happens, Kadir will be safe. But that's not entirely true, and deep down I know it. When Zahid Bin-Asfour is gone, someone else will take his place, just as someone else will take Hakim's place. Kadir is so determined to bring change to Kahani, that's all he sees, and I'm afraid he won't take proper care of himself." Again she looked Sharif in the eye. "So I want you to do it."

She thought that Sharif would refuse out of spite, since he didn't like her at all, but instead he said, "I'll resign my post and take over as Kadir's head of security, if he will have me." A crooked smile twisted his lips. "After the debacle at your flat, he might not want me."

"He will."

"I failed."

Cassandra smiled as she stood. "I can't know for sure, but I have a feeling you don't fail very often. After allowing Hakim to sneak up on us once, I don't imagine that sort of thing will happen again."

Sharif's answer was a low growl. She took that as an affirmative, and reached for his unbound hand to shake on the deal, such as it was. Kadir would be in good hands, and nothing else mattered.

"You know," she said as she ended the handshake, "if you had a girlfriend you wouldn't be so irritable all the time."

Her boldness shocked him, and his dark eyes widened.

"You've grieved long enough. Amala wouldn't want you to live your entire life in pain."

"You do not understand the pain of which you speak," he said in a soft voice.

"No, I don't," she admitted. "I can't even begin to comprehend all you've been through. But I do understand love." A week ago she hadn't understood love at all, but now… "Not completely," she added, "but more than I once did."

"Until Zahid is dead, I can't—"

"No," she interrupted. "Until Zahid is dead, you *won't.* There's a very big difference. You're hurting yourself, not him, by carrying all this rage in your heart. I don't think Amala would approve."

Sharif did not agree, of course. Did he ever agree with anyone about anything? Likely not.

But she felt quite sure he would protect Kadir with his very life.

The waves near the villa did not soothe Kadir today, not at all. Instead they reminded him of another bit of ocean, and another seaside home that was not his own.

He had a new security detail in place, a new secretary and a new aide, courtesy of the ministry. Everything appeared to be back to normal—or as normal as was possible, given the circumstances.

His home was filled with strangers…and though they had all been cleared by the ministry, he did not entirely trust them. Would he ever? Betrayal from within was his greatest fear, and that fear had come to pass, thanks to Hakim.

His new secretary, who was achingly young and eager, stepped onto the balcony. "Excellency, you have a guest." The young man glanced over his shoulder, obviously nervous about this particular caller.

Before Kadir could ask who had called, Sharif stepped through the door and onto the balcony, sparing only a quick glance to the vista before him. His shoulder and one arm were bandaged, he used a cane and favored his wounded leg…and he smiled.

"I didn't expect you until tomorrow," Kadir said. "Did the physicians release you early?"

"No, I left on my own." Sharif looked at Kadir and the smile widened. "After receiving a very important phone call." Sharif didn't smile often these days, and never like this.

"What sort of phone call?" Kadir asked.

Sharif did not trust easily, either. He glanced at the new aide, and Kadir sent the young man inside with a nod of his head.

When they were alone, Sharif said, "If you remember, I told you I had a man inside Bin-Asfour's organization."

"Yes."

"I know why he's been trying to have you killed."

Kadir turned to his old friend and waited for more.

"It is his plan to make a move back into Kahani, to establish a stronghold here. He knows no one will fight him as strenuously as you, so he attempted to be rid of you before he made his move."

"You are just as much a danger to him as I am."

Sharif smiled crookedly, and without humor. "I do

not have your influence, Kadir. I'm a soldier who can be taken out at any time, without raising too many eyebrows. You, on the other hand, would be missed. Your death, when it comes, will be newsworthy."

For a moment they watched the ocean. Kadir waited for more—he knew more was coming—and then Sharif said, "I can't remember the sound of her voice."

Kadir turned to his friend. He knew who Sharif spoke of.

"At first I dreamed of Amala often, and in those dreams she spoke to me. In those days I could remember her voice, I could see her face so clearly. Now my memory fails me more often than not, and I haven't dreamed of her for a very long time. I still want Zahid dead, and now that he's in Kahani again, perhaps I can make that happen. But it won't change anything. It won't bring back the sound of her voice." Sharif glanced at Kadir with sharp eyes. "She would like your Ms. Klein. I know that much."

"Yes, she would."

"It's a shame things are as they are," Sharif added simply.

"Yes, it is."

There was a change in the way Sharif held his damaged body, as he changed the subject to that of business. "To continue with the reason for my early release from the hospital and my visit today… We know where Zahid is going to be tonight. There's a rather large drug deal taking place, right here in Kahani, and because it's so large, Zahid will be participating person-ally." Again, that humorless smile. "Wounded or not, I will be there. No one can keep me away. You?" His eyebrows lifted slightly.

"I wouldn't miss it."

He did know better than to believe their goal of the past fifteen years would be met tonight. Still, simply knowing it was possible lifted his heart.

Sharif turned his gaze to the sea. He sighed, as if he took the same pleasure in the sight that Kadir often had. "When Zahid is dead, do you think we can move on?"

"I don't know."

Sharif sighed again, but without the peacefulness that had marked his appreciation of the view. "Neither do I."

She should've expected everything to go wrong, and all at once.

Cassandra's parents arrived at her flat Saturday morning. Her dad had his favorite tux with him, and he declared it was just fine—even though it fit too snugly and the shirt had blue ruffles down the front and on the cuff. He swore it was not out of style, and never would be. The tuxedo was, in his opinion, a classic.

She managed to intercept Mrs. Thatcher, but wasn't sure she could keep it up all weekend. Maybe she'd tell her mum all about the exciting events of last Saturday in a letter. Someday, *not* someday soon. She certainly didn't want the news to come from a nosy neighbor.

Lexie showed up right after lunch, red eyed from crying after her ugly breakup with Stanley. There had been a time when Cassandra would've been tempted to remind her sister that she'd been warned about that man more than once. Today she just gave her sister a hug—or two or three—and then rummaged through her closet for a proper gown. The gala would surely cheer Lexie up. Cassandra and her big sister wore the same size, so finding something for Lexie to wear was easy. In the back of the closet hung one royal-blue satin dress Cassandra had ordered from a catalog and never worn. It didn't suit her at all, she'd decided after the fact, but it would be perfect for Lexie. Lexie liked flash in her wardrobe.

Ms. Dunn was in a dither—but that wasn't all that unusual. She called half a dozen times with questions or orders for the coming evening. Cassandra had to be at the palace early to make sure each and every one of the ambassadors was greeted in the proper way. She was not alone in that assignment, but she had to be there.

Lexie helped Cassandra style her hair atop her head, and she did a fine job of it. When that was done, Cassandra reached for the plain black dress she planned to wear.

"You're kidding me, right?" Lexie said as she grimaced at the gown.

"It's fine," Cassandra said. The dress was plain, floor-length, black and simply cut. No one would notice her in the black gown, but that was fine. She was supposed to blend into the background, not stand out in the crowd. The gala was fun, for most, but for Cassandra it would be an evening of work.

"Fine is not sufficient, little sister. I'll wear the black, you wear the pretty blue. I'm in mourning, after all."

Cassandra didn't point out that Stanley was not worth a moment's mourning. To Lexie, he was worthy. Nothing else mattered.

So Cassandra ended up wearing the royal-blue gown, leaving the black for Lexie. She left for the palace, knowing her family would join her later. She'd likely be too busy throughout the evening to spend any time with them, but they had each other. The gala was always a spectacle, and tonight everyone would be vying for a glimpse of the pregnant princess, and there would be a spectacular fireworks display at the end of the ball. It was scheduled for midnight, of course.

Cassandra arrived at the palace early. Along with Ms. Dunn and several other diplomatic aides, she made sure someone would be available to greet each ambassador in their own language, and that the food and drink served to them would be suitable. No fish for this one, no wine for another. No meat at all for that one, and this one had a fondness for fine champagne. One of the ambassadors had gained a reputation for grabbing the tushes of the prettier aides. Timothy Little had been assigned to see to all that ambassador's needs.

Once the guests began to arrive, Cassandra's job was almost done. All she had to do was cross her fingers and hope the evening went well and there were no blunders. If there was a blunder, she'd be available to fix it.

There would be no relaxing, no dancing, no curious peeks at the pregnant princess. Not for Cassandra.

She gave half an ear to the announcements of those dignitaries who arrived. Familiar names drifted in one ear and out the other as she wandered around the room keeping an eye on the ambassadors—and maintaining a distance from Timothy Little's tush-grabbing ambassador. The crowd grew steadily, until the ballroom was teeming with well-dressed guests who danced or flirted or conversed. Cassandra didn't participate in any of these pastimes, but she did listen. People speculated about Prince Reginald's murder and Lord Carrington's marriage. They whispered about royal scandals—some partly true, others entirely false.

Not long into the evening, Cassandra decided she should've worn the black; she drew too much attention in the blue satin. Men stared. They smiled and bowed and even winked. She ignored them all, of course.

She caught sight of her family, once or twice, and sighed at her father in his outdated tuxedo. And then a moment later she grinned widely. He was who he was, and she loved him. Her mum and Lexie both looked fabulous, of course, and Lexie even smiled a time or two. Good. The relationship with Stanley didn't deserve an extended mourning.

Half listening, Cassandra heard the announcement, "His Excellency Sheik Kadir Bin Arif Yusef Al-Nuri…" She spun around and moved to the side so she could see the arriving guests, as the announcement continued. Out of the corner of her eye she saw her mother and Lexie, with Dad right behind, hurrying to join her.

She had never seen Kadir in his traditional dress, not until tonight. He wore a small turban, loose-fitting pants, Kahani boots, a loose shirt and a vest. The colors of the costume were brighter than his usual attire—green and gold, primarily, with a touch of blue a shade darker than her gown. Two men flanked him, and they, too, wore traditional costumes. One was a large, muscled stranger; the other was Sharif. He'd trimmed his beard a little for the occasion, and limped with the assistance of a cane.

Kadir's eyes scanned the room as he stepped into the crowd. It didn't take him long to find her, and when he did he smiled widely.

"Oh, my God," Lexie whispered. "Who is that?"

"That's Ka…" She stopped herself. "Sheik Kadir, the director of…"

"No, no, no," Lexie said, her hand on Cassandra's arm. "The one on the left. The guy with the beard and the stare, and one arm in a sling and a cane."

Cassandra turned to look at her sister, aghast. "Sharif?"

"You *know* him? I take back everything I ever said about your job being boring. You have to introduce me," she whispered as the men drew closer.

"What about Stanley?" Cassandra asked.

Lexie laughed lightly. "Stanley who?"

Something odd happened as Kadir walked toward Cassandra. His stomach flipped over. His heart fluttered.

She was beautiful, even more so than he remembered. All sounds, the faces, movements and greetings of the revelers around him faded to nothing as he moved toward the woman he loved. And he did love her, more than he had imagined was possible.

The blue evening dress Cassandra wore hugged her body and showed off her perfect shape, but that wasn't what made her so beautiful. It wasn't the gown that made his heart flutter. It was the smile. It was the hope in her eyes, as he drew close enough to see them well.

When he reached her, he took her hand and bowed sharply. "Ms. Klein," he said in a low voice.

"Excellency," she responded. "I didn't expect to see you this evening."

He caught and held her eyes. "I didn't expect to be here." He greeted Cassandra's mother, and was introduced to her father and sister. The sister had eyes for Sharif, and she didn't even try to hide the fact. She moved right past Kadir and offered her hand to Sharif.

"And who are you, exactly?"

Sharif's eyes widened slightly. "I am the bodyguard," he responded.

"A wounded bodyguard. That's interesting. I'm Lexie, Cass's sister. Can you dance with that cane, or do you have to stick to your boss's side for the entire evening? I mean, it's not like anything's going to happen *here*."

Kadir gave Sharif a signal, a simple lifting of two fingers, and then turned to Cassandra's father. "Sir, may I have a moment of your time? Privately, if we may leave the ladies to their own devices."

He walked away with Cassandra's father, leaving three very curious ladies behind.

Cassandra watched the two men leave, her eyes slightly narrowed. What on earth was Kadir up to? Her father, in his too-snug tuxedo, and Kadir, in his traditional costume, walked with purpose toward a corner of the ballroom. Halfway there, Kadir leaned down and began to speak.

In rapid Arabic, Sharif ordered the other bodyguard to follow Kadir but to keep his distance.

Lexie asked Sharif again if he danced.

"No," he answered curtly.

"Oh." Lexie was not one to give up easily. "Well, you do talk, don't you? In English? What happened to your arm and your leg? Were you wounded in the line of duty?"

Sharif looked at Cassandra, casting her a quick, questioning glance. She shook her head very gently. She hadn't told her family anything about that night—and perhaps she never would.

Sharif then gave Lexie a stare that would chill any other woman. "Did you say your name is Lexie?"

"Yes," she said, thinking she had the man's attention.

"Sounds like an automobile."

Lexie laughed, not at all offended. "I suppose it does. It's short for Alexis."

"Ah, Alexis." The name rolled off Sharif's tongue

slowly, and Lexie looked as if she were about to melt into the floor.

Then she sighed. "Honey, you can call me Alexis any time."

It didn't take long for Sharif to quit fighting Lexie and just talk to her. He kept his eyes on Kadir and the oddly dressed man he spoke to with such passion, but he also listened to the woman who was so obviously infatuated with him. Once or twice, he even smiled.

After just a few minutes, Kadir and Cassandra's father headed back toward them. They both looked smug. Satisfied. Manly. Kadir didn't take his eyes off of her, not even for a second. He came directly to her, took her hand and asked for permission to speak to her privately.

A part of her wanted to hope that this was what it looked like...but she didn't dare to hope that much.

Kadir held her hand and led her to a large balcony. There the music and the voices from the ballroom were muted. Another couple shared the balcony with Cassandra and Kadir for a moment, but soon they drifted into the ballroom, arm in arm.

When they were alone, Kadir took Cassandra in his arms and kissed her. Softly, gently, but with more than a touch of real, true hunger. Cassandra sighed and laid her hands on his back. His arms were wrapped so warmly and possessively around her, she reveled in the touch. She had told Sharif that she hoped Kadir would come back to Silverton now and then, but heaven above—could she stand it? Could she bear to hold him and let him go, again and again?

For now she simply enjoyed the kiss. If she was going to learn to take what she could get, she'd have to enjoy the moments when she had Kadir—rather than worrying about how she'd feel after he was gone.

The kiss slowed, and Kadir dropped his arms. "Zahid Bin-Asfour was killed last night," he said as he took his mouth from hers.

Her heart experienced a little jolt. "What happened?"

"Late last night…early this morning…Kahani soldiers interrupted a very large drug deal. Many of Zahid's followers were killed. He almost escaped, but a few of us followed. He did not expect such opposition. After a short chase he was cornered and shot."

She touched Kadir's face. "Who shot him?"

"It doesn't matter."

Him, she thought. Or Sharif…or possibly both of them.

"All that matters is that Zahid is gone. This doesn't mean the danger is over," he said heatedly. "There are others out there who will be eager to take his place. There are others in Kahani who don't want the country to move forward. Some of them will fight. Unless I'm willing to change my name to Joe and hide myself away, there will always be the potential for danger."

She knew him too well. "That will never happen. You're no Joe." He had never fit well into that role.

He smiled down at her. "Cassandra Klein, my life is not entirely without risk, and the lives of those around me are not as safe as I would like them to be. Any woman I love might be a target of those who oppose me. I tried to walk away from you once, deciding that I would not put you in that position of danger, but I was wrong to make that choice for you. You're an intelligent woman, you know the dangers life with me will bring and the choice is yours. I have asked for your father's blessing, Cassandra, and received it. I love you. Will you marry me?"

Before she could answer, an explosion rocked the palace. Kadir's response was immediate and instinctive. He threw her to the ground and held his body over hers. His arms protected her head, and she was completely trapped beneath him. The balcony shook; in the ballroom, people began to scream. She smelled smoke.

In just a few seconds, amidst the panic and screams from the gala guests, it became clear that the explosion had originated elsewhere. Close by, but not directly beneath or beside them.

Kadir rose to his feet and assisted Cassandra, taking her hand and steadying her as she stood. Immediately they turned toward the ballroom. They saw Sharif headed this way, with Lexie and their parents gathered together. He and the other bodyguard were shepherding her family in this direction. Beyond them, there was pandemonium as guests ran for the exits. Kadir moved forward as if to join them.

"Wait!" Cassandra called, tugging on Kadir's hand and forcing him to stop the escape.

He turned and looked at her, his face grim. She saw in his eyes what he expected her to say. The explosion coming when it did might be seen as a sign of sorts. This would be her life from here on out, Kadir's eyes warned her. Uncertainty, the potential for violence at the most unexpected moments.

And yet…

"Yes," she said. "I love you, Kadir. My answer is yes."

Chapter 17

The explosion that had interrupted the Founder's Day Gala had taken place in the medical wing, and it had clearly been intended to kill the ailing king. The comatose ruler had not been injured, but his surgeon, Dr. Zara Smith, had been knocked unconscious in the blast. Dr. Smith had not yet recovered her memory. Investigators were hoping that perhaps she'd seen something before the explosion, and would soon be able to give them a lead.

Those same investigators had quickly determined that the materials used in the medical wing explosion were not of the same type as those used to destroy Kadir's yacht. It was still possible that the same culprit was responsible—that the events of that night had been set into motion before Zahid Bin-Asfour's death—but that was unlikely. Bin-Asfour had tried to kill Kadir more than once, but he had no reason to assassinate an elderly, ailing king who would soon be stepping down from the throne—if he survived.

Those events were days past, and the morning was a quiet one. Cassandra checked her luggage for the third time, trying to make sure that she had everything she needed. It was almost time to leave for the small airport where she had met Kadir a little more than three weeks ago. Lexie had promised to pack and ship the rest of her sister's belongings, but Cassandra didn't want to get to Kahani and find out she needed something that had been left behind.

She'd loved this flat for a long time, and even after the frightening events that had left Sharif wounded, it had felt like home. But now…she wasn't only ready to leave everything she knew behind, she was eager.

Kadir crept up behind her and slipped his arms around her waist. "Stop worrying, love. Anything you leave behind can be replaced."

Cassandra turned in his arms. "I know. I'm just trying to be an organized wife." She wasn't a wife yet, but within two weeks she would be. Her entire family would travel to Kahani for the wedding.

Her heart fluttered as Kadir kissed her. The life he promised her was not the one she'd planned for herself, but it was everything she wanted. Would every day be secure and totally safe? No. Would Kadir protect her? Yes, he would, just as she would protect him.

His fingers tangled in her hair. "Are you ready to go home, Cassandra?"

She grinned. "I'm ready to go home."

Six weeks later
Tuesday night

> *Dear Mum,*
> *Lexie arrived yesterday, and she's fine. She and*
> *Sharif spent most of today touring Kahani, and I*
> *believe they have the same activity planned for*
> *tomorrow. I offered to show her around myself, but*
> *she prefers to allow Sharif to be her tour guide.*
> *Finally I think she's found a man worthy of her.*

That was an understatement. It was so cute, the way
Sharif called Lexie Alexis, the way she hung on to his
every word and ignored his occasional glares. Lexie
made Sharif laugh. Sharif offered Lexie a sense of peace
she had never known. They suited one another well,
even though they both still had issues. For once, Cassandra approved of her sister's taste in men.

> *I hear that things in Silvershire are in an uproar*
> *once again. I always wanted to be right in the*
> *middle of all the royal scandals, but I'm very*
> *happy to be here, instead. Not that we don't have*
> *our own scandals, now and then.*
> *I know you always want to know what those*
> *scandals are, and what a shame that the Silver-*
> *shire Inquisitor doesn't have a correspondent here*
> *in Kahani so you can be well-informed. ☺ The*
> *man who took leadership of Bin-Asfour's follow-*
> *ers after his death is very much against bringing*
> *Kahani into the twenty-first century, but he's shut*
> *down Bin-Asfour's drug operations, finding them*

distasteful, and he's in favor of peaceful change. He doesn't agree with Kadir on what those changes should be, but he makes his point by yelling a lot, not shooting people. He doesn't like me at all, but what do you expect of a man who wants to take an entire country back a thousand years? I met his wife last week, and I like her very much. Once the men excused themselves to talk privately, we had a very interesting conversation. She seems to think her husband will come around to Kadir's way of thinking, eventually.

Wouldn't it be marvelous if two women from very different backgrounds had their say in the changes that were due to come to Kahani? Cassandra knew she would have to take her part in the participation slowly, but still…she was off to a grand start.

From the beginning, Kadir had included her in his day-to-day business as much as possible. They'd made a few short trips out of the country, and they had created their own scandal just by getting married and working together. Talk about photographers! Everywhere they went, around the world, men like Simon York snapped endless photos.

So far, her bare legs had been kept under wraps, thank goodness.

For the most part, she and Kadir had spent the first month of their marriage here, at this villa by the sea. Her fondest moments with him were all by the sea, either here or in Silvershire. She could not hear the waves crash or smell the salty air without thinking of her husband.

Cassandra was living in a foreign country, surrounded by people she was just beginning to know, and yet this was the home she'd searched for all her life.

I saved the best news for last. Kadir and I are going to have a baby. I can't tell you how excited I am, how happy, but I guess you know well enough what a wonderful feeling it is to begin a family. I'm terrified and excited and elated, all at the same time.

Kadir walked up behind her, reached around the chair and laid a hand on her flat belly.

"Feel anything different yet?" she asked, her pen poised above the paper.

"Not yet," her husband answered. "I'll try again in a few minutes." He leaned down and kissed her on the side of her neck, then left her to finish her letter with a wide smile on her face and a new shimmer beneath her skin.

Do you still get those flutters and flips when you look at Daddy? No, don't tell me. I don't really want to know everything that's to come. I only ask because I get those feelings every time I look at Kadir. I know we're newlyweds, but somehow I think they'll stick around for a good long while.

She couldn't imagine ever settling for anything less than what she and Kadir had, now that she knew what real, true love was like. Had she really thought that she could plan how and with whom she'd fall in love? Had she really thought she could dismiss what she felt for Kadir because it wasn't convenient? Trying to stop love was like trying to stop a freight train with a well-placed pea.

Thanks for all the good advice, and the stories
about love at first sight. Eight months from now,
I'll be an almost-psychic mum like you!
Love,
Cassandra

She prepared the letter to post, and set it on the dresser in the bedroom. Kadir stood by the nearby wide window that looked out over the sea. Cassandra joined him there, wrapping her arm around his waist and leaning in. This was her place in the world, and she would not trade it for anything, or anyone.

Cassandra shared a lot with her mother in her weekly letters, but she hadn't yet mentioned one small fact. Perhaps that fact was insignificant, and not even worth mentioning. Perhaps it was just a coincidence, and to mention it to anyone would be silly. But to her, it wasn't silly at all.

Her husband was the owner of a very fine white horse.

A sneaky peek at next month...

By Request

RELIVE THE ROMANCE WITH THE BEST OF THE BEST

My wish list for next month's titles...

In stores from 16th March 2012:

❏ Claimed by the Italian — Diana Hamilton, Christina Hollis & Kathryn Ross

❏ Reasons for Revenge — Maureen Child

3 stories in each book - only £5.99!

In stores from 6th April 2012:

❏ Capturing Her Heart — Nina Bruhns, Caridad Piñeiro & Kathleen Creighton

Available at WHSmith, Tesco, Asda, Eason, Amazon and Apple

Just can't wait?

Visit us Online

You can buy our books online a month before they hit the shops! **www.millsandboon.co.uk**

0312/C

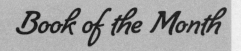

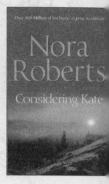

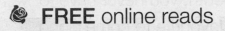
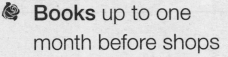

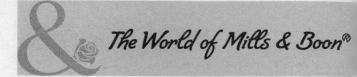

You've just finished your book.
So what did you think?

We'd love to hear your thoughts on our...
Have your comments hand...
www.millsandboon...

- ❖ Easy to use
- ❖ Short questionnaire
- ❖ Chance to win...
  voucher